D1664535

GALAXIAN
THE SEARCH FOR ICOL

BY:
CARL SHEFFIELD

TABLE OF CONTENT

CHAPTER
1

From a side street, I was concealed in the shadows of a building. Standing with my back to a wall. My vision was not good; objects were blurry. Pain rushed through my head. I could see beings were moving around. Many thoughts were rushing through my head. Who were they, yet what were they? There were species of all kinds. I couldn't remember how I got here. Who am I? Looking at my hand I could see, I was a human or appeared to be. I was weak. I turned my face to the sky to feel the warmth of the sun.

My back against the wall, I slowly slide down to a sitting position. Crossing my arms over my knees letting my head rest on my arms. Many thoughts were running fast, yet I had no answers. How did I get here? Where was here? I was trying to gather my thought when a hand touched my shoulder. A voice said in a whisper. "Come, my friend, it is not safe here."

I ask, "Where is here?"

The voice answered, "a long way from your exile, come we must hurry."

The voice sounded human; the touch felt human. Even his words sounded human. Taking my hands from my knees, I placed them on the wall trying to stand. Looking in the direction of the voice, I stared into the eyes of a species of some sort. A solid flash swept through my thought. "Do I know you," I ask?

"How could you not know me? My friend, we have been together for many, many years." He answered.

"I do not know you. I don't even know who I am," I replied.

He said, "The crash has taken your memories, they will return I promise this."

"Yeah, when," I asked? The being told me, he had found a place outside the city, a place of sanctuary.

"Sire," he said, "the sentries are looking for us. Come with me, I will explain to you everything. Please, Sire, we need to move." Following this being through the street stumbling several times finally falling to the ground, finally he picked me up.

"Come, sire, we must hurry," He said.

"Go," I said to him, "I'm too weak; leave me."

Replying, "I will not leave you, sire."

"Sire," I replied. "Why do you call me that?"

"Let's go," He said. Helping me from the ground, somewhere between here and there, I went cold.

Strange dreams of a beautiful woman I had throughout the night. Who was this woman I dream of? Do I know her? This woman always coming to me. Her hair went to her mid-back, black as the night, dressed in a white robe. Her eyes of emerald green, that sparkled in my dream. Why could I not remember her? Were we lovers, were we mates? My eyes opened. I looked around me. I was lying on the floor, of a place I knew not. My friend or so he said, was lying by a small fire. I made a grunt that brought him awake.

"Ah sire, you are back with the living. You have been gone for several days as on this world."

Staring into the flames, "What do you mean this world," I ask? He glanced at me with a slight smile. "Sire, days do not last long on this world, only a few hours." I watched him as he moved around the fire, not knowing what to expect.

"Sire," he asks, "Are you hungry?" I thought, was I hungry.

He said, "You know, eat, food." With the sound of the rumbling in my stomach, I was hungry. I tried to stand; I almost fell.

"Take it, easy sire," he said. There was that word again.

I said to him, "Why do you call me that?"

"That, what you are, you are my King," he answered.

"King! King of what," I ask?

"Sire you were exiled from our world of Galaxo, we fought a good fight. We were surprised by many coming into the castle. Drex had placed his men all around the village, through the streets he struck without warning. Drex and his rebels killed hundreds of your people, as many Claxton's too."

I replied, "Claxton's, what is a Claxton."

The being said, "that is my species, we are called Claxton's.

3

You do not remember sire?" I told him no, I don't remember much of anything.

Setting back, he looked at me, "Your brother did this out of greed and jealousy. Drex took his band of rebels, overtook the castle, slaughtered many, destroying so much. You, sire, was sent to prison on Advair. Since I was your advisor, he sent me with you. Twenty years we were there."

"You say, my brother, I have a brother," I ask him?

"Yes, sire, and a very beautiful wife." I do not know what happened to her, I was wounded trying to protect her. It was my belief Drex killed her. I have stood by your side for many years."

Looking at him I ask, "Where are we know." The being told me he was not sure about the name of this world. He handed me a slice of what looked to be fruit, with a cup of tea. I sat by the fire for a long while. I was thinking about what he said. Looking across the fire spoke.

"Sire, there are several types of species here. There are humans here too. Sire your human. You do have alien blood. Your mother was human. Your great, great, grandfather came from a place called the Moon of Corning. I believe several hundered years ago."

I ask, "Tell me, what is it your called?"

Replying he answered, "Tenna, I am called Tenna."

I asked "Tenna what was this war about, with my brother," Tenna handed me another slice of fruit.

Tenna said, "The war started long ago with Drex. It ended with him wanting your wife for his own. He wanted the throne for his petty difference, Drex wanted Shara mostly."

"Shara," I said.

Tenna was telling me how beautiful she was. He described every detail. Long black hair, eyes so green."

"Yes," I said out loud, "I know, I see her in my dreams."

Tenna asks, "You dream of her." I told him every time I close my eyes; I see her running to me. Always the same, always.

"This is good sire," Tenna said.

"Please don't call me that," I said.

Tenna asks, "Then what shall I call you?"

Looking at him I said, "My name, call me by my name until I reclaim this throne you speak about. I'm no different than the wind that blows across this place."

He said, "As you wish Icol."

I ask him to tell me more about her. Tenna told his tales, somewhere in the night I fell asleep. In the still of the evening by a small lake of blue with the trees swaying in the rhythm of the gentle breeze, she came to me again. Looking around at the place, a solid flash hit me, I have been here before.

Her arms were reaching for me, come to me she would say. Come to me, reaching for my hands as always. Our hands would touch, our eyes would meet, her lips would touch mine so softly, the gentle feeling of her embrace was so intense. Then she's gone.

Sleeping as it was, bits and pieces of my memories would come through. I could not see the castle to say, just bits and pieces. Could this be the kingdom, Tenna told me about?

Tenna said I was a king. I see myself not a king, just a man. I knew nothing of the years I've been away. Tenna said the hit I took to the back of my head had taken my memories. If all is true what Tenna said, why would I want to remember? My life, my world, my children. I moved to wake Tenna. I Pushed at his leg, "Tenna," I called. Coming to a standing position Tenna asks. "What is wrong?" I told him I saw an image of a castle.

Tenna said, "Good Icol, your memories come."

"I suppose Tenna," I said. "There slow Tenna, yet they come."

Tenna said, 'Icol in a few days you will be strong enough to leave."

"Leave," I said, "Tenna where would we go. We don't even know where we are."

Tenna replied, "Have a little faith Icol, you will see. When daybreak comes danger will come with it. The guards will be out on patrol. I tell you; we are searched for. The ship that brought us here crashed; we escaped. I don't know why we were brought here."

"I don't know either," I said, lying down close to the fire

Tenna said, "It was as if they wanted us to escape. Icol, you really don't remember, do you?" I told him I remembered a few things. I do not remember being in a prison or being a king. As far as I know, you could be a king Tenna, I could be your server.

He stood from the ground, "That is not true, you are my king I swear it. I would die before I would deny you. Fight to my death to protect you. I am a Claxton warrior, loyal only to you." It took several minutes for Tenna to settle down.

I ask, "Did I have children Tenna?"

Answering with a snarl, "No, just you and the queen. I do not know what has happened since. There was a captain on a ship, I befriend him. He told me Drex had locked her away in the castle. He told me she was a prisoner in her own home. He is mean, kills anyone that defines him. He has taken all the young females to have children for him, he is trying for a son. That was long ago, it was reported Drex took his head in the market square."

I ask, "How long have you been a guard?"

Tenna replied, "All my life as I remember."

I ask, "Then you knew my mother and father?"

"Yes, Icol I knew them. I was young when your father acquired me."

"What, you were a slave," I ask?

Tenna said, I was not a slave, I was acquired. I left the home of my father, in the city of the Claxton to live with humans. Your father took me in, he trained me to be what I am. You were only a few days old. You're a warrior to Icol, this I tell you. I trained you myself, your mother gave me her permission to do this.

Only in secret was I allowed to train you. When you were eight years, I took you to the mountain of the Trion. For another eight-year, I trained you hard. The eight years you were in the city of the Claxton's you become a great warrior. You took the trial of the warrior. You have the seal on your back to prove it. Yes, my friend, you are a warrior. You left the castle a child returned a man.

Your father was so upset with me, he had the guards chain me to the walls of the castle. I found it quite humorous.

In four days, he released me, he said he could not sleep for me calling his name in the night. Only one bad thing happens while you were away. Your mother gave birth to Drex. From the moment, he came into this world, Drex was evil, evil to the core. When Drex was sixteen he made you a king by killing your father. It could not be proven, yet I know it to be true."

Tenna stopped talking. He sat poking in the fire for several minutes. I had to know.

I ask him. "How do you know it was true?"

Tenna said, "Rest now Icol, the fire will die, when the night comes, we must leave."

"Tenna, you did not answer me," I said.

Replying Tenna said, "The people talk Icol. Believe me when I tell you Drex is evil." I closed my eyes somewhere in my dreams she came to me. This time it was more real than before. Walking to me with a gentle embrace, it was like magic, I was in her arms.

I could hear her speak to me, "My love, our people have suffered the wrath of Drex.

I know this was only a dream, I told her, my memories have left me. I dream of you, think of you, yet, I know you not. My memories are not whole. Tenna tells me of you, he tells me of the throne I have, he calls me sire. Tenna and I escaped on a ship as stow ways I'm hurt. Here in your arms, I feel so warm.

For some reason, I left her, before I could hold her. She was so perfect, so graceful, she was a true queen."

Tenna was shaking me awake. "Wake up Icol, someone comes."

Tenna eased his body to the small opening. Looking into the darkness Tenna said, "there's six of them sire."

"Tenna, you say I was a warrior."

"You are Icol," Tenna said, "A furious warrior you are," I told him, I'm not sure I can fight.

Tenna said, "Just follow through, six is no match for us. If we are discovered, we will fight. I will not go back to that prison. I rather die here. In this place is where we will stand."

I said, "I will fight by your side Tenna, maybe it's my destiny to die here."

Tenna replied with a smile, "Icol, your destiny, is on the throne of Galaxo."

CHAPTER 2

I sat alone in my prison cell, waiting for Icol, my husband, and the king to return. I've waited for so long. In my heart, I know he is not dead. I feel him each time I close my eyes. I see him in my dreams. I thought, am I fooling myself. I think not, I love my husband, I know he is alive. Drex has told me for twenty years he is dead. The dream I had last evening, was so real, so magical as if I held him.

All this time I have held on to the hope someday he will return. If Icol is alive he will come for me someday. Alone in my solitude; I'll wait. Only a few times a week am I allowed to go to the garden. Escorted by the guards of course, once loyal to my husband.

Sitting alone in the garden smelling the fresh air. I heard a voice as the guard approached me.

"You are to come with me," he said.

"If I don't," I replied.

The guard said, "I will drag you. You mean nothing to me. The king wishes a counsel with you." I said to him loudly, so loud the few birds flew away.

"He is no king. He killed his father, sent his brother to prison. Drex has told me several times he was dead. I tell you; he is not dead; Icol is alive you once were a loyal guard to him, look at you know."

The guard stepped closer, "Please come", he said. "My lady, what you say may be true, for some of us to remain alive, we had to serve him to save our families. He surely would have killed them as he has so many others. Drex has killed over a hundered of our people over a hundred Claxton's. Just because they would not call him king. Drex said as he took the throne. Only the strong survive. Remember this"

I said to the guard, "Only the coward in him is why he lives."

"My queen please," I told him to call me by my name until Icol returns.

The guard said, "Then I will call you by your name for a

long time because he is dead." I walked past him like he wasn't there.

He said, "Shara please, come with me?"

Walking through the garden I said, "You know he is alive."

The guard replied, "I know nothing, if you say he is alive I would say you are mistaking." I told him I was with Icol in my dream.

"Shara, please."

I ask, "Where do you take me, I am a prisoner remember?"

"Yes, you are, you need to remember that. Drex has killed for less. Drex will speak to you."

I looked at him, "You don't call him king. Very well, where is he in the castle."

He answered, "No Shara, he is in his chambers."

"I will not go there, if Drex wishes to speak to me he can speak where there are people. If not, take me back to my room." Walking back to the tower my home for so many years I told him, go to him tell Drex what the queen has said. Tell him I will not come to his room; I would die first.

Locking the door, the guard went to Drex. In the chambers of Drex, the guard knocked on the door.

"Sire," he said, "The queen said she would die first before she would come here, to your chambers." Drex was mad you could see in his eyes his blood was hot. Drex was dangerous. He took nothing from anyone.

Drex said with a sharp voice," Very well I'll go to her, I'll kill her myself. Something I should have done a long time ago." Walking down the long corridor to the outside walls of the castle, Drex caught a faint breeze. It was a feeling he did not like, something he had not felt in many years. There was something he felt in the wind.

Looking out the window a ship thundered overhead. Drex knew from the marking on the ship it was from Advair. Drex watched the ship as it landed on the pad. The hatch opened; two men walked from the ship. Sentry's made their way from the ship to form a circle. Drex thought to himself now what. Drex's mind went to Shara, then he whispered through a soft voice, she will have to wait. The Advairian was not due for several weeks, why were they here now.

Drex turned to leave. Shara, I'll deal with her later. Drex sent a sentry to escort the captain to the council. I watched them go. I watch them come into the council. Walking to Drex the captain bowed, "King Drex."

Drex asks, "Captain why are you here, you're not due for another month." The captain began to speak.

I reached through the door unlocking it. I made my way to the council chambers. Standing just beyond the reach of Drex, I listened to what was said. It was my castle I knew my way around, dodging the guards. In my heart, I knew some of the guards were still loyal to Icol. They did what they had to do to stay alive. I knew one of them was. I heard the captain say to Drex.

"Sire there has been an accident on a planet several galaxies away. Several days ago, a ship left Advair, at that time two prisoners went missing."

There was silence. "What does that have to do with me," Drex asks?

"Sire one of them was your brother, the other one the Claxton. I believe you called him Tenna. I gasp, not loud enough to be heard. Backing up I turned into the guard.

"What are you doing here Shara," He asks?

I smiled, "Did you hear him, you did. Now you know he is alive." The guard escorted me back to my room. The guard said to me, "I can't protect you forever Shara. Someday this curiosity of your will gets you killed." The guard pushed me into the room as the door closed behind me.

I said. "I'd rather be dead than to let him touch me." As the guard locked the door I pleaded, "Go, see for yourself, if it is true come to me, let me know."

He asks, "Shara how am I to find out." I told him to walk

among the guards. talk to them Tankko.

I said, "You know he is alive."

Tankko replied, "I know nothing." Then walked away.

In the chambers of Drex, the captain ask, sire, are we to look for Icol. We were told the ship crashed on Gara."

Drex asks, "Were there survivors?"

"Yes, there was," the captain said. "It was told to me two walked away we are looking for them. It was reported we have no idea who they were. We tracked them to a small village where we have a trade agreement. If it was your brother and the Claxton, we will find them."

Drex said, "If you find them do not take them, prisoner, kill them where you find them."

The captain walked to the door of the council. Stopping he saw a female being escorted by a guard. He was leading her down a long corridor. Thoughts ran through his mind. Could this be the queen; he had been told she was alive. "Captain," Drex called, "Something else you want to say."

"Know sire, I will be gone."

Drex said as he walked into the corridor. "Kill them where you find them. I wish not to be burden with this again."

The captain left walking down the long corridor; between two small steeples, he caught the scent of a female. There was no doubt the queen _was alive. The captain approached his ship. Tankko was talking to the sentry as the captain neared the ramp; he called to Tankko. "Sir who are you."

Coming to attention Tankko replied. "One of the King's guard sir. Just making conversation, always wanted to serve on a ship. Never had the chance."

He got close to Tankko, "Is the Queen alive."

Tankko replied, "I know nothing of a queen, Drex has many females in the castle."

"Tankko we look for Icol, its time he comes home. If you are the man, I think you are, you will pass the word only to the ones you can trust. Someday he will return this I promise you.

I give you my word as a captain."

Tankko asks, "Why are you telling me this?"

"This king of yours, he scares me Tankko. Now I'm going to push you, believe me, he is watching. The captain called to his guards."

I fell to the ground with weapons drawn on me. The captain smiled, walked on to his ship.

Inside the castle, Drex walked very fast to the room where Shara was. Opening the door walking in.

I ask, "Drex, what is it you want?"

Drex said, "I've come to you one last time, marry me or die." Shara walked to a small window stared out for several minutes. Drex asks, "Shara what will it be." Shara took her robe, ripped it open so her breast was exposed. Shara's breast was as a mountain peak. So, beautiful so full for a woman of Shara's age. When Shara exposed her breast it almost took Drex's breath away.

"Take your sword Drex, push it deep into my chest. I'd rather die than be anything to you." Drex stared at me. Sweat beaded his forehead, drool dripped from the corner of his mouth.

Drex said, "Please Shara, I beg you, I love you."

"You're a pitiful excuse of a man, your nothing as your brother, your useless. Kill me now you have tried so many years." I knew the words I wanted to say, now they come so easily. "You say you love me Drex."

"Yes, Shara yes, I love you," Drex replied.

"Oh, Drex, you love me with the twenty-five-young girl in your chambers."

Drex said, "I'll kill the one that told you that."

I replied, "Yes Drex I'm sure you will, you have killed for less.

Drex stood looked at me. "Shara you will die here in this room."

I ask Drex, "Do I die by your hands Drex, or some pity

guard who is not worthy to take the life of a queen? You are a coward Drex, a stupid moron. If my husband was alive, he would kill you himself."

Drex said, "Your husband is dead Shara because he was weak. I took his throne I have his wife. In this very room, you will die of old age. I will damn you to that Shara. I will order no one to take you to the garden or to speak to you again. If I find they have broken my order, I will have their head."

Drex as I have said, "You have killed for less."

Drex turned to walk away. I said to him, "Your no man Drex, you a stinking coward." Closing the door behind him I went to the small table taking the quail and parchment. (*I'm Queen Shara, wife of Icol. Drex has me in prison in the east tower over the city. Look at darkness you will see a single light.*)

I took the letter folded it dropped it from the window. A small breeze took the parchment through the courtyard into the door of a market. I thought how did that happen.

A young girl was sweeping the walk, not old enough for Drex to take yet. She was old enough to read, taking the small parchment the young girl read then gasp. Folding it she placed it in the pocket of her apron. Her father was watching.

"Shila what have you their child," he asks?

"Oh, father it's just a piece of parchment I wish to keep."

Her father asks, "May I see it Shila?" Looking at her father she said. "Father please it's nothing."

Shila's father said, "If it is nothing Shila, let me see it."

Shila took the paper from her apron started to hand it to her father when a guard come in. "Drex wants his payment storekeeper."

Shila said, "If the real king was here, you would not be alive." The guard laughed out loud. "Store keep tell you, daughter, to mind her mouth. You will be next to go to the castle." Leaving the store, the guard thought of what she said. If Icol was here would things be different?

Shila's father asked, "Shila the paper?" Taking the paper

reading it he staggered caught the counter with his hands.

"Shila where did you find this," he asks?

Shila replied, "It blew in the store father."

Coe said, "Shila, do not speak of this to anyone, ever."

"Father how much longer are you, and the others going to be ruled by a madman."

"Shila, not a word to anyone." Shila turned walked back to the walk.

I've watched my child grow into the girl she is. Raising her from birth alone. She had her thirteenth birthday in the summer. When she reaches the age of fifteen, she will be taken to Drex. She despised Drex, I'm afraid she would kill herself before she would go.

Shila asks, "Father may I have a leave to visit a friend." I nodded my head. Walking to the baskets Shila placed several pieces of fruit in her bag. Leaving the shop, walking to the gate she was stopped by the guards. "Where do you go child?" Shila told them she was going to visit a friend for fruit and tea. I won't be gone long she told them.

Walking along the road many thoughts ran through my mind. I continued walking along the trail to the plains.

Sometimes I could see things from afar. I've never told anyone about my visions. Even when I watched the King's guards work. I was going to the home of the man in my eyes, was the greatest warrior of all. He would tell tales of his travels when I visited. Basco had a son the same age as me. I knew he was teaching him the skills of a warrior, a Claxton warrior. Claxton warriors were superb fighters: they were the best.

In the early morning air walking alone as the sun showed my shadow on the ground. I felt a strange feeling; It was a creepy feeling. I hurried my way to the house of Basco. Walking to the stoop, Basco, was in the backyard. He was working on his scruple.

"Morning sir," I said.

"Shila, how do you fair this morning," Basco asks?

I looked around Basco said, "Dris is in the house Shila. What do you have in the basket." I told him I brought him and Dris some fruit.

Basco said, "Let's go inside Shila, Dris will be pleased to see you." Walking into the front room Dris, stood with a smile on his face.

"Morning Shila," He said. I told him the same. The talk was going on when from nowhere come a question to Basco.

I ask, "May I ask you a question, Basco? Did you know our King Icol?"

Basco looked at me, "Shila, why do you ask me this."

"Basco I have no reason. One more question."

Basco said, "Go ahead."

"Will you train me as you do Dris." Basco gave a hard laugh. He was so powerful, he had to be six feet three. Dris at thirteen was tall also. Basco was so powerful, his hair was down to his shoulder his chest and arms bulged with muscles.

I ask him, "Did you get those from working or training."

Basco replied, "You ask a lot of questions for a little girl."

I jumped up from the table, "I might be a little girl. This little girl will do two things."

Basco asks, "What will that be Shila?"

I said, "I will go to the mountain of Trion, I'll have the Claxton's to train me. Then I will find our king, and I will kill Drex, you will see."

Now all the time the talk went on Dris, son of Basco was listening to me.

Dris said, "Father I feel the same. Father, you are a great warrior. The Claxton is the greatest of all. Father, you fight as they do."

Basco said, "Son I fight as they do because I was trained by Tenna, the grand warrior of the Claxton's."

"Basco I will return tomorrow for your answer," I looked at him, "either way, sir I will be trained by you or the Claxton."

"Basco before I leave there something I want to show you."

I pulled the paper from my pocket, this made its way to the store this morning. "

"What is it," Basco asks? I handed the paper to him. Reading the paper Basco asks, "Shila, who else knows of this." I told him just me and my father. He told me not to show it or speak of it to anyone.

Basco asks, "Then why did you show it to me?"

"Basco beside my father, you and Dris are the only ones I can trust? Even now I ask myself, I can trust you." My queen is locked away in her castle, while her husband has been exiled or killed, I promise you I will find out. The queen should be on the throne, not Drex."

Dris was at the door, "Father someone comes."

Basco replied, "It's the guards." I told them I was coming for fruit and tea. Sitting cups and fruit on the table we were sitting at when they come through the door. They never knocked just walked in. Basco stood his arms were so full of muscles, reaching for his sword.

"Can I help you," Basco asks?

The guard asked, "What are you doing here?"

Basco said, "My house, I need not answer to you."

The guard asked, "Only the three of you?"

"Is that all you see," Basco asked? I admit I had a smile on my face a little tingle in my stomach. I was thrilled to hear Basco stand up to them, I love Basco.

Basco said, "There only two here, sometimes Shila comes to visit my son. The guard looked at me.

The guard said, "Basco do not get close to her. She will be going to the castle soon."

"I jumped up I will die by your hands before I go to that place," I said.

The guard looked at me. "You have spirit, I'll give you that little one."

Standing with my hands on my hips. I moved to one side. I still had my hands on my hips. "I mean it, you remember this when the time comes. Tell that coward when he sends for me, send you. You come to get me, you or I will die, it won't be me."

The guard said, "I could kill you for that." The guard started to pull his sword looking at Basco with his hand on his. He knew Basco from long ago, he knew Basco was a warrior.

The guard said again, "I could kill you now for those words." I told him, do it your no man, your nothing without that thing you called king. Please tell him in two years when I'm of age, tell him to send you. The guard left Basco looked at me then to Dirs.

Basco said, "Dris pack only a few things. Shila you cannot return to the village today if you plan to go to the Trion's."

The day went on Basco worked out with his training. Basco told us we were waiting for darkness to come. Basco told us he didn't want to cross the plains in daylight."

"Basco you will train me," I ask?

Basco said, "Shila I will take you and my son to the Trions. I will speak to the Claxton, I promise you nothing."

I ask Basco, "Will they let me speak."

Basco said, "I will ask Shila, there's only one thing that bothers me."

I ask him, "What is that?"

Basco replied, "The Claxton's, has never trained a human female."

I ask Basco, "Have they trained Claxton females."

"Yes Shila," Basco replied, "several."

I said, "If you ask them if I can speak, they will train me."

Basco brought his scruple from a hiding place, we started packing it. The craft was small walking around he took a rock knocked out all the lights. Dris and I waited inside for darkness to come. Dris walked to me, Shila are you afraid.

"I stood looked at him, I will become a warrior Dris. I will free my queen. I will find our true King or die trying. I don't know him, I've never met him. I have talked to several of the people that came to my father's shop. You know the older ones. They say he was a true king, took care of his people. Drex will never be my king." Basco came from the stoop to the table where Dris and I were, "I knew Icol very well," he said.

I have said to you, "Tenna trained me, I was a king's guard. There were only twenty- six Kings guards. The rest were guards, and sentries. Drex took his rebels into the village, Icol was captured before he knew what had happened. It was that quick, Tenna was placed in chains, it caused a war between the humans and Claxton's. The Claxton's thought it was Icol, later found out it was Drex."

Basco sat at the table eating some bread with a bowl of soup. Looking at me he said, "There were many that died that day before the fighting stopped. The Claxton's went back into the mountains of Trion. Drex has sent his men there several times, none have ever returned."

I ask him, "Did they kill them or capture them."

Basco replied, "I don't know Shila, no one has ever returned that has followed Drex orders. As I speak Shila we may not return."

I smiled as I looked upon the big warrior, "you will see Basco we will return, between you, myself your son Dris, we will return our king to power. I will find him if he is alive."

CHAPTER 3

Drex was screaming as he left the chambers of the queen. Running to his throne, find Tankko he said, bring him to me. The guards nodded as they left Drex. Drex saw the Advairan captain when he pushed Tankko. What was that about, he said to himself. I will find out why.

Sentries were sent all over the castle, was looking for Tankko; he was not to be found. Reporting back to Drex about Tankko absence's, Drex screamed at the sentry's, "find him," I said.

Drex sent a guard to the hanger where the ships were. Guard bring me a captain of one ship, "Sire as you wish." Returning to the castle the guards were summoned to Drex. Tankko entered the room filled with guards.

Drex stood looking at him, "It has been brought to my attention, someone has been conspiring with the queen. Let him step forward." Tankko took two steps forward.

Drex watched. "Tankko you, you have spoken to her?"

Tankko answered, "Only when you ask me to sire. You ask me to walk with her to the garden. Take her back to her quarters never do I speak to her any other time."

"Tankko are you loyal to me," Drex asks?

Tankko said, "Yes sire always." Drex turned as the captain of the ship come forward.

Drex said, "Tankko you and ten others, will go with the captain. The rest leave now." As the guards left the chambers Drex walked to the door looked down the corridor saw nothing.

"Captain," Drex said, "Take these guards, go to Gara find the Claxton that is called Tenna, and my brother, kill them."

Tankko looked as he spoke to Drex. "Sire I thought he was already dead. How do you kill someone already dead?"

Drex replied, "You have your orders now go. Speak to know one of this."

"As you wish sire., Tankko said. The ship from Advair left hours ago, Drex told the captain to follow them. If they do not carry out their mission kill all of them do you understand. Captain If you don't find them and kill them don't come back here. If you do, I'll kill you myself."

Captain Meric made ready his ship. Waiting for the guards, many thoughts went through his mind. How did it come to this, as he thought back twenty years ago when the Claxton's were here, how the queen would walk among the people? I wish it was like that again. Meric waited as Tankko boarded the ship. Walking past the captain speaking only so Tankko could hear. "I wish someday someone kills him."

Tankko said nothing taking his place on the ship he remembered what Shara said. The one she spoke to was not on the ship. Tankko thought he must find Icol first. Several days as it was in space Tankko went to the captain.

"Sir, may I have a word with you," Tankko asked?

Meric waved his hand, "Come in Tankko, what are your thoughts."

Tankko said, "What you said when I come aboard the ship."

"Ah yes," Tankko. Someday someone will kill him."

"Captain you have been around a long time. Did you know his brother Icol? Meric looked at Tankko. Leaning back in his chair, "Yes Tankko I was his father's pilot on many journeys to many other worlds. I mean we had the ships we needed to go somewhere.

"Do you think he has allies," I ask?

The captain thought, "I'm not sure now. Tankko why do you ask? It has been a long time."

Sir did you know the queen, is locked in the castle in the east tower. Captain Meric was pouring tea it went all over the floor.

"Tankko you are mistaking," Meric said.

Tankko replied, "I assure you, captain, she is alive."

The captain said, "Tankko she died over twenty years."

I ask him, "Did you see her body?"

"I was not on Galaxo when it happens, Tankko. I was told of the affair later.

"I tell you, captain, she is alive, locked in the east tower.

Drex had me stay with her no other. I walked with her to the garden every day."

"Tankko why would Drex go through the ceremony?"

"I think captain to hide it from the people. When Drex took power from Icol, he showed him in chains, that was to show how powerful he was. He told all he killed Icol and the Claxton Tenna. I believe in my heart if Icol was here he would take back his throne. There's no doubt if the people knew in time Drex and his rebels would not have overrun the castle. Drex slowly brought his men into the village dressed as farmers. No one suspected what was going on until he stormed the castle. I believe if he came back, he would be most powerful."

I stood to leave, "One more thing sir."

"Yes," Tankko what is it. The Advairan captain looks for Icol to bring him home not to kill him."

Meric said, "Icol would die Tankko before he could rise to power."

I looked at the captain, "What if the Claxton was with him. The Claxton's led by Basco."

Well, Meric said, "There's a name I haven't heard in a while. Basco was a furious warrior what I remember he was trained by the Claxton's."

"He was I said, so was Icol trained by the one they called Tenna, in the Trions long ago. The Avarians look for him, there tired of Drex. They're tired of him taking the young girls for his sexual pleasure. The people of Galaxo are tired of it too."

Meric said, "I have heard of this too, Tankko."

I told the captain before I left, the daughter of a storekeeper and Basco's son Dris, Basco will train them you will see she is a brave girl.

Meric rubbed his face, "Tankko the Claxton will not train a woman."

"Your right sir they will train a girl, especially Shila, something about her. It is not for me to say." I went back to my quarters with much on my mind. Several planets were looking for him, was it possible he was still on Advair, I think not. I was loyal to Icol, I had to serve Drex, so my mother would live. Drex would have surely killed her. I tried to take care of the queen, give her the things she needed. I told her of the guard that was beheaded in the square. She wanted to know why. I told her he brought word of Icol, Drex took his head himself.

CHAPTER 4

Night had come to the village of Galaxo. Shila's father walked to the edge of the courtyard, looking to the east tower of the castle. In the window of the tower, it was as he had seen written on the parchment, a single light. She was alive he thought. Drex has lied to us all these years. Well, that comes as no surprise. Several people from the village looked up, they saw what I did, the light.

One said, "A single light who is there. There has been no one there in years."

I said to them, "You mean that we know about."

Another said, "It is where Icol took Shara on their wedding night."

One said, "Do you think it could be her, after all this time."

"None sense," one said, "Watch your tongue Drex will cut it out," Coe remembered his daughter was not home. He asks everyone if they had seen her.

One man said, "maybe Drex has her, she is almost of age." I told them she has two years left. "He took one the other day, she was thirteen," one said.

As everyone stood talking, one woman said, "Icol would have never done this."

I spoke as they listen, "Drex has our Queen. I say to everyone, keep quiet of this. I tell you now our Queen is in that tower. Shila found a parchment on the floor. I tell you the queen is there." I told everyone I had to find my daughter.

I knew I could not go to the palace. I knew I could not ask Drex for help. I was thinking this morning when she asks to leave, she was going to the house of Basco. I no Basco son was sweet on Shila and she felt the same. Shila at thirteen she was not old enough to go to Drex or old enough to go with a boy. Shila was at Basco, I know this. Maybe it just got late Basco told her to stay there for the night.

I knew my daughter, she would have come home unless it got late. Shila may be thirteen and a strong-minded girl. I feel in my heart Shila has a strong destiny. I suppose I should tell her of her ancestors. The blood that runs through her veins. She will discover this as she grows. I went to my home closed the shop took my jacket. The light was the only thing I need to see. It was true after all these years. How could Drex keep her hid without someone knowing?

I tried to clear my thought, walked out the door to the courtyard. I suppose it could be done, hiding the Queen. Anything was possible with Drex. I have never seen a more spiteful man. Drex never cared for his people, even back to his birth. When he was a young child, playing in the courtyard and the garden, he would always run over the other children. Being the son of a King, the people just let it go. Our people have suffered greatly since Drex.

I walked through the gates of the palace. A voice called, "Where do you go, Coe?"

"I go to look for my daughter. This morning she left to visit a friend. It's late I must find her."

The guard said, "She was reported to be at Basco. That where she was going, Coe."

"If you leave you must return before we raise the gate." The guard said.

"I understand," I said. I walked across the bridge to the road I heard them laugh as the gate went up. I thought a planet as advance as we were, why do we have to put up with the likes of that. Someday the laughter will come from the other places. The guards are always taunting people, there are no laws here, only Drexs law.

I made my way down the makeshift road I realized it was very dark. The moon on our planet shined all the time. Looking up I noticed lights moving in the atmosphere it was high. They looked like stars moving from place to place. I remember back to a better time, back to the time when ships would come here, they come no more.

Every now, and then an Advairan ship would land, pick up people Drex did not want here. He would send them to Advair.

In my lifetime, I've never seen them bring anyone back. Where ever they take them, they take them to their death.

Walking on for a while the home of Basco appeared. Edging closer I heard a small craft. Turning the corner Shila was stepping into the craft.

I said, "Wait, as Basco jumped from the craft with a sword in hand."

Shila called, "Wait, Basco, it's my father."

Basco said, "Old man, why are you searching in the dark?

I look for Shila, my daughter," I replied. "I can't go back tonight the guards have pulled the gate," Basco told me I could stay here. Shila told her father we got to go.

"Go Shila, go where?" Basco told me it's best I didn't know.

Shila asks, "Father had you rather I go to Drex, or go with Basco."

I ask, "Could you at least come to tell your father?"

Basco said, "Coe we got to go."

I ask Basco, "Why are there no lights on the craft?"

Basco replied, "I don't want to be seen crossing the plains."

I ask him, "Where do you take her?"

"Old man, say goodbye, we leave," Basco said.

"Basco she is my only child."

"Coe, I know who she is. Maybe you would like to see her in the arms of Drex," I ask?

"I would not like that Basco." "Then say goodbye let us go. I will take care of her with my life. If someone asks of her, tell them she ran away to escape Drex. Tell them she went to the north."

Shila said to her father, "Just remember I love you I will return someday with our true King I promise you."

I stood watched Basco talk the craft with my daughter until the darkness took it from my sight. Basco told me I could stay at his place until morning. Going into many thoughts ran through my mind. I knew the only place Shila would be safe would be the Trions, with the Claxton's.

The chief had a daughter little older than Shila. Cousins, yet they did not know this. Another part of her life I should have told her about. Basco left hot bread on the fire, with fruit and cooked vegetables. I made fresh tea sat for a long time before sleep took me.

During the night, stepping to the stoop looking skyward I saw ships slide through the night sky. Who they were, where they were going? Then I thought of Shila my child she has always been Destin for a bigger thing, maybe she will find what it is with Basco. I do know one thing Basco was a good man, trustworthy.

Lying down I toss and turned then fell asleep. Outside a noise woke me. I kept waiting for the door to open there was no other sound, nothing, silence all around. Shila was so tired of Drex taking the girls making the storekeeper pay him. Drex gathering the girls for his pleasure. This made her so angry.

Father, if I must go to him I'll catch him asleep, then I'll kill him. Shila has told me several times she had rather be dead than let Drex touch her body. To have a child by that madman, she has said in her heart it would be hard, yet, I would kill the child myself.

Daylight came with the sun over the eastern mountains. looking around Basco's house I must say he was a knowing man. He had placed his cupboards full for a day to come. I made tea had a plate of fruit, started my way back to the castle. Guards had started their patrols, why I was not sure no one ever comes here.

Stopping by me one guard asks, "Storekeeper why are you away from the gate so early." I explain the account with the guards and the gate. I told them I was looking for my daughter, I have been out all night One of the guards said he saw Shila at Basco place. "I saw her with my own eyes," he said.

I looked at him, "She is not there now. I went all the way to the plains. Please if you see her bring her home." The captain told me he would watch for her." When they left, I started to smile, I didn't know I was so good.

Basco flew the craft to the east of his villa. Shila threw out her coat. Basco said, "Let's get out and make tracks all around." Basco Dris and I got back into the craft. Basco turned the craft to the west straight toward the mountains of Trions. Thinking all the time we must reach the Trions before the guard's search there.

Basco said, "I know a place to hide the craft. I promise no one will find it. There are no ships on the mountain after you reach so high no place to land. Besides no one can see the city of the Claxton's its hid.

My son asks, "Where do we go once we're there. I told Dris, and Shila it would be a two-day walk up the mountain. Then we would wait for the Claxton's to come to us. You must be welcome.

CHAPTER 5

Drex waited, sitting on his throne looking at what was his. Yet as much as he had he still wanted the queen. He wanted her so bad sometimes he hurt in his private areas. Just thinking of her drove him insane. Why did this woman lay so heavy on him? Was it the fact he could not have her, that had to be it? Thinking of her got him in the mood, he got aroused. Stiffer and stiffer he got. He almost wanted to scream out in agony. He could stand it no longer.

He went to the chambers where he kept the young girls the youngest one was the one the guards brought yesterday. She was so beautiful the desire he felt in his loins was about to leave him. You, there, as he pointed to the girl, come here. Drex led her to his bed, as he was getting ready he told her to unrobed. Drex took off his robe turned to face the girl his penis was fully erected swollen if nothing else, Drex was a full male. All Drex wanted to do was explode. Drex told her I said for you to unrobed.

The young girl said, "I tell you again I have something to say."

Drex said to her, "I don't care what you have to say, tonight you will be mine."

The girl stood looking then she said to him as she moved closer to him. "Really sire, can you have sex with your daughter." The feeling he had was gone in a moment, a moment he will never forget. The look in his eyes when she said that, Drex's eyes went pure evil.

"You are my daughter," Drex asked?

"Yes, sire all of us are, you have had sex with several of them all have children by you. You are talked about from here to there. If you want to have sex I will. I tell you now it won't be before I claw your eyes out. You are a pitiful man. How many of your children have you had sex with, how many have had children, all girls? Your no man. I don't know what you are your no man and you'll never be a king." The hatred builds inside Drex he was mad so mad, she blew everything for him.

Drex reached for his robe, "I could kill you for talking to me like that."

"Yes, father I suppose you could. You have killed for less. Tell me, father, how do you live knowing you have got your daughters pregnant. Your daughters." Drex screamed at her to shut up.

Drex said to her, "Leave here now never return."

Father, she said," Drex said never called me that."

"Father, twenty-five girls in your chambers are your daughter, several are having your babies.

Drex said to her, "If I ever see you again I'll kill you."

The girl turned to leave she said, "Father you're not man enough to father a boy you will never be a king."

Drex stood in shock at what she was saying. No one has ever said to him such words and lived. Walking around the bed, Drex slapped her on the face. Back and forth he just would not stop. Blood had started flowing from her nose then her mouth. The harder he slapped the girl, the harder she would laugh. Drex beat her to the floor then started kicking her with wild fury. Beating her lifeless until two guards ran in. Sire, they called please do not do this.

"Take this bitch to the Queen. Show her what I do to females that defines me. Take her now!"

Sire one guard said, "You have given strict order, no one goes to the Queen."

"Who is the King here?"

"You are the sire," one said.

"Then do as I say," Drex commanded. Going back to the chambers, Drex took to more. The girls saw the blood on him, it scared them.

"Are you my daughter," he asks? I've been told you are. Come here let me show you what will happen if you tell anyone that you are my daughter." Walking to the queen he let the girls look through the door.

Screaming he said, "That's my daughter, now leave this

place if a guard comes to you. Tell them only you are pregnant."

"Yes, sire," they said. "Now go, leave this place," Drex commanded.

Drex let the other girls go he had inside the chambers. Falling to his knees why can't I have just one sticking son. Then his thought went to the queen. Oh yes, she would give me a son. How can I make her see this? How can I make her see I love her? I'll go to her, tell her I have set all the girls free. I'll tell her I love only her. I'll give her anything I just want her for myself. Rising from the floor Drex went to his bed stretched out fell asleep.

In the village, the girls went running through the streets. The guards ran to the girls thinking they had escaped. The girls told them what Drex had done. The guards could not believe that Drex would do such a thing. The guards held the girls until the sentry went to the castle.

Returning the sentry said, "It is true, Drex has released the girls." The girls ran to where their homes. Stories were being told of the girl that Drex had beaten. The girl's mother came forward.

"Where is she my daughter, she is still there," she asks?

One girl said, "In the east tower with a woman."

"What woman," she asks?

The girl's story was the same, they all said, "We never saw her before."

"Who do you think she is," the question was asks?

The girls said, "We are not sure."

One old woman stood. "Mary, you have something to say." Heavy tears fell from her face. "I was only hoping he would return someday."

"Who Mary, who are you talking about?"

"Icol, my King," Mary replied.

Coe had walked through the gate to his shop, People were standing in front. There was much talk about what had happened. Coe like the others could not believe what had happened. Drex had freed all the girls except one.

I ask Mary, "What about the girl.?" Mary told me, she was placed in the tower where we saw the light.

I ask, "Did you say anything of this to anyone?"

Mary replied, "No, I haven't."

Mary asked, "Did you find Shila?" I told her I looked for her all night until sleep overtook me then I came back here. I hardly open the shop when the guards come in. "Storekeeper where is your daughter." I don't know, I looked for her last night. I went to the plains. I met a patrol the captain said he would look for her."

I ask, "Why do you seek Shila?"

Replying, "Drex had dropped the age. Drex wants a son for the throne. You would think after sixty-five girls he would give up." I said. The guard slapped me across the face.

Replying, "How dare you speak of your King like that."

"He is not my King," I said. The guard bound my hands took me to Drex. The guard explains to Drex, what had happened.

Drex asks me, "Did your daughter run away. I will find her store keep until she returns you will stay in prison."

"Then I will be there forever. I fear she is dead. Sire before you pass judgment on me, may I take care of my affairs. I need to close my shop. Sell the things I can. Let my friends know I'll be leaving. You will not tell anyone where you go. I will need two days sire."

"Very well, you will return here in two days," Drex said," I told him I would.

Drex snarled, "If I come for you I will kill you where you stand. A guard will be with you most of the time, there's no need sire. Where could I go." A sentry came to Drex.

"Sire," he said, "A ship comes to port." I thought this could be a sign, it could work. Leaving Drex I saw the captain coming up the corridor.

I ask the captain, "Sir do you plan to take on supplies."

The captain replied, "that's why I'm here." I told him to

come to my store. I said as he walked away I was selling all I have two days to do this. I told him I had the shop next to the inside pad. Walking to my shop I watched for the captain. In the back, I had two big crates I brought them from the back of the store. Placing them in the center of the store taking the tops off placing things in one of the crates. What seemed hours the captain finally appeared.

I had made fresh tea. Cookies Shila had made before she left. Suddenly I thought of my daughter where was she now where did she go. The captain speaking to me brought me back to myself. Two guards were with him, King's guards, Drex was having me watched as he said.

The captain said to them, "Leave me I'll be fine."

I ask him, "Would you like to have a cup?"

"Ah yes thank you," he said. The deal was made, the crates loaded the ship left.

On the second day, Drex asks, "Has any of you seen Coe, the store keep?"

One said, "Sire, yesterday he sold all his things to the Advairan captain. Drex sent for Coe to come to the chambers. The guards searched the village he was nowhere to be found. The guard went to Drex explained to him about the search.

Drex went crazy, find him, he is here somewhere. I'll have his head go beyond the village go to the plains he has got to be here somewhere. Bring him and his daughter to me. Twenty-five guards left the castle the search for Coe led them to the house of Basco. Looking around still no Coe. As the night come upon them making a camp one guard said it's as if he flew away.

Drex head guard said, "What did you say."

Repeating his words," He flew away."

"He nodded, yes that's what he did. Coe left on the Advairan ship.

"Sir no one saw him go aboard the ship, we were there."

"I know, he went aboard in the crates. When the sun comes we will go to see Drex. I'll tell him what has happened. Drex will send a ship to find them you will see."

CHAPTER
6

I eased my way to the window, "Tenna there's six of them." I said as I peered out the window.

Tenna said, "Watch the back Icol, there's two coming around." Taking the stick, I used as a crutch I waited as the men come to the corner, I was ready. Tenna told me I was a warrior, at this minute I was scared.

I whispered to Tenna, "We must take one just to find where we are then you can kill him."

"Ah sire, I have no problem doing that." A craft came from nowhere. Two guards stepped out, there is no one here let's go. A relief came over me I was not ready for battle; if Tenna had stood well I would have too.

Each guard left looking my way, they knew I was there. Leaving with the other he pushed a box from the craft. I was not sure why he did that.

Tenna said, "Icol I was going for the box. I believe they're far enough, so we can't be seen."

I said, "Tenna, let me go. I'll retrieve it, maybe it's food. I am hungry." I started to go to the box. The scooter came screaming back. It was a trick, yet they did not stop. They just kept on flying. I waited this time watching the guards. When the guards were out of sight I went for the box, it was food.

Sitting around the fire Tenna told me if we leave now we might find their camp before sunup.

I said, "Tenna, not even a Claxton likes to move around in the dark."

Tenna said, "Well not on a troop mover anyway."

Tenna said, "It's my belief Icol, they did not go far."

I ask Tenna, "Why would we want to find the camp?"

"Sire," I said, "If we overtake their camp, take their craft we don't have to walk. When we find the camp, there might be a fight, nothing we can't handle."

"I don't know Tenna," I said, "I'm still weak. I do see what you say is true. I will try to keep up Tenna lets go. Tenna you must promise me if I fall you will leave me." Tenna mumbled something under his voice I could not understand what he said.

Later he told me what he said. It made me smile kind of made me forget our troubles. Tenna and I were hunted men, no doubt Drex was behind this. Tenna told me there's no doubt there will be others coming for us, such as hunters, you will see.

We walked through the night. I wanted to stop, my head was aching. My vision was beginning to go blurry. My mouth was dry I needed a drink. I was walking behind Tenna, he stopped suddenly.

"What is it Tenna," I ask? Tenna stretched out his arm.

In a very low whispered Tenna said, "Someone is out there sire."

"How do you know," I ask? "Tenna I can't see you, yet I hear nothing.

Tenna said, "Remember your training Icol."

"Tenna I don't even remember me, you talk of training."

"Sire look with your mind, listen with your mind," Tenna said. Closing my eyes, I stopped for a moment. Letting my mind go wild, in a meditated state of mind. I found what Tenna was saying. I touched the shoulders of the big Claxton there, "Tenna there is what we seek."

"There's no fire that we can see," I said.

Tenna said, "Icol, it's uphill they could hear us coming." Tenna caught the wind the breeze is against us, that will help.

I ask, "Did you see what kind of weapons they have."

Tenna said, "I will take my sword that's all I need. Some will be asleep the others will be sitting together; the surprise will be ours." Moving a few meters, we come to the top of the hill.

As the wind blew the wood smoke to us, Tenna said, "it's a fire all right." We could not see it for the rocks.

"Let's go, sire," Tenna said, "The craft will not be where they are. Maybe we will get lucky we could use it." Walking away from the fire I thought, Tenna was right. The walk to the craft wasn't a long walk from the fire. There was no guard.

The wind blew the smoke our way. The guards were cooking

something on the fire. It smelled as if they had killed something. I prefer fruits and vegetables. Some people as I remember on Galaxo did eat meat. When they could find it, it was something rare.

Tenna stopped me. "Look, sire, the craft is there. They're no guards." Like wild animals, we came closer and closer until Tenna reached out to take hold of the craft when a guard stood. Tenna hit him with everything he had I heard it pop when he hit. The guard hit the ground as another one come from the darkness. I took him out. Tenna said, "Now sire, jump in, we're leaving."

Since I was not all here in my thought Tenna took the craft to its highest-flying altitude. One thousand feet we had a flying craft how long we kept it, well that would be another story.

Tenna said, "Icol, we need to find a village or a city. It is my belief the Advairan had not come this far."

I was not sure of this myself. I do know we were moving. From the flying machine, we could see for many, many miles. We were looking in all directions for any kind of light. For what seemed several minutes we flew taking the craft up again to extreme heights.

Tenna said, "Icol," Turning to face him Tenna pointed, "there on the horizon to the east a white shade, a city from the looks of it a very big one.

Tenna sat the craft down just outside the lights of the city. Making our plans before we entered the lights of the city streets.

Tenna said to me, "We need to have a bath, a change of clothes." The clothes, we were wearing we would be spotted as an Advairan prisoner. We had taken the craft I would hate to trade it for something. We need it to travel to other places. The craft wasn't worthy, yet we need to travel.

Reaching in my pocket I took out a gemstone maybe this is worth something. Tenna looked at the stone.

"Sire where did you get this," he asks," I told Tenna, I have had it for a while. I took it from the place they made us dig. The color reminds me of the color of her eyes.

"Icol, if you had been caught with it, you surely would have been killed," I told Tenna I didn't care I was dead anyway.

Tenna made his way to the top of a ridge. Straining my eyes, into the lake of lights, I told him my memories were returning. I told him I will never go back to that prison, where we were for so long.

"Tenna I tell you this, I will find my way home if it is in me. I will find Drex, I will kill him. I will take his life with my hand in the market square for all to see. Tenna I will make you a promise this night. We will go home I don't care who I must kill to get us there."

Tenna said, "Icol that's your training, I'll stand by you to the end. I will fight for you. I will fight with you. We need to find out what is going on here. First, we need a bath and new clothes."

Tenna placed the craft in an alley on a side street. Shadows were looming all around. Looking down the street people and beings were everywhere. I walked into the street of this fine city. A man was standing beside a shop. The man looks at me strangely when I ask the name of the city.

"Are you daft, man," he asks?

"I do apologize, sir, sometimes I forget my name," I said.

The man said, "You're not from here, I can tell you don't speak with our dialects, your attire is different too." I told him I just come from a freighter. I have a friend we seek sanctuary.

He asks, "Are you running from the Advairan, they're everywhere." I told him I will not lie. We stole the craft from them on the plains then come here.

"Ah Then it is for sale," he asks? I told him it was.

The man looked very happy, "I will give you six hundred pieces for it." Well, I had no idea what that was. I took the stone from my pocket showed it to him. I ask, "Can you help me sell this?" Looking at the stone he reached for it.

"I tell you this, if you can sell the stone for me I will give you the craft. If you tell where you got it, I will kill you or the Claxton will." He stared into the eyes of Tenna. Tenna was standing in the shadows, stepping out into the light the man gasps. "You are the ones they look for," I knew it. "Show me the stone," he said. I open my hand showed him the stone.

"Oh yes," he said, "very nice indeed." The man told us to come from the street.

Tenna asks, "Are there other being here."

He said you are draft, "There's every kind of being from every universe I can think of.

He told us the Advairan said, "They must find you, they have their orders."

Tenna asks him, "What is the name of the planet."

He replied, "Gara, the ship you were on crashed outside of Oma. It is a village where we trade. There is a reward for you. Sell me the stone I will help you." The man looked at me. "I know your Icol, I know you're a King on your world."

I ask him, "How do you know me? How can you know me? We must be a long way from my world of Galaxo."

He said, "Several hundered light-years. I'm not sure where in the systems."

He replied, "There are others that do. I fear bounty hunters will be looking for you. Yet I have not heard of this."

Still looking at Tenna, then he said, "Come let me get you off the street. Come inside this is my shop. I assure you it is safe. If I cross you Tenna will kill me."

Tenna smiled, "Oh I will do just that." There were fresh fruits of all kinds, meat was roasting. I know I was hungry. The bread was dry the fruit was tangy I did not try the meat. He gives me a drink I've never had before. It had a taste of fruit. The man called it the nectar of the Gods. I took a drink of it. Moments later I was talking and walking funny.

I said, "Tenna, something is wrong." I fell to the floor.

I was looking for the owner when the doors open wide two Advairan guards walked in. The shop owner behind them,

I killed the three of them. I was light-headed, holding to the counter I locked the door Icol was laid out on the floor. Walking back down the stairs I picked him up. Come on friend walking up the stairs was all I remembered. Somewhere in the night, I woke up.

Icol asks, "What was that Tenna." I told him I had no idea.

"Icol strip your clothes, take your bath," I said. "Then I will take mine. I have acquired clothes for us. Hurry we must leave this place. We will take supplies the guards will look for us."

I had wished for a long bath, yet I knew we needed to go. Tenna also had to take one. Tenna was taking a bath, I placed the fruit in the pockets of the guard. I placed the currency in their hand. It would look as if they were stealing.

I ask Tenna. "Why would he turn on us?"

"Remember he talked of a bounty. There was a poster of us just no currency was offered."

"What do you think Tenna?" I ask?

"Icol, the guards could not know we were this far. I mean how long had it been since we took the craft in the plain, eight hours. I tell you there's no way they could be looking for us. The guards could not have walked here that fast. Six days since the crash, news travels fast on a ship. Think of it a ship leaves Oma, they heard about the crash, two escapes, it is possible."

I walked to the back of the store looking out everything looked as normal as I guess it could be. This was a strange place I didn't know their ways. Returning Icol said he had a headache. I took the pack I made, I told Icol to let's go. Walking to the door looking out, wait someone was there. I told Icol someone was there."

"Kill them as you did the guard Tenna," I said.

"As you wish sire," Tenna replied. Starting out the door the man appeared. I mean you know harm I'm just looking for food. I told him to wait, stepping inside I told Icol we need to go. Walking outside I told him to help himself. Dark as it was he could not tell who we were. Icol and I made our way to the craft, threw the pack in, went aboard. Once again, we left for parts unknown.

CHAPTER 7

Basco found the place he had used before. Dris and I helped push the craft into the cave, in the lower part of the mountain.

I ask Basco, "You have used this place before."

Basco said, "It was a long ago, little one. Tenna brought me here. I was a small boy, smaller than Dris." Leaving the craft, Basco took us to a place in the woods by a mountain of rocks.

"I smiled." Turning around in a circle looking at the enormous mountains that appeared before me.

Dris ask, "Why are you smiling ShIla?" I told him I'm one day closer to my training one day closer to finding my king.

Dris sat on the ground, lie back on his arms, "Shila you have never met the king." I told Dris, your right I haven't, I have read of him. Dris took a straw placed it in his mouth staring at me.

"What is it Dris, why are you staring at me," I ask?

Dris said, "My father, was trying to teach me words. He said I will make a good warrior, I need teaching." I told Dris I will help you if you want. Basco returned with wood for a fire. This place is used a lot by the Claxton's they come here to wait on humans or ships.

I said, "Basco, I thought they were all in the mountains."

Basco said, "The first rule of your training nothing is as it seems. There is always someone, somewhere Shila. The hand is not quicker than the eye Shila. If you have been trained properly," looking at his son, "isn't that right son."

Dris answered, "Yes father, it is what you taught me first." Basco continued to talk as Dris and I listen. Always be aware of your surrounding, always when you make a camp look to the horizon. Here in the mountains is no different than in your house.

In your home, some things can hurt you as here. Basco told Dris while there is light, show Shila your stands on how to hold the staff. I will prepare us a meal.

Shila was thirteen years old. I could tell by the way she walked, the way she carried herself she would be a great warrior. At this point in her life, I did not know how great she would be. If the Claxton's will not train her, I will. She will be a great warrior as my son already is. Yet I never let him know this, I only tell him his training is good. He is just as good with a sword as he is with the staff. Yet the Advairan had powerful weapons. I made a crude meal told them it was not much.

Shila said, "Ah Basco it is fine, I know there will be days and nights we will go without." I thought little one you just don't know.

Dris ask, "Father is this the place we wait on the Claxton's."

Basco replied as he stretched out, "No son it's a two-day climb. They know we're here, I promise you. Shila took out a book, Dris ask of it.

She said, "It was very old."

Basco asked, "Shila may I see it?" I passed the book to him. Turning a few pages, he asks about the person. I told him I had no clue of it.

"Shila he said, "This is about the ones that come before us. This woman is what I was taught, was from Earth very long ago. Lola came to the planet our ancestors were from. Then to the planet that disappeared."

I said, "Basco, I do not know of that. I remember my father told me stories as a child of our first King and his wife.

Dris was reading the book as Basco talked to me. Basco told me Dris's reading had improved so had his skill as a warrior. I told Basco I love the way Dris showed me how to stand. I loved the way he showed me how to move my body, how it lets me sway like the wind.

Basco said to Dris, "Son, show Shila, how to run the rocks. Shila this is something you must learn. It can and will save your life someday. It will help you escape others, it's not only rocks, it is as I said, but rocks can also turn into a building if need be."

In no time Dris was up Shila watched him with every dire of her body. When he moved her eyes never left him. In her thought, Dris was like his father. At the age of thirteen, Dris was a warrior. When he was finished with the rocks, Dris and

I talked for what seemed hours. Talking of the only thing we knew, the village.

Basco woke up "Children sleep, you will need your strength for tomorrow it's a long climb."

I watched them make their beds. I knew it would be hard on Shila. She never had to endure the work like Dris. I feel I will have to carry her, which will mean leaving supplies behind. Drifting back to sleep for what only seemed a minute when Shila was shaking me awake.

Looking up I ask, "Shila what is wrong."

Replying, "Basco something comes or someone. I can't wake Dris he is in a deep sleep." Basco crawled to Dris, he was lifeless.

"Basco, what is wrong with him," I ask?

"Dris wake up son." Basco said, "Shila his spirit has left his body." Looking at Shila, tears were flowing from her eyes.

"Basco why has this happen," I ask? I placed my hand on Dris, wake up Dris, please wake up. Whatever was moving outside our camp come in. It was a Claxton boy about my age. He told Basco, let me have him. Reaching in his bag he had a pinch of dust blowing it in Dris face.

He is strong my friend. "I saw you last evening. I was on my way to the plains there is a ship coming soon," He said.

I spoke, "How do you know this."

He smiled, "You are a human female."

I said, "Yes I am."

"You must turn, go back now," he said. You will not continue females will not be allowed to enter the city."

Shila jumped up, "What is your name?"

Replying "I am called Oc."

"In this city of your, you have no females."

Oc said, "yes, of course, there's many."

"What makes them different than me," I ask?

Oc said in a whisper, "You are human." Basco if your son is strong he will survive. What has happened to him is a test?"

Oc told Basco to look at his neck. There was a small dart in the neck Basco took it out. I have seen this before, long ago, we must leave Shila, I must carry him you will need to carry his pack.

"I will Basco, do not wait for me, I'll keep up, I promise. I will make you proud," I said.

Basco took Dris in his arms as we started to move. The sun peaked the eastern sky. The sun on my world came quickly and stayed long, this made it good for travel. Basco stopped several times. I told him I know why you stop, do not stop for me, I will keep up.

For the next three hours we walk walked up, I thought I would fall. My legs got so heavy never one whimper did I give. My thought was always the same.

I knew when we arrived at the city of the Claxton's it would be hard for me. I started to do something, I meant to see it through, I would be trained by the Claxton's. I would fight them if I must. Then I thought how far I would get with that. I laughed out loud.

Basco said to me, "Something you want to share little one." I just kept walking at least it would show them I was strong. Finally, we stopped.

Basco said, "We rest here for the night."

I said, "Basco he has made no sound all day."

Basco replied, "I know little one, yet he breathes." My legs were shaking as I placed the pack on the ground.

Basco said, "Shila I'll gather wood for a fire." I sat with Dris holding his hand, Dris open his eyes.

"Shila," he said, "I was so happy, I kissed him on the face as tears fill my eyes.

"Oh Dris," I said, "are you ok?"

Dris ask, "We are not where we slept?" I told him what had happened with the dart, they shot you in the neck.

Dris ask, "Why?"

Basco said, "It was to test your strength."

Dris said, "Shila it's as my father said, they know we're here." Take your scarf and wrap it around your neck put your coat on." The time it took for me to do this, three darts hit my neck I fell to the ground. I fell beside Dris Basco saw the darts ran to me. "Shila!"

I said to him, "Let me play Basco."

Basco said in a light whisper, "I understand."

I whispered in a very low voice, "Let me lie as if the poison has entered my body." Basco picked me up placed me on his coat he called to Dris.

"I'm fine father," Basco told Dris, take care of her.

Basco made food, Dris took some of it to me in the darkness of our camp Dris took small pieces fed me. Basco watched in the firelight I watched him as he smiled. I knew then he realized what I was up to. Dris lie beside me all night. I heard a noise that woke me. Someone came into our camp. Dris and Basco were fast asleep.

How could they sleep? How could they not hear them? I'm not a warrior I'm a little girl I hear them. Closer and closer they come until they were over me. Whoever it was, pushed me with a stick, then a foot. I wanted to smack his ass, yet I remained still. Dris woke up yield. Whatever it was run from the camp into the darkness.

Basco jumped to his feet. Dris he called." I'm okay father, whatever it was tried to take Shila."

Basco said, "It was a Claxton warrior son, only a test. In a low whisper, little one.

"I'm fine Basco," I said.

Basco said, "Yes, Shila I can see that you cheat."

"I'm a woman Basco, I play by different rules, besides what difference does it make I'll show these Claxton's," I replied

"Little one, I think you already have," Basco said as he went to the fire.

Basco turned to go back to sleep. Dris came close to me, it was the first time in my thirteen years of life a man or boy has lie beside me. I could feel the warmth of his body as he turned with my back to his stomach, with his right arm over me. I do admit, I liked it.

I whispered to him, "Dont get used to this, I will become a warrior."

"Shila," Dris said, "Even a female warrior needs to be comforted by a male."

The sun came quick, opening my eyes it was full daylight. Basco and Dris were still asleep. I come to my feet walked to the edge of the camp, I let out a scream. Basco and Dris come alive.

Basco called to me, "Little one."

I stood tall yelling, "I made it, you think you could discourage me so easily." Dris walked to my side, I took his hand held it high. "We both made it, your medicine is strong, we're stronger."

From the rocks, high above the camp three Claxton's warriors sat watching. Listening to what I'm was saying, I shouted at them. They didn't know what to think of this human female. They made talk among themselves. Dris and I returned to the camp Basco stirred the fire then added more wood.

Sitting around the fire I ask Basco, "Now what?"

Basco said, "We climb, again after tea we packed our thing left for the trail All day we went up higher and higher into the mountain. The air was growing thin, it was kind of hard to breathe. Yet we kept climbing.

Basco turned after an hour, "Shila, do you need to stop?" I looked at him as I went past Dris.

I smiled, "Dris might need to, I'm fine."

Dris said, "I'll get you for that." I laughed out loud Basco had a smile on his face. I loved Basco.

We kept climbing, the grass had turned brown the air thin. Topping out on a mountain, to a clearing you could see forever.

Basco said, "we'll make camp here." I never said a word. I was thankful, I was tired.

Later I ask Basco, "Is this where we wait?"

He said, "No little one."

"Basco you said two days," I said.

"Yes, I did, yet we are not there."

"Very well," I said. We go ahead tonight."

"We cannot Shila the forest is not safe at night. We could walk off into space." I was sipping my tea as I listened to him.

"I understand what you said, Basco."

"What would that be," Basco ask?

"Basco, Remember, you said the hand is not quicker than the eye, it takes training. I just saw someone dart into the bush. I thought they were smart Basco."

"Shila they're cunning warriors, little one, maybe they wanted you to see them."

"Well, Basco It works I did see them." I eased myself to the right picked up a small rock walked to the edge of the camp. Basco or Dris had no idea what I was about to do. I turned suddenly, I let the rock go where I saw the Claxton, I hit something. I heard a grunt, walked back to the fire.

Basco asked, "What was that?" I told him it was an animal.

Dris said, "Yes Shila, a two-legged animal, Dris and I laughed. I went to my pack, Basco told me to go to sleep. Maybe an hour later I looked at Basco and Dris they both were fast asleep.

It was very dark in the camp. Basco told us to make aware of our surrounding. Do this just before dark, see what is out there. I saw a small bush that I thought was a perfect hiding place. I crawled to the bush very easily. I had no clue why I was doing this. I just thought it was something I needed to do. Something told me to sleep by the bush.

I took my coat placed it where I slept covered it with my cover. Under the bush where I crawled, I lie waiting, for what I wasn't sure. Closing my eyes, I thought of my father. I thought, was I missed in the village. If Drex harmed my father, well I would deal with Drex when the time comes. I'm too close to let distraction take over, too close to my dream. lying under the bush I could see Basco. I have loved him, for as long as I could remember. For some reason, Drex did not bother him.

Lying still, looking at the stars through the branches of the bush, was that a movement, what was it. I had my staff lying on the ground beside me. The one Basco give me before we left. Little one, keep this with you, learn how to use it, watch Dris. Shila if you will listen to me, I will teach you.

Every time we stopped Dris and I would work out with the staff. Basco and Dris said to me, the five days we have been together I have already shown the makings of a true warrior. Basco told me if the Claxton's did not train me he would. I told Basco if he trained me we would have to leave this planet

Basco asks me, "Why is that Shila?"

Answering I said, "If Drexs guards find us, it will be death to us, you know that. No disrespect to you Basco, the Claxton's will train me."

Dris said, "You sure are full of yourself."

"Dris if they will let me speak they will train me."

Watching and listening to the sound of the night from my hiding place, I made out a being a man. I could tell, it was a Claxton. Closer, and closer he came. I moved my right hand placed it on the staff. He made his move I slapped him on the knee joint. He was not expecting that, I was expecting him.

The warrior went to the ground. I placed my left foot all in one motion, just behind the back, he went forward. The Claxton turned to his back, my staff went into his throat. Basco and Dris come alive calling me.

"Over here Basco, I've caught me a real live Claxton," I said with a smile. Oh, he was mad. He snorted like a wild animal, yet he was caught. I told Basco there are two more out there. I pushed the staff harder into his throat, "call then," I said.

"I will not," the warrior said.

"You will call them, or I promise you."

A voice called there's no need for that." Dris more wood on the fire. Basco made give a signal. I had him I felt good.

Basco said, "Little one let him up."

"Know Basco, I like him where he is, on the ground. Basco if I let him up he will try to hurt me. I have the advantage at this moment." Like lighting, he came from the ground. I thought well I might die here so here we go. He made a dive at me the rocks moved under my feet, I fell slapped him again.

Basco stood in ah, as the other two Claxton's laughed. I then learned a lesson more than any training. I took my eyes off my enemy. It was a mistake, I'll never do it again.

"The Claxtons said, "You are a female." It was dark, they couldn't tell until the fire showed on me. I turn to say to them when I was hit hard in the side. The Claxton was on top of me. I was kicking screaming get off me, you coward. Your no warrior fights me like a warrior. Hitting me when I wasn't looking that's what cowards do.

"Dred stop," came the call from the others. He jumped up offered his hand. I hit him in the knee joint again taking him down once more. I grabbed my staff all in one move placing it around his neck applying pressure.

Basco called, "Shila let him go."

"Very well," I said. I kissed him on the side of his face, whispered in his ear, "I kicked your ass. A thirteen-year-old human female kicked a Claxton warrior's ass." Then I let him go. He jumped up, the next thing to happen I did not expect it. I was waiting for anything. He bowed to me. I bowed to him never taking my eyes off him. In the few days of training Basco or Dris never told me that. He backed up where the other two were, he said something to Basco then left. Later that day I ask Basco what was said.

Basco answered, "Little one they said tomorrow someone will come to us. we must wait here."

I hate waiting I said as much. Most all-day Basco showed Dris, and me how our stands should be. I was tired, I needed a bath. I said as much. Dris showed me a stream just past the camp.

Dris said, "Shila if you don't undress I'll wait with you."

"Dris I need a bath, not a wash. Go beyond the rocks I need a bath. When I'm finished you can take one, you need one too."

Dris said, "I'll wait."

"Oh well," I said. "I just thought you might want to sleep next to me again. I don't want no smelly man close to me."

Dris said, "Ok Shila, I'll take one," Returning to the camp Basco talked to us about the day. Little one, they might not let you come. Stand your ground, you will know what to say, and what to do. Dris you will be asked to follow them. I will be asked also, remember ShIla stand your ground." I slept very well this night I was the first up. Dris watched every move I made. Looking at me funny.

Dris said, "Someday Shila I will take you for a mate, you will see.

CHAPTER
8

Several hours after leaving the planet the Advairan captain went to the storage area. Taking the top of the crates, Coe looked up.

Thank you, sir, "Captain, little do you know sir, you have saved my life. Drex surely would have killed me."

The captain said, "It's time we remove him from power. Coe why did Drex have you sell your things."

"My daughter Shila ran away. A warrior named Basco, took her and his son left to parts unknown. Drex had sent for her to join his sexual pleasures. Like he has done with the other girls some of them his daughters."

The captain said, "It's time we place Icol back on the throne."

"Icol," Coe said.

"Yes, he is alive, or I think he is, somewhere on Gara."

Coe said, "I do not think so sir."

The Advair government planned his escape. We also planned the Claxton's. We just did not know the ship was going to crash, that we did not plan. We have looked for days for them. The Claxton and Icol we know went into the village of Oma. That's where we lost then, now they could be anywhere. Drex told me if I returned without them, he would kill me himself."

"Captain, Drex will kill you this I promise you."

"It will be several days before we reach Advair, Coe, make yourself comfortable. The captain said.

Walking back to the control room the pilot asks, "Sir where to?"

"Set course for home," the captain said. It would be a great day when we place Icol back on the throne. I wonder how he survived in the mines so long. Icol was tough.

When things started happening to the guards Drex kill several, that's when the government took notice. The leaders were brought in meeting after meeting then our King said.

"Drex paid us well for the two prisoners. I give him my word that Icol and the Claxton would be work to death. We never knew he was the King of Galaxo. When we found out we staged their escape. I am sorry for what has happened.

Several days it took to reach our home world. Seeking a meeting with our King. I reported the meeting of Drex.

The King said to me, "Captain we will never go there again." I told him of Coe the storekeeper. It would appear his daughter ran from Drex with a warrior and his son. She was to go to the castle for Drex, she was thirteen."

"Captain this is not the first time I have heard of this. This Drex needs to be killed." Captain go take this Coe, to find Icol make it your highest priority."

The captain said, "Yes my King, as soon as we can resupply I will l be gone."

The captain went back to the pad, told Coe what the King had said.

"Coe, you say your daughter is with a warrior?"

"Yes, she is I saw them leave."

"Then we should not worry about her. This warrior will take care of her. This Basco you speak of, you know him well." I told the Captain I know him very well, all his life. The captain kept talking. I looked out the portal watching space go by. I wondered if I will ever see my Shila again.

Captain, I said, "I know where they'll go. I didn't know at first now I do. Basco will take them to the mountain of Trion."

Captain Paso stopped. "Coe the Claxton's will not accept her. They will, sir it's a long story."

Paso said, "Yes, I'm sure, one I wish to hear." Walking to the bridge the captain and I stood as the pilot made a course to the base of the mountain.

"Sir, if you're doing what I think you're doing you will never find them."

"I know Coe, you are correct. I know the Claxton's I have met them they always have a runner. You will see."

It took several days to reach the mountains. Paso stopped the ship in orbit. He told me we will go to the planet with the sun. I sat thinking of the planet. What if Drex waited for the ship to land. I said as much to the captain.

He said, "I would not worry much about this. We will land with no problems. you will see."

Taking a shuttle from the ship captain Paso and I left. Following the base of the mountains, Paso went to the place where Basco went.

Paso said as he looked around, "There's only one trail, Coe no one has returned." Sitting in the shadows of the mountain a young warrior appeared. "See Coe," Paso talked to the young one. They both laughed as the warrior made signs with his hands. He made a sign what looked to be five feet, then another one about a foot higher. I heard Paso say the little girl did that.

The warrior left, back into the shadow of the mountains. The captain told me, let's go back to the ship. Smiling he said, "Coe, have I got a story for you."

Several hours on the ship, Pao telling his stories. I found myself in disbelief at what I heard. My little girl, this was not Shila or was it. I somehow knew this was going to happen.

Paso said, "It seemed she was headed to the city of the Claxton's. Her training has already begun. The Claxton's shot her and the son of Basco with darts, they survived. Shila got into a fight with one of the warriors, she won." The captain told me he had sent word to Shila that you were with me.

I ask, "Coe do you want to stay with me or return to your village?"

I said, "I will stay here with you. We can find Icol together."

Minutes had passed when Paso said, "I told the runner, give a message, I told him, tell the chief we look for Icol. We are placing Icol back in power."

The runner said, "I will go none stop. I do not know Icol, it was before my birth. I do know the name. If the Claxton's go I will follow. Icol is a Claxton warrior. This I've been told."

The captain told me, the Claxton's will not train the girl. Before the young one left he told Paso. I will train her, teach her all I can. If Shila, Dris, and Basco leave to find Icol I will be with them. I will defend her with my life." I stood looked at Paso.

"My daughter will be the only human female trained by the Claxton's.

Paso looked at me, "You know something I don't know Coe." I told him someday I will tell you the story you wanted to hear.

The captain said," Yes, you will Coe, I insist."

Somewhere on the mountain, Shila watched Basco and Dris work out. then it was her turn.

Shila said in a low voice, "Basco, I noticed several times you held back on Dris. I promise, you hold back on me I will try and hurt you."

Basco laughed hard bent over at the waist. The first mistake, I took him down with my knee joint move. Just as before, with the Claxton. I saw madness in the man's eyes as he came to his feet. He came up like a wild animal. He did not see that coming. I learned my lesson on the trail to where we are now. I won't make that mistake again.

Basco came from the ground. He had a look on his face, "Little one you will not get that chance again." So many times, Basco would take his eyes from Dris. The way I see this, the enemy will not do that. What I learned was my enemy will try to kill you and will if you're not working to stop him. I don't want to die. I watch for any given chance, I'll take it.

Basco was off the ground coming at me with full force. Swinging his staff at me. I could feel the wind from the staff as it passed my face. I fell flat he tried to recover I rolled to my right side, I took the big man down again. I've watched Tankko, Nordic some of the other guards, watching the mistake they make.

"Basco you say I was lucky to take you down. Therefore, I want to be trained by the Claxton's."

Basco said, "Shila you were lucky to take the Claxton's down too.

I smiled at him, "Yes, I'm sure I was Basco, yet I did it."

Basco got up, I've had enough between you and my son I'm tired go little one rest. Basco knew I would turn to go to the campfire. I turned to leave throwing my staff above my head.

Smiling as I turned, "Basco you are a dangerous man, after you."

Walking to the fire Basco ask me, "Shila why did you keep this hid from me." I told him I was afraid he would not take me to the Claxton's. When I came to your house. I was hoping you would take me and Dris. Look where we are Basco, one more day closer to my destiny.

Basco asks, "What is your destiny Shila."

My answer was, "Basco, it is to be trained by the Claxton's, find my king."

Basco said. "Then what Shila?"

Taking my staff, I brought it over my head in one motion, how it happened I'm not sure. I hit the bush, I split it in half.

I replied to Basco, "And to kill Drex." I said it with a smile.

Dris ask, "Shila what is wrong with you?" I told him if you were a female you would understand. Many thoughts ran through my mind when I said that.

I said to Dris as I recovered from my stands, "I only want one man. Who would want me if I was sent to Drex, I hate him." I looked at Basco for the first time with a look of hate.

"Basco, I will kill anyone that stands in my way of full filling my destiny.

Basco said, "Shila who is dangerous now?

"I'm not dangerous now Basco when I have finished my training I will be."

Walking to the fire I thought of what Shila said. She was a strong girl. Watching the training of the guards was no doubt very good for her. She was better than Dris. I would not tell her or him that, the training of my son the fight with the warrior, if she can enter the city we will not be there long. Sitting by the fire having a cup of tea I thought of the village.

I ask, "Shila where was this place you watched the guards work out."

"Basco," I said, "remember I told you I didn't know if I could trust you."

"I remember little one." He said.

"Basco, now that you have brought me here. I will tell you something my father doesn't know. My father's shop was one time used as a quartermaster. It was storage for the king. I don't know this for a fact just talk. My father said the king at the time was Icol great, great, grandfather. Maybe three- hundered years ago. In our history, I find this to be true.

In the root cellar of the store under our house, I found something my father doesn't know. I found a passage to the training area. I would ask my father to let me go to someone's house. The passage was covered with old boards and dirt. My father would never know.

The passage would travel several feet then up by an old tree. When you stand up you were in the middle of bushes and flowers. There would be no one that could see you. Like I've said Basco I'm a woman I play by different rules."

Basco asks, "Could a full-grown man walk through this passage?" I told Basco two men could walk down the passage side by side.

Basco said, "That's how Drex got so many men into the castle without being seen."

"Basco my father took the shop two years ago. Before that, we lived outside the village. Drex had to know about the passage. Maybe as a small boy, he watched the guards come and go caring supplies to the castle."

I started to take a sip of tea. I jumped to my feet. "Someone or something is out there."

Basco said, "I hear nothing." Dris said the same. Then a loud sound we jumped behind the rock.

Basco said, "Little one, you will make a great warrior."

In a soft whisper, I said to Basco, "I promise I'll make you proud of me."

Basco replied, "You already have."

Dris ask, "Do we fight?" The three of us came from the rocks, made a circle, facing outward. I told Dris as we stood to wait.

"Dris you ask if we fight. I say yes by all means."

Dris said, "Watch for darts." Two young warriors come from the trees.

"The female that fights," one said. You have started history in the village of the Claxton's. We have been sent to bring the males."

I said to them, "You speak of history, come let me show you a little more history. Let me kick your ass as I did your brother.

"Shila," he called. I moved when he said my name.

"We cannot take you. You must go back, you cannot come." Then we fight here and now I told them.

"Shila, my chief said no."

I went into my stands. "Then you fight me now, prepare yourself, Claxton."

CHAPTER 9

Drex had waited for several days for word. There was no guard no ship no nothing. Drex walked to the balcony looking over the village. People were moving around. Drex was so mad he wanted to kill someone. His thought went to the first time he killed. A message was sent to his father. There had been an accident. Running to the edge of the village, Drex was waiting. Drex killed his father placing the Queen in charge.

The queen was told of Drex. She sent guards into the village. The talk was Drex killed the king. Several of the Claxton's were training the guards. Tenna was one of them. Drex knew it would be a matter of time before his mother died, he would make sure of that. When she died he would make sure she would pass the crown to him. He told her more than once. Mother Icol is not fit to be a King, he is weak.

Drex had several counsels with the queen. Each time Drex put Icol down, only made her want Icol in power, at least Icol was intelligent. The queen told Drex if he wasn't satisfied, he could leave the castle. This upset Drex.

Drex left taking several men with him. in his thoughts he would show her how weak Icol was.

One morning the queen summoned Icol and Tankko. In her council, she expressed what must be done. Tenna and Tankko spied on the band of rebels. Several weeks passed when the two reported to the queen. In their report to the queen, they told her how strong Drex was growing.

The Queen said, "We must post a guard." They both agreed. Several months later Drex returned to the castle. He carried herbs in a pouch on his side. The Queen's maiden was watching this. Drex had no idea she was around.

She watched him place the power in a vase of tea, he took it to his mother. She drank the tea as Drex ran from the room, the Queen died. Placing Icol in power, the Queen's maiden told what she had seen. Drex ran through the village telling everyone Icol had killed the queen. Icol poison my mother.

Drex was talking to a crowd. He was telling of the event.

One man said oh you mean like your father.

Drex said, "Who said that?" A guard stepped forward.

Drex said to him, "When I take power I'll kill you."

"My name is Basco. I am and always will be loyal to the King and Queen, now they're dead. I'll stand by Icol and his queen."

Now that did not go the way Drex thought it would. Several times Drex sent guards to kill Basco, they never returned. Several years after Icol took power, Basco went to Icol. Basco wanted to mate with a girl he had loved since childhood. Icol, Tenna, Tankko was waiting in the chambers when Basco arrived. Telling his story Icol granted him his request. Icol set him free from the guard ship.

Icol asks, "Basco if I ever need you, will you be there." Basco looked at his King, hand over his chest. I may leave you services sire, I'll always be loyal to you, and the queen.

Walking around, "Who is left in the chambers," he asks?

The guard said, "I'm not sure sire." Walking to the maiden chambers opening the door no one was there. Drex's thoughts went to the girl he threw in with the queen. Drex ran to the window, all of this is mine. Why can't I have her?

Falling to his knees Drex said again, "Why, why can't I have her, with hate in his eyes looking out the window I love her. The hate grew in him, then his thought went to the girl, she said she was my daughter. I could kill her as fast as I could kill a rat. Walking down the corridor Drexs thoughts went to his brother.

I could kill him. I should have done that long ago. What would I do if Icol did return? He will have her, then I feel he will kill me. I do not worry about Icol my guards will not allow that. My guards are loyal to me all of them.

Drex slowed his walk stopping again, he thought of the girl again. Drex felt sure by now the people in the village knew what had happened. Down the corridor, two guards stood by a door. Drex started toward them reaching out his arm.

The two guards crossed swords. "Sire at your request, no

one enters, no one goes to her. Only the maiden that carries her food."

Drex screamed, "Get out of my way your stupid fool." Drex was saying this as he hit the guard. You think you can keep me from her, I am the king. The guard picked himself from the floor threw the sword down.

"Then guard her yourself." He expressed. Drex ran for him then stopped, as the guard turned to face him.

"Kill me Drex if you can." Other guards had shown up.

Drex shouted, "Kill him.

One guard said, "I rather not sire."

"Kill him, or I'll kill you,"

"Sire, then kill me, I will not draw arms on a man for doing what he was ordered to do."

Drex stood with sword in hand, "Very well leave this place, the castle, the courtyard. Guard if you ever return I'll kill you.

The guards backed up leaving the corridor. Drex thought yes this is good. There's no one to help her, no one to come to her rescue she will be mine. Walking to the door where Shara was, trying to open the door shaking the handle it would not move. The small window came open.

Shara responded, "So the coward returns. Drex what is it this time, you would think by now you would give up? Did you come to beat me as you did your daughter? You are a pitiful man, Icol is coming to Drex. Every day Drex, he comes closer."

Drex screamed, "Shara, open this door, why is it locked?"

"Go back to your chambers Drex. First, let me show you something. I brought the girl to the window. She was black and blue, her eyes still swollen together her mouth still ran blood after a week. I said to him, this, this is what makes you a man," I spit on him. "If I had a sword I'd kill you myself. You say you love me Drex. You're not capable of love, look what you have done to this child."

Drex yelled, "I did nothing Shara, it's you. If only you would give me your hand in marriage."

"You want me Drex," I ask?

"In a pleading voice, Drex answered, "Yes Shara.""

"Drex I will marry you, stand by your side forever if you wish. Drex you have to give me one of two things."

Drex said, "Anything Shara, anything. Just tell me what it is." I looked upon the man I most despised in my world.

"I will marry you if you grant me this. Bring me Icol or his head, until then leave never to return until you have granted me this."

Shara closed the door walked back to where the girl was. Drex was pounding on the door. "You're crazy Shara, your insane. Open this door, Shara."

I said, "Go Drex never return until you have granted me my request. "Drex went back to his chambers. Looking through the window he saw two guards talking, then four. What was this it would seem they're not as loyal as I thought?

Drex was sitting alone in his chambers, he was furious. The sun showed midafternoon. Drex sent a sentry to the gate with a message. Close the gate come to the chambers. The message was sent to all the guards. It was said for them to meet in the chambers of the king.

Drex was sitting on the throne when the guards appeared. He walked amongst them, Drex stopped. Looking around he said, "it has been brought to my attention" Silence, was on the guards as they listen.

Drex said, "It would seem some of you are not very loyal to me. Of course, you know of the others leaving."

"Sire," One spoke,

Drex asks, "You have something to say?"

"Sire, I have been with you from the beginning. I've killed people that did not deserve to die. This I did because you said ordered it. Never have I ever stood for anything but you. If you had given me an order, not to let anyone go to the queen, that also means you. I would have done the same as the others."

Drex asks, "Are you loyal to me."

The guard replied, "I think I have proved myself to you sire. I cannot speak for the others."

Drex asks, "How many others feel this way. This is my order, go to the gate turning to the man that spoke. Take six men, go find the ones that left, kill them, bring me their heads, prove your loyalty to me. Guards, if you return to me without their heads, I'll kill you myself."

Bliss was the head guard. He had been with Drex since he had taken power from Icol. Walking into the guard's room, Bliss told the ones that Drex had picked, "Gather your things we are leaving now." Walking outside to the hanger Bliss asked the captain for a craft.

"We'll take the scruple, that will work," Bliss said.

The captain asks, "What is it today?"

Bliss said, "A mission I wish not to take. I must find the guards that left, take their heads, bring them back to Drex."

"Captain, I do not wish to do this. Some of us have families, Drex will surely kill them. My daughter is almost of age. I do not wish for her to go to that place. Captain, if I do what he says their safe. Two years she will be thirteen then she will go to that place. I swear this day I will kill him myself."

"Go, Bliss, take your guards and do what you must. If I was you I would take the big ship, go to Advair."

Bliss replied, "Captain, they could not have got off-world there only a few hours ahead of us."

"Bliss, take the ship, go to Advair, start your search for Icol." The captain said.

Bliss said," Icol is dead. Drex made sure of that long ago."

Replying, "Yes I suppose if that is what you believe. Like he tells everyone the queen is dead. Yet he keeps her locked in a room in the east tower."

Bliss said, "You think Icol is still alive. My crew and I just returned from off-world, we were told they escaped from Advair. Now go there I will try and watch your family. Bliss search for him until you find him. Icol the true King is alive this

I promise you."

I stood in the hanger looking at the ships. The captain said, "take that one." He pointed to the smaller one, it was even smaller than it looked. Yet would serve the purpose. My men went aboard walking to the bridge. I watch all take their stations.

The pilot asked, "where to captain?" I told him to set a course to Advair.

Traveling at the speed it took several days to reach Advair. The ship came to a stop in space. The pilot told me we were in orbit above the planet of Advair. He had called for landing clearance. The Advairan ask our reason. I told them I needed to speak with their government. I was told the story again. I was told how they help Icol escape.

"Bliss we here on Advair do not Condon what you king is doing. He is not my king, he is Drex. I serve him, so my family will live. I was a guard when Icol was in power. Walking to the window looking out, "now I face my daughter at the age of thirteen going to him."

The chief said, "I was lead to believe the age was fifteen." I told him It was until he found out he was having sex with his daughters.

"That is ridiculous," the chief said. I told him it's the truth. Even Drex didn't know. One was taken to him, she told him, Drex beat her almost to death. Locked her in the room with the queen.

"Ah, so she is alive." The chief said.

The chief and I talked for several hours, then I told him it was time to go. He told me to go to Gara. The ship they were on crashed on Gara. I'm told in a village of Oma. Bliss went back on his ship told the pilot to set course to Gara. We will start our search in a village called Oma.

CHAPTER 10

Tenna or I had no way of knowing that the Advairan were looking for us to carry us home. We killed the guards thinking they were going to take us back. Leaving the store, we placed our packs in the Scruple stepped aboard. I told Tenna it sure does get dark here quickly.

Tenna said, "Yes it does sire." Knowing there was no ship at one thousand feet we went up. Flying what seemed hours with no light in sight. The gray light into the east told me it was coming daybreak. The sun would be up in no time.

In the gray early dawn, Tenna looking down saw a huge rock outcropping, looking around he found what he was looking for, landing we made a crude meal.

Tenna said, "Sire you rest, I will scout see what is out there if a ship comes close do not move from the overhang. The Scruple is out of sight, it can't be seen."

Tenna left to do what he had to do, I was tired. Lying back under the overhang somewhere in the early morning sun, I fell asleep. I had no idea how long I had been asleep when a voice called to me. My love, I have waited so long. I see her running to me as I was running to her. Her long hair her eyes the kiss, yet I could not remember being with her.

Tenna said my memories would come back, this I wish would happen. Something brought me fully awake. Looking around I said it was just another dream. She is so beautiful I must remember her. I sat with my back to the wall it was already getting dark. Nights were so long here. I sat waiting for something, yet I knew not what. I began to worry about Tenna. What could have happened to him? If he does not return, what do I do?

Tenna was a warrior. He knew his way around, even on this strange world he managed. I sat straining my eyes to see anything that moved, I dare not make a fire. Yet if I did maybe he could see where I was. If he has not returned by daybreak, I must search for him. Tenna said I was a warrior. I knew nothing about tracking. Just as he calls me sire, he said I was a king. I do not feel like a king.

Sitting alone in the darkness I stared into the night, the stars did not give off enough light. I was wondering about something else, where was the moon. We have been in this world for over two weeks. I have seen no moon. Maybe that's why it gets dark so early, maybe this planet was a moon. Could it be this is the moon of our world, I think not? Yet it was nice to think of my home, my wife Shara.

Wait, why did I say that, have I heard Tenna speak of her, or maybe my memories returning as Tenna said they would. Shara yes, my wife I do remember her, the woman in my dreams. Advair the mine Drex the overthrow of the kingdom. I was mad, a feeling went through me it all came back. I stood let out a scream that could be heard for miles I suppose. Tenna came around a huge rock."

Tenna asks, "Sire what has happened?" Sitting on the ground I placed my head in my hands.

Tenna I said, "My memories have returned, all of them. Tenna we must get off this moon."

Tenna looked at me, "A moon Icol. Why would you think we're on a moon?"

"Since we have been here, have you seen a moon," I ask? Tenna brought the wood back, sitting on the ground placing the wood to build a fire.

Tenna replied, "You know sire I have not, just stars." Tenna started a fire told me of the scouting he had done. He told me off in that direction as he pointed, was a farm.

He explained, there was a small craft come with one man. I take it was the farmer and the pilot placed several boxes on board. There must be a village or town to the east.

Tenna had the fire going. Rest sire you still need rest so do I. Lying on the ground we both fell asleep.

What seemed minutes Tenna touched my arm. "Sire someone or something comes." Tenna stood facing the noise when three men come around the rocks.

I heard one say, "What is that? Looking at Tenna I told them he is a Claxton he's not from this world."

One of the men said, "Well you're not from here either."

"Your right we want no trouble," I said. They started laughing.

Tenna said, "We're just passing through."

The big man standing close said in a silly voice. "You want no trouble. How is it a being as you can speak our words like us."

Tenna said, "I assure you there are several planets where humans like yourself, and other being that can speak words. I've never heard of this. He said.

Tenna replied, "I'm sure there's a lot of things you have never heard of."

The man said, "Well if it's not trouble you want its trouble you found. The rocks are mine. You will pay to stay here maybe you are wanted, men." Turning to his two friends, "Yes he said, that's it you are wanted. We will be taking your belonging."

I jumped up, "You will take nothing from us, I will give you a sword. They moved so did I? I took two of them Tenna took the other.

Tenna smiled, "I see your back, you still have one on me. I noted I am back except for the girl my wife something is still not there. In time Icol, it will come. I helped Tenna place rocks over the three. Placing our things in the Scruple we left our night camp in search of whatever lay east. The early morning came to this world as we flew into the air. Tenna was in silence for a few minutes.

We traveled on when Tenna said, "Sire look a village." It was small, yet a village. Tenna sat the scruple down on the pad next to a ship. I did not know the ship. Tenna told me to watch myself. Be aware we do not know what to expect.

I looked at Tenna, "Always my friend," I said. We stepped from the scruple, we were waiting for what I was not sure of.

Tenna said, "Well sire, let's see what kind of trouble there is." Entering the street from a small alley didn't take long. Walking around a corner, now you have seen places you've been you didn't want to be. This was one of those places you don't want to come back to. This was one place I wish we had never stopped. The village was called Maki.

Humans just can't let things go. Tenna came from the corner two men were turning the corner, Tenna ran into them. It was an honest mistake.

Tenna said, "I do apologize sir." We kept walking.

"That's ok, whatever you are." one said. We started to walk on.

One called, "You, you just keep walking." I told him again, we apologize, sir. Now humans can be so stupid.

He said, "Know you don't we fight here now."

I looked at Tenna, "Well there's two of us, which one are you referring to.

"The ugly one, he said.

I looked at Tenna, "Well my friend, I think he is talking to me."

Tenna said, "Icol these humans have no sense of humor." By the time Tenna said that a big stick went past my head. I looked with a look of disbelief. I started to say something when he pulled a sword. Well, that was good enough for me. I thought, An invitation.

I did take pity on them, not like the ones in the rocks. Maybe I wasn't in the mood to take another life. I punched one, turned on the other. Tenna smiled at me go Icol go. Watch it Icol. Then it was over, they were lying on the ground. Guards came running to us. I thought we are caught."

Tenna whispered, "Not yet there's only three of them. Let's see what they say, if they're not for us I suppose we could kill them."

I said to Tenna "Ah yes, I'm for that." Tenna smiled as the guards approached us.

"What is the meaning of this," He asks? I explained what

had happened.

The guard asks, "Where are you going with this thing?" I told him, Tenna is very intelligent, his race is called Claxton's. Please don't refer to him as this thing.

The guard said, "He is not human."

"You are correct, yet he has more intelligence than the two on the ground. Look we don't want trouble, we are just passing through."

The guardsman asks again, "Where are you going?"

"We were in Minot looking for a ship," I answered.

He asks, "Why do you look for a ship." I told him we wish to work on a freighter.

The guard replied, "Well if you go two days to the east, the largest city on the planet is Rulla. It also has the largest port."

I said, "Planet you say."

He replied, "Yes I do say."

"Tell me," I ask, "Why is there no moon here?"

"What is a moon, you have seen this thing you call moon? There is no such thing here," he answered.

"I'm sorry," I said, "a moon is a beautiful thing. A huge light in the night sky."

The guard said, "Maybe someday I will see this moon. For now, finish whatever you are doing then be gone. If you go to the east side of town you will find a place to sleep." Going back to the scruple we found the place the guard sent us.

Tenna said, "Icol, the news of us has not reached here yet." I wonder in Minot if they had received word of us. I was not going to worry about a small fire I lie back on the grass and went to sleep.

CHAPTER 11

A ship landed in the small village of Oma on the planet of Gara. Two tall guardsmen walked off. Walking from the ship's pad a word was passed. The man he asks pointed down a small street. Walking to the local magistrate's office looking around before we entered.

The magistrate said, "I saw the ship come in, we don't get very many ships here we are on the back side of the planet.

Tell me, captain, "What is your mission here," he asks?" I told him we look for survivors of the crash weeks ago.

Let me introduce myself, "I am called Bliss."

The magistrate said, "Well the crash happened weeks ago, the Advairan said they would come to clean it up. The ones that walked away the Advairan has sent for them."

Bliss said, "Then we leave you."

"Well, there were two that did not go. One had been seen in the village, the other one was from another world. What are the species called?"

I said, "They're called Claxton's, very intelligent. There also warriors very capable of killing a man. The Claxton's comes from the mountains of Trion, of course, that's on my world."

I was told of this after the crash. If I was asking Bliss, I would say they were trying to land here for some reason. As I have said, we don't get many ships. I can show you where the ship is"

"It should have been gone by now, yet it is still there."

As I said, "It should have been gone by now, it would be nice if they would clean it up."

While the magistrate got his things ready to go, I sent the guard back to the ship. I told him to tell Taso to come to me. Tell the pilot we will be here a while. You also come back.

The guard said, "As you wish," then went out the door. It took an hour for Taso to come to the office.

Taso asks Bliss, "How can I help you."

Bliss responded, "Your training came from Tankko, he taught you how to track. Then come with us, the magistrate is going to show us where the crash happened. He said one man was seen. He also described the Claxton."

"We will try to start, yet it gets dark here fast." The magistrate said.

Leaving the magistrate office Taso ask me, "What are we doing?" I told him we are looking for a Claxton.

Taso asks, "Why are we not doing what the king ordered."

"Is that what you call him," I ask Taso?

"He is my King Bliss."

I looked at him, "Yes, so was Icol. If Icol was here would you follow? We're not the only ones searching for Icol. The Advairan are searching, the Claxton would if they had a ship." We walked to the crash site it was not hard to find.

The magistrate said, "Well here is what is left." The ship was damaged badly. What I don't understand the magistrate said, is why they let him go?"

"What do you mean," I ask?

"Bliss when they come here they took the ones that were here, then left. They didn't look for the other two. The captain had guards dressed like you. "Tankko!"

"Yes, that is what he called himself."

I will be honest sir, I told him the story of the overthrow of the girls the magistrate looked in disbelief.

"The people of your village let this go on." he asks?"

I said, "Drex has over two hundred guards they are very loyal to him. Look the village people are afraid of Drex. They give them food supplies even their daughters. There was a fifteen-year age. Now I'm told Drex drop the age to thirteen years."

"Bliss, surely you can find another colony that would help," I told him, it's us and the Claxton's. When we find our king, then it will be our turn. Drex or Icol will die. Icol's Queen is still alive in her castle, she is a prisoner. I assure you Icol will fight for her." In the middle of our talk Taso return. I didn't look outside. It had grown very dark.

Taso said, "Bliss I swear I've never seen a place so dark."

The magistrate said, "We only have five sometimes six hours of light." He told us he was one hundred thirty years old. It's always been this way.

I ask Taso, "Did you see any kind of trail."

Taso said, "There's a trail it is old, yet it is there. I do not wish to move around in the dark."

The magistrate smiled, "That was a smart move." I sent the others back to the ship I told Taso I would come later.

Taso replied, "I wish to stay Bliss, I know you will say more. I already know what you will say, I see it every day. Bliss I'm loyal to Drex." I told him I was too at one time. Taso what if your son was a girl how would you feel knowing she would go to him, so he could have a son.

Taso said, "If that is his wish I must for fill it, he is king."

"Taso return to the ship, maybe you would like my position," I said.

"I want nothing," Taso said. I do not wish to take your leadership. I wish to do what Drex sent us to do."

"Taso the ship returns to our world tomorrow. If you wish you may go with it. When the sun comes tomorrow, I go look for the Claxton called Tenna, if he is alive so is Icol. Icol needs to be back in power." The queen needs to be freed from the tower where Drex has had her for twenty years."

Someday Icol will be back in power, that will be a glorious day Taso. Now go to the ship." The magistrate and I talked for hours. I heard something off in a distance.

The magistrate said, "Bliss your ship leaves." I ran to the door three guards were walking toward me.

"Taso took the ship Bliss," the guard said. He told us if we were loyal to Icol get off, we did. Taso said he was going home the fool, saying that out loud. I told them tomorrow we follow the trail of the Claxton. The magistrate showed us a place in his office where we could sleep.

"Bliss something you should know. As I have said, daylight does not last long. You will need a craft; I have one it is a six-man craft capable of space travel. Maybe it's time I leave Oma."

"Sir if you will let us have the craft, come with me." The gray had come to the morning sky as the magistrate woke us.

"Would you care for tea," he asks? I took the cup, with his hand outward.

"My name is not uncommon here. There are several Bunns here, no reason it is just our ways. We must hurry. I took my guards walked to the crash site. Walking through the village every being watched. A small boy walked after Bunn.

The small boy asks, "You look for the ones that stayed in the old house in the field."

I ask him, "What do you know of them?"

"I know there was a human, not sure of the other one. He looked human just not so much as a human. I was hiding when they come from the village. The human was sick or injured, I'm not sure. If you follow the street through the village to the plains, you will see. In a field close to the forest, you will see the house."

The small one asks, Are you a guard?" I told him I was.

"Someday," he said, "I would like to be a guard."

Walking to Bunn, I ask, "Do you know the place?"

"Bunn said yes, "it's outside of the village," I told him of what the boy had told me. I'll stay on the ground you stay with the ship, I'll come aboard at night. Leaving the village, we found the house, just as the child said. I found the camp, footprints all over. Searching the grounds, I saw where two left on foot to the east. The trail was cold, yet it was there.

For several hours, I followed the trail until it got too dark to follow. Bunn landed the ship I told him I found the place where the guards had slept. They have a scruple know.

Bunn ask me, "How do you know this?"

"I found where it was parked, they pushed it out only two sets of prints," I said.

Bunn said, "Then Minot is the next town. We will leave at first light."

Bunn and I walked outside looking at the stars.

I said, "No moon again."

"What did you say," Bunn asks?

I said, "No moon, a light in the sky so you can see how to travel at night. When it is full, it's almost like day."

Bunn looked at me with a skeptical look, "I've never heard of this besides why would anyone want to go walking into the night."

"I'm not saying that Bunn, it is just beautiful. You should come to my world sometimes you would see what I mean."

Bunn replied, "Well Bliss maybe someday I will. I took a writing tool a piece of parchment wrote down the grid of our galaxy where we were from.

I was watching skyward as you could see ships far into their atmosphere. I told Bunn this.

He said, "They all look like stars to me." I showed him at least ten.

Bliss said, "I've never noticed that."

Bunn asks, "Bliss you have a daughter?" I told him I do. In two years, she will be of age. Bunn let me tell you this, I'm a man that loves his family."

Bunn said, "I feel sorry for the people of your world. Maybe we will find your king." I told him I know he will try to go home, I feel it.

"Maybe," Bunn said.

My thought went to Tankko, where was he. Has he found Icol, I feel he doesn't know we're looking for him? I also no Tenna, he's a warrior, he will do everything to hide them, day or night. Maybe they have already found a ship. Only my thought, yet I feel they're still running. Tenna will seek a port city.

It would take a big city, one where they would blend in.

I ask Bunn, "What is north?"

He said, "Nothing as I know of, to the south just farms. The farmers gather their crops. They take them to Oma, Maki, Minot, and Rulla. Rulla is the largest port city, it lays three days ahead of us."

I said to Bunn, "Trust me, someone will know if they pass. If they see Tenna they will remember. No one forgets a Claxton, I promise you. We rest now tomorrow is another day."

CHAPTER
12

Mornings come, yet they go. It had been two weeks searching for a ship. Tenna watched every day for a ship to take us home. The journey we left behind, has ended. Our journey ended here n Rulla. Rulla was the largest port and largest city on the planet. There was nowhere we can run from here. Sometimes, I sat thinking of the men in the rocks, the man in the shop. The lives I took, so I could be free.

Tenna talked to the captains of the ships. Each time they would tell him no. You will not find a ship going there. It has been passed to the words of the other ship, it was a bad place to go. The captains said it was said the king had been known to take heads in the streets.

I sat alone on the barrier thinking, what happened to my home my world. It must be a wasteland. I waited for Tenna to return, he was talking to the captain of another ship. Tenna knew what to say and how to say the words. I only wanted to go home. The day was coming to another end, as the sun left the sky. Tenna came from the shadows.

"Sire I have found us a ship. We will meet the captain this night. There is a shop from the Port where we are to meet." I walked the floor wondering what to expect.

Several hours passed when Tenna said to me, "Icol, it's was time to go." Walking through the door I turned to see a parchment on the wall. The parchment was in large print. Wanted in Minot for the death of a shopkeeper. I took it down, a voice from behind me said.

"I was going for that. I am a hunter, are you?" I did not know what to say I just looked at him, I said nothing.

He asks, "Maybe we could partner up." I told him I already have a partner. I'm here to see a captain. I feel the poster is old. I feel they have already left the port. It was said they boarded a ship for parts unknown."

The man looked at me with those empty eyes. Eyes that could look through to a man's sole.

Tenna walked to me from the back of the shop, "Come, my

friend, our appointment." I never took my eyes from the man, I told Tenna of the poster. You know I just don't understand humans. We were trying to be nice. Tenna being the person he was, me the same. All we wanted to do was go aboard a ship leave here. Why is it humans always metal where they have no concern?

I wondered if they do this on other planets, then I felt sure they did. Well, it wasn't funny.

The captain said, "Do you know this man."

Tenna said, "No sir."

"He said I was on Zoop a while back, I have no clue where that is." I jump in sir we don't know him. The hunter came up whispered something to the captain.

Tenna said, "Icol, here we go." Well, I backed up, the hunter came first. The other one Tenna had on the ground, bleeding from the mouth.

Tenna asks, "Did that hurt." Well, I smiled at him lying on the floor.

"You know Tenna I bet it did," I said.

Two more jumped in, one said, "You can't do that in here." Tenna hit one I took the other. Then we were back to back.

One said, "He's defending that alien. Someone kill him."

Tenna looked at him, "Sir would you like to kill me."

He replied, "I have no weapon."

Tenna kicked one to him, "Now you do."

"I'll kill you, you bloody alien." He bent over to pick up the weapon. Tenna kicked him in the mouth.

"Did that hurt," Tenna ask?

I said again, "Oh yeah, I'm sure it did look at the blood." The man got up ran out the door. I looked on as the hunter pulled himself up from the floor just, to go down again. His two friends were moaning in the corner.

The captain said, "Well you will do, you are hired."

Our newly found friend said, "We leave in two days, when the supplies are loaded were off to Eden."

The captain gave his approval to move on the ship. I can't say I wasn't happy to leave Rulla. Never seen a place so dirty.

Tenna said, "That's the way it is in a port city Icol." Tenna had been with me for a long time. I knew he was with my father too. I'm sure he traveled with him on his travels. I wonder sometimes, where did they go? Did they ever go to the place of his grandfather? This I will ask him someday. I wondered if he ever had a mate. So much I know, so much I don't know.

Later that afternoon we were sitting on the deck, watching the other ships come and go. Far to my right, I saw movement.

Tenna asks, "Icol, may I see the paper?" Taking it from my pocket I handed it to him.

Tenna said, "Someone's to my right." I saw him hiding moving closer for a better look.

Tenna said again louder this time. "Sire it would appear you will be having a guest."

"I shook my head, I Know, no one here."

Tenna said, "Oh sure you do. The hunter is coming to see you. I think he wants another round with his newfound friend."

I said to Tenna, "Well then, I don't want to disappoint the man."

The hunter started aboard Tenna said to him, "Sorry friend you cannot come aboard."

He said, "I have business on board with the captain." I told Tenna, let him come I'll send him back to you, I'll whip him again.

The hunter said, "You were lucky, very lucky, next time he said." I told him to let me hurry this time up. I jumped off the deck to the ground where he was, here it is.

The hunter replied, "Here what is." I told him the next time. The hunter made his move to the right. There was a very loud sound. I looked at the top of the deck. The captain stood with a weapon in his hand.

"Well I can't have people hurting my crew, now can I." All this time I turned to see what was going on with the hunter. He was lying on the ground with blood coming from his chest.

Our captain said, "Check him, see if he is dead."

Tenna said, "Oh he is captain he is."

"Tenna, come to my quarters bring your friend with you." The captain said. Tenna and I cleaned up the body of the hunter.

Tenna said, "Icol there will be more."

I ask, "Tenna, do you think it's the Advairan that sent him."

Tenna answered, "Sire it's hard to say. Could be the Advairan, sent word to Drex. Could be Drex sent them. It's hard to say who sent them. It possible it could be the Gara government." I told Tenna, I never thought of that.

Since the dealing on the deck one hour had passed. Knocking on the door of the captain, enter was the words that come from within.

The captain said, "We would be leaving soon. I expected to be here for another day. Yet everything has been loaded. looking at Icol the captain said, look you two I run a tight ship. I must have everyone's trust. If I can't trust you, we have a problem." Taking a paper, he looked at it. Then looked at Icol again then he looked at me.

"Tenna," he said, "What is your race called."

"I am a Claxton, my race as you say are trained to be warriors from birth. Captain all Claxton's are very intelligent, in my world we have no ships. Yet I can fly this very ship."

"Why are you trained Tenna," he asks?

Tenna said, "Sometimes other planet calls on us for protection. I tell you now captain no four men can take me. No eight men can take us both."

"Very well," the captain said. "Now this world of your, where is it."

"The planet of Galaxo, Tenna said, "Very far from here."

The captain asks, "Every thought of going home?

I looked at Icol he gave me the sigh, "Captain" I said that's what we are trying to do. The trouble there, no captain wants to go with their ship."

"Very well Tenna. Now that brings me to you," looking at Icol. "Icol that's your name."

I looked at him, "It is sir, the name my mother and father give me at birth."

He looked at Tenna then ask the next question. "How long has he been with you? I looked at Tenna.

Captain in our years I'm forty-two years old. He has been with me since before I was born."

The captain said, "Well how is that Icol?" I told him, he was my father's advisor." Well, I could see he was looking for an answer.

"Then Tenna trained you, he said.

"Yes, sir since I was eight."

The captain asks, "Your father was a powerful man?" He leaned back in his chair.

Tenna said, "Captain, why all the question. I am his guard now. I will defend him until my death."

"Tenna I mean no disrespect." He answered. The captain talked on for several minutes.

"Icol," the captain said. "The way I see it you must be of power on your planet. If you will allow me I can help, I have this paper." The captain showed it to us. The same paper Tenna has in his pocket.

The captain asks, "Can you explain this?"

Tenna asks, "Why do you think it is us?"

"Tenna, I ask for your trust."

"Very well," Tenna said, "He befriended us then turned us in."

"Turn you in, the captain asks, turn you in to whom?"

Tenna said, "The Advairan."

Turning to me he asks, "Why?" I reached into my pocket. I took out the stone placed it on his desk.

"Yes, very nice," he said. Where did you get this?"

"Captain," I said, "The stone is yours if you do not ask

questions. If you wish we can go back ashore. We Tenna, and I are honest and trustworthy. We just want to go home, captain I must go home. I took the stone for passage to pay for myself and Tenna. I know it is valuable.

The captain pushed the stone back, "Icol I don't want the stone, it is yours."

"The paper said you killed a man in Minot, I wondered why. I now wonder why you are running when you are in power somewhere. We will talk later now go find you quarters we leave shortly."

The next day the captain call Tenna and me to his chambers. He told us it was a hundered and twenty-seven-day journey to Eden. When we arrive, you can go off the ship if you wish. I will talk to the general for you. Maybe he can help you find a ship back to this planet of yours.

The meeting Tenna and I had, we give our thanks to the captain, we turned to leave. The captain spoke we both turned to look at him. He had a smile on his face.

"Of course, there is an alternative. We stood listening. "You could stay with me, stay with me I'll help you gather information. Just be honest, now go think of this. When you're ready come to me tell me all."

I looked at him with a smile. "Betray me, captain, I'll turn Tenna on you. There is nothing more vicious than a Claxton warrior."

Captain said, "Oh Icol, I believe you, I really do."

CHAPTER 13

From the forest two warriors came from the rocks, then three more. I told Basco as we were waiting for the Claxton to move. I yield loud, come on cowards.

The Claxton in charge said to me. "I do not wish to fight a female,"

"Then it is settled let's go," I said.

He replied to me, "You are a brave one Shila. Oh, you look surprised I know you. Your battle has reached our city. I was sent to bring them. I was told not to bring you."

"I go with you, or we fight here now," I announced. I took my staff started to twirl it in many ways. I started in a half-circle. The Claxton started smiling.

I yield, "Hey don't smile, fight. This thirteen- year old human female has already kicked a Claxton's ass."

"Shila, I or my warriors, do not wish to fight you."

I stood straight, "Yes," I said, "You like to hide in the bush as a coward, jump someone when they're asleep." I think I touched a spot.

"Shila," I am chief of the village."

"Then chief, you fight me. I know you should be better than a warrior. Who knows, maybe I'll get lucky, maybe I'll kick your ass also." Everyone started laughing. "Chief," I said, you will fight me. If Tenna was here he would train me." There was silence.

The chief looked at me very strange, "Shila, what do you know of Tenna." I told him only what I've been told and have read in our archives before Drex closed it.

"Sir Tankko, Basco, Dris, I will place our king back on the throne. I need to be trained. Sir, as I said taking my eyes from him, hoping he would take his chance. I was right he did, he had only one thought, I would not be expecting It, I was.

He made his move I made mine. I took the big warrior down everyone stood in ah. Looking at their chief on the grown by a human female. My staff on his throat please sir train me, I know so much now. I just need to complete it." I offered to help by giving my hand, he declined.

"I must speak to Basco." He said. The chief and Basco walked off to the far side of the camp. The other warriors come closer.

One said, "You are a good warrior now Shila." I told him as I have said, there is so much I don't know. Several minutes passed, the chief came to me.

"Shila, we have never trained a human female before. The reason they're so weak. You have made history in our city, our homes. From the cave where Basco hid the craft you have been watched. You and the son of Basco. Shila I have watched you before now. Someday you will find all the answers you seek."

The chief asks, "Will you finish what you start."

"Even if it kills me, I just want to place my king back on his throne."

The chief said, "Oh little one, you will hurt, I assure you. The first sign of weakness you will be asked to leave. I told him I accept this.

Basco spoke, "Chief I will train her, and my son." One from the crowd spoke. A Claxton very strong being. A master Claxton, like Tenna. Tenna was a grandmaster.

"My chief."

"Yes, Kash what is your bid."

"My chief, I will take her, train her."

The chief looked at me, "Dred has asked to train her."

"I've already beat him," I said.

The chief said, "Shila you did not beat him, you caught him off guard. You will see as time goes on. When we reach the village, you will wait for final approval.

"Sir, you said."

"I know what I said Shila, you will wait." It must be approved by the council.

"If I'm not trained, I know the way here," I said.

"Shila you will not remember when you leave. However, I see no reason why you should not be trained. What you already know with Basco speaking and myself to Dred; I do not think there will be no problem." I ran gathered my things looking back I saw a smile on his face.

Coming back to Basco I said in a low voice, "I'll show him and make you proud all at the same time."

Basco said, "You already have, little one. I wonder about what he said to you." Slinging my pack on my back, we left in a single file. The climb up the mountain was easier than before. Rounding a Huge rock, I saw a mountain that shot skyward.

Dris said, "We're almost there." Walking to the base of the biggest rock in my world, something happened. the Claxton moved the rock. A giant hole appeared.

I said out loud, My words."

"Come little one," Basco said, "hurry."

"Basco, what is this place," I ask?

He replied, "The doorway to the city."

The sound was so great, I turned to see the rock close. There was nothing but darkness before me. Then from nowhere, yet somewhere lights were everywhere. There were lights from their walls, the paths we walked on. I fell on my knees I had this strange feeling come over me as I've never had before.

Basco said, "Shila." I told him only in my dream have I seen such a place. A city that is so full of love. Claxton's were everywhere. I've never seen so many, yet the ones on the mountain are the only ones I've seen. I could see they all were looking at me. What were they looking at me for? A strange-looking female.

I wasn't sure what to do so I stood still, looking around at the beauty of this place. A young female met us.

She bowed to me, "You are the first human I've ever seen. Others have seen them. I knew you were coming. I am Fina, sister to Dred. We laugh when he tells the story of you. I too am a warrior, I have been trained since I was three. I started to tell her my name. She pushed out her hand palm out.

"I know who you are ShIla, there is a word the humans say,

I believe it is called friends." I was not expecting what was next, especially some being that wanted to be my friend. I reached out my hand, she took it jerking me to the ground, I hit very hard, she caught me off guard, my body went flat. I was up as fast as I went down.

"Ok bitch, a word I never use much, yet this bitch pissed me off. "Come on let's see what you got," I said." I knew she was a warrior, just the way she held herself. She was maybe fifteen. Her hair was very long and straight It was the color of a sunset.

Fina made her move. Basco has told me several times never rush a fight, let it come to you. She did, she took me down again. Well, the word I called her, was bad enough. Her taking me down twice, was the worst.

"Shila", she said smiling, "Your second mistake. You first were giving me your hand. The second one showing me your hurt."

Going in a circle limping a little I was not as bad as I let on. I took my staff as a crutch limping around I moaned out loud once.

I looked at Basco he smiled as to say, "Do what you must." Thinking I was hurt she made her move to go for the kill. Fina did not know what had happened. Fina found herself looking at the sun. She was lying on her back with my staff pressed against her throat.

With a gauged voice she yelled, "I can't breathe." A stern voice from the right. Enough! It was Dred.

I said, "Falling to a thirteen-year-old human female fall in your family."

"Little one," Dred said, "Let my sister go," I told him I like her here. Dred made his move. Dris took him down with a rolling block to the knees.

"Shila," Dris said, "We have them both on the ground, now what." Little did we know all of this was planned. Basco said as much when he ran to me. Dris and I stood looking at them clapping, smiling.

"Basco," I said, "Funny way to welcome someone," I said. Fina shot up from a lying position to her feet. She came to me with her hand out, I declined it.

"Shila I was being serious when I ask you for your friendship, I truly was. Yet I had to test you myself to see if you were worthy of my friendship."

"Well, I said, am I?"

She laughed out loud." I said, bitch."

She said, "I don't know that word." I told her if you are worthy I might tell you, someday.

Fina said, "Yes, you will or will kick your ass."

I backed up, "really," I said.

Fina turned to the chief. "Sir with your permission I will show them where they will live."

"Very well Fina, Shila you and Dris will start your training tomorrow. You will not need your staff. Leave them in your quarters." I looked at Basco he gives a nod. That was good enough for me.

I watched everything carefully. Fina showed Dris and me to our cabins by the river. I placed my things on the table.

Fina asks me, Shila would you like a bath." I told her I surely would. They had all the facilities as we did, yet I saw no power source, I never ask. Before we arrived, there were clothes placed for Dris and me. They knew we were staying, as she said it was all planned.

Fina asks, "Shila, the move you used on me, the one Dris used on Dred. Could you show them to me?

I said, "If you will stay with me, help me when you can."

Fina said, "Dred, is my brother he is a great warrior. I only hope to be as good as Dred someday. Tomorrow he goes for his promotion he will become one of the highest warriors there is. Each time a warrior advances to a higher level he or she is tested. There are not many female warriors, they wish not to be. Most take mates early in life. It is said, this I think is true the firstborn of all Claxton's are males.

"Shila, Fina said, "you have spoken of one of the highest warriors. It was Tenna, I never knew him. In our archives, it is written several pages of him. Kash you have met, there are a few more. I told Fina I would like to read of Tenna.

"Fina said, "It will be part of your training. When you're not training you will learn to read and write." I told her I already could do that.

She smiled, "The words are not of your language Shila. There are other worlds out there. Training for you and Dris will be hard because of your age. By the time I was six, I could speak six languages, one time our people traveled to other worlds until the overrun of you king."

"Fina that's why I'm here," I said. "Once I am trained Dris, Basco, and I will go out to find Icol. We will bring him home."

"Shila you forget one thing. I will stand by you too. I will become your friend and advisor." Standing from the pool my hair fell to my waist, my body was full, full as a thirteen-year-old should be I suppose. I think my top was as full as any grown female. Fina watched me leave the water. I saw her staring at me as I placed the robe on.

I ask her, "Why are you staring at me?"

Fina said, "I've never seen a naked human before. Does Dris, look the same as you." I told her no, there's was a difference in us. Fina took off her clothes. I saw no differences in our body I said as much.

Fina said, "Someday you will, it is not for me to say." Her long sunset hair hung low to her back. Her blue eyes, her skin looked a little different. The water came to her chin. Fina pushed her hair behind her ears, there it was. She had pointed ears. Fina lay back in the water, let the water come over her body.

"Shila, she said, "When you dress there is a white shirt on the bottom never train without it. Trust me it holds down your breast, so they don't bounce When she stood I saw her come from the water. Dris walked in, Fina never moved she dried off as if she was the only one in the room. Dris stood with his mouth open.

Dris said, "I've never seen a woman naked before. I waited for Shila to bathe once, I never saw her."

Fina asks Dris. "Do you like what you see?" I don't know if it made me mad or jealous. I walked to Fina, open my robe let it fall to the floor. Standing in front of Dris were two beautiful women from the neck up we were different, from the neck down we were the same. Except for the skin, it was kind of different.

Bosco walked through the door. "Well, what do we have here. Dris, son you are seeing something a very few men will ever see."

We told Dris, at the same time, "Look hard you will never see it again, for a long time."

Fina's breast was so full I could not believe it. It was like they were calling me. Come to me Dris, touch me take them in your hands caress them. I didn't know what I was doing. Shila's breast was full to be her age. They were not like Fina's, so nice beautiful as a mountain peak. I found myself reaching for them when my father stopped me. I got scolded. Yet I wanted to touch them both at the same time.

Basco said, "Dris touch a female Claxton, before your wed, means death."

"Father there here, before me how can you not."

Fina said, "Dris your father is right. To touch a female Claxton is death. Yet I would not have said a word to the council. I can't speak for ShIla. I wanted him to touch me." Basco looked at me standing without clothes on. I told him I don't know what I was doing I just thought if Fina was doing it, it must be her way of saying hello. I didn't want to be left out."

Basco said, "Dress girls we are called for dinner, in the hall."

I ask, "Basco, you've been here before?" Basco smiled as he walked away.

I heard him say to Dris. "You should learn to move faster

son."

Dris replied, "I will next time father."

Basco said to Dris. "It will be a long while before that happens again. Claxton women only get that way, once maybe every two years. It only lasts a couple of days then it's gone. This time tomorrow the feeling she is having I assure you, son, it will be gone, or it should be. I tell you this Dris, do not go to her again."

"What about Shila, father," Dris ask?

Basco said, "Dris, Shila is still a young girl, let her train first. You also need to keep your mind focused if it is permitted for you and her to be together it will happen."

The Claxton dining hall was as large as our castle. Well maybe not that big, their table was Huge. There was food of all kinds, yet I never saw anything growing.

I ask Fina about this, "Shila I do not know where it comes from, it is always here. Our dinner went well.

The chief came to us, "Fina go home you will need to rest for your training.

"Yes father," she replied. I started to say father when the chief said, "Dris you too must go. Shila had already gone.

I left on the run, I had to tell Shila of this. Running to where Shila was I went inside. "Shila the chief is, Dred and Fina's father."

Shila said, "She played us again that little. Dris we must get her back for this." I agreed.

CHAPTER 14

Several weeks Dris and I trained hard. At the end of the day, I was so tired. Climbing the mountain with Basco, I hurt from that climb, not as this. Sometimes I think they were trying to get me to give up. Well, that wasn't going to happen. When Dris and I weren't training in the daylight, we trained at night. There were times we were awakened to train.

I always looked for opportunities to get Fina back. I hate to say it, Fina, was very intelligent. Dred was a great warrior and a great teacher. He was better than Basco, yet sometimes Basco would stop in to see how we were progressing. Basco was my hero, always has been, if I was older I think I would mate with him. Basco was a very handsome man, very handsome indeed.

Our training was over for the day. I was tired to my bones. I went to the pool. I was lying on my back completely relaxed. I open my eyes to see Dris standing over me, it kind of startled me.

"You know Dris," I said. "I never realized how the water can make you feel, this water anyway." I was floating on the water; my naked body could be seen. I never made a move to hide it. I mean, after all, Dris, had seen me naked before.

I ask, "What can I do for you, Dris?"

Dris said, "Shila, you are a very beautiful woman."

I answered, "Not yet Dris."

Dris said, "What does that mean. Shila you are so complicated."

"Someday Dris, I'll explain."

Dris said, "I'll wait by your bed."

"You know Dris, there no reason you can't get in with me."

"I can't Shila, my father said to stay away from you. If it is meant to be, we will be together."

I reached for him, "I pulled him a little closer Dris." Dris stepped two steps closer. "Now bend down." I pulled his head close to me, I placed my lips on his. Kissing him was something new for me, I liked it. "Now you can go wait by the bed."

I stayed in the pool for a while. Placing the robe on I wasn't ready for bed yet.

Dris ask, "Shila you want to talk." I told Dris I want to study. Fina and Dred have told us we must learn to meditate.

Dris said, "Shila I can't do it, I've tried so hard, I just can't. My mind won't do what they want. Dred said if we have a problem we should come to him."

"Dris, Dred is so smart he can help you. You must do this to pass. Fina has helped me. Dris I want to go farther than here. I want to go to other worlds."

"That hit from the staff has got you talking crazy Shila," Dris said.

I told Dris I want to see if I can go to my father. I try hard not to think of him. I hope he got away from Drex.

Sitting on the bed, Dris took my hand. "Shila I'm sure he did. I'm sure you will see what you wish when we finish our training and find Icol. When Icol takes the throne back I'll ask for your hand, if you will have me."

I said to Dris, "I do have a strong feeling for you, I've never hidden that. I promise you Dris, there's no other man I'd rather be with except.

Dris said, "Yes Shila, I know my father. Dris how did you know?"

CHAPTER 15

The ship flew through space. Coe had never been on a ship before. Well not until he left Galaxo with us. Growing up on Galaxo with the ships, he never had a chance to go, however, he said he watched the ships come and go Shila.

The captain called for him. "Coe," he said, "If you like you may stay on Advair. I assure you your safety. Drex your King will not send a ship there. If you wish you can stay with us. Join the search for Icol with the ship ahead of us, I think Tankko is on it.

Tenna and Icol have no way of knowing we look for them to help. They think we look for them to carry them back to Advair. I suppose they will find out in time. I sure hope so, I don't want that Claxton loose, not on my men.

I sat for several minutes captain I said, "If it's okay, I will stay on Advair. Shila has always said if she was a warrior she would kill Drex. I truly believe she will.

The captain asks me, "Do you think they will train her?"

I replied, "If they will train anyone, it will be Shila. Captain, I must say with the mind of Shila, she will be a vicious warrior. I also believe she will kill Drex.

Captain asked, "Didn't you say she stood against Drexs men." I told the captain, that she did. Taso to be exact of course she stood to several of them. I had the parchment of paper, then the light in the tower.

The captain said, "Yet you can't be sure." Tankko told me she was alive.

"Captain, Tankko would not have said it, if it was not true," I answered.

"Tankko is ahead of us by several days," The captain said.

We had landed from our mission from the Trions. The ship from Galaxo sat down beside us. Bliss came from the ship. Bliss looked at Coe, then to the captain.

"Don't worry Captain, we're not here to kill him, we're looking for Icol. It's time for him to come home." I told Bliss, Icol and Tenna escaped weeks back. I have no idea where they could be. Feel free if you like to look around. Were at home Coe, has asked for asylum. He now is under the protection of the Advair government. If anything happens to him, I'll come for you. We're leaving we are sincere about looking for Icol. We want to take him home.

The captain said, "Bliss they're several ships looking for Icol. If someone finds him bring him here to Advair."

The captain turned looked at me, "Coe, they have no idea where to look. Coe in three days we leave, I think you should come with us and meet our government."

We set several hours talking. I give them thanks for helping me. The captain showed me where I could stay. I told him I would stay on the ship.

"Very well Coe, as you wish," the captain said.

All-day and night the crew carried supplies onto the ship. I never knew what was going on. I only thought of Shila somewhere in another world she waits for something, hopefully, she is well.

I wish to find Icol, I remember back when his father was king. I was a child, I remember when word reached the village, the king was dead. The word was he was killed by rebels. This placed the queen in power. Drex was compassionate to his mother. The more Drex downed Icol, the more determined she was to place Icol in power. This she had planned all along.

By the time Icol married Shara, Drex poisoned his mother. Icol took the throne. Several years he reined. To this day we still don't know how so many rebels got into the courtyard. Icol was like his father. He was a good man, cared for his people. The only thing Drex ever cared about was Drex.

The captain came aboard. "Coe," he called. "There is much to tell you. Last evening one of our ships come to port. There captain told a story of a being and a human running together on Gara, in the city of Rulla. That my friend is where we will start our search."

I ask the captain, "Is there a word of my daughter?"

"Coe I'm sorry. You said this Basco took her to a place on your world."

'Yes, captain I know he took her to the mountains of Trions."

"Good Coe, which is more important, finding Icol or your daughter."

I said, "Let's find Icol, even if we went back, they would not let us enter."

The captain took the ship up. It seemed like seconds we were in space. It was so beautiful streaking through space. It was like the lights were going by we were moving so fast. I went to my quarters to sleep. Sitting on the side of the bed I had such a feeling come over me. It was as if my daughter was reaching out to me. It was like I could hear her say words, impossible.

I lie on my back went fast to sleep. Morning came as it is in space. I was sitting on the main deck talking to the captain.

The captain said, "It has been several weeks since we left home. According to the pilot, we should be over Gara in about three hours. We'll take a shuttle to the surface. I want to start in Rulla."

The pilot sat the shuttle down on the pad after landing clearance was given. The captain opened the hatch, walked to the ramp, "are you coming to Coe." I told him, yes, I'll wait here on the port, I'll ask questions around the port.

The captain replied, "Very well I won't be long."

I walked around the port it was a fine port. Dirty as they come, yet it was a fine port. There were being here I've never seen. Some I've never heard of. The only reason they were here was to deliver or to take on supplies. Some of them were good, some would kill you in a flash. Walking around as I did, I walked to a human.

I ask, "Sir may I inquire about a person." He had a look of him to be mean. He set a small parchment down. "Yes, sir how can I help you. You lose someone," he asks? I told him I did, a human with a being called a Claxton. Maybe they were here.

"Tell me, why you are looking for them. We here on the

port do not talk of the shore man." I told him the Claxton was a dear friend, Icol was my son. Of course, I lied.

"Your son you say. I do remember them. Caused quite the problem in the eatery. In the city, several weeks ago. The captain took them on, he comes here maybe every six years."

I walked back to the ship with a smile. The captain had returned to the ship as I walked up the ramp.

"Coe," he said. "I had no luck. The Gara government, well they're looking for them for a killing in Minot. Only for questions nothing more."

"Captain if they did this they were challenged. I know Icol, he is not a bad person. The Claxton, well if someone tried to hurt Icol, well that's another story."

"It doesn't matter Coe the paper it's only good on this planet. It would have appeared, they're not here." I told him what I had found. The only thing the dockworkers would say is they were going to Eden. He was not sure where that was. I told the captain I had no clue either.

Walking to the control room the captain told his pilot to enter the coordinates for the planet of Eden.

The pilot replied, "Sir it is quite the distance."

The captain said, "Well we best be on our way."

CHAPTER
16

In my prison staring through the window at the morning sun, wishing for someone to talk to. It had been weeks since Lama was brought here, she was lying on the floor. Lama was healing from the beating she had taken from Drex.

My thought went to the ships. Drex sent them to find Icol. For some reason, the coward had not been to see me, which I was thankful for.

Lama was on a cane mat. Drex went wild when she told him, she was his daughter. He never knew the girls were his daughter. Lama had healed some, yet she still carried the marks on her back. Drex never sent a doctor. He was as useless as a bucket with a hole in it. The girl moved brought me back to the surrounding of my prison.

For weeks, Lama laid helpless, trying to speak when she could, today was no different. Lama had long beautiful hair, lying in dried blood, her hair matted together. From what I could tell she was very beautiful before that man beat her.

Lama had a full body to be thirteen not yet a woman. How can a man have the desire to bed a girl that was not a woman? I can't imagine a man doing this to a little girl, especially his daughter. What kind of man would do this? I kept telling myself over and over, Drex was no man.

I took a wet cloth, washed her face. Opening her eyes, she looked at me smiling. "My lady, I know I'm getting better, at least I can see you."

I ask her, "Lama do remember what happen?"

Through a chores voice, she said, "My father." Tears streamed down her face as well as mine. "How can he do this to me? I'm not a grown woman my lady."

I held her hand, Lama I said, "Some men are just mean. Someday Icol will return." Lama went back to sleep, I went back to the window. Looking down on the village as the people went about their affairs, I remember when Icol was King we had a thriving place. Ships come and went all the time. They would bring the supplies we wanted from other planets even the Claxton's.

I jumped when I said that, the Claxton's. Tenna was with Icol. Tenna was a supreme warrior Icol had told his story. When he was a small boy Tenna took him to the mountains of Trions.

The Claxton's were respected by all our people. I remember the Claxton's would come to our village. They would trade for some of the things we had, not that we ever had much. We were simple people except for Drex. Drex was a mean and cruel person.

I never knew the Claxton's had pointed ears. One night Icol and Tenna were working out with the staff, I walked into the chambers. Their skin well I can't explain it.

It was said that some of the Claxton's took humans as their mates. I have seen some very handsome Claxton's. I was told once they lived in the village to the north. This I don't know, yet some of the females have left the village, never to be seen again.

The guards here always wanted to be trained by Tenna. Tenna took several of them at Icols request. Basco, Bliss, Tankko, there were others. The training was hard. Icol said there is nothing more vicious than a Claxton warrior. Tenna would tell us to be trained right, you need to start at two or three years old. This way you can learn many different languages.

Tenna took Icol at the age of eight. He stayed until he was fifteen. When he returned four men could not take him down, this pleased his mother. It made his father mad. Later he told Tenna he was free to do as he pleased. Tenna thanked Icols father. I will stay, the young one will need me in the years to come. Tenna was always beside Icol.

Lama moved brought me back to reality. I thought of the parchment I wrote on. It seems so long ago when I let it fly from the tower. I know someone found it, I wonder who it was. Of course, I wonder about a lot of things.

The door lock moved, I looked at the handle. Someone was there my heart stopped, could it be Drex, could he have found Icol. I thought, could he have his head to show me then the door open. I heard that awful voice, as he told his guard to wait.

"Yes, sire," as you wish.

"What is it this time Drex, do you have another thirteen-year-old you have beaten," I ask? You could see it made him mad.

"Shara I have come to let you know a ship has returned. I come to let you know the ones onboard have betrayed me. The others Shara, are on the trail of the Claxton and your husband, I ran at him. Drex started laughing.

"You are lying a thief, he is alive."

"Oh Shara, all these years he has been in prison on the planet of Advair." There was a vase of water on the stand. I placed my head on my arm braced the wall. Drex touched me I took the vase I smacked him on the head with it. I told you Drex not to come here again unless you brought me Icol or his head. I hit him so hard with the vase, Blood was running down his face.

"I should kill you for this Shara," Drex said.

"Why not just beat me as you did your daughter, you have practice."

Standing in front of me I could see he was mad. Drex ran to me, grab my hair jerking my head back I was laughing at him.

"Drex, you're a pitiful man, all you know is how to beat a woman. Beat me more Drex, hurt me." He turned with my hair in his hand, dragging me to the floor. Letting me go he started for Lama.

I screamed at him. "No, Drex leave her alone." I ran at him hitting him in the back with my shoulder. The blow took him to the floor. Someone grabbed me from the back pulling me away. Drex got to his feet. I'm going to kill you for that.

I screamed, "Go ahead Drex, you've killed for less."

Drex wiped the blood from his face. Blood had run down his neck soaked his shirt.

Drex shouted, "you're a miserable bitch Shara, I thought I was in love with you. Now I see you will never love me."

I had to think fast, "Drex, I will do as I said. I will marry you, I made you a promise. Bring me Icol or his head and I'll marry you that day until then Drex don't come back here."

Drex took his hand touched her face. Make plans Shara, your wedding, it will happen before you know.

I said to myself, "if that happens he will be dead within a week. I'll kill him myself, one night in his sleep lying beside me. I may have to endure sex with this madman. I won't like it, I will do it just to gain his trust, then when he sleeps I'll kill him." I turned to look at Lama. In my thoughts will she ever be the same.

For the next several days I took care of Lama. Several times I heard her call for her mother. I had to do this for her, I took a big chance. I took a parchment wrote on it, hopefully to someone that was not loyal to Drex. Lama is with me in the tower. I am Shara, wife to Icol, your King. Drex has beaten her almost to death. For several weeks, after the other left, she has been with me.

Tonight, I will light two candles then you will know she is with me. Please believe me someday Icol your King will return. There has been word Drex has sent his guardsmen to kill him, so far, the guards have failed.

Tenna the Claxton is with him. I folded the paper let it drop from the tower. I could not tell if someone found the paper. That night I lit one candle then two. Far to the east of the tower, I saw two small lights. I knew they had found the paper.

Alone in his room, Drex sat looking from the window. He could see the people as they made their way to their homes. Tomorrow, I will send a patrol to the plains. Their mission will be to find Basco I want Basco dead. The storekeeper's daughter, and yes, Basco's son, kill them all. Drex thought of the girl, where did they go. You don't just disappear. He thought as he said that it was true.

I know where they went. They went to the Claxton's the mountain of Trions. Walking to his throne, I will send a patrol there. I will tell them to go to the mountains again. Drex knew as soon as he said that they would not return yet he would send them to the base of the mountains.

Drex called his guards as the day ended. Telling them what he wanted them to do. The guard's question Drex decision. "Sire, we have lost so many."

Drex replied, "Go anyway." The morning came as the sun appeared. The guard was up early left as the sun-filled the sky.

"If there is a man among you, you can go to the mountains," Drex told them they were the best of the King's guards. Taso, Bliss, Tankko, trained you, now go bring her to me." Six men went aboard the Scruple. Six men would not return. Drex did not care, he had many men.

The guard's lives meant nothing to him. This would be no problem for him. If they die he didn't care. Everything about Drex was about Drex. Then his thought went to the queen. Damn her for what she has done to me. Cutting me the way she did. A woman, so full of passion, so full of hate, so full of nothing for me. Then he thought of his daughter lying on the floor. He never knew her name, he didn't care. It didn't matter. She would have been in my bed if she had not spoken up.

Drex thought, "How many women in the city have had his child. How many were his daughter? Drex thought everyone must be laughing at me. Drex called two guards to him. Walking to the window as the guards entered the room.

In a low voice, Drex said to them. "Go into the city, dress as they do, find what they say of me. Speak evil of me if you need. Find out what they say, then come to me."

"As you wish sire." The guards replied.

Drex went back to the window looking around as the guards went into the city. They found no one that would speak badly of Drex. They knew what Drex was capable of. In a small shop, they started talking bad about Drex.

One man stood. "Sir if the guards heard you speak of the King the way you speak. They will behead you. I say this, it is wrong what he has done with the girls. It is worst what he has done to his daughters, yet he is still King."

One guard said, "It took nerves to said that." The guards left the shop.

One woman said, "How could you stand for him."

"I didn't stand for no one," He replied.

She said, "I heard what you said."

Replying, "Do you not see what they do. Drex is bored he is looking for someone to kill. He sends his guards to try us. Pass the word that is loyal to Icol."

The woman said, "I thought everyone was."

"Maybe," the man said. "Just tell them what Drex does. I'm sure there will be others. I tell you Icol will return. I have it on paper, from someone."

Everyone gathered around, "Tell us where he is."

"Drex exiled him with the Claxton Tenna, I was a young man then. Drex paid the Advairan."

One said, "I have heard this. Drex paid them to carry him and the Claxton to Advair placed him in the mines. Icol has escaped alone with the Claxton. I'm not sure how long it will take him to return yet return he will. It is said a ship returned without Tankko, and Bliss they search for Icol."

One asks, "What of the disappearing of Coe, Basco, his daughter, and Basco son? Drex sends patrols to the plains every day, looking for them. Think about it."

A woman in the back stood. "Do you think the queen is alive?"

The man answered, "I do, in fact I know she is. She has Drex's daughter in the tower with her. Drex beat her almost to death. He had chosen to bed her, when she told him who she was, she told him of the others. The ones he had fathered a child with. I tell you now when Icol does return, I hope Icol lets the people decide Drex faith. I promise you, I don't want to send him to prison. I'll kill him myself."

CHAPTER
17

In the early evening, the sun seemed to hang on our village, a man came forward. I'll go to the plains tomorrow, to everyone I see. I will tell all the guards, someday Icol will return. I packed a few things in the dim light of my room, waiting for the morning light. I would be ready to go when the light comes from the east.

Stepping from the stoop to the small craft placing everything I was carrying with me. A voice said, "Sir, take me with you." From the shadow of the house, I looked at the place where the voice came from. The voice sounded female.

She said, "Drex will send for me, I'm thirteen today. I'm not his daughter, he surely will send for me. Please take me!"

Now, I surely did not want to see any young girl go to that man. Maybe ten minutes had passed when I saw her. She was a small girl, with short light hair and blue eyes. She was just a plain girl. This I assure you did not matter to Drex. I was told he took a cripple girl once, then had the guards kill her after they were finished with her. The girl stood with tears in her eyes. She put her hand in her pocket took out a digger. I will kill myself before I go to him.

the young girl placed the digger toward her stomach.

"I will kill myself before I have a child by him, or even let him bed me. Just the thought makes me sick to my stomach," she said.

"My name is Pru." a voice called to her from the house.

Looking at me the woman said, "Sir what have you done to my granddaughter."

Pru said, "I'm thirteen today grandmother, I was trying to leave with him. I don't want to go to Drex. He will send for me this very day." She looked at me I said the same.

"Grandmother if the man will take me, I'm going. Then Drex can't find me."

"Pru, when he returns what then?"

Pru said, "I'll deal with that when it comes." Pru picked up her pack threw it in the back we left. Passing Basco house she asks my name. I told her it was Pena. There was no need to stop, I already knew Basco was gone.

Pru asks, "Where did Basco go?" I told her they just left, several hours later we made a camp. I told her I had a friend on the plains. Tonight, we make a camp, so we can sleep without a fire. If the guards, see the fire they will be here at first light.

Pru said, "Pena, the girl that is with Basco, I know her. Her name is Shila, we're friends." We talk for an hour when we had the chance.

I ask, "What would you talk about? You and Shila."

She looked at me with a smile. "We plan how we would kill Drex if we were ever brought to him."

"We must go, Pru," I said. "It's still a way to the house of my friend. Drex has his guards everywhere. If we are stopped by them we're going to see your grandfather."

"I understand," she said.

Making our way through the plains today was easier than when I was Pru's age. There had been so many changes since Drex took over. Stopping under a Huge tree, where the limbs touched the ground, is all that saved us from the patrol. lying flat in the tall grass that grew under the tree.

I heard a guard say, "I thought I saw something."

One said, "Just an animal." I told Pru after they left, now we can make a meal.

We reached the home of my friend early morning. I told Pru it doesn't take long to come here if it wasn't for Drex. She nodded her head as she understood. Walking on the porch knocking on the door. A young girl answered the door.

"Pena come in quick. The guards will be here soon. My father is in the garden I'm watching for them." Tears filled her eyes.

"Pena, they killed my mother last week. They came looking for me, she died over me. The guards killed her. I was hiding in the dugout under the floor. She died protecting her daughter. They will come for me this time they will find me. The guards have a list of names of all the girls, they'll come for me. I know they will be back, this time they will find me."

The girl looked at me, "I think all girls should have the right to choose who they want to be with." Pena introduced me.

"This is Pru," Pena said. "She is hiding from the guards also." A sound was made from the door, the girls ran to the back, opening the door it was Urea. I embraced my old friend.

"Pena, you have come at a bad time, we're leaving," I told him that's why we are here. I told Urea, Icol is alive he is out there somewhere. The girl with me is Pru, she is running from Drex.

Urea said, "Pena we need to hide." I told my old friend I know where a cave is. Hidden in the outback of the Trions. It's where all Claxton's come to wait. "The Claxton's will let us stay in the cave."

Urea said, "That's a three-day walk."

"Ah my friend, I have a scruple."

Packing a few things in the scruple we waited until dark. Urea closed the hatch we flew just above the ground. The sun was making its way over the Trions when I found the cave. I called to the girls.

Pru said, "It's tight in here, there's another scruple in here." I told then it was Bosco's craft, I knew they were here."

Urea said, "If Basco knew the cave was here, the guards do too. Since he was a guard himself."

Pena said, "I don't think so Urea. If they did, they would have been here waiting. I don't know much of these Claxton's. I do know if they want you to go to their city they must take you."

Urea said, "Let's take the supplies out we can live here for days if we're not seen. We can have a fire at night the guards will not move around on the plains at night."

On our first day out from Urea's house, night came to the plains. Long after the girls went to sleep. Urea told me of a half-breed Caxton, that come to his place with a woman he called mother. Buried her next to my wife. Urea told me, the Claxton was a son of Tenna. I could not believe what he told me, yet it was possible.

High above the cave in a remote place, a young warrior watched. The warrior saw the scruple come from the plains to the cave. Off to the south, he saw another one. He thought that will be the guards.

Making his way to the other side of the cave to another location. He sat as the guards come to the base of the mountain. The warrior showed himself to the guard. This made the scruple turn to keep them from spotting the cave. The course they were on, they would have seen the cave.

Stepping from the clearing where the craft landed. The warrior watched as the guards come from the ship. Cautiously the guards looked around. Walking to the forest the warrior appeared, "come no closer."

"Why are you here," the warrior asks?" Today, yesterday the day before, you were here. What are you looking for? This is Galaxo all owned by King Drex."

The warrior replied, "He is no king." These mountains are home to the Claxton's. It is part of a treaty by the true King Icol. Leave here send no more guards. I will let you live if you leave now. The guards started laughing. The warrior killed a guard the head guard shouted stop. The rest of you will die if you come closer.

The head guard said, "If we go back without anything he will kill us."

The warrior asks, "Then you are loyal to him?"

Replying, "Yes," he said.

The warrior replied, "Take your craft go to the open plains. In two days, a ship will come. Go with that ship, swear loyalties to Icol, help find him. Tell the captain what has been said here. If you come closer or try to follow me into the mountains you will die, this I promise."

Now the guards have heard of a guardsman that disappearing in the mountains. Drex has sent several patrols into the mountains to search for the Claxton city. He has sent ships flying over the mountains several times the captains come back, each time with nothing to report. This would make Drex very angry. Drex was an awful man.

Think about it, this man will take a thirteen-year-old girl to bed, even his daughter. This kind of man would not hesitate to kill you, he has killed. Drex himself has killed many of his guards. Drex will soon destroy Galaxo, then it will be as before, only the Claxton's and the mountains.

CHAPTER 18

I was summoned before the council. I was waiting when Fina come in with Dred. The chief said something in the Claxton language. A motion was made, I stood bowed to the chief.

He asks, "Basco do you understood?" I just shook my head I replied in their language. "Yes, chief I understand."

The chief said, "Bring Shila and Dris." I was skeptical of what was going on. I sat watching the chief as my son and Shila come into the council. Standing in front of him they did as anyone would do. They both kneeled on one knee, out of respect.

The chief told them of their training here, "Shila, Dris, I've never seen two humans so determined. From the time, you have been here you have shown much progress. Dred has told me much has been accomplished. Both of you have met and conquered each task, that has been placed before you. What you have done would have taken someone years to do.

The chief moved to the right. You may stay here longer if you wish, there is more training. It will be mostly language. However, there is a journey I must send you on. This could prove to be very dangerous.

The Chief asked, "Will you do this?"

Shila replied, "Yes my chief."

"Dris will you?"

Dris said to the chief, "Sir, together we are the strongest."

"Yes, Dris I know I have watched you." the chief said.

"Dris, Shila, Basco will not go with you, my daughter will go." The three of you will go to the plains. In a few days, a ship will come. It was told to me by a warrior that the very cave, where Basco placed his scruple. Humans await there, you must see them safe to the craft. The young warrior said guardsman was waiting to join the ship."

"Shila, you Dris, and Fina under no circumstance are to bring anyone here, is that understood."

I said, "I swear it, sir."

"Fina," the chief called to her.

"Yes father," Fina answered. "You will lead them, die defending them if need be." I raised my hand.

The chief said, "Yes Shila."

"Sir I will protect her I promise."

The chief said, "Shila I'm sure the three of you will do fine. Now go ready your packs there is no need to return here, pack and go."

As the three turned to leave the chief spoke. "Shila you will be judged on this trail, all three of you," I told the chief, yes sir I understand. I will make you proud. I can't speak for Fina or Dris. Both looked at Shila strangely. I swear I heard Fina whisper a word, I know she got from ShIla.

The three gathered in front of the cabin. Fina was the first to arrive. Fina said, "Shila you will not need to bring anything but food."

"Fina, I will bring my sword," Shila replied.

Fina said, "Dred will lead us to the rock."

Dred said, "There will be others you won't see them."

Dred led us to the opening at the big rock. "Shila, Dris, Fina you will see humans, guardsman's if they try to take you. You know what must be done, do not hesitate. If you are captured, they will take you to Drex. The humans in the cave, the warrior said they were from your village. I also believe they look for Icol. When this is over, return to the city. In a few weeks, you will be asked, to leave. Basco will take you on your journey. This will take you to other worlds."

Leaving the opening, I never give it another thought of what Dred said. That night we made camp in the place where the Claxton's shot me with the darts. Lying on my pack it suddenly came to me, we were leaving Galaxo. I stared at the stars then I stood.

"Fina, Dred said Basco would take us on our journey. Does this mean you will be coming with us?"

Fina said. "Shila I have had a council with my father. He said I must stay with you until you no longer need me. Then I will return to the mountains."

I said, "Fina then you will be with me for a long time. I will always need you. We have spent so much time together. Now I ask you this. "When I place my King back on the throne, do you think I can live in the city of the Claxton's?"

Fina said it is not permitted for humans to live there, over the years we have had humans come for training. It was before I was born. Even you King Icol was trained, I think he was there for a long time. He to Shila is a warrior, trained by my father and Tenna. Tenna was a powerful warrior, acquired by Icols father. He was about my age at the time I believe. It's all in our archives.

I said to Fina, "I know of the place, it is a most interesting place."

Dris said, "There is so much to learn. I see it would take a lifetime to do."

Fina told Dris when you learn to completely clear your mind, learn how to meditate. Fina looked at me, you will be surprised at how powerful the mind is. Dris you must learn how to do this, you must. Remember when we reach the cave we must search out every place a person could hide. I have never been there you have, remember what Basco told you about your camp. Always look around be prepared for what is there. Sitting around the fire a thought came to me.

I ask Fina, "How do we go to another world? The Claxton has no ships."

Fina said, "Shila ships come and go, we are not forgotten. If we were humans would not try to find us. Drex only wants to find us to destroy us." Let me tell you now, he does not have enough men. The guardsmen he has it would take maybe a day or less to destroy them."

I looked at Dris then at her. "Fina why have you not done this."

First Fina said, "Shila it is not our problem, we have been here thousands of years before the humans came. We will be here thousands of years after. Second, we have not been asked, Claxton's have never fought a fight unless asked."

I ask her, "Why do you train?"

"In case we need to fight," Fina replied. "Shila, I suppose somewhere in the past maybe someone got bored, they just started training. Then it went from that, to what it is now. You see Shila that is the problem, I love being your friend. Unless I'm killed in battle, or fall from a cliff, you will die long before me. Claxton's live to be very old by your standards. Don't worry Shila I will be by your side when you and Dris have your first child."

"Fina, I swear you are way out there," I said.

Fina said, "Do you not wish to mate with him? I have heard you say when this is over you will."

I said, "Fina that will be a while."

"Shila I did not say it would be tomorrow. I never said it would be next week. Yet I did say I would be by your side."

Dris looked at me, "That will be the day I live for."

Fina said, "Dris you have seen me naked, Shila too. Please don't let that stand in your mind."

Shila said, "Oh Fina, let me tell you now, he will I assure you. That day he will never forget. Two naked women standing before him he could not have either."

Dris just lie there with a big smile. I told ShIla, we could take him now. I would love to have sex with a human. I think in my mind it would be wonderful.

I said," Fina, I believe you would love to have sex with anyone."

Fina laughed out loud. "I've never had sex ShIla."

"Well, Fina neither have I," I said.

Fina stood, started to Dris, "Let's take him now Shila."

Dris ask, "Don't I have anything to say about this?"

Fina and I said at the same time, "We was just joking Dris. We wanted to see what you would do." Dris started to speak.

I said, "Go to sleep Dris tomorrow is another day."

CHAPTER 19

The gray sky to the east has a different view of the morning sun, high in the mountains. I had a small fire going when the girls sat up.

"Morning my ladies," I said. The difference between human and Claxton female I was not sure. Fina's skin was a little different. Of course, she had those pointed ears. I was staring at Fina sitting on the ground.

I ask Shila, "What is with her." Fina placed herself into a meditated stage. As soon as Shila set up, she never said a word. Easing her way to the fire.

"Wow," she said, "That was fast."

Dris ask, "Shila you think she is well. I was not sure of anything these Claxton's do. Besides Shila how do you tell if a Claxton warrior is well? I mean at this moment she looks pure evil. Shila, I swear I saw her eyes glow. What is she doing ShIla?" I told Dris I had no idea she is lost in deep meditation.

Dris said, "Where ever she is Dris, she is out there."

I wish I could see what she sees." Dris said. I no longer got the words out.

Fina said, "If you and Shila would learn to meditate you could be with me, our minds as one. You must learn to control your mind."

Dris replied, "I have tried Fina I have."

Fina said, "When we camp above the cave tonight, I will show you one last time."

I ask her, "What about Shila."

Fina answered, "Dris, Shila has learned to clear her thoughts. She has journeyed with me several times."

I looked at Shila, "You really can do it," I ask?

Shila said, "Yes Dris, I saw my father, Dris he got away. My father is on a ship, he looks for Tenna and Icol."

"This can't be," Dris said. "I'm as good as she."

Fina said, "It's not about being as good as anyone Dris. It's how you use your training."

Dris ask, "Then what is that look, you have when you do

this, you look evil.' Fina told us she knows nothing of this. Fina walked to the fire, I give her a cup of tea. "Drink this," I said, "we need to move."

Now the chief of the village and Fina's father knew before we left, we may need a guardian. Basco and Dred stood above us listening to every word Fina said. What he wasn't ready for is what Fina told them. Basco looked at Dred.

"She is right Basco, I was with my sisters in thought. Together we went to the plains. Someone will die today, it won't be us. There is a man in the cave, he is with others. He will die trying to save the girl. This I tell you, so you will be prepared when they reach them. He will come from the ship.

I said, "Dred let's get there first, and stop it."

Dred shook his head. "I am sorry Basco, we cannot interfere."

I ask Dred, "Them tell me who gets killed."

Dred dropped his head. "The guard from the ship kills the man from the cave. Shila kills the guard. That's when we join them. I'm truly sorry Basco, faith has been written."

I said to Dred, "I know about faith." As the day progressed, Dred and I ran down the trail. By the time the three of them stopped for a lunch break, we were miles ahead. I told Dred, today we have done good, by nightfall we will be by at the base of the mountains, by the cave. The sun going down, brought the night stars.

Dred said to me, "I've noticed you do not meditate, is there a reason. Tenna trained you with respect, he trained several guards, you trained several." Tell me, Basco, If you come upon one of your students, he pulled arms on you, could you kill him." I sat thinking for a moment.

I replied, "Dred it would be hard to take up arms against my friends or student. Dred, if any man pulled arms on me I would kill them, even my son."

Dred looked at me, "Then my friend, you are truly a warrior."

The time you have spent with him before coming to the

city. You have trained him well. Shila, what of her."

I said, "ShIla I would defend her to anyone. She is a daughter I never had. I feel her, and my son will come as one someday."

Dred looked at me, "Basco, then what becomes of the father."

"I'm not sure Dred. Maybe when we place Icol back on the throne, there won't be a need for a warrior. Look at it this way the only people of Galaxo are human. In the village, a few are in the plains. These people are simple farmers. The Claxton's of the mountain, and the other Claxton, I live and fight to see us united again."

"Then Dred, your people can come and go as you please. I know it would make me happy. That why we are doing what we are doing. This planet belongs to your people, we were welcomed by the Claxton long ago, long before we come here from a world I hope someday to visit."

"My lifelong, I was told of this. Hundreds of years ago in the very ships we now have in our fleet. I was told the ship belongs to a planet that disappeared. The ships were given to them, I know not of this. It was said my people come from there, settled on the moon of Corning. Corning was overrun some escaped to this planet. It was told, only your people were here when the ships arrived.

Dred looked at me, "It is true Basco, almost in those exact words. It is written in our archives. I was also told the people were mixed between human and a being of long ago. Where that planet went no one can say. I only think of this. How much power would it take to move a planet or destroy it? Well so much for history, let's move Dred.

Dris thought as he ran, tonight he would let Fina help him. He told Fina before they moved, your right we need to become one. I need to try to learn this, he looked at Fina then at Shila. Let's go I'll lead for a while I remember the way. We ran for several hours. Stopping at a stream for a drink.

Fina said, "Oh my, would you look at that, it's a beautiful

sight. I've never seen so far; is there no end." Fina was looking at the plains at two thousand feet up.

Shila moved as Fina caught a movement from the corner of her eye. Falling to the ground Dris and Fina fell, as Shila said down.

Dris said, "Maybe the people from the cave."

I said, "Could be the ones your father was talking about. It is men in uniform." We watched carefully. There on the horizon to the south, moving around a clump of rocks.

Fina ask. "What are we looking at?

"There I said, "A ship on the floor of the plains. It's as big as a mountain." Fina looked with the sharpness of her eyes.

"Shila," Fina said in a low whisper, "There are several men. I told her she didn't need to whisper, they can't hear us.

Fina spoke again, "Look there're the people from the cave."

Dris said, "Your father said there were guard's men around." From two thousand feet, the three of us started down to the cave, Fina took the lead. We had run several minutes Fina froze, Dris and I did the same. When you train as we have you learn to become one. Fina pointed to the bush. A young girl was picking berries.

I said, "That's Pru, she's from our village."

Fina said, "Do not call to her, remember your training." The girl stood up as if she heard something. Looking over her shoulder a man came from the bush.

"Come here," he said to her. Dropping her berries, she started to run into the forest.

The guard shouted, "Come here, stop." Pru just ran faster. Dris and I started to make our move, Fina took hold of Dris's arm. She grabbed me by my shirt.

"Don't be hasty to die, my friend."

"Fina he is going to catch her," I said.

Fina replied, "I'm sure he will, six others come from the woods. Seven guards ran into the forest after the girl.

"You see my friend, now we can go, now we know who we

fight," Fina said.

"They will follow her to the cave," Dris said.

Fina said, "She will not go to the cave." Fina was right, Pru ran down the path to the plains. Running into the bushes of a stream One thing I can say of Pru, she was smart. Going into the stream she found what she looked for a dugout where the water ran. Roots had grown over the water. Crawling under, she was completely concealed.

Wet and very cold she shivered as she waited for the guards to leave. The guards stood on the banks of the stream looking.

Several got into the stream, one said, "She could not have disappeared into the air. I tell you she went into the water. Maybe she is one of those Claxton's she heard one say." The guards search for hours lying in the cold water hid under the bank the guards give up went back to the ship.

When the guards went back to their ship, I jumped into the water.

"Pru, it's Shila," I called several times before she came from the undergrowth of the stream. Pru was so cold, the water fresh from the mountains of Trions deep from the mountain lakes. I told her, let's go back to the others.

Pru looked at me, "Shila, there are no others, just me."

"Where is the girl, and the two men," I ask?

"Shila there's only me now. The guards found us killed her, her father Urea. Pena tried to fight them. The guards killed him trying to protect me. Urea said to me, run I'll try to keep them off you, go girl run." Pru was crying as she said, "Urea died protecting my getaway." From behind a Huge tree, a guard stood as bold as the sun.

He said, "Well little one we met again. Did you forget about me?"

"No, I haven't," I said.

"Come with me, it time to go to your king." He expressed.

"So, you have found Icol," I said.

He spits at me, "No Shila, I have come for you as I said I

would." I walk to him before he knew what had happened I took his hand. Making a move I was famous for I took a leg. As he fell I took his life. Basco and Dred had reached the ship to stop what was to be. Little did they know it had already happened. The ship left two days later, another ship came, it was an Advairan ship. We placed Pru on the ship. Fina, Dris, and I returned to our home in the mountains.

Returning to the city of the Claxtons, I went to the pool. Fina went to the chambers of her father.

My father said to me, "Go, Fina, rest tonight." Ra came to the sleeping room.

Calling my name," Yes Ra what is it."

Ra said, "Father has called for you and the humans to come to council." There had been a celebration for us. We had been named warriors. Shila started to go, then stopped.

"Shila you have something to say." The chief asks?

I ask, "The mission was for us. Why did you send a guardian?"

Fina said, "What are you saying?"

"Fina your brother was there," I told you this, in your meditation.

"Shila, Dred, and Basco were there only as observers. What you did was faith, part of your destiny. I bowed to the chief, I would not hesitate to do it again.

The chief said, "I believe you ShIla."

CHAPTER 20

Captain Lux landed his ship on the planet of Eden. Several months we spent in space. Believe me, I wanted off the ship. Tenna said the same. Eden was a beautiful planet. A tropical, most radiant place I've ever seen. Millions of people lived here. Everyone moved with ease as the morning breeze moved the trees. The smell was like nothing I've experienced

Captain Lux asks, Tenna and me to join him as the crew unloaded and reloaded the ship. A craft of some kind picked us up, moved us to the city. There a smaller place we need to visit. Moments later the craft stopped. Icol the captain asks, "Have you thought of my offer?"

"Yes, captain, "Tenna and I have decided to stay with you for a while." "Why are we not helping with the ship."

Lux replied, "You are my guest. Besides Icol you're a King, how can I make you work."

I just looked at him, "You treat me no different than your crew."

"Icol please you are my guest. Come inside I think you will find this interesting." The captain moved with swagger, he was, however, an established man. Well respected by his crew. Taking a table, drinks were sent to the table.

The waiter announced, "Captain Lux, "the general has asked you to join him in his office."

Taking our drinks, Tenna said, "This is very good." I find it very strong, of course, I was not one to drink.

"Why are we here," I ask him?

Lux said, "You will find out." Entering the general's office, introductions were exchanged?

The general said as he handed Lux an envelope. Taking the paper out, Lux handed one to Tenna, one to me.

Tenna asks, "Why do we need papers."

"Lux is going to a different galaxy, there will be hunters there." The general spoke to Icol. "I know of your troubles in your world. Captain Lux ask me to gather information, this I have done. Your wife is alive."

The captain said, "When we return, we will go to my world. I gave you my word. If there anything I can do, we will return here in six months. Then I will go to Advair. There's no need to worry, they'll never find you. This I'll make sure of."

Going where you're going with the captain. Icol all ship that comes to port must be cleared by me. None can land or take off without my permission. This is the way it has always been. Therefore, I will stop them as they resupply. A small craft took us back to the ship.

I ask Lux, "Where are we off to?"

Lux said, "I have been asked to go to the Star of Joni. A colony several light-years away. We will be traveling for quite some time. Come aboard we need to go. "

Tenna asks, "What is the Star of Joni?"

Lux said, "A planet of misfits, rebels, and killer and cutthroats. Only ships go there are killers and ones that will hide. If you go off the ship, be careful. Lux said, "Icol, they don't like humans."

I replied, "I'll stay on the ship, sir."

The ship flew through the emptiness of space. The thing about space was it was always dark. I went to the bridge with Tenna. We passed by several planets that were not habitual to anyone. Day after day we flew through space. Early one morning Tenna come to me.

Tenna said, "I have overheard the men, there is a mutiny to take the ship when we reach the Star. I have been asked to join." I told Tenna we give our word to the captain. Tenna, if we do any less it would be no different than Drex overthrowing me. I have given him my word."

Tenna replied, "Go to the captain tell him I'll join to keep up with what is going on. Icol I give you my word when the time is right I'll be there for him. I made my way to the captain's quarters. I told Lux what Tenna had said.

Lux said, "It was not the first time, when I pick up other crews from other planets this happens. Dont worry Icol I'll play along."

"Just remember captain, the Claxton is very much for you."

Tenna or I had no idea it was a setup. A member of the crew was a hunter, he came aboard in Eden going to Joni. The hunter did not know the Advairan had canceled the contract on me or Tenna. All he could see was the gold or the precious stones. He would come out of hiding as the crew tries to overthrow the captain. Tenna was listening as the outlaws told him what to do.

One of them said to Tenna, "You have been talking to your friend, we asked you, what will he do?" Tenna told them Icol wanted no part of this, all he wants is to go home. He is either with us or against us.

"Then I must tell you, he has given his word to the captain, he will stand for him.

One of the outlaws said, "Tenna you will kill him." I told them I would not he is my friend. I agreed to help take the ship. I only agreed to do this because you promise safe passage home. I will not pull arms on my friend, he will give you no trouble.

The hunter stepped forward, "I will kill him for you. I am a hunter; I have tracked these two across the space of time. He is mine when we land on Joni.

I started to leave the hunter said, "I will take you to Claxton."

In a low voice, I whispered, "You can try taking me, hunter. I will promise you a swift death." The closer we came to the Star of Joni, the more the tension builds.

Twenty-seven days on a ship in space was a long time to be closed in. It reminded me, of the prison on Advair. I haven't seen Tenna in three days. Tonight, I will meditate, see if our thought can come together. In my training, I remember I have always been able to do that. The Claxtons village of the Trions, Tenna taught me well. I was told by a young warrior I learned very quickly.

The warrior was a great help to me as the years went by. My thought went back to that day. At my mother's request, Tenna was to teach me so I would have the skills when I became king. I think Tenna was looking for an excuse to go home.

I thought of my friend from time to time. I have even asked Tenna of him. He would always say he is training. I'm sure after the years have passed Dred has become an established warrior. When Tenna said it was time to go I took the seal of the Claxton's. Leaving that day, I've never returned, yet sometimes I think of my friend.

Sitting alone in my room I still can't understand how the Claxton's know when a ship comes. All ships, not just ours. I sat thinking, how long would it take to go home? How many planets were between us and there? My thought went to my wife. The general said she was alive. I had a different kind of life, it seems a lifetime ago. The last time I held her, the way her eyes looked when I left her watching me go. I'll never forget that.

The day Drex said to the rebels, "Kill the Claxton's first, they pose the biggest threat. Kill them the others will fall. May the power and the life last long enough to take back what was once mine.

Three days to port. Writing on parchment at my table in my room when a knock came on the door.

Speaking through the door I ask, "Can I help you?"

"Icol, open the door," Lux whispered.

"Come in captain," I said.

Lux said, "Icol you must come with me now, to my quarters." In the corridor, the captain walked very fast. Entering the captain's quarters' locking the door a shadow came from the closet. Moving as fast as I could I had the shadow on the floor gasping for breath.

Lux said, "Icol he is my aide." I told him he shouldn't hide in the shadows with a weapon.

Lux said, "I will talk to him of that." I offered my hand, I'm sorry I told him.

He said, "I'm just glad you're on our side."

I ask the captain, "What is going on?"

Captain Lux said, "I need to talk to you. Tenna sent word, they plan to take the ship tomorrow."

I ask, "I thought it was three more days to port?"

"Icol," he said, "We have made good time." The captain continued to talk, I listen.

The captain said, "There is a hunter on board, he came aboard on Eden. This happens every time I go to Joni. It will be my last time here. The cargo was too good to turn down, it pays very good Icol."

"Sometimes, captain there's more to life than money," I said.

"I suppose Icol, I suppose." Just outside the captain's door was a loud noise. The captain called there was no answer his aide open the door Tenna fell in the door, falling into my arms. Tenna had been beaten badly.

I looked at Lux, "Now what?"

Tenna took hold of my hand. "Icol a hunter is on board, he has a green shirt, he's bad Icol. It took six of them to take me." I told Tenna I'll go for him.

"Captain lock the door," I said, "do not unlock it for anyone. When I return I'll give you the name of my wife." I went to his ear so only he could hear I told him the name in a very low whisper. I simply said, "Shara." Outside the door I stepped cautiously, two of the crew stepped out.

They ask, "What is going on?" I told them someone came aboard while on Eden, they want to take the ship.

They ask at the same time, "Where is the Claxton?" I told them he was beaten very badly.

One asked, "What are you going to do, get yourself killed?"

Look I said, "It took six to bring him down, the one with a green shirt, I want him. How many on this boat can you trust?"

He replied, "Several." I told him to go to them tell them when we descend to the planet they will come to take the ship.

One asks, "If they take the ship what become of us. We are

so far from our home base."

"Just where is your home base," I ask?

They both looked at me. "Icol its Advair."

I ask, "You mean the captain is Advairan?"

He said, "Icol we all are."

"Then you know who I am."

"Yes, Icol, why do you think we're helping you. The Advairan have lifted the bounty on you. They have paid several ships to find you. We have you, we are to take you home. The hunters we have no control over. There several ships looking for you even from your world."

"Then let's take this ship, make sure the captain doesn't lose it. Go to you men, I will go to the galley. Tenna said that's where they're at. I must face this hunter, walking slowly down the corridor I watched each one from the side. Coming to the galley I looked inside.

The hunter was sitting at a table alone. I scanned the room there were several of them. I didn't care I was mad at what they did to Tenna. I entered the galley.

King Icol, he said, "I must say you look nothing like a king. You smell like a thieving Claxton."

"I assure you a Claxton has never taken a thing from anyone," I answered.

He replied, "Yes they can't fight either." The three at the table laughed. I never said a word, I turned to them pulled the sword killed two of them. I turn back to the hunter. "It took six of you scum suckers to take him down. That to me is a coward, a filthy coward."

Now, these boys had no clue I had been trained by the Claxton's. They thought I was an easy target until they moved. I cut two of them as they moved around the table. The others made their move. A cut on the arm, a cut on the leg, cut two ears then the hunter came for me.

I told him if he stopped this munity, I will promise you a fast death. Look around you, I have already killed all that's with you. When we arrive at the port of Joni, you leave the ship, or I will kill you. Tell the others to stop what they are doing. The hunter came fast, he will come no more. Several other crew members entered, I told them the same. You stop this or come here to the galley, I'll end it here.

I sat in the galley for several hours. I stood to leave when scum suckers entered. The captain's crew come in from behind. I heard the captain call my name. I killed three of them went to one knee as one went over my shoulder, I killed him, stood went to the captain.

I said, "I ask you to stay in your quarters, it is over. Captain do what you will with them." Lux place the body in the air shut. I'll pull the handle myself.

Lux said, "Icol, I thought you were a peaceful man." Looking around at the dead on the floor I said to him, "I am, this is war. I won't be defeated so easily." I told him I assure you if you let them live, you will fight them again someday. I walked back to the captain's quarters. I give Tenna his sword. Tenna whispered, "Icol." I told him it was over, there were only three left.

We found the Star of Joni just as the captain said. There were several different kinds of beings, that come to unload.

Lux said to me, "No one can pass the cargo deck." All the cargo was unloaded captain Lux closed the hatch.

"Icol, tell the crew, I won't be here long."

I looked around. "What was that all about," I said.

Veeta said, "It looks as if the captain has a first mate."

"Oh, no you don't, I just want to go home," I said. Veeta told me over tea as we waited for the captain's return. Veeta me he would follow me as he would the captain. Icol you have done a great service here today. It wasn't just for me or the crew. You did well for the captain too. I told him he would have done the same.

I ask Veeta, "When do you think the captain will be going home."

Veeta said, "I'm not sure Icol, there are other planets we must go to. I feel sure he will go there. It is several light-years away. It was a planet that once was a moon, to the planet that disappeared long ago. Of course, that was hundered of years ago. How can a planet disappear? Does anyone know for sure? The Moon of Spores." I told Veeta I would like to see this moon.

Veeta and I talked for several minutes. A crew member ran inside the galley.

"Veeta, the captain is in trouble." He announced. The door opened the ramp went down, I stepped from the ship. I looked around walked down the ramp to meet ten beings. I do remember the captain said to me they didn't like humans, here. My sword in hand, Lux on the ground. I was staring into their eyes of some beings I've never seen before. Lux was bleeding from his head.

I looked over him, "sir," I said.

Replying Lux said, "I'm fine Icol, just help me aboard."

I ask him, "Did you get paid?"

Replying no, "Icol they would not pay me."

"Which one captain," I ask? Lux pointed to an odd being.

"He did not stick to his barging. The contracts said ten beings of any race. He only brought three." I stepped one step closer to him. I told him if I had my way I would have placed them all in the airlock. You see captain what I mean. How much does he own you?

The beings started laughing. "What are you going to do, all by yourself," he said in a silly voice."

"He's not alone? Look above you the first sign of trouble you will be the first to die. Now pay the captain or die. I believe it was one thousand credits."

He said five hundred. I told him no, that will not work. You see your boys tried to stage a munity. Your boys beat the captain. I believe one thousand sounds good. How's does that sound to you Tenna.

Tenna said, "I think that will do it, as long as he pays now. The longer we stay, the more it's going to cost."

I hit Tenna on the shoulder, "Man I love the way you do business." He passed us a large envelope, "it's all there."

The being said, "You have not seen the last of me." I hope I have I told him. Helping the captain on board we went higher into the darkness of space.

Traveling through space I was no expert. I've never been on a ship until Drex sent me to Advair prison. Tenna, well Tenna had been in space several times. He would accompany my father on several of his quests. I wonder now, why he never went back to Claxton city.

Tenna said to me once he was told never to come back when he left. When Tenna would talk to me about space he would say, I rather have my feet on the ground, so would I.

The thing about space it is dark and cold. It seems to go forever Captain Lux let me stand beside him on the bridge when we approached Eden. Again, when we approached the Star of Joni. They're just big balls floating in space when you look upon them.

Veeta walked with me to my quarters. I told him I needed to check on Tenna. Tenna had gone to the galley when we went aboard. Tenna had recovered from his wounds.

I ask Tenna, "Would you walk with us to the captain's quarters."

He stood, "Look, sire, he said I'm back." I told him he needs to work out. I told him I will join you. First Tenna we need to go to the captain.

Entering the quarters, the captain said, "Tenna, Icol, I have already thanked my crew. I'm truly sorry for the beating you took. I do think you for your help.

Tenna said, "If we are on this ship, we are part of this crew."

Lux looked at me. Well Icol, I hear you found out who we are. Tenna looked at me.

I said to Tenna, "Sorry for the trouble, I forgot to tell you."

Tenna asks, "What?"

"Tenna the captain and crew, well there Advairan," I said. Tenna took two steps back.

"Tenna wait," The captain said, "I mean you no harm. The Advairan have dropped the bounty on you and Icol."

Tenna said, "What is this Icol?" I told Tenna the Advairan and others who wish to help with the overthrow of Drex. Tenna please I'm your friend, we want the same as you. We want Icol back in power, it must be that way. I'm sorry Tenna I did not get the chance to tell you. Tenna there several ships looking for you, and Icol. Some of the ships come from your world."

Lux said to me. "Icol I know how you must yearn to see your wife, take back your throne, there is much to be done. The general has sent word, high in the mountains, a warrior named Basco has taken refuge. He has taken his son and a girl from the village. This you do not know. I must finish my run, then to my world. Once there, we will make plans to go to your world. I promised you this Icol when we left Rulla."

"I'm a man of my word, you believe me don't you." Icol looked at me with a believing look.

"I do sir," I said. "I will stay with you. Betray me as I have said, I'll turn the Claxton loose on you. I just want to go home."

Captain said, "Icol it will be several months before we get there. The hurting the longing the burning makes you stronger. That's what will keep you alive. It will keep both of you going."

The day had gone. Veeta, Tenna, I sat long into the night. Veeta told us space stories. He had been with the captain for sixty-one years. I looked at him.

"How old are you," I ask him?

Veeta said, "I think ninety we don't age much."

I thought I was very young compared to the others. I had no children, know travels. I did tell of the trip to the Trions. Yet I was very small at the time. I told Veeta of my family coming from a moon somewhere. I believe it was called Corning a hundered years ago. That's how we met Tenna people.

His race was the only one on the planet. The Claxtons befriended us, there were times, there were hundreds of them. My grandfather would say it is written in our archives.

Veeta said, "This planet you speak of, the one that disappeared." I told him there was a great war. Some of our people took the ships went to Corning. You could say we started a new world on a new planet with the help of the Claxton's. There was talk between us.

I said to Veeta, "Have you ever been to Galaxo,"

He replied, "No, I've never heard of it until I met you. Icol I have asked the captain for my leave when you reach your world. I to will stand proud, by you and Tenna. It would be my honor to do this. I'm also a warrior, I'm not as good as you and Tenna. I have not had the training." Standing he touched a weapon of some kind. "Trust me I know what I'm doing."

Tenna smiled, "We would be honored to have you."

"I agreed." The next morning, I spoke to the captain in the galley. I ask about Moon of Corning. Lux told me all he could.

Icol he said, "I have been going to the moon several years." He told me after the moon he needs to go to the Moon of Spores, then to Bangor. Then Icol we will go home." I told the captain as we sat, that the Moon of Corning was the place of my ancestors. Three hundered years ago I believe they fled the moon. Captain Lux placed his hand on his face.

Well, Icol he said, "I do remember reading of this, something about a war with a planet. The overthrow of a moon, it's been so long I don't remember. The thing I do remember is said the planet disappeared. I'm not sure how."

I told the captain I have been told that my whole life. It was said a man named Kohl, took our people from the moon. Kohl himself was from the planet that disappeared. Kohl took his wife come to the planet of Galaxo.

Lux said, "It has been several years since I've been to the moon."

I said, "Captain, I do not believe anyone would know Kohl

now."

Lux asks, "Do you know the name of any of your ancestors."

I said, "His name was Kohl. Our first King of Galaxo. All I know is what I've been told the archives are full of our history. I was exiled so I have no idea what my brother has done. Kohl had children passed the royalties to them, then to my father then to me." I set for several minutes.

I ask, "Captain why after all these years that have passed, why now?"

"I'm not sure what you are saying," The captain said.

"Why have the Advairan government changed their minds," I ask?

Lux answered, "The government was growing impatient. Complaints of our ships, the way Drex is treating our men. Mostly the way Drex is treating his people. The worst is he takes all the women past the age of thirteen and above to have children, hoping for a male child. The last count was sixty-five."

It is said Icol, "Most of the girls that gave birth, was his daughters." I looked hard at the captain.

You have my word, "If I get the chance to face him, I'll kill him myself, I swear it."

Lux said, "Icol, he is your brother, just send him to the mines."

"Captain as I stand before you, that will not happen. Drex is my true blood, sometimes the brother must die."

CHAPTER 21

I was up within two hours when Lama sat up. "Good morning," I said to her.

Lama said, "My lady I was listening to you, and that dreadful man, my father you know. My lady how can a man do this to his daughter." I told Lama, he has done the worst. "Taking his daughters to bed. It has to be the worse, I just know it."

"Lama the day Icol takes his throne back, this will never happen again. It will be a law, I promise. I just want to live long enough to see someone put a sword through him." I said.

Lama asks, "My Queen do you believe he is still alive?"

"I want to believe he is Lama," I replied.

My lady, "My father is trying to have a son of pure blood. Would it not be pure blood by another woman not related?" I told Lama it would be.

Lama asks, "Then why does he do it?" I could only stare out. Lama would sit up to talking to me. Each time a noise would sound outside the door, she would run to me. Tears would fill her eyes.

"Please my lady," she would say, "don't let him take me. I cannot endure another beating. I'd rather die than to let him touch me." It had been weeks since Drex had been here.

One morning Lama, and I was having our morning tea, without warning the door flew open wide. Lama screamed I jumped up. One of the guardsmen Looking at both of us. I looked at him Lama was behind me.

I said to him, "If you want her, take her." The guard took a step. What I said made him stop.

"First you must tell me. Why you want her?"

"Drex gave her to me," he answered.

I replied to the guard, "If you want her, you must kill me. It's the only way you take her from this cell." Standing before him I open my robe let it fall to my waist, I let my breast show. They were still firm always have been as the peaks of a mountaintop. My waist was slender my hips were wide. A perfect body for a woman my age.

I said to him, "Come in, take me, letting the robe fall to the floor, take me again," I said.

"I cannot Drex would kill me." Standing before him, my long dark hair hung to my waist. "Take me again," I said. "There is no one around except Lama." I don't know what made her do what she did. Lama stepped out, dropped her robe. She still had the bruise from the beating.

I said to him, "Come on in, two naked women stood before you. We can have some fun, you and the two of us." Sweat rolled down his face his mouth was dry. Slowly his hand went down to his private area, touching himself.

I said, "Wait come let me do that, let me touch you there. Let me show you the touch of a woman." Again, he said Drex would kill me.

Lama said, "You want me, come here lie here on the mat, take me here, I'm ready."

"No, no, no," was his reply, as he backed out of the cell." I placed my robe on so did Lama.

I said, "You're a poor man if you're not man enough to kill me or mate me your no man at all." The guard backed out the door went running down the hall.

Looking at Lama I said, "First time for everything." We both started laughing.

Lama and I spent most of our time talking about the people in the village. The changes made since Drex took over.

"My lady," she said, "Everyone hates him. Only the guards bow to him. Mostly to keep their family's alive. When it's time for their daughter to come to him, they just bring them to Drex."

Having our evening tea Lama said, "My lady it has been a week since the guard was here, I wonder why." Lama no more got the words out when the sound came, Lama looked at me.

"Please don't let him have me?" Lama ran to the corner of the room. Speaking through the door, it was the guard.

"You show me again," he asks? "I'll give you fruit if you will." I looked at Lama. We had already planned to get him in the room. I had taken a chair, made the leg so it would come off quickly. We had planned to get him in the room beat him to death. We had placed a Curtin to divide the room.

"Come in, I said. "I'll show you a real woman. I have not had a man in twenty years."

Standing at the door he asks. "What about her," looking at Lama.

"If you want her I said to him. You must kill me."

"You have already shown me your body. Let me take her." He said.

Lama called, "Come in, we can go behind the Curtin."

He replied, "No later, someone comes." The guard ran down the corridor. I knew by the smell it was Drex.

"Shara he yelled, your husband will be here by the end of the month. Shara," Drex called in a long word. "Are you planning our wedding day?" I looked at Lama, walked to the door. Drex opened the window. Drex I told you not to return until you bring me my husband's head or him, you scum sucker. I do not need to know when you bring him Drex, just bring him.

"So be it," Drex said "I will not give you his head Shara. I want you to witness the weakness of your husband. I King Drex will place a sword through your pathetic husband. I'll cut out his heart as I take his Queen."

I said to him as he walked away. "Drex you will never be a king. How can you be, you're not even a man?"

"Shara," Drex yelled, "you will change your thoughts when he lies before your feet, his heart in my hands."

The thing about time, it never stops, even when you are dead it goes on. The month was coming to an end, still, Icol was not here. The gray light of the morning told me another day comes. Something in the courtyard was happening. A ship had come to port. Could it be the one Drex had waited for?

Lama sat up, "My lady, what is wrong?" I turned to her as my eyes filled with tears.

I said to her "There's a ship Lama. One I've never seen

before."

Lama asks, "Do you think it could be.?" I told her to help me. Pushing over the chair I climb to the window, so I could lookout. There were three guards with uniforms I knew not. The guards had a man in chains.

Jumping down smiling, "It's not him Lama, it's not him."

The ship landed, then left. What seemed hours a guard come past the window. I called to him.

"My lady I cannot talk to you. Drex would kill me." Reaching in his pocket. The guard took fruit hurriedly give them to me. "For my family, I do this, I truly am sorry."

"Please tell me," I said, "Who was on the ship?"

He said, "Two hunters, they brought back a runaway guard." Drex will take his head in the square as he has others before him. He will do this to show the people he is still in power, I must go." I told him, Icol will return.

"My lady," he said. "I wish he was here now," I told the guard, go find others tell them Icol is coming. The guard turned the corner and was gone.

I said in a low voice, "I just don't know when." Turning to Lama, I handed her one of the fruits the guard gave me, it was so good.

"My lady," she said, "When the guard came the one we undressed before him. I know about things my mother told me. I ask you, what is it to share a man's bed with him. I mean to let him have you for the first time." I told her a woman any woman can share a man's bed. The first time it must be love, if not it is meaningless, it's just sex.

Most men Lama can and will settle for this. Marriage is for life Lama. There are men like Drex that will force themselves on you. I have heard of men paying women for sex, only love Lama.

She said, "As you have for Icol."

"Yes, Lama like that, then and only then should a woman share his bed. Lama, you're a young girl. You haven't even started your cycle yet. Lama, there will come a time when you mate with someone. Your first time will be uncomfortable for you. When you get that feeling, there is no feeling in any world that feels like that, this Lama, I promise you. That's why when a woman and a man mate should be for life. I hope someday you find someone like that. Someone you wish to spend your life with."

Lama looked at me, "I already have my lady. I want the guard that came before us. Before I give myself to him we will be free of this cell. I make you this promise. I may taunt him; I will tell him until we are free I will stay here." I told Lama that might not be wise. He could trick you just to gain your trust. Then have his way with you then turn you back to the cell. Looking at me lama said, "Then my lady, I will kill him."

"Lama, remember, if I die here, I have seen my life from inside this cell. Drex may find my husband bring him before me. I may have to marry Drex. I may have to let him have his way with me. I promise you I will not enjoy it. When I win his trust, I'll kill him while he is sleeping. This I promise you, Lama. You have the right to tell him."

Lama said," My lady why would I tell that man anything." I told her because he is your father.

"He is not my father; my father would not have done what he has done to so many," Lama told me as tears fell down her face. "My lady if I get the chance I'll kill him myself. Besides my lady what kind of father would do this to his daughters." I moved back to the window, give thanks to the man on the ship that it was not Icol.

In heavy thought with the morning sun on my face, I wish to be outside in the garden. Lama touched my shoulder to get my attention.

Turning to ask, "Yes Lama what is it."

Lama said, "Someone at the door. I'm not sure who it is." Walking to the door. Drex I told you what to do.

The voice said, "It's not Drex my lady. My name is Rand, I

never knew your husband, I have made several inquiries about him. Most of the people will not talk of him. They're afraid of what Drex will do to them. The guard that came to you, the one that took you to the garden. I ask him who you were."

The guard said, "forget what I saw. There is talk in the village of a note you wrote on parchment. Drex does not know of this yet. Shila, a store keeper's daughter found the note. She has fled the city with a warrior named Basco. My lady, do you know him."

"Basco," I whispered. "I have not thought of him in a very long time."

I ask Rand, "How do you know the girl is with him."

Rand replied, "My lady guards talk. It would have appeared one of the guards has a run-in with the thirteen-year-old girl. She told him when it was time for her to come to the castle, have Drex sent him. She told the guard she would kill him herself."

Lama stood, "My lady I know Shila, she is full of energy. My mother said Drex would never tame her, he would kill her for sure or Shila would kill herself." I told Rand I knew Basco, I knew him well. He was captain of the guards. Basco was number one to my husband."

My lady Rand said," I thought Tenna was."

I said, "Tenna was my husband's advisor."

Rand said, "Drex has ordered us to kill all Claxton's on sight."

I laughed out loud," Good luck with that. If you see a Claxton it will be because they want you to see them. If you are after them, you will see then, when they kill you."

"My lady, someone comes, we will talk again."

I ask Rand, "The other guard, what is his name?"

"Nordic my lady." Then he was gone. I smiled at Lama.

"My lady, what is it," Lama asks?

I said, "Now you know his name, your guard it's Nordic."

Several thoughts went through my mind that day. Late in the evening, a light warm breeze blew through the window, bringing the fresh smell of the new flowers from the mountains. This was called the new season. Sitting in silence for several minutes, sipping tea, my mind was clear. Lama said as she took her tea walked around.

"My lady, "Who was the guard that took you for your walks."

"His name was Tankko Lama. He took Basco's place when Basco left the guard to be with his wife, until her death years ago. Basco turned all his attention to his son. That's what I was told by the guards."

Lama said, "My lady, his name is Dris. I know Dris and Shila very well. My lady, I wish we could go for a walk in the garden, walk among the flowers, dabble in the stream. Do you think Drex will ever let us go?" I never said a word to her, I walk to the window felt the warm breeze.

I dropped my head, "Lama, If Icol doesn't come soon I'm afraid we will die here."

Hours had passed, darkness had come once again to the world of Galaxo. I tried to clear my thought as I sat in my chair. Being as young as Lama, she was so full of questions, she began to ask questions of the ancestors. Closing my eyes in a more relaxing mode, just waiting.

"Lama," I said, "I only know what I've been told. The archives would tell you more than I could."

Lama replied, "Drex has forbidden us to go there. He locked the doors, posted a guard with orders to keep all out."

I said to her, "Of course he did. Lama, can you read."

"Yes, my lady we were taught from our family's, or others, we are smart. Reading and writing, well my lady Drex has not taken that yet. Drex did close the learning center." A loud noise got my attention, standing on a chair I could see the people. Six girls were escorted to the castle within minutes I heard them walking in the corridor.

"Guards open that door," Drex ordered.

"You bastard, I shouted," I told you never come here

without my husband.

Drex started laughing, "No woman tells me what to do."

"Drex," I said, "You're a poor excuse for a man." I was screaming at him when the six girls come closer. "Oh Drex, I thought you loved me, this is what you called love."

Drex replied, "Shara this is what you make me do. If you would only give yourself to me." Drex told the girls this is what will happen to you if you don't do as I say.

I shouted as loud as I could. "Girls your father will bed you, then turn you out into the streets of the village."

Two girls came forward, "It's true, you are the Queen, wife off Icol." She gasped as she looked down at the sword that Drex ran through her. She fell to her knees, Drex killed her, in front of everyone.

Falling to the floor, holding to the door, "My lady, I'm sorry. My name is."

That was all, she said. Five other girls were pushed into the corridor. Drex did not search then when they were brought in. One pulled a long slender knife give it a throw it was a good shot. I yelled as he tried to pull it out.

"Drex, too bad it wasn't your heart."

Drex cried out, "Help me." Then shouted to the guard, kill that bitch kill them all. That's just what they did. The guards killed the five helpless girls.

Night time was coming to the village of Galaxo. In the mountain from where I could see the trees swayed with the evening breeze. I went to Lama, my sweet little girl, lying on the floor. The senseless killing of the girls. Sobbing as she laid on the floor.

"Come here, Lama," I said. Sitting on the floor I took her in my arms.

"My lady," she said. I knew them all, as I do most everyone in the village. My lady, do you think anyone will miss me when I'm gone."

I told her I was going to write a letter on a parchment. Drex has killed all six girls. I dropped it from the window. Looking into the area where the candles were. The candle's flames come to life. There was one, two then all six. I knew they had found the note.

How many more senseless killings before it stops. If I went to him, it would all stop. No, no I can't, I hate him. I want to kill him with everything inside of me. How much longer before Icol comes.

My thought turned to Basco, where did he go. Did he take his son and the girl Shila? Then it occurred to me, maybe Basco took them to the Trions? Basco was a Claxton warrior. He had the seal of approval. The seal to come and go as he pleased into the city. That's why Drex wanted him.

Yes of course, what did he have planned. Basco was a warrior this I know. Basco, Tenna, Tankko, there were so many I have forgotten them. I know they are still loyal to Icol.

Checking on Lama she had gone to sleep. She had recovered from the beating that Drex did to her. Only a few bruises still on her back. lying beside her somewhere in my thoughts sleep overtook me.

Somewhere in the night, I went to him in my dreams. I could see him. Where are you, my love? What is this place, I have never seen you in such a place? I went to him, hold me how long will I last. Icol Drex pressures me every day, he has killed six more girls his daughter. Lama spoke to me brought me back, to the darkness of the cell.

"What is it Lama," I ask?

"Someone comes," she said. Looking out the window I could see it was still dark. Even the cool gray morning had not come. The gray dawn to the east told me it was coming daylight.

I whispered to her, "Lie still." A small knock, a light whisper, it was Nordic.

"Lama," he called in a very low voice. "Please come to the door." I put my hand up.

"Nordic why are you here," I ask? "Drex will kill you if he catches you."

"Drex is in bed. The wound in his shoulder was great he is out. The other guards are all asleep."

I ask him, "Did you come to get another look?"

He replied, "No my lady, I'm truly sorry you did that."

"What is it you want Nordic," I ask?

Nordic said, "I just want to talk to her." I looked at Lama nodding my head, go ahead Lama. Lama walked to the window, I listen as they talked.

Lama said, "Nordic I'm not a woman yet. I promise you this, you said Drex give me to you."

Nordic replied, "Yes Lama, he did." Lama told Nordic, in this cell I will stay with my Queen. If the day comes we go free I will give myself to you and only you forever. I want no other man. I care for you know or I would not have done what I did. I showed you my body, now it's yours forever. You must tell your friends this.

Nordic said, "They already know. I come to bring you and the Queen this." Pushing a loaf of bread through the window a container of soup. Lama handed the food to me. Lama stood in front of the door as Nordic touched her face, closing her eyes as she tilted her head to the left; to lay her head in his hand.

Nordic said, "I love you, Lama." I told him, I will in time, love you only you. I will love no other. Nordic kicked the door. Lama jumped back I thought she would scream. I ran to the door.

"Nordic," I said, "You must be quiet."

Nordic said, "I should go kill him while he sleeps. "

"Nordic, Drex's time is coming. Icol will take care of him. Do you no Rand." Nordic said, "Yes he is a friend." I told him to find them tell them Icol is coming.

CHAPTER 22

I had a different look at life this morning. It had been six weeks since our mission to the plains. It was a training mission. I had taken a life. only six weeks ago, yet it seemed a lifetime ago. Funny I've never said a word of the mission. Fina and Dris speak of it often. Basco has sent for me.

Walking from the archives, my language class had ended. There was so much of their history to learn. The chief said I did not need to know more of their history. The thing I find is when you start you can't stop.

The chief said to me, "little one if you learn more of our history I may not let you leave." I looked at him with a smile. "If not for Icol," I said, I would not want to leave."

I have met several people that I have grown fond of. I have been approached by several Claxton's men that ask for my hand. Ra was one of them, now in my life, I just wanted to find Icol, returns him and the Queen to where they belong. Ra and I sat long at times talking about my training. The fact of me becoming a warrior. I told Ra when I return to my village, I would not be accepted as a warrior.

Basco spoke behind me, "little one you will be surprised what you find that awaits you in the village." I smiled at the man. Basco was a man I loved so much. I have said on several occasions, if I was older I would mate with him. I did not care about the age. Yet there was Dris, I have a strong feeling for. Yet somewhere I feel in the future Basco will find a very strong woman, I just feel it will happen.

Smiling at the man I ask, "You sent for me?" The chief was sitting on the steps to the castle.

The chief said, "Basco there coming."

I ask, "Who is coming?" I waited for what seemed several minutes. "Basco," I ask, "What is going on?" Dris, Fina, Dred came to the steps.

The chief said to us. "Come to the council hall." We gathered in the council, waited for what I was not sure of. A door opens all the council members came into the hall went to their seats.

The chief nodded to the members. The chief said to Dred, "My son come forth." Dred went to the council stood in front of them and bowed, then turned his back to them. Placing a cloak around his shoulder draped over his back to the ground.

"My son you have achieved the highest award of a Claxton warrior. Fina rise, you are my daughter, all your life you have trained. You have received a title of warrior." Dred and Fina walked to the side.

"Dris, Shila, come forth." Walking to the council we both bowed to the council, then to the chief.

"Dris, Shila with your prior training before you came to us. Basco has done the Claxton's proud, he is a high warrior; he also is a true friend. It is my honor to award you with the achievement of the Claxton, you are a warrior." Looking at the council each one bowed their head to us.

There was a million thought running through my mind. The one I was thinking was, what is next. Standing as he was, the chief said to us.

"There will be a feast tonight, in your honor, enjoyed this.

He took Fina and my hand, "Come with me." Basco and Dred took Dris.

"Shila, after the feast, come to me in the early morning. Fina, you know what must be done." Fina bowed walked away. The chief was asking me a question about their history. An hour had passed when Fina returned with a small metal staff. She placed it in the fire, turning to a table she opened a vile. I knew it was a dye of some kind, I just didn't know what it was for.

"Shila," he said, "This is the true seal of the Claxton's. All Claxton's and a few humans have the seal. It is a must, I assure you will find it to be true in the years to come. It is given when training is through. I kind of got choked up. I knew I was leaving.

In a deep voice, he said, "This seal gives you the power to train others. It is our way of giving our approval to do this."

Fina said, "Shila, it gives you the right to come here when you desire."

The chief said as he turned the staff in the fire. "Shila, there are only a few places a female can receive this. Right shoulder, high arm."

I looked at Fina. I said, "I often wondered what the painting was on your shoulder."

Fina smiled, "Yet you did not ask." I told her it was not for me to ask. I thought it was a private thing.

"Shila," the chief asks. "Where will you receive you?" Taking Fina's hand I turned to the chief.

"The same place as my sister," I answered. Tears filled our eyes as we embraced.

"Forever," Fina said.

In front of the chief, I did as I did with Dris. I let my robe drop to the floor. My naked body was exposed to him. Fina looked shocked.

Fins said, "Shila, you have a habit of dropping your robe in front of men."

"Fina, he is your father, I see nothing wrong with it. Besides, it will be easier this way," I said. The chief never looked at me as other men would, in the village. I was fourteen years old now. My body was at full potential. My legs, hips, and as Dris would say my full luscious breast stood as if they were peaks of a mountain. Fina stood beside me, her body was as full as mine or maybe fuller. Even at our young age, we were too grown women.

Standing in front of the chief, I ask him, "What must I do."

"Take this Shila, place it in your mouth, this will hurt." He explained. Fina took my hand.

The chief said, "I can give you an herb to make you sleep."

I ask Fina, "Did you take the herb."

She replied, "No ShIla, I was strong, it did hurt clear your mind go somewhere. Where ever you go you will find peace." I did as Fina said.

I found myself floating around the tower of the castle. In my thoughts, I saw my Queen. Shara was so beautiful I've never met her, yet I knew who she was, I'm not sure how. I can see why Drex wanted her.

My mind when to another world somewhere I've never been. Where was I? Why was I here? It was a world of humans and some other beings. It was a beautiful planet. Why would I think of this? I was told to go to a peaceful place. Yet I know not this place. I opened my eyes to Fina shaking me.

"Shila wake up." I held on to her, looking at her. "Wow!"

I said, "Fina you will not believe what I saw or where I went." I felt a little pain in my shoulder.

I said, "Is it over, did your father do it yet."

Fina answered me, "Several hours Shila, you were lost in deep meditation. I have sent for my father." It wasn't long before everyone come in.

Basco came to me first, "little one you give us a scare." My chief in all my training turning to Basco I said to him, "I went to the castle; I saw her Basco."

Basco asks, "You saw the Queen?"

"Basco she is so beautiful; her hair is dark and long. There is a young girl in with her. Turning to face them, "then I was suddenly swept to another world. There were humans and other beings. Tell me, what does that mean."

Dred said, "Shila, Fina, Dris you must come with me. One more journey to make, one more trial, before you leave. All your questions will be answered." Basco looked at me then at his son.

The chief said, "Shila in five days a ship will come. That ship will take you to search for Icol."

I said, "In five days. Look how can you tell me a ship will come on a certain day? How do you know this?"

The chief asks, "Shila do you doubt me.?"

I smiled at him, "Chief that is something I would never do."

Dred called to us, "We leave, take nothing with you, we will be back tomorrow."

I ask Fina, "What are we doing?"

"Shila," she said, "I have no idea."

Dred led us to the edge of the river. Going aboard a small craft, we left Claxton city. I thought to myself, how beautiful it was. It was as we were outside, yet I knew we were inside the mountain. I could see why the city could not be seen from the air. Where does the sun shine come from and the moon, I know, I have seen them? Rolling down the great stream we passed several small villages. I was curious, yet I said nothing.

Turning a small bend in the river a Huge light appeared. The closer we got the brighter it got. Going through the hole, the sun was so bright I had to close my eyes. Seconds later I looked at Fina, she had done the same. Looking around we had appeared into a Huge lake. I've never seen so much water in one place in my life.

Closing my eyes again, in my life I could never imagine a place like this. I called to Dred as I open my eyes.

"Dred, what is this place?" Great rolls of water come rushing at us. I thought it was beautiful. Dris and Fina looked scared, yet never said a word. I turned to look behind us I could not see where we emerged from the mountain. In my mind, I would never have pictured such a place like this in my world.

Dred stayed close to the shore as the vessel continued to roll on its power. I started to make a conversation between us, as Dred watched the shoreline. I wondered what it was, he was looking for. What seemed an hours Dred headed to the shore?

Dris and Fina said, "What is this place?" I told them to come on, I won't let anyone hurt you.

We talked as we walked deep into the forest. Even here, the trees were so big, like I've never seen. In my thoughts, I wondered if this place had even been touched by any being. I listened for a moment, I could not hear the waves any longer, Dred stop.

"I whispered what?"

Dred said, "We wait here, someone will come." A voice spoke as it came from the rocks.

"We are here Dred, we have been waiting for you." Well, you know me.

I said, "You knew we were coming.?"

Replying "Yes, little one," he said, "we knew."

I ask, "How do you know me?"

The warrior said, "That is Dris, you are Shila, this is Fina. My lady how are you."

Fina said, "I am fine Ru."

I looked at Fina, "We need to talk, you and me."

Dris said, "Yes we do."

Dred said, "There will be time for that later."

Ru led the way to the base of the mountain. Looking around there was another Huge rock. Ru moved the rock, it opened into another village, almost as the Claxton city, where we came from. There were a sun and a moon. I just looked around shook my head. The Claxton's all laughed.

I ask Dred, "Why are they staring at us?"

Dred said, "Many have never seen a human Shila. Especially a Claxton human warrior.

Ru said, "They know of your accomplishments Shila, you, and Dris."

I said, "What of Fina?"

Ru said, "We have waited for the princess for some time."

I said, "You know, I got another name for her."

Ru smiled, "What would that be?"

I smiled, "Someday maybe I'll tell you."

Fina said, "Yes she will, I would like to know myself." I walked by her smiled well maybe I will tell you someday too.

"Dred and Ru said at the same time, "Wait here." What seemed thirty minutes Dred returned.

Dred said, "Shila you must show your seal."

I started to drop my robe, Fina took my arm. "Shila," she said, not all the way. I swear Shila, you drop your robe for anyone. Only the shoulder. You and I must talk about this. Right after you tell me the name you have for me."

I laughed at her, "Right Fina, that's what we will do." The three of us walked past what appeared to be a guard.

I whispered, "Well whatever is here is protected."

Fina said, "I know these people, yet I've never been here."

Dred said, "My sister, these are the elders, the most intelligent of our race. We must wait here," Dred said. A place on the stone floor with a groove cut in it. Shila you must answer truthfully. You and Fina will go to the old one. Dris, and I will wait here."

Hand in hand Fina and I walked to the steps. She held tight to my hand as if she was afraid.

I whispered in a low voice, "Dont worry I won't let them have their way with you."

Fina expressed, "Shila if they try, don't you dare stop it. If you do when I get you back to the lake, I'll kick your ass."

I said to Fina, "You're such a primadonna."

Fina asks, "This is what, Shila?" I told her I would tell her someday.

"Oh yes, you will Shila or I'll kick your ass."

Fina and I stopped at the steps waiting. The stairs lead up six tiers to the top. I swear the Claxton that sat there had to be two thousand years old. The Claxton's that appeared, they were very old too.

The old man said in a low yet chorus voice, "Come little one."

I whispered to Fina, "I think he is talking to you."

Fina said, "You're a bitch Shila." I told her I took after her.

Fina started to rise, the old one said, "No my lady, the other one."

"Ah," I said, I suppose that's me."

Fina said in a low voice, "You're still a bitch." Walking up the steps, I bowed to him, the old one said, "Kneel Shila." All the Elders were looking at me as if they have never seen a female before. The old one that spoke I assumed was the head of the clan, little did I know. It has been said to us as he made a jester with his hand.

"You have gone to another world?" he asks.

"Yes, that is correct," I said.

"How can this be, you're a human."

I said, "That too is correct." I told him with a well-trained mind you can go and do almost anything.

He said, "Your mind, it has this training."

I simply said, "I'm a Claxton warrior."

"It was said you went to your home, beyond the Trions. Tell me little one was it your first time." I told him no, I saw my father once.

Several seconds passed as they said something in their words. When you went to this other world, tell us, what did you see.

I explained, "It was so real my chief. I can't explain it; it was as if it is now."

The old one said, "Come to me Shila." Yet I did not see his mouth move. Now I was afraid, what is happening to me.

"Shila, he said, a warrior you are. In your blood is a mystery of the ones that come before you." I didn't say anything, I kind of knew he had already seen something.

Placing his hands on my head. "Dont worry about what I said Shila. It will work out in time, clear you thought. Take me to this other world." I sat with my head bowed in his hands, I did as he requested. I was getting good at this. Before I knew it, Fina was beside me. I was leading the old one down a path to a city.

Fina asks, "Shila where are we?"

The old one said, "In a world far from your world. Yet the world from where Shila's ancestors originated." Then it was over, I stood up, look for Fina, she was still at the bottom of the step. She had never moved, yet she was there. The old ones talked to themselves in their words.

"Shila, your training is complete, go now find your destiny."

"May I ask a question, sir?"

A faint smile came to his face, "You may have one."

"What is my destiny," I ask?

He replied, "That is up to you." Search your mind Shila, you will find what you seek. Life is ten percent of what you are, ninety percent is what you do with it." The old one called to Dred.

"Yes, wise one."

"Come forth Dred," he said.

Take them to the water, wait until its daybreak. There's a ship coming, you must reach the plains. He spoke again this tie to Fina.

Fina said, "Yes, wise one."

"Fina, Dred, stand with her and Dris. Dred will be your leader. Basco will go with you, he will make many stands with you. Bring the power back to Icol." The old one looked at me, "Yes, Shila, I know him, with your mind and others you will find him, now go."

The night was coming to Galaxo. Dred had made a fire behind a Huge rock. It was not the first time a fire had been built here, I could see this.

"Dred may I ask a question?"

Dred replied, "Yes Shila.

I ask him, "How is it you, or the Claxton's always know when a ship comes to the plains. I see no way to call or talk to anyone. Yet you always know when it comes."

"Maybe ShIla, we call with our minds. Maybe we can send a signal to the ship with mind thought."

"Dred, I thought of that. I ruled that out."

Dred asks, "Shila did you not go to another world, even your home? So why can we not call someone with our mind?" I told him I suppose it was possible, yet I doubt it.

Dris said, "We still have two hours of daylight left, we could make it back to the village."

Dred looked at each of us, "Dris there's a reason why you must do as others say. Especially when the words come from the old ones."

Watching the sun go down, sitting by the fire felt good. For the first time, I felt a strange feeling, I was cold. I said as much.

Dred said, "It's the air from the water. Let's go close to the shore, something you must see." Walking from the rock to almost to the shore the wind was forceful, waves were twenty feet high. I tell you it was a sight to behold.

Dred said, "You see Dris, what would have happened if we were on the water."

Dris said, "I see what you mean." Dred put out the fire we went further into the forest. We'll stop here, Dred told us. You could see what would have happened if you were on the water. Remember Dris, there a reason for everything. Dred told Dris, you must learn to meditate. Fina was with Shila and the old one.

I told them it was a place of my ancestors, before coming to Galaxo.

"Why do you think you saw this place," Fina ask?

I looked at Dred. I ask, "What do you think."

Dred replied, "Shila, I believe this place is where everything will come together. You only see what you need to see, be ready."

"So, what are you saying," I ask?

Dred replied, "I believe this place, this world of your ancestors is where you will find Icol and Tenna." I told Dred that is what I think. How will I know him?"

Dred said, "It is not for me to say. Basco will know him, trust in him. I've never said this to anyone. When Tenna brought him to the city to be trained I was his friend, as Fina is to you. We took the seal of the Claxton's together. He was my friend. Many years have passed since. I would not know him if I saw him.

Fina said, "I know how I would know him."

I ask her, "How is that?"

"Fina said, "Tenna would be with him."

I moved my lips, so she could see me say, "You're such

a bitch." Fina smiled. I made my bed in the grass and leaves, I pushed together. Cuddle next to Fina I had a very pleasant night. Daybreak was showing through the trees. Dred called to us.

"Shila, Dris is gone," Dred said," We must hurry." I found a trail that led up the shoreline, this was not good. Dris knew better than to leave on our quest. Walking along the shore we saw him picking berries.

Dred asks, "Dris, have you eaten any of the berries."

Dris replied, "No, why." Dred told Dris, the berries are poison, they would have made you very sick. Throwing them down Dris wiped his hands on his shirt. You are new here, you have no idea what to eat.

Dris said, "Sorry I was only trying to help." Dred led the way to the vessel. During the waves, it had been washed up on the shore. It was still tied to the rock. Dred and Fina took one side, Dris and I the other. We carried the craft to the water, went aboard. We were on our way back to Claxton city.

Arriving at the dock as the morning ended. I told Fina I wanted to go to the pool. Basco greeted us with a good morning. Taking my hand helping me to the dock. I embraced the man I thought hung the moon.

"Little one," he said, "Go rest, we leave at first light." Fina and I went to the pool, I sometimes believe it cured all. Fina and I dropped our robes stepped into the water, it felt so good covering my body.

Lying back, I cleared my thoughts, somewhere on top of a mountain I saw a vast land, a ship flew by. What is this place? The wind blew hard, picking me up sailing me through the air. I was flying, or I appeared to be? The wind seemed to set me down on the bank of a small stream. Looking behind me was a vast mountain range that I stood on. Yet I had no idea where I was.

I noticed the air was clean, the water was pure. I scooped a hand full to taste. Walking cautiously down the stream looking all around. Somewhere I could hear voices, people talking, children playing.

"Hello," one said. I thought who are you.

I greeted them, "Where am I, can you tell me?"

The man said, "It's my home, I live here."

"What is it called," I ask?

He replied by saying, "Silly girl, it the Moon of Corning, do you know me." I ask?

The young man said, "I do not know you, yet I know who you are. The one you seek is not here. Someday he will come, you must be here to greet him." I told him I seek no one.

He said, "Oh but you do Shila."

I ask the young man, "Is there was a city here." He pointed off in a direction.

He said, "It's over there, go you will find it." I started to move when my head went under the water. I started to cough and gag. I had no idea what was happening. My head was under water again. Fina was pulling me from the water, "Shila," she screamed. I woke up still coughing.

"You almost died Shila, you must never meditate in the water again. You go too deep. It was all I could do you pull you up, I tried to find you. Dress Shila, before the others, get here." Fina handed me my robe, I was still coughing from the water. I could tell the way she looked at me she was pissed off.

"I tried to find you Shila." Dris and Basco ran through the door Fina told them what had happened.

Basco said, "Don't do that again little one, I need you alive if we are to find Icol."

"I was there again, I talked to people, they told me the one I seek was not there. A young man said I must be there when he comes. I had settled down so had Fina, yet she was still mad at me.

I ask, "Basco, do you think we can find this place?"

"I give you my word Shila, we will find it, this place you see."

Dris looked down at me. I told him I was fine. Fina and I watched as Basco walked out the door.

Smiling I said to Dris, "You missed your chance to see to naked women again."

"I missed nothing Shila," Dris said. "Oh, I saw you ShIla, and Fina, as I ran to get my father, believe me, Shila I looked," I told them I was going to bed. Fina said, "Tomorrow, we leave early." Fina walked up the steps to where she lived. I told Dris you know I just thought of something, I've never seen her mother.

Dris said, "She was nowhere, I've looked."

The morning was coming quick. Fina came to Dris and me.

"Shila, Basco, and Dred, they're ready to go." I slung my pack on, walked to where the others were. I had to go and ruin something. I ask of Fina's mother.

"She is gone Shila, that's all you need to know. My father raised me, with the help of Dred."

I started to ask, "Where is she when Fina stopped me. Let it alone Shila, someday I will tell you, just not today."

I thought, what could have happened to Fina's mother. Several hours had passed when we stopped. I guess you could say I come back to myself. Looking around I saw we were at the place where the Claxton's shot me with the darts. Basco told Dred will make a meal here." Dred agreed.

"Fina and I sat with our backs to a rock. I told her I was truly sorry for what happened this morning. I told Fina, let's talk about the mission. Dris came over to set down. I told him we would be on the plains one day before the ship. We should go to the stream where you killed the guard.

It was the first time I had thought about it, it was the first time I had thought of Pru. What had happened to her? Dris would not stop? All he could talk about was the way I sliced that guard.

He boasted, "I'll be glad when I kill my first." I told him it was sickening to hear him say that. We made our way further down the mountain. The sun in the evening breeze felt good on me. I was happy when we stopped for the night. Lying my pack on the ground, I went to the stream for a drink. Returning to my pack, placing my head on my pack I fell asleep.

I was the first one up as always. The steel-gray dawn of the morning had approached the mountains. You see Basco taught me well so did the Claxton's. I cleared my mind I let it take me to the trail. I was a Claxton warrior. I didn't have the experience as Drod, and Basco has. I was as good as Fina maybe better. Yet I would not tell her this.

In several months, I've been in the village, I have come close to her. Closer than anyone in my life that I could remember. She was the sister I never had, even if she was a Claxton. Fina and I may be a different race we were one in mind, we were sisters. I could not say Dris was as a brother.

I do have a strong feeling for him, even looking at his father the way I do. Basco was a beautiful man. He was so handsome the way his muscles would budge under his shirt. His hair long dark to his shoulder with blue eyes. Yes, sir a beautiful man. As I've said, if he was my age I would mate him, now.

My mind followed the path to the cliff down the side of the mountain. Where the path split is where the warrior said the ship was. Others were seeing the ship. In my mind, I could see they were from my village. Drex had sent them to the Trions to die.

My mind took the left path to the bottom. There were twenty-five guards. Six at the small craft that made thirty-one waiting for us. There were four of us more than enough if we caught them by surprise at different times. The six would be no problem.

"Shila, Shila wake up." The sound of Dris voice brought me back to myself.

"I jumped up, Basco they wait for us."

Basco asks, "Who wait for us Shila?" I told him of my little journey down the path. There are six of them at the craft.

Twenty-five at the bottom of the mountain, there is a scruple in the clearing.

"Little one, did you go there," Basco ask? I shook my head. Basco told Dred we don't need to fight them at the same time. Maybe two of us go to the clearing. Dris and Fina can go to the clearing. We will wait on the trail out of sight. If a patrol comes by we can take them.

Basco told me to head down the path, I went in my mind. Slinging my pack on I left in a run. Fina behind me for over an hour we ran. It was still a way to the top of the ridge, still, we ran. Within the hour, we stopped on top of the ridge. It was the place where Fina said, she could see forever. The first time she was here. Again, she said it goes on forever.

Turning to Basco she asks, "What is on the other side?"

Basco said to her, "I can't say, Fina, I've never been there. I've only been to a few farmers on the plains."

Dred said, "I have never left the city except when I went to the village once, when I was a small boy or when I go to the mountain to look around."

Fina said, "How do you know, there are not others out there?"

Dred said, "There are others my sister. There are clans, fourteen of them."

"Are there bigger cities," she asks?

Basco said, "If there was we would have known."

Dris took the led down the slope to the stream. A thought went through my mind. The warrior that brought the message to us was Ru. How did, I mean it made no sense. How did he get there, he never came from the city? He didn't come up the trail. I feel someday all will be revealed what I want to know of these Claxton's. I have studied their history been trained by their warriors, yet I did not know that much of them.

Someday I will ask Fina if she does not tell me the truth I will kick her ass. Thinking of what I just said, I laughed out loud. Everyone sitting around, looking at me. Everyone said at the same time, "What!

We made our way down the stream to the lower part of the mountain. Each step I felt myself slip away. It was as if I was leaving home. For the past year, I have been safe, with no worries, I still have no worries. The guards, I do not fear them. Standing on the ridge I could see the scruple. Basco and Dred walked over to me.

"Basco," I said, "I pointed to the clearing, see there."

Basco said, "Just as you said ShIla." Fina, take Dris, go to the ship to find out why they are here."

I said, "Basco, Drex has sent them here to find you. Drex wants you, me, Dris Dead. Basco, maybe it should be me, and Dris."

Fina smiled looking at me, "Basco she is right."

I said, "Maybe we should not let them see Fina and Dred."

"Shila may have a point," Fina said. If they think we are working together they might try and storm the mountain. This Drex he would never find the city. Yet if he brought his guards, many would die. On both sides."

Basco looked at Dred, "You are right. If anyone comes beyond the clearing, they would be killed."

Dred said, "All the years no one has ever found Claxton city without us showing them.

Basco asks, "Fina what do you think?"

Fina replied, "Basco it's your mission. I must agree with ShIla. Let her and Dris go." It was settled, Dris and I went to the clearing. The guards came bearing arms, as we knew they would.

Halt one said, "Who are you? Ah, one said, "the storekeeper daughter, the female Drex has sent for." I never said a word.

One guard pointed to Dris, "You are the son of the traitor Basco." Dris lips crinkled up.

"My father is no traitor, you are a stinking scum sucker. If there's a traitor, it's you for turning on Icol. That thing you called king placed him in a prison."

He answered, "Icol is dead the queen is dead." I stepped one step closer. I told him the queen is in the east tower, with a young girl Drex has beaten so bad it was hard for her to walk. He tried to bed her, his daughter. You know it's true.

The guard said, "Well I think we will bed you here, forget about Drex." Dris was mad I have never seen him as he stood before me.

Dris said, "You will die here, that is what will happen."

"So, you think the two of you can take us," one guard said.

I said, "Oh you mean the others at the cave below. Look I know you have heard of men going into the Trions never coming back."

The guard said, "Girl we will have our way with you, kill your friend." That was all that was said.

Dris move so fast I hardly had time to think. It was, well I can't explain how it made me feel to see Dris in action. Dris had two on the ground, he was running for the others. Another one hit the ground, the last one ran aboard the scruple left. I started running Dris behind me. I ran past Basco and the others.

Fina call, "Shila," I never slowed down. Looking behind me, all was running the scruple never slowed down. It never went to the cave, it headed to the castle. The guards at the cave had no idea what had happened; or what was going to happen.

Basco called, "Little one wait." Stopping we set on the ground in a circle talking of the plan to kill the guards.

Basco said, "We would wait until tonight then we take them out. We will surprise them while they're sleeping. They'll not expect that."

"Remember," I said to Basco, "One got away. He probably will return with others."

"Your right Shila, we can lower the odds. We have today and tomorrow. If they return, we should be gone. We should go to the area where the ship should come. It is still a good walk. We sat talking about things when I told Basco. You know Basco you would have been proud of Dris today. The way he moved on those guards. He killed two of Drex's guards. He did that before I could pull my sword.

Dris said, "They should not have said the thing they said about you Shila. I will defend you to the end, with my life. I wish not to say what I'm about to say. Yet I feel it is important, I have learned to meditate. What I must say should be said in private. Now I know what I must say, should be said so others can hear. I love you Shila, I have always loved you." Dris looked at his father.

Basco said, "I know your feeling son, I have seen this." Dris turned back to me. "Shila we left our home long ago, one year now. I loved you then I just did not know it." Dris went on talking, I went somewhere else. Coming back to myself, as Dris stood.

Dris said, "Shila someone has chosen you. In my sleep, I have seen you with someone. You have been chosen to kill Drex." Dred spoke for the first time.

Dred said to Basco, "I have also seen this, I have not said a word. Even the old one has seen this." Fina looked at me, never said a word. Moving her lips to say, "You are a bitch." I hid my face to keep from laughing out loud. I loved her she was so funny.

We had a camp well off the path. There was a noise as an animal would make. I looked over the rocks to see nine guards. I motion to Basco and Dred to come to me. Waving my hand to stay low. Looking over the rocks they saw what I did. I crawled to Dris and Fina.

I said to them in a low whisper, "Guards below." Basco and Dred crawled to us.

Basco said, "Look the trail is climbing here. He pointed with his hand its four feet from the trail. Fina you and Shila take the point. Dris in the middle we will take the end."

Moving in to place you could hear them talk. The one guard I knew, I saw him work in the courtyard. My father said, when he would come into our store he was still loyal to Icol. It was a shame, yet I knew what was going on. Since the year I've been gone, I have grown up some. Before I kill him, I will give him the task to be loyal again.

One guard said, "Drex will be proud of us, no guard has ever been this far into the Trions. We will make history."

"You're a fool," he said. "The only reason we're this far is there letting us come."

The guard said, "these Claxton's really, have you ever seen one." The guards stopped we moved into our position as they talked their words never left my ears. The words Dris said had never left my ears either. Somehow, I was a chosen one, how could this be? How could anyone know I would come alone?

I tell you one thing, I will be mighty pissed off if I don't get the chance to kill Drex. Everything I've put myself, my body through. Claxton this, and that.

Speaking one guard said, "Long ago, I saw them come and go from the village, there odd looking. They look like humans you know like us, except they have pointed ears, their skin is different. I knew Tenna very well. I tell you now, believe what Drex tells you if you will. I had rather take on ten guards than one Claxton."

One guard said, "Your joking right."

The guard said, "They're here now, looking at us, watching us."

Another guard said, "Well if there is a Claxton anywhere within the sound of my voice, let him show himself, I'll personally kick his ass."

Dred said to Basco, "I just got an invitation." Dred dropped from the rocks to the rear. Fina to the front. Dris and I watched for what seemed seconds.

Dred said, "Well I'm here, I did not want to disappoint you, are we to fight."

Fina said, "I'll take the front."

The guard said, "A woman."

Fina smiled, and said, "Yes I am, and a very dangerous

one." That was mine and Dris's cue. We dropped from the rocks to the middle. The lead guard threw down his weapon. This is my time to be loyal to Icol.

The others said, "You fool, they will kill you anyway."

Fina said, "Go pass them, wait. If you run I will kill you myself."

I promise you the fight was swift. Eight men lay on the trail. One was still alive yet dying. He called out to Basco, Basco kneeled by him,

"Tell the queen I'm sorry, tell Icol it was my faith." Then he died. Walking past them to the guard that waited.

Basco looked at him, "You are Nordic." Basco asks him, "How many more guards are here?"

Replying, He said, "Maybe fifteen, or twenty. I am loyal to Icol. Basco, you must understand I was a very small child when the over-through took place. I needed to survive, I have seen the queen. The one that is with her I love her. She will be my mate someday.

Basco asks, "Then why do you lead them?"

"Basco I knew we were dead, yet we were ordered," Basco told Nordic if he looked a hundred years you would never find the Claxton.

Dred said, "You would have been dead before you reached the top of the trail."

Fina said, "Basco, the cave is just beyond the rock test is loyalties."

"How would you do that," Nordic asks? Fina walked around the guard looking at him.

"Nordic," Basco said, "If I was you I would do as she says."

"She is a bitch." Fina's eyes darted to me. Then back to Nordic. "Send him to the cave, bring the other." Before he could move, Fina cut his arm. Blood flowed down his arm.

Fina said, "I just wanted them to think you were in a fight."

I said to Fina, "you're enjoying this?"

Fina replied, "Oh yes Shila I am. I just hope someone comes

to me. I just want to cut someone."

Nordic looked at Basco, "Basco she is out of control."

Basco said, "Nordic, she's a Claxton warrior."

Dred asks, "Basco, do you think this will work?" Basco looked at me, I saw a half-smile.

I said, "Well no need to scare him too bad. I think it will work."

Fina smiling that little smile she has, "Let's go kill them all."

Dris replied, "It's now or later." I said, "I'm for now."

Fina whispered, "Basco I do not wish to scare him, if he doesn't come through, I will kill him. The only way for him is to bring out the others." Dred started to move down the train. Walking by Nordic, Dred told Nordic to come with him.

Walking toward the cave Dred said, "Now go." Nordic left without a weapon. Walking straight to the cave, going inside it took only moments for them to come from the opening of the cave. What Nordic didn't know was Fina, Dris and I, followed him.

I must say, Nordic was not in the cave very lone when the guards ran from the cave; there were seven of them. That was no match for Dred and Basco. I mean really, Dred could have taken them himself.

We waited for the guards to come from the cave. Three of them come outside to the cull-de-sac. Dris jumped, hit the ground, we did not see the scruple as it flew by with guards on board. The three guards that came from the cave lie dead or dying. I saw one fall, Fina killed him. I had two on me. I turned to see one of the guards run from the craft.

Picking up Dris, I threw a digger at one. It took him through the leg. Dris had been hit by the scruple. He had been hit hard. I could see blood flowing from his head. I screamed for Fina.

I said, "Kill them." Fina cut two guards, as she ran to Dris side. Two more guards ran from the ship, then two more.

I looked at Fina, as I prepared to battle them. I know Dris was in bad shape, blood was running fast from the gash from his head he was unconscious.

The four-guard that came from the ship was running for me. I was doing a good job holding them away from Fina. I was flipping, cartwheels, sliding all over the place.

A big guard came to the ramp, "Enough," he said. I just kept slashing.

"That one," he said, "Is a Claxton. The other one is the storekeeper's daughter. That's the one Drex wants, get her the boy is the son of Basco."

I smiled, "He is no boy," I said.

If he was conscious, he would kill you himself."

The guard said, "Then I'll kill him while he is out." I told him if he comes close to Dris, he would die here today.

The big guard boasted, "Two girls against eight men. I told him don't underestimate us girls.

Fina said, "Unless you are prepared to die, I suggest you leave." Then Shila laughed out loud. It made the guard mad.

"What's so funny." He asks?

Shila said, "If you stay here you die if you go back to Drex you die. Throw down your weapons we will treat you fairly."

The guard said, "I don't think so, you discard your weapons."

I ask, "You will die to defend that bastard. A man that will bed his daughter, just to have a man-child. How about your daughter. You will take her to him?"

I could tell I was getting to him. Then as he lifted his sword he shouted "Guards." The fight was on.

Basco came from one side, Dred from the other. I stood, my blade in his stomach, I kneeled beside him.

I ask, "Was Drex worth dying for. You fool now you will never live to see your daughter again."

In a dying voice, "Please," he said. "Tell her I love her." The guard coughed blood then died. I told Fina I knew the girl, when we go home I'll tell her. Little did I know at the time, Drex had already killed her.

Basco picked Dris up carrying him to the cave. The guards

had left water for tea. Taking a towel from his pack Basco poured hot water on the towel started to clean Dris 's wound. Basco told me it wasn't so bad. I looked at Shila, she was the color of the clouds. I told her he was fine, he will recover. He will be good as ever. Dred asks, "What do we with Nordic?"

Basco replied, "Let him go, he did what he said he would do."

Nordic said, "Go! Go where? "I can't go back to the castle, Drex would kill me for sure. He looks for someone every day to kill." Basco told Nordic of a farmhouse from across the plains. A friend lived there, he is dead now. Take a scruple from the cave, go there Nordic, we will come for you. I'm not sure how long it will be, I tell you now I will come.

The morning came slowly. I lie beside Dris all night, he was talking to me when the others came to the fire. Basco placed the other scruple in the cave we started walking to the landing where the ship was to come.

CHAPTER 23

Drex was sitting on his throne when he received the guard that ran from the mountains. Drex asks him, "Why have you returned alone."

The Claxton's sire, they killed all my men, the patrol sire, they killed my squad." Drex looked on as sweat beaded his brow. Drex stood to walk to the window.

"Thirty men sire, all dead."

Drex shouted, "Thirty of my guards, dead, thirty men against, how many did you say."

"Sire I do not know, they come from everywhere yet nowhere. I swear there were so many." Drex looked back out the window.

Drex asks, "Anyone else with the Claxton's."

"Yes, sire, two humans," the guard said, "the store keeper's daughter and the son of Basco."

Drex looked hard at him, "Come here," he said. "How is it you got away?"

"I needed more men. Sire, you know how awful those Claxton's can be."

"Did the boy and girl fight, Drex ask?"

"Sire it happens so fast, I did not see much. I just wanted to come to tell you. Sire, I'll get more men then return. Even as I tell you this I know they are all dead. I can tell you this sire, Basco was with them, he killed four of the guard by himself. Sire if I can have more men."

"Guard," Drex ask, "Are you loyal to me."

"Yes sire," he replied, "Sire I have always been, from day one. These Claxton's, I'm afraid to say what I feel to you. I feel if they marched on us we would be doomed. There's got to be thousands."

Drex told the guard to go to the hanger tell all the captains to come to me. In minutes, all six captains were inside Drex chambers.

Drex asks, "Where are the other two captains."

One captain said, "You sent them to look for Icol."

"Yes," Drex said, "Icol, can't I go through one day, without hearing his name. So many years went by, so many years living my way until they let him escape. I should send the ships to attract them."

Drex stood from his chair, walked to the window. Turning around with his hand to his chin.

"Captains, go to your ships fly over the Trions. Find and destroy these Claxton's, place men on the ground invade the mountain."

Sire the captain said, "Every time we go there we lose men, we have no reserve."

Drex screamed, "Find them and destroy them, once and for all. Do you understand me? Now go!" In the hanger, the captain and the others ready their ship.

The captain said, "I'm done with him. I'm taking my ship, I'm going to Advair."

The other captains said, "Let's go before the guards come." In the heat of the moment, all six-ship left without the guards. Higher and higher the ships went into the darkness of space, on a mission to Advair. Weeks later the Advairan government saw a fleet of ships traveling in their airspace.

The controls told them the ships were from the planet of Galaxo. Several ships were sent to intercept the Galaxian ships. In minutes, a call was sent. Galaxian you're in the Advairan airspace. What is your intention, reply?

Replying, "We mean you no harm, do not fire on us. We need a council with your government. I am the high command of the Advairan government." All the Galaxo ships came to a stop. The Advairan ships surrounded them. Docking was easy. Walking aboard facing the high command. The greeting was exchanged.

The Galaxian captain said, "We mean, you or no one harm." I told him of what Drex wanted. We want nothing to do with his orders. Sir we wish not to kill the Claxton."

"You mean if you could have found them." The Advairan

command said.

"Sir, Drex sends men there almost every day. They never return within the last month over fifty men have gone into the Trions, none have returned."

The commander said, "My government has traded with them for many years. We would land do our trade then leave. We have a ship landing there today. The captain will be picking up five. Three humans, two Claxton's." I just looked at him.

Captain, would you join us on our quest." He told me the humans were Basco, his son, and Shila, a storekeeper's daughter."

I looked at the commander, "How did they know?"

"Captain you must remember, the Claxton's since the overrun they have a few human friends. Now captain let's go to my government see what they say I will present your case. Are there more ships?" I told him we have eight ships. Drex sent two of them to find and kill Icol and Tenna the Claxton.

The commander replied, "Good luck with that one."

The captain of the Galaxo ship said, "Commander it would be a great time to overrun Drex. Only if we had Icol here."

"What of the Queen, could she not hold the throne until Icol is found."

I sat back looked at him strangely, "I'm afraid she is a long time dead."

The commander placed his hands on the shoulder of the captain, "Captain I assure you she is not dead. How, how long have you been in the service of Drex."

The captain said, "From the beginning."

"Haven't you heard the stories of the queen? Let me tell you a story the commander said. I'll make it quick. Drex paid the Advairan government, I must say, very well to take the Claxton and Icol. We were to place them in prison. Years past, it was brought to the attention of the government about the way Drex was doing.

We at the time did not know Icol, was the true king. Let

me tell you, the government is highly upset with him. The way he has treated his people and our people. We made the arrangements for them to escape, Icol and the Claxton. It was to take place on Gara. We did not know the ship was going to crash. Well, they were to be escorted to the Trions, where Icol was trained."

"Commander I assure you, Icol, was never on the mountains of Trion."

"Oh, captain I assure you, Icol is just as much of a warrior as the Claxton he is with. Now come my government awaits you." Hours later we stood in front of the council.

The high council said, "What you have said captain, just concurs with what we have heard of this Drex. We could overrun him. A lot of people would die. I feel if we tried to overrun him he would kill the queen for sure. I feel she is too valuable, she must be protected. As bad as I hate to say, I think it will be best to let her stay where she is."

"Council members, I tell you she is dead. Drex killed her long ago. I saw him place a sword through her. Then took the head of several guards because they would not swear loyalties to him."

"Believe what you want captain, my son was killed by this Drex. He told me of the queen. Captain how can you not believe, yet you're here asking for our help." The council continued.

"Our council will decide this. Commander, take your ship go to the planet of Eden. There you will meet our passages. The search for Icol will begin, this I promise you. The Advairan government wants no part of Galaxo. Know more than what we have. We want no problems with the Claxton's."

"Commander this council places you in charge. Go, ready your ship, take the captain with you. Let him tell Basco of the thing that Drex is doing. Let Basco tell the captain of the queen. The Advairan ship is leaving Galaxo today. You must meet them in Eden."

CHAPTER 24

Drex went crazy when the ships left without the guards. Taking his sword, he started to slice one of the guards. Jumping back the guard pulled his sword.

Drex said, "How dare you to pull a weapon on your king."

The guard replied, "Sire, I have served you since your rein began. I will not let you kill or wound me. If you try I will fight you back. I will not make it easy for you." Drex threw down his sword ran from the chambers. Drex thought as he ran down the corridor. My men pulling a weapon on me, how dare they. I was their king. Drex's thoughts went to the queen, as he ran.

I will take my rage out on her, or the tramp with her. Running to the tower Drex stopped just outside the door. Waiting and listening to anything he could hear, there should be talking.

Walking to the door, opening the small window looking into the room. Lama stood in sight naked. She thought it would be Nordic. When he began to speak, Shara's heart started beating faster.

"Drex did you bring my husband," she asks?

Drex said, "Know Shara, I brought me. Today Shara you die. I've waited long enough. You and that tramp."

"Drex, that's no way to talk about your daughter," I said.

There was silence, Drex said, "I will kill her as fast as the others."

"Oh Drex, we know how you have killed others. One day you will die by the hands of a girl." Drex started laughing, reaching down to the handle. It was locked.

"Shara open this door." He demanded. I walked to the door started pampering him.

"Oh, the king can't get in? What's wrong with the King." Lama was still naked.

Walking to the middle of the room, "Father," Lama said, "Look at my body, you want to kill a body like this. Lama was right she did have a nice body.

"Father, this is one body you will never touch again. Drex was screaming you tramp, you bitch, don't ever call me father.

Turning around Lama placed her robe on, walked to Shara taking her robe from her shoulder. She exposed Shara's full breast. Breast that Drex wanted to touch so. Sweat beaded the forehead of Drex.

Lama took her right hand from the bottom of Shara's breast she pushed up on Shara's breast. Drex couldn't do anything but watch. His mouth was so dry, trying to swallow he started screaming.

"You bitch, open this damn door." Drex had got excited he wanted her now, bad. He meant to have her, now, today. Drex took a bench rammed the door. Shara still taunting him with baby talk.

"Oh Drex," Shara said, "Did you see something you like. Oh, wait, as Shara took both of her breasts pushing them up to Drex in front of the window.

"Do you like this Drex." Drex stood screaming at her.

Shara let her robe drop, "All this can be yours Drex if you bring me Icol."

"I swear I will kill you Shara, you and that tramp with you. Shara said to Drex through the window, speaking softly.

"Bring me Icol or his head. I will marry you. I give you my word months ago. You have failed Drex. You failed me, your men your kingdom as you say. This kingdom belongs to Icol."

Drex stood outside for several minutes without saying a word.

"Shara, I will do as you ask. Before I marry you, Shara, I will chain that tramp with you to a bed naked. I will line up all my guards let them have their way with her, all of them."

Lama said, "Father, at least it want be you. Father, it sounds like fun. Father if I get the chance, I'll kill you myself. I love you father."

Drex screamed, "Don't ever call me that, you bitch."

"I love you, how can you be so cruel to me."

"Shut up you bitch." Drex started to run down the corridor. He could still hear Lama calling him father. Turning from the window my robe was still down.

Lama said, "My lady, you do have nice breasts."

"We both laughed, "Well I think that went well. Shara smiled, you have grown up Lama."

Taking a piece of fruit Lama said, "I would still kill him."

"Yes, I said, "I do believe you would."

I took a piece of parchment sat at the table thinking long before I wrote the words.

"I'm Queen Shara, wife of Icol. Tell the mothers of the girls I'm truly sorry." I turned to Lama, I said, "Let's leave the door locked, thanks to Nordic."

Lama asks, "My lady, where do you think he is?" I told her word would come don't lose faith, without it, you would have died long ago. Lama my faith is strong, my husband will come. When he does there will be a fight. Drex, will keep me here until the last minute, then barging me to Icol for his life.

Lama asks, "What about me my lady?" I told her nothing would ever happen to her if life was in me. She threw a blanket at me. I turned quickly, you little, well I see you're feeling better.

"Yes, my lady," Lama said. "Do you think after all of this is over my lady, Icol returns to the throne, I go home to my mother. My lady, you think you will remember me."

I went to Lama took her in my arms. I could tell she had tears in her eyes, I did. I told her the time you have been here. You have been as a daughter to me, despite your horrible father. You will always have a place in my heart.

If you like when power is returned to Icol, I will make you one of my maidens. I feel all my maiden that was is no longer. You are very special to me always and forever, Lama embraced me.

Replying Lama said, "I feel I will die before that happens." We had talked for hours of all things around. Looking out the window nighttime had come again to the village. Standing on the chair I looked out the window a single light, then two then all six. I knew they had found the note. Lama went to bed for the night. Before going to sleep Lama asks.

"My lady, Did they find the note?" I told her they had. In the silence of the cell the darkness all around I made myself a promise. Someday when I'm released from this cell I'll visit all the families of the girls Drex has killed. I will tell them of the one that put a dagger into him. I lie quietly in the cell thinking wishing for Icol to come.

Almost in a daze of sleep, a knock came on the door opening the window, I could tell it was a new guard. He had brought our meal. I told him its very late for a meal. I thought everyone had forgotten about us. Drex has cut the water from us. Only lets us have a small amount. I opened the window I could tell he was a young man.

I ask him, "Where is Nordic."

The guard replied, "He was on a patrol in the Trions. I'm sorry to say he is dead. The story is he was killed by the Claxton's." I looked around Lama had stood up.

"I'm ok my lady, Nordic is still alive, I feel it. He may have been in a fight. If the Claxton's were there he would have survived I know this. He said he was loyal to Drex, to stay alive. Nordic would have given up his weapon if forced. I will not fear this."

I ask the guard, "Can, you tell me what is going on outside." Looking over his shoulder in a low whisper.

My lady, "The ships left, Drex order them to go to the Trions kill and destroy the Claxton's. The ships left without the guards, Drex went crazy. The chief captain said they had enough, they took the ships to Advair. My lady no one knows that for sure." The guard turned to leave then come back.

"Who are you," he asks, "why does Drex have you hear?"

I simply said, "I am Queen Shara, wife of Icol." I thought he would choke.

"I must leave," he said.

Lama and I sat talking about things women talk about. The towers were over one hundred feet in the air, yet we could hear sounds from the street. I looked at Lama, something is going on. Pushing the chair over to the window Lama and I stood to look out the window. I told her this could be it.

Lama asks, "It could be what, my lady?

"Maybe the people have had enough," I said. There were shouts from the street calling Drex. Guards were sent to hold back the people. It only took several minutes for Drex to appear.

"What is wrong with you, have you forgotten who I am, what I can do?"

One from the crowd said, "Release the queen."

Drex screamed with excitement, "Who said that?"

A big man came in front, so did several others. "You must release the queen now."

Drex called guards. "Somewhere a shot was fired from a weapon the guards stopped."

"Think about it Drex, that could have been you. Now release the queen."

"I know nothing of a queen," Drex shouted.

The big man said, "She is in the east tower, there Drex, see. The man pointed to the east tower.

Drex shouted, "Guards kill any, and all that comes close to the castle. Drex turned, walked away. Standing down, I told Lama, he will come, he will try to get in. Drex will try and break down the door.

Lama said, "I'm ready for him my lady. Nordic helped us with the material to make a lock inside, only we could unlock it.

Drex was screaming, "Shara, what have you done. I swear I will kill you, Shara." He was running hard as he rammed the door. That door was not going to move, we had a lock on the inside. Drex had tried to knock it down before.

"Shara open this damn door, now, I mean it Shara. I have said it before, today I swear Shara, you die today." Lama walked to the door.

"Father," Lama said.

Drex screamed, "Don't call me that."

"Father if only you would touch me, please give me your hand. If you will touch me I will unlock the door." Drex stopped looked at her through the small window.

"I only want to be a part of your life father." Well, I had no idea what Lama was doing.

I said, "Lama no, don't do it. He will only use you."

"All I want is to hold your hand, my lady."

Drex still looking through the small window, "My hand that's it."

"Yes, father that is all."

Drex said, "If I let you hold my hand, you'll open the door."

"Yes, father."

"Lama no please don't do it," I said.

Drex screamed, "Shut up Shara, you're in enough trouble." Drex fell for it, I never thought he would. Drex pushed his hand through the window. Lama took it touched her face, then kissed it. Then with a jerking motion, she pulled the whole arm through the window. Drex had no idea what was about to happen. Lama pushed down hard, Drex's arm snapped like breaking a stick.

Drex screamed, "You bitch, I'll kill you for that. Drex went screaming running down the corridor. Running from wall to wall as the pain went through his body, screaming until we couldn't hear him any longer.

Walking to Lama I said, "Let's recap the month. He has been turned down. We give him a strip show. Broke his arm, looking at each other as we laughed yes, it has been a good month."

CHAPTER 25

Shila was sleeping, Dris lying beside her. I pretended to be asleep. Dris places his buskins on, walked to the stream. Basco was up as usual. My brother was in a meditating stage.

Well, I was feeling a little spunky, so I took from the ground a leaf that hung from the stick. I thought it would be perfect for what I was going to do. I touched Shila on the upper lip. She jumped up slapping like something was on her face. I pretended to be asleep. Lying back down with her back to me I touched her on the ear. She jumped again. This time I could not hold it in, I started giggling.

Shila came from the ground, "Fina I'm going to kick your ass." Shila grab me started rolling around on the ground. Basco came running, I was laughing so hard I could see through her. She tried so hard to be mad with me for waking her, yet as we rolled she started laughing too. We both were laughing so hard Dred came from his state of mind ran to us.

Basco bent over us, we looked up at him. Such a beautiful man, his arms so thick with muscles. His long hair lying on his shoulders. I thought if I was older, Basco, you would be mine. I, of course, would not tell Shila this, if I did we would be rolling in the grass again. Basco looked down at us.

"Girls," he said, "What am I going to do with you?" Well, that just made us laugh harder. Dred stood looking at us lying on the ground. Basco looked at him.

Dred said, "I have no reason why she does this. Claxton is supposed to be a serious being. Sometimes, I think she is part human."

Dred turned to walk away stopping he said, "Basco a ship comes." Looking skyward we saw nothing.

Dred said, "The ship has drop from hyperspace it will be here within the hour" Dris ask if we were afraid to go on to the ship, I told him no.

Fina came over smiling at me. "Dont worry Dris, I will hold your hand, yours to Shila."

"You no Fina," I said, "One day, one day." We both

laughed. Making our way to the fire Basco had made tea passing it around.

Dred said, "The ship comes through the atmosphere, Basco." I stood beside Fina as the ship came into sight. I've seen ships before, I've even seen our ships at our hangers. I've never seen a ship as to what was coming before my eyes.

It was the biggest ship in the world. we waited for it to land. I stood waiting. I admit I was a little shaky. My thoughts went to the old one on the coast of the Trions. Taking me on my mind thoughts to the land I was from.

My ancestors, will I go there. Thinking of our ships, they were made by someone we inherited them from. A planet that seemed to disappear. I will find this mystery, meet it head-on, I'll solve it. Little did I know at the time that's exactly what would happen.

Fina toughed my shoulder, "We must move Shila hurry."

I ask, "Why must we be in a hurry."

Fina screamed, "Run." I turned to see a hundred men on foot some on scruples. Turning to face them when Fina hit me in the knees, we went rolling. I was glad she did, the scruple would have run over us. Basco and Dred picked us up from the ground. My sword was out I took one of the guards across the face blood went flying.

I shouted to Basco, "Put me down, let me fight."

Basco said, "This is not the time to fight little one." Basco had me under his arm. We followed Dred and Fina aboard the ship placing me on the floor, I saw the ramp go up. The door closed we went higher into the darkness of space. Then a feeling I've never had I think it was more like a thrill.

Basco said, "Welcome to hyperspace, Shila."

I said, "Wow what a rush."

We got our footing turning around ten of Drexs guards were facing us. I had my sword in hand as I called to Basco.

Shouting I ask," Basco what is the meaning of this?"

The Advairan commander said, "Place your swords back

in their sheath." I moved toward the Galaxian captain. The commander stopped me.

"Basco," he said, "You must listen to the captain." I never took my eyes off him. Dris and Fina were watching the others. As the captain told his story. Dred started to walk to the three of us.

He said, "I believe him."

"I do not trust them," I said.

Dred said, "Shila clear your thoughts, you're full of hate. Go somewhere with your thoughts, remember your training." Dred said all this in a low whisper. "If you do not trust them Shila, trust me."

What Dred said had meaning. I did what Dred had instructed me to do. In seconds, my mind was blank. I found myself flying through space. Something touching my hand, turning to the right I saw a Claxton. One I've never seen before. We were on a mountaintop, on a planet, I've never been. Suddenly Fina appeared.

The Claxton said to me, "You have come a long way. I see you're in good company little one." Fina talked I listen to them.

Fina asks him, "You are Tenna?"

He replied, "I am." The warrior went to one knee.

I ask him, "Why did you bow to her."

"Little one, you thought all this time she was the chief's daughter, which she is. Fina is a Claxton princess, her father is the King of the Claxton's. He only goes by the chief."

"So, Dred is a prince," I ask? "How did we cross paths?"

"You look for Icol little one, I protect him. I too look for you, as you look for us." Dred touched my shoulder brought me back.

Dred smiled, "Better Shila." I told him yes, much. Yet I still do not trust them.

The captain said, "We all want the same thing. You are the daughter of Coe the storekeeper. He escaped on an Advairan ship. The same as us, the guards on the ground, we are not part of them.

Our captain kept talking as we flew through the darkness of space. My mind still going a thousand miles per second. Then he said to me that brought me back.

"Your father Shila, is on an Advairan ship, looking for Icol, as we are. Several ships are looking for Icol. We don't know if he will ever come back some of the men are still loyal to Drex." Sitting down the captain said, "I'm afraid some always will be until the end. The guards, Tankko, Bliss, Taso now are looking."

Basco said, "Maybe if we see them, I could speak to them."

Shila said, "There's only one thing. It has been for told by the old one of the Trions." I reached out for Dris taking his hand, I said to them, "It was said by Dris first."

"I will say this only once, by my hands Drex will die. Anyone tries to stop this, I will kill them as fast as stepping on a bug." As the captain contained to speak he said to Basco.

"Basco, we are heading to a planet called Eden. I know that's where Icol and the Claxton went with the Advairan captain Lux. From Eden, I'm not sure. I feel when we arrive on Eden, we will prevail in gathering the information we seek of Icol."

I listen to them as the commander said, "Of course, if we know they went their others will too. There are hunters out there, with your people that don't know we have lifted the bounty on him." The commander told us to follow him as he led us into the corridor to our quarters.

The commander said, "Shila I have waited to meet you. I have been told great things. Believe me, when I tell you this, we will find your King." Basco and Dred shared a room the three of us in the other. Dris was the first to drop his pack. I told them I still did not trust the guards, Fina said the same. Dris said he was not sure. Fina and I dropped our packs.

Then I dropped my robe. Fina yelled, "Shila you will drop your clothes anywhere. There's no one here but us, Dris has seen us naked before. I have me under clothes on Fina, what is the deal with you. Take your clothes off relax.

Fina asks, "Shila what if my brother or Basco comes in?"

I ask Fina, "Have they seen your bare ass before."

Fina replied, "Well yes."

I said to her, "Then what is the problem? Undress come over her take my hand." Fina did as I ask. Joining hands, we went to a happy place, we went home "Home to Claxton city."

Fina was speaking to her father I knew how they could see the future. This is how Dred knew the ship was coming. He went there in his mind, after all this time after all the training. I have found out what I've always wanted to know.

Opening our eyes with a start. Someone was knocking at the door. We scrambled to our feet, my breast was exposed so was Fina's. Dris open the door as we placed our robed around us.

Fina smiled, "See what I mean."

I whispered to her, "You need to grow up Fina. Waiting at the door was a young Galaxian guard.

"Please," he asks? "May I speak with you." Fina looked at me.

Fina ask him, "Why do you look for us on the mountain?" He explained about Drex.

Fina said, "I should kill you now."

Replying he said, "I mean you no harm."

I ask him, "What is going on at home?" The guard told his story.

Dris ask him, "Have you seen the queen."

He replied, "I have always been told she was dead. Now I know different. Drex still takes the girls from us. Last month he killed six of them. The month before he beat his daughter almost to death. Yet everyone is afraid of him. I'm not afraid, yet I'm only one man. I would love to kill him myself."

I listen to him talk yet something was not right. I told him my name, he looked up at me.

"He said," I know who you are," I told him according to

the old one in the city of the Claxton's, I would be the one to kill Drex. The guard I cut on the ground, I to will kill him. My friends with me will help. We all are Claxton warriors. I showed him my seal. He looked at it, I know nothing of this. It was placed there with a red-hot iron, from the fire in the city of the Claxton's.

"Maybe someday, I will see this Claxton city," he answered.

I laughed, "You, I think not you could never find it."

We didn't pay much attention to him moving around to the door. Somehow, he opened the door, two guards ran in with swords swinging. Dris was on the floor as Fina and I flip over to our packs where our swords were. Blood was oozing from Dris's chest, he gasps for breath. The three guards were slashing cutting, yet they were not reaching me or Fina. It's as if they could not see us. Dris was in bad shape, Fina screamed very loud. That brought Basco and Dred running.

There were two guards behinds them, Dred took them, Fina and I took the ones in our room.

One guard on the floor said, "You rebels as long as there is life in me you will never take the castle. I walked to him I took his head Basco picked Dris up went to the commander.

Dred looked at me. "Shila you are a supreme warrior, yet sometimes you scare me." I walk to the Galaxian captain placed my sword to his throat.

Captain, I said, "If another one of your guards crosses me again, I will kill them in front of you. Then, sir, I will kill you, do we have an understanding." He just nodded his head.

I told Dred in front of all that was there. Speaking out I told them all I have two things I must do. I do not trust you, as far as I am concerned you are loyal to Drex, this proves it. I trust only the ones I come on this ship with. My faith, my destiny is to kill Drex.

I started to leave, one of the guards ask, "What is the other one."

I looked at him, "Kill anyone that tries to stop me from

doing this."

He replied, "You will have no more trouble with us Shila, this I promise you."

Fina took my arm, "come on Shila, let's go see about Dris." Leaving I heard one say she just took his head, she didn't think about it, she just cut.

In the sick room, the captain said, "I never thought they would do that."

I ask him, "How many men do you have on this ship."

He said, "There are six more."

"One guard said, "Shila, the one you took his head, was my brother."

I said, "I'm sorry for your loss, he came, he paid his bill, just let it go. Why he was loyal to a man that would rape, bed his daughter I cannot say. Fina knew I was taunting him, well he was not even a man. You're not a man to let this go on. Stay out of my way, cross me or my friends without hesitation we will kill you."

The brother said, "We want no trouble Shila after this is over, I will seek revenge for my brother."

I smiled at him, "You will die as your stinking brother. Revenge is best served cold.

He said, "I will never die by the hands of a woman." He made a final mistake he slashed out at Basco as he was coming to let us know Dris would recover. It was the last thing he would do, he died on the deck of the ship.

"I looked at them, there's five left, who's next," I said.

CHAPTER 26

Tenna and I made our way to our cabin. The captain left the Star of Joni, going higher into space. looking from the window portal the star was a dot in space. We had been several hours into the flight when Lux sent for us.

"One month," he said. "We will be in the Spore's galaxy. We will not take the ship to the surface. A shuttle will be used to transport the supplies to the Moon of Corning. Then the ship will continue to the Moon of Spores. Crew members spoke among themselves.

I said to the captain, "Sir, Tenna and I, we're still in a hurry to go home. Yet when we reach this moon, I would like to go from the ship to talk to some of the people."

Captain Lux said, "They're human Icol, they're other beings too. Icol if you wish you may stay there, you and Tenna. I'll make the run to the Moon of Spore's, then I'll return. It will be on the way home." I told the captain, I think it will be safe for me. I can't speak for Tenna.

"Sire I will go, with you," Tenna said, "you cannot rid yourself of me so easily. I will be with you until you are placed back on the throne. Then, and only then will I ask for leave to go to my home. Then, sire, I'll only be gone for a short time."

I told Lux it would be fine. I told him I would like to see this Moon of Spores. I have read in our archives there were two moons there. One of them had a purple haze that comes from it. Some say the planet that disappeared, is what controls their climate. I do not know this for sure, it is written."

Lux said, "It would take four months to make the journey to the moon and back. Icol if you wish I can talk to the chief justice for you. He will see no harm will come to you." I thank the captain, Tenna, and I walked to the galley for tea.

As the captain said, it took one month to reach the Moon of Corning. I felt the ship come from hyperspace to impulse. I knew we were in the moon's galaxy. I sat up quickly. Tenna came to me with the captain. My stomach was all knotted up. I was going to the very place my ancestors come from. There was no doubt I would walk the same path they did.

How long had it been since the planet disappeared? The ships we have were sent to another planet. They were sent here for some reason. I remember the writing now, it was after the war of the planets. The planet was tired of the fighting; all ships were sent to the Moon of Spore's, then to Xon and Corning.

Boldlygo was the name of the planet that disappeared. The old man in the archives was Quad. Late one night he loaded the ships with all kinds of supplies. Three hundered years ago. Kohl and his wife left Corning never to return. I'm not sure about this, I hope to find my answers. I told the captain I was ready.

"Icol the shuttle will take us to the surface. The big ship will stay in space. I only have a few things for them remember Icol, I will speak for you."

Lux told me it had been several years since he was here. Landing on the pad, I walked from the ship looking around. I thought the climate was the same.

Lux was welcome by the dock officer. He just looked at me and Tenna. Lux ask to speak to the chief justice. The docking officer pointed to the building. Walking from the pad knocking on the door the chief said "Enter." Lux introduced me then Tenna.

A big man leaned back in the chair, "Ah yes the Claxton. I have heard of your people."

I started to give him my name he said, "I know who you are Icol, and you are Tenna."

Tenna asks, "How would you know that?"

The chief said, "Captain I have papers for a murder on the planet of Gara, the town of Minot. Yet they have done nothing here."

Lux said, "They are trustworthy, I give you my word on that."

"What is it you want Captain," the chief asks?

Lux answered, "Icol wants to stay here. It will take me four months to make the trip."

"Captain I know the Moon, I send supplies there all the time. I also send lawbreakers there."

Tenna said, "We have broken no law, this I tell you, the man in Minot betrayed us, he paid his bill."

"Lux said, "If you have papers on them, then you know who he is."

The chief said, "I'm not sure the papers do not give that."

I interrupted him, "He is King Icol, King of Galaxo. His brother exiled him to prison. Drex, Icols brother, overrun the castle. Killed his mother and father."

Tenna said to the chief, "Sir Icols people were from here." The big man looked at me skeptically like.

Looking at me he asks, "Is that true."

I said, "I don't know for sure how long ago, maybe three hundred years. All I know was, this very moon was overthrown. In the archives of my world, it is written his name was Kohl his wife, Joy. His wife's father, his name was Quad.

Standing he pushed out his hand. "Son if this is true of what you say. It's an old story, the Platonians fought with Quad. He is welcome to stay if he wishes, the Claxton too. My name is Redda. I've read of the war, all about the people of Boldlygo."

"Boldlygo, sir."

"Yes, Icol," he said. "You will never find in this life or other people, more intelligence than the people of Boldlygo. They were very brilliant. The old one called Bota built the first ship. I have one of the ships here, so all can see."

I ask, "May I see it?" He granted it, walking down the stairs to the archives he just kept on talking as if he knew me a hundred years.

"These people were so brilliant, they made the whole planet disappear. Some of the people stayed on the Moon of Spores some went to the Moon of Xon. Late one evening the King and his daughter disappeared, with Bota never heard from again."

Stopping at a desk, Redda called for a female. Redda called her Lori. She was a beautiful woman. She had blue eyes with long brown hair.

"Redda said, "Lori would help you on your quest." Here underground you could hear the ships come and go.

I said to Tenna, "The port here is very busy."

Lori said, "Ships come and go all the time. Now, how may I help you." I explained to her what I wanted to see. Turning from me she walked down the aisles of books.

Tenna whispered to me, "Sire she wants you." I told him I was a married man.

"Go, sire, I won't say a word."

"Tenna if I did that, I would be no different than Drex."

"Sire," Tenna said. "Who would know," I told him I would. Lori came back after several minutes.

Icol she called, "Come this way, what you seek is here. There were four large books, there must have been thousands of words. I told Tenna I wanted to read. I told him to go look around. Redda said there were no boundaries. Sitting down I started to read.

Tenna left walking to the top of the stairs down the hall to the door. Redda called to Tenna.

Redda asks, "Is Icol in the archives."

"Yes, I said with Lori."

Redda said, "Tenna I feel I must warn you of a hunter." I told Redda the general on Eden cleared us of those charges.

Redda replied, "I know him, how is the old man." I told him he was still in charge, we only met briefly.

"Tenna it is the moons law, when a hunter comes here they must clear themselves with me. I will tell them what you say."

I said to Redda, "I would like to walk in your city."

He asks, do you have stones?" I told him I did not, yet I have gold coins captain Lux give me."

Redda said, "You know Tenna, I could use a man like you. I have a ship bound for Earth."

"Earth," I ask, "What is Earth?"

Redda said, "It is a planet very far from here. It would take almost four years to go there and return." I told Redda that would be too long. Icol and I want to go home, soon. I told him of Drex. What he was doing to the girls.

Redda said, "Then you need to go home, take care of this. Tenna If you want to see the city, go. When you return I'll show you where to go retire for the day."

I walked the streets of the city. Named from the planet.

I ask, "Is there other cities?" I was told by several of the people I talked with beings and humans in the shops, each of them said the same. There was no other city on the planet. I was told few people lived on the plains. They're farmers mostly.

I saw a building that seemed to touch the sky. I knew I was not far from the port. Ships would come in, do their trade then leave. There was a small ship that came to port that did not leave. I wondered if they live here or was it a small freight carrier. My thoughts went to the time Icol and I were in Rulla. Rulla was the largest city I've ever seen, now I think Corning was.

The front of the shops was made of what was called glass. I've seen glass before just not so much of it. My thought went to Icol, I wondered if it was like this when his people left here. I walked up and down the streets most of the day. Mostly talking to the people. The afternoon had turned to even I need to return to Icol. Redda did say return to him before sundown.

Leaving the streets to the archives. I walked to the bottom floor. Icol was talking to the young girl. She was showing him things in the books.

"Sire," I said, Icol turned to me.

"Tenna," he said. "I have read so much. Lori has helped me find what I seek." The girl asks Icol if he would come back tomorrow. He told her he would be here for four months.

Leaving the archives to Redda office. Entering the office Redda motion for us to sit. Walking to the window Redda spoke in a low voice.

He said, "There's a hunter here, landed in a small craft

several hours ago."

Tenna said, "Redda we want no trouble."

Replying, "I know Tenna, I know I have sent watchers to watch his moves."

Tenna said, "Redda if he comes at us, I will kill him, I promise you this."

"Tenna I hope it won't come to that. We in my eighty years in office had only one killing here on the moon."

Icol said, "Eighty years' sir."

Redda said to us, "We don't age here as on your world, here the Moon of Spores the planet that disappeared. It was said if you stay on the planet, you could not die. Icol you will find, some of the people lived to be over one thousand years old. Maoke, Bota, who knows how old they were. It was said three hundered years ago Bota took the King and daughter of Xon, left one evening never to be seen again. Bota dated back to the beginning.

Icol looked at Redda. "My ancestors come from there."

Redda said, "Only two people come from Boldlygo to live here. Pep when his wife went to Earth." Tenna turned to look at me, "Then Kohl, Redda said to Icol you will learn Icol when you read the archives you will find our past is the same. The hunter we must face him. I have sent for the authorities. When they arrive, we will send for the hunter together?"

I said to Icol, "Sire the word Earth comes often." Icol looked at me. I told him Redda wanted me to go on a ship to Earth.

Icol asks, "Do you want to go?"

Smiling Tenna said, "I just want to go to Galaxo." Sitting in the evening sun Icol dozed off to sleep. I touched him on the shoulder shaking his head. "What is it Tenna," I told him someone comes. The hunter enters first then the guard. The hunter looked at both of us then stepped off to the side.

Redda said to him, "I have asked the guard to bring you here, these men are no longer wanted by the Advairan government. They were pardoned by the general on Eden."

The hunter said, "They may have been pardon on Eden. The Advairan I know nothing of. They are wanted on their world, by King Drex."

Icol said, "Drex, is no king, he, however, is my brother. He takes his daughter to bed, has children by them. He has my wife the rightful Queen of Galaxo in prison, sent me and Tenna to Advair to be imprisoned."

The hunter said, "I have nothing against you, it's business. Chief if you will sign here I'll take them, I'll be gone. The men have broken no laws here I'll sign nothing."

"Well then sir, I'll just take them back dead. The bounty is dead or alive, the one you call queen said to Drex, bring me Icols head or him, I'll marry you Drex." Icol staggered, the words to his ears were devastating.

"Tenna she has forgotten me," Icol said. I told him, sire Drex has said this to the hunter, all these years Drex has told her you were dead. Sire, remember the dreams.

Icol set in a chair, "That's all they were Tenna, a dream."

Tenna looked at the hunter, "Icol go there in your mind, you will see what I say is true."

The hunter replied, "It's me or the guards, they also look for you." He told us he met one of the guards named Taso on Gara.

Icol answered, "I do not know him."

Redda said to the hunter, "I will not hand them over."

"Then I will take them." The hunter said.

Redda said to the hunter, "You do know who that one is."

The hunter said, "I'm aware of the Claxton. I also know he is a warrior. Yet I must take them back." I looked at the hunter, I told him I have sworn my loyalties to Icol. The hunter never said another word. I drew my sword cut him in half.

I ask Redda, "Where can I place the body?"

Redda and I talked for several minutes while the guard left for a cart. Several minutes later, I help him place the body in the cart.

Smiling, "I'll take care of this," the guard said.

Redda said, "Tenna you are a very devoted being, I'll give you that." Redda carried us to a cabin across the way. You will stay here while you're on the moon.

"So, we are confined," I ask?

Redda said, "Know Tenna you're not, you may go as you please. Icol can go to the archives you may stay with him or check out the city." I'm sorry for what has happened. I must report this, we are under Palatonian rules. I'll try to hold off for a while, give you some time." I told Redda don't report it at all if there's not a body there's no crime.

Redda replied, "I like the way you think, I could sure use a man like you."

I smiled at him, "Redda," I said, "I'm sure you have several guards that would defend you." Redda left the cabin I told him I would see him tomorrow.

That night Icol slept restlessly. I woke him early before the sun came. Icol looked at me with that morning look.

He asks, "What is wrong Tenna?" I told Icol, you were having a dream.

"Yes, it was a bad one Tenna," I told Icol I had a dream, the dream woke me. It was as if Dred was calling to me."

"Tenna isn't he the one that went through training with me. How could that be, were galaxies apart."

Tenna said, "Icol you surprised me, you know what a well-trained mind can do."

Icol asks, "Why have you not tried to go to the castle?" I told him I have. There is nothing I can connect to. I decided to keep the meeting at the stream with Shila, and the princess to myself.

"Icol," Tenna said. "Clear your mind, go to her, you can do it. Tonight, you must meditate. Icol let your mind go, clear it of all things. Let your mind go to a happy place, you and she once shared. I to will meditate, I must find if Dred is trying to reach out to me."

Walking from the cabin the sun was high in the morning sky. I told Icol my plans for the day. I will stay with you for a while. I would like to go outside the city. I was skeptical of the ships coming and going.

Icol said, "Go, go, do as you wish, while on the moon. I will spend most of my time in the archives."

Inside a small eatery, we had a simple breakfast. Icol could see the city very well. Having the last cup of tea, Icol explains the writing he had read, how the small outpost started long ago. I find it as Redda says, they don't age as we do. I told Icol all planets and moons are different.

Redda said, "The Moon of Spores, the people from the planet that disappeared lived a very long life. Some over a thousand years old."

I said, "That true. I remember reading that on Galaxo. Even in the archives on Galaxo, it speaks of Kohl and Joy. I think when they left here, Kohl lived to be over eleven hundered years old. Tenna what I don't know is where did they go. I remember when my father and mother died, where did they go there's no accounting for them."

I told Icol I could not answer his question. I've seen death in Claxton city we cremate the bodies."

"I don't understand Tenna. I think I will walk in the city amongst the building. Maybe I can get some idea of the pass. What we see here maybe someday we can build a city on Galaxo.?"

I looked at Icol, "That would be something." Icol I don't think the council would approve it. If they did sire, I've got the perfect place. There is a river that runs far away from Claxton city. I fear someday the Claxton's will be discovered."

Icol said, "Then we must go to the far side of the planet to build this city. Of course, I would stay at my castle."

"Of course, sire," Tenna said. Icol walked down the street looking at the building.

Stopping suddenly, "Tenna, have I ever been here." I told

him no not, that I know of. "Tenna there is something about this building. I can't put my finger on it, yet it has a familiar feeling about it."

"It is said sire, there are things you can't explain, been places you've never been before. I can't explain it, yet it happens." I walked beside Icol for a long while.

Tenna, I'm going to the archives. There is so much to learn, over three hundered years of history. My ancestor walked these very streets. I'm sure it was different back then, yet it is still the same.

I walked inside the building past Redda's office. I walked down the stairs to the huge room, there were many books. Parchment lay on the table. The caretaker came from a row of books.

Lori asks Icol, "Would you like to start where you left off."

I said, "There is so much to read." I told Lori I would like to read, one hundred years before it started. I was overwhelmed to be reading about my family's history. Tenna told him he would be leaving.

I walked up the stairs leaving Icol in good hands with Lori. I walked down the corridor overhearing Redda talking to someone. Walking to his office a big man stood over him. He was dressed in a plain black shirt with a diamond and a star.

I stood listening for a moment. I knocked on the door, the man said, "you need to mind your own business." Well, you know, I had a feeling like he was threatening me. I replied, "He is my business. I'm his guest from a world you know nothing of and will never go."

"I am a Palatonian, I go where I please," he said.

He stood talking to Redda kind of rude. The big man took a punch at me. I moved, he went to the floor. Trying to get up, I kicked him in the face. Turning over he sat up rubbing his face.

He said, "No one has ever knocked me down."

I said, "Well now they have." Picking himself up, he told Redda high council would not be amused by this being."

I smiled at him, "Then don't report it. I think we should just leave it alone." I told Redda I would return later, as I walked out the door I could hear him say something to Redda.

Going to the street from the building a voice spoke to me. I started across the street. Turning a young man stood on the corner.

"I have a hovercraft," the young one said.

I ask, "What is a hovercraft."

He answered, "It's a four-man craft you can tour the city, or most anywhere on the planet as long as it is short-range." I walked with him to the small craft I must admit it was something to see. He explains how it works.

He asks, "Would you like a ride?"

Sometimes I wonder what else is waiting for me. Stopping in a section of town I did not know, it was different; It was more run-down. The young one told me his name was Tosh. Tosh told me it was the original part of the city. Over the past years, the new city was built around the old one. Tosh told me he must stop at a shop. I sit in the craft, Tosh jumped from the craft running inside. Tosh wasn't gone long. Returning he had a bag.

Tosh said, "It's food, we will be traveling outside the city." Traveling in the craft he handles the craft very well.

Tenna," he said,

I looked at him, "I never told you my name."

Tosh said, "Oh I know. I know you, I no Icol. I will explain later."

Higher up the ridge, the craft topped out, it had no trouble climbing. Topping the ridge, I saw an awesome sight. An inland lake with miles of water. Tall trees of a different kind, humans, and beings everywhere.

My mind drifted back to the time when I was a small boy, in Claxton city. The river flowed into the lake, where so many times I went as a boy. My father would always tell me after I return, standing on the dock he would look at me and say.

In his stern voice. Tenna, you should not go to the lake

alone. Then he would say you will be a great warrior son. Thinking of this I thought to myself, only a few humans have ever seen the lake. Icol, Basco that I knew of. I often wondered of Basco. He was a young king's guard when Drex sent us away. Yet Basco was a warrior, I trained him myself. Tosh shook me, bringing me, from my thoughts.

Looking around I ask Tosh, "What are they doing?" There were hundreds of people.

Tosh said, "They were families having lunch." I told him I've never seen anything like this. In my thoughts, this was great.

Tosh said, "We do this when there is no threat of the Palatonians coming. We always know when they come, thanks to Bota many years ago. I'm not sure how long ago. It is written in the archives."

I ask Tosh, "Who is Bota?"

Tosh answered, "Bota was a very intelligent being, from the planet that disappeared, some say he moved it."

I smiled at Tosh, "My friend no one can move a planet."

Tosh asks, "Can, you explain its disappearance, no one can?"

I said to Tosh, "I think your writers place that in your books."

Tosh said, "Tenna that is not true." Tosh seemed just a little agitated with me. Finally, he said, "Tenna the story is no legend it is facts. Still taught in our schools today. Even the Palatonians talk about it. Tenna you know it's as anything else, people say things and do things as they write it down. Hundreds of years of things placed in your archives, you're not sure of."

"Like what," I ask Tosh?

Replying he said, "Well do you remember the humans coming to your planet. They came from somewhere, even the old ones here as on your world would know." I told Tosh, I see what you mean. Tosh walked to the back of the craft.

Looking at me he said, "We need to leave Tenna." Tosh gave three long blasts from a horn, people started to scatter.

Tosh said, "The Palatonians you had words with, they come.

Dont worry about the people. Come, my friend, we must go."

I ask him, "Where are they?"

Tosh said, "They're coming over the ridge." I told him, then I will stand.

Tosh said, "Tenna they don't fight with that primitive weapon." Tosh jumps in the craft.

I ask, "What do they fight with?"

Tosh answered, "With weapons that have a roar. It can cut a man into. I've seen this with my own eyes. The Palatonians come for my mother and father. They took them away, it has been two years since I've seen them. I don't know if they're alive.

Hundreds of years ago when Icols people fled, the Palatonians took over the ones that were left. They were treated badly, all this time they have left us alone. They come and go yet never bother us. They come to collect the resources and leave. I think we should fight them. Redda said we all would die. They would kill us from space."

I told tosh the guard wants me. They will continue to follow us unless I face him. There is so much of this planet I wish to see. I need to know who is following me.

Tosh said, "I understand Tenna, I do. There's no harm in running away to fight again another day."

"Tosh Claxton's are a race that is not accustomed to running," I said.

"I'm sure," he said. "Hold on Tenna, we leave."

Tosh made his way with the small craft to a small stream. Following the stream, Tosh brought us to a huge waterfall. It was no doubt a beautiful place. Tosh looked at me with a smile.

He said, "Hang on Tenna, we're going to get wet." Going through the water under the falls opening to a cave, a room so big you could have placed three hundred men.

Tosh said, "We will be safe here. Only I know of the cave. Tenna I have placed things in different places, it's always there when I return." Tosh took me further into the cave until the roaring of the rapids did not hurt my hearing. There was an opening at the top. Climbing up the wall at the top of the opening, looking down I could see the Palatonians.

Tosh said, "You made him mad Tenna."

Going back to the bottom Tosh asks, "You never said why he is after you?"

I looked at Tosh, "Ah he'll get over it." Tosh told me the Palatonian followed Tyler, a human from the planet that disappeared all over Earth. When they thought they had him, Tyler would move? Finally, in New Mexico they had him cornered. Lucky for Tyler, Dorn showed up with the fleet, along with others from Xon and Valorian. Our teaching tells us they defeated them returned to Boldlygo, just to disappear."

"Even the people from the Moon of Spores will tell you. I believe Graf was in power. He lived to be very old. His people could still be in power as Redda is here."

I ask Tosh, "What do you mean?"

"Redda is a descendant from Quad and Joy. Joy was Quad's daughter, she married Kohl. Tenna, I'm very intelligent not like some of the ones out there."

Tosh dried himself with a towel, made a small fire. He asks, "What was my planet like." I begin to tell him.

He asks, "Do you live with the humans." I told him I did. Yet there is in the mountain a grand city, it is hidden in the mountain of the Trions. Only a few humans have seen it.

Tosh said, "You mean like Basco, Icol, Shila, and Dris."

"Tosh, what kind of trickery is this? You can't possibly know of them." I said.

Tosh smiled, "Yet I do." "Tenna they come."

I ask Tosh, "Who comes?" He told me, Basco.

I said out loud, "So Drex has hired him to find us, no doubt to kill us."

"Tenna if you will sit I will show you something you won't believe. Only I know of this. I will never let anyone know."

"So, it's a secret," I ask?

Tosh said, "As I have said, only I know this."

I ask him, "Then why do you show it to me."

Tosh said, "Tenna, in my forty-three years of life, you are the only person I've met I can trust. What I'm going to show you, is your city you speak of. A human girl, a human boy his father, and two Claxton's are on a quest to find you, and Icol. They're looking for Icol to place him back in power. Dred and his sister Fina." I told Tosh I've been gone too long. So, Dred is a warrior.

Tosh said, "As his sister, the two humans, are also. I have followed them."

"I don't understand, how did you find them," I ask.? I told Tenna in great meditation we crossed paths in the very stream the Palatonians search for you. We met in the stream higher above the falls. There still a long way off. Tenna, it's a long way to your planet. Yet they follow the path you and Icol took. I have tried to call her to tell her to come back.

I looked at Tosh, "You are draft. Even in my meditation, I can't find them." "Come with me Tenna, let me show you." On the floor was a small puddle of water.

"Tenna," Tosh said, "Clear your mind of all you think. Look into the water Tenna, let go. You will find everything you wish to see." I did as Tosh said, I found myself getting up off the floor. It was full dark outside; Tosh was sitting by a small fire. I woke up looking around calling a name, I was calling Shila. I told Tosh I met her in a stream once. The day's event turned into the late evening. The Palatonians had left, we returned to the city. Icol was upset.

"Tenna," he said. "It is past curfew, Redda said you had a Palatonian after you."

"Ah sire, that is true, I feel he will die." Tosh was with me as we entered the cabin. Tenna told me as we entered the cabin someone looks for us."

"I know Tenna, several of them," I said.

"Sire Dred, your friend from the city of the Claxton's. Dred,

his sister Basco his son, and a girl. Trained by the Claxton's."
Icol at first, looked a little skeptical. A female Tenna, trained by
the Claxton's.

Icol asks, "Tenna you know this how.?"

Tosh introduced himself, "I will tell you everything.
Everyone has their reasons, Icol. You to find your past, me to
find my future. I have not found it yet. I believe I will die here
on this moon. One thing I will tell you is this. Never let the
Palatonians know where your homeworld is. Maybe if I don't
die here I will let you see your future, if you let me come to
your world."

In the many generations that have passed, we are from the
same blood. The ones left, the ones that stayed behind. I will
show you this as I showed Tenna. When I do, then it must be
destroyed. You must promise me if something happens to me,
you will do it Tenna. It is my belief if it is found it could be used
for evil things.

Tosh talked, as Icol looked at me in disbelief. Tosh said, "I
will stay here tonight, we will take my craft and leave, at first
light."

We talked for several hours about the day's events. I told
Icol about the lake where people were having their meals
together. I tell you Icol it was a beautiful thing.

Icol said, "Tenna maybe one day when this is over, we may
do the same for our people." Icol had made tea. I offered Tosh
a cup.

Taking it Icol asks, "Tell me more of the ones that come?"

"Good sire, you remember Basco. He was the head
guardsman even at a young age. Sire if you remember Basco
was the only guard that was trained by not only me, by the
Claxton's too. Basco carries the seal of the Claxton. Now his
son and the female called Shila have the seal, they are warriors.

"Basco son I never knew," Icol answered.

I said, "The boy and the girls are very young sire. Dred your
friend, his sister, Basco, the two young ones, it will take many

to stop us." Tosh told me they take the path we took. Unless we can call them. Maybe we can reach them in meditation.

Tosh said, "Maybe the pool will let you see what you need to see." Icol went to bed, leaving Tosh and me to talk. Tosh sat on a small mat on the floor.

Tosh said, "Come Tenna, join me." I tell you this, in my lifespan I've never seen a human so strong in meditation. Together across the universe to the very world of ours, to the village of Galaxo, in front of the castle. Tosh and I Walked among the people. Funny how dark it was on the moon to walk into complete daylight.

People were gathered outside the castle looking up at the east tower. My very quarters where I once lived. Where I fell in love with a human female. I told Tosh to follow me. Going to the tower I could read his thoughts, she is beautiful.

I said to Tosh out loud. "You should have seen her twenty years past. "Shara, hear me," then we were gone. A strong pounding, someone was knocking on the door. I reached for my sword walking to the door I looked through the window, opening the door slowly, Redda stood with a concerned look on his face.

I said, "Redda, it's late for you."

Redda said, "Tenna, you and Icol need to leave. The Palatonians are coming. Their ships will be here by dawn." Icol had come to the front wanted to know what was going on. We explained, Redda told us Lux had been captured.

Tosh spoke, "Redda I can hide them, they won't be found."

Redda asks Tosh, "Where will you take them."

Tosh replied, "Best you not know."

Tenna asks, "Why did they take the captain, he's a freighter. He has no weapons on board just supplies."

Redda said, "Tenna it's just the way of the Palatonians. Conquer, that's what they do. Only the planet that disappeared has ever beaten them.

Redda said, "Icol, we have no forces or means to fight. We

are a peaceful race, we wish no trouble with the Palatonians. We are tired of living under their laws. When they came they took all according to the archives?"

"Quad stayed, wanted to fight it is written. Late one night several ships had been given to the Xonians by the planet of Boldlygo, these ships came to port. The captains told their stories."

Quad told Kohl, to take his family, take as many that will go. It took two weeks for the six ships to load all they could."

Icol said, "Tenna that's why our people come to Galaxo, to the Claxton galaxy."

Tenna said, "If they ever come to Galaxo we would destroy them, this I promise."

Icol asks, "Tenna how would you do that? I've never seen a weapon anywhere in the city. I've never seen large weapons anyway."

Tenna replied, "I know Icol, yet it is there. The only reason the ships of the village were not destroyed, was because they were from the village. The Claxton's did at one time before me, or my father, a distant planet did come and tried to overrun us. We destroyed all that came."

Icol said, "Tenna I've never heard that story before."

Tenna said, "It was removed from the archives. The old ones in the ancient city would know of what I'm saying."

Tosh said, "Gather your things we must leave." Walking out the door I told Redda we would be close.

The three of us went to the craft. We placed out few things in Tosh craft. Leaving the city following the course of the river, approaching the falls, Tosh stopped the craft, I jumped off the craft. I told Icol and Tosh to wait here.

Making my way through the forest. It was as I expected two guards were at the falls. I made my way around to the upper side of them. Looking down a slight incline I could see they were both asleep. I thought as I came to the small fire that burned, how easy this will be. Sitting on a stone I took my sword touched them on the foot. Jumping up to a sitting position one said to me.

Looking at each other, "Who are you, yet what are you?"

I simply said," I'm a Claxton, I'm going to kill you." One went for a weapon that laid by his side. I took his head. I pointed to the other one, leave your weapon, take him to the city. You will have a ship coming, tell them to let the captain go. The one your captain captured on the Moon of Spores.

He said as he picked up the guard, "If it takes me the rest of my life I will find you."

"Guard," I said. "If you look for me I will take your life, as I did your friend. Now go tell them what I have said?" I watched him as he loaded the body in the craft. He went higher in the air then made his way toward the city.

Icol and Tosh made their way to the falls. The water came rushing over, millions of gallons of water. I jumped on the craft going under the falls to the large cave. I took a log dragged it to the water's edge. I also placed a large log on the fire before we left. It was still very hot.

Tosh said, "We have enough supplies to last several weeks. Each time I come here I always bring something." He showed me all kinds of things he had brought to the cave.

Tosh said, "No one has ever been here. I found this place by accident. I was on the bank looking for gold. Fish would go under the falls then come back. Fish are funny if they go they will come back. I went into the water, the force of the water hurt my head."

I went under the water to the pool coming up that's when I found it. I was a very young man then." I listen to Tosh talk as I made my way to the pool. It was swirling around.

"Tosh," I ask? "Why is it doing this."

Tosh said, "It's hungry is what I find when it does that."

Icol asks, "Hungry for what?" Tosh told Icol to come a little closer, clear your mind of all thoughts, then gaze into the water." Icol did as Tosh said, moments later he was asleep calling Shara. Icol woke up shaking as if he was cold. Weak from whatever had happened.

"What was that Tenna, what happens?"

I said, "Sire did you see Shara."

Icol replied, "She is being held inside the tower. Drex is going to kill her. You were right Tenna, Drex wants to marry her, yet she clings to me. Tenna we must go home." I told Icol soon.

CHAPTER 27

My group with me had been on the ship, for forty- eight days, as it is in space. Our captain told us we would arrive on Eden tomorrow. Everyone was sitting in the galley I was ready to embark from the ship. I wanted to feel the touch of the ground beneath my feet.

Basco asks," Captain, how long will we be on Eden?"

Replying, the captain said, "As long as it takes. We must see the general. He will tell us where Lux went." I was excited to be there, to walk among people on the ground, "know offense captain."

He replied, "None taken little one." Fina well Fina was Fina. She and I were as one, together all the time. Dris was always around.

The captain said, "Shila, everyone can go off the ship, look around. There mostly humans, some other beings. I will plan to meet the general. When he is ready he will send for us." Yes, Shila, there will be others there too." He explained.

I ask, "Everyone sir?" Replying he told me every one that wanted to go.

The day came to an end. Shila and the others excused themselves to their room. I sat long with Dred talking about the event to come. The night was long I thought I would check on the girls. You know sometimes a man just doesn't think. I never knocked I just open the door. On a mat in deep meditation, Shila and Fina both had the robes off their shoulder. Sitting on the floor they never moved.

Both girls had their breasts fully exposed. I never said a word. However, I will tell them to lock the door when they do that. I closed the door took a deep breath, wow I thought. I walked on down the corridor. Inside the girls told me later they laughed.

Fina said to Shila, "Do you think he liked what he saw?"

Shila laughed, "If I was a man I would." I loved Basco.

Dris was sitting with Basco, "Father this is exciting, just a few more hours we'll be in another world." I told my son, your life is full of exciting things Dris, you have been wounded in battle. Trained by the best. Now you're on a quest to find your king. There will be several quests, in your life my son. I ask my son, "Dris, have you learned to meditate. Dris it is as important as your skill with a weapon."

Dris said, "I have in some ways father. I can't go as Shila."

Dris said, "Father She scares me sometimes."

Basco smiled, "Yes son she sometimes scares me too."

I let my mind go, I have not meditated in years. I think the reason I haven't, is sometimes I don't like what I find at the end. Everyone can meditate, a person must be completely in solitude. You must clear your mind of everything. When this happens let your mind take you where ever you wish. I told Dris to let your mind go son find her.

"Find who father," Dris ask?

"Go find Shila and Fina," Basco said.

Dris closed his eyes, cleared his thoughts until he found himself floating in darkness. Dris found himself in the girl's room. Their body was there; their minds were gone. I searched my thoughts, Shila I called, where are you. I found myself calling her several times. Shila, Shila thousands of miles an hour I was traveling. I jumped up my father took hold of me. I yelled out loud, father I said as I fell into his arms. I was sweaty mouth was dry. I looked at him then I passed out.

Opening my eyes lying on a table, my father was beside me. Shila and Fina running down the hall, the girls said at the same time.

"Dris you did it, we heard you. We tried to reach out to you."

Raising I said, "Wow what a trip."

Basco told us all to sit. "First, I would like to say how proud I am of you. Shila you and Fina need to keep your door locked. We looked at each other laughed out loud."

Dris looked puzzled, "What," he asks?

Basco said, "Tomorrow we will be on Eden. When you

leave the ship stay close, and please stay together. When the captain seeks council, we need to be prepared to go. I'm sure, you would not like to miss it. Dred will also be with us. The Galaxian guards will stay on the ship."

"I do not trust them," Fina said. I said as much.

Basco said to all of us. "Go rest Shila, you and Fina, do not meditate tonight go to bed, sleep. If you're not here in mind and your mind clear, well let me say mistakes could be made you understand." I nodded to him.

In our room, I told Fina and Dris I was going to do as Basco said. I cleared my thoughts the next thing I remembered was feeling the ship come from hyperspace. In our training, we learned the difference between hyperspace and light speed. Hyperspace your traveling two, three, sometimes four times the speed of light.

Coming to a complete stop we scrambled to get dressed. Running to the galley, Basco and Dred were waiting. Fina went for tea as Dris and I sat down.

I ask her, "are you thinking only of you this morning Fina."

"Oh Shila," she said. "Would you like tea," I told her no I'll take hers?

Fina said with a smile, "Shila, sometimes, I just want to kick your ass." Then we laughed out loud, everyone just looked at us.

Our captain came in the galley, "Basco I have received word from the planet. They're several ships on the floor. Three Advairan ships, to ships from Galaxo, two hunters. Their seeking counsel with the general. I assure you; he will see us all."

"Basco one other thing, "You may want to find what the Galaxo guard's intentions are. I can't let them run free on the ship. Maybe I will take them to the floor send them to another ship."

Basco said, "I agree, Captain."

I said, "Basco, there is another way."

The captain asks, "Shila I'm afraid to ask?"

I smiled at Basco, "You could let me kill them, I promise you I would have no problem. I'll make it quick I promise. I'll even enjoy it." The captain told me sometimes I scare him. I told him I've heard that before.

Fina called loudly, "Why does Shila have all the fun. What about me?" Basco looked at me, and Fina shook his head. We sat for what seemed an hour.

The captain said, "When we reach the docks, the guards will be waiting. We have land clearance."

It took almost an hour to sat down on what I thought was the largest port I'll ever see. There were several ships as the captain said and places to land many more. Our captain's ship was a fully armed battle cruiser, all Advairan ship was, except for the freighter. The captain spoke to Basco as the ramp went down.

"Basco," he said. "I'll go first." He told us to stay onboard until he called. I could see him talking to the other ship's captains. They all looked up the ramp, we were far enough so we were hiding. As the Advairan captain walked to the Galaxo ships, the Galaxian captain appeared.

"I am the captain of this ship." He said.

"I am Tankko." Tankko introduced Taso."

Taso said, "We have a different mission, we will settle it later." A smaller ship landed when two others come forth.

Taso saw then, "Bliss." Taso said, "You're a trader." Drawing his weapon Tankko hit his arm.

"We will not fight on this dock." Bliss walked to the crowd.

"Tankko," he said. "Thing must be bad at home if Drex to sent you."

Bliss said, "We look for Icol."

Tankko said, "Yes to return him home. Looking at Taso, we will place Icol back in power regardless of how others feel."

Everyone talked for several minutes. I wanted off this ship. I told Basco this.

Basco said, "Shila we must wait."

Fina said as she smiled, "Yes Basco, Shila is reckless."

Our captain said to the crowd. "Maybe you need to walk with me down the walk to my ship. I assure you when we leave here, we all will be in accordance with each other. Believe me the general will make sure of that or you will not leave port."

In front of the ship, our captain called out to us. Everyone walked down the ramp at the same time. Tankko saw Basco first.

"Well, well the great Basco," Tankko said. Then he saw me and the others captain.

Tankko asks, "How many others do you have?"

Tankko bowed as he saw me. "Well, little one you have grown up. How long has it been?"

I answered, "Just over a year Tankko, in front of my father's store. Oh, by the way, Tankko the guard I told to come for me when Drex sent for me. Just to let you know, I killed him as I said I would do." I'll kill anyone that tries to take me from Drex. I have trained hard to do one thing."

Taso came in front of Tankko. "Does that mean me also?"

"Taso," I said. "You're no match for me."

Taso replied, saying with a hateful remark, "I will kill anyone that tries to keep me from taking Icol back to my king." It was the last thing Taso will ever say. I ran my sword through him as he was falling to the ground I took his head. Everyone saw this, the hunters come close they had never seen a female take a life. I told them as I turned in a loud voice.

I said hear me now, "For the ones that don't know me. I am Shila, any man or race of being that is here, stand in my way to find my King and return him to our world I will kill them just as easy." Two guards come from behind me I did not see. Fina saw them, they breathe no more.

Fina said, recovering from the event, "That goes for me too." Fina turned to the hunters pointing her sword at them her sunset hair hung long on her shoulders.

Fina asks them, her sword pointing, "Do we have a problem?

The bounty has been lifted on the King, and the Claxton, join us or leave. I promise you if you leave, the next time I see you I promise you a quick death. Fina started to walk toward them Hands went up as they moved back.

Tankko saw this, I heard him say to Basco, "Got your hands full."

Basco said, "She is a Claxton warrior."

"Good to see you, Basco," Tankko said.

Tankko said to Shila, "One of the Advairan captains said to tell you, your father is on his ship."

Tears were filling my eyes. I looked at Fina, placed my sword in my sheath.

"Fina would you come to meet my father," I ask?

Fina replied, "Shila, it would be an honor."

It took two days for the general to see us. For a small fee, the hunters said they would join us. I sent my Dris to ask Shila if she was fine with this. I told Dris I had no problem with anything Basco did. Shila came from the ship strapping on her sword.

Shila said to Basco, "I have only one objective, you know what that is." Walking down the small walk, a small ship set on a small pad. Bliss walked to the ramp, Bunn speaking to him. Dris walked to the end of the dock. Dris stopped.

"Ah master Dris, I'm afraid all grow restless."

Dris replied, "I can almost feel the tension." Returning to my father I told him all that each said.

Shila asks, "What is happing Fina?"

Fina said, "It would have appeared, the general has sent a messenger Shila." Everyone was waiting at the clearing when the messenger gave his speech.

"Today, at a given time, the general will speak. All captains will join. The general will talk to everyone. The hunters and all others will wait by their ships at the time I will come with a means of transport, please be ready to depart." When the messenger left I stayed to talk to Shila and Basco. Dred never said much mostly listen.

Basco said, "I can tell there's tension building between the Advairan and the Galaxian." I told Basco we need to stop this before it gets out of hand. He agreed.

Basco and I went to the Advairan. We talked to the captain telling him what was happening. He told Basco he would go talk to his men.

Basco said to me, and Dris to come with him to the Galaxian. On the walk approaching their ship, several were standing outside. Several of the guards were talking bad about Basco. One of the guards talked to the other of the events on the ships with Shila. The one speaking said no woman will ever call me. If that had been me I could and would have killed her. That was the wrong thing to say, Shila heard them.

Shila said to them, "You are a bone face liar, you ran as a beaten animal, all of you. I was mad. I called all the ships, I will tell you now. I'll give you the chance to leave if you want. If you are loyal to Drex do not go back on that ship." Three guards stepped forward.

"Your right we are loyal to Drex. It is only for our families. We do not want them dead. Then help me find Icol place him back in power. I wasn't around then, wasn't it a better life. Think of your daughters, do you want them to go to him. Would you want them to have a child by him, a man that would sleep with his daughter? Think about it all of you." I kept talking others come from the ship.

One said, "How can you be sure Icol is alive." I told them if Icol is dead I'll make you a promise this day. I will by myself overrun the castle and do what I'm supposed to do. I will kill Drex, no one, and nothing will stand in my way. A few cheers and a few nos.

One asks, "How old are you?"

I replied, "I am fourteen."

He asks, "Can you fight."

I smiled, "I'll take you down." Everyone laughed at me. I took my staff looked at Basco. A smile was all I needed. My sword I placed in its sheath.

I pointed to them, "You, you, you, come to this fourteen-year-old female." They all come at once, back in Claxton city everyone knew I could get myself out of a tight fit. Everyone that traveled with me knew I could do what they were about to see. I hit one on the head with the staff. Swept the legs of the others moving so fast I jumped up flipped backward, did to flips forward took out the third.

I tell you now it was something to see. Basco gave a hand, everyone did.

I simply said, "Anyone else. If not, then stay out of my way. Stay out of the way of my friends. If you can't do this, you will feel my sword this I promise. "Please!" I said, "Let's find Icol so we can go home. He waits for us, so does his queen. Just ask Tankko."

A hush was upon the crowd. Everyone thought she was dead except Tankko. The secret he kept of the queen, so many could live. Loyal to Drex never. Small sounds come from the crowd. The Advairan never said much. The Galaxian watched as Basco stood by me. Bliss went to one knee.

"Basco," he said. "I swear my loyalties to you as a leader. My crew also, let's find our king and go home. All that was on the pad did the same. I thought now we have an army.

Later in the afternoon, all sat around waiting. Fina felt a little frisky, so she started teasing Shila. She was lying in the afternoon sun. It was ashamed to mess with her, yet well you know me. Shila was lying on the soft grass when I eased my way over to her.

I said, "Yawing, Shila you're a bitch."

She opened her eyes, "Fina I've had a bad day."

"Oh, let me see," I said. "You're still a bitch." Shila came from the ground grabbed me before I knew what was going on, we were rolling on the ground. I was laughing so hard. I grabbed her in the side.

"Fina, I'm going to kick your ass," I told her it would be

hard I'm on my back bitch. She took hold of me, I was still laughing when she started to laugh rolling on the ground, we rolled into the messenger from the general how embarrassing. Looking down Basco was beside him. Girls will you ever grow up. Well, we started laughing again. The messenger started to speak as Basco give us a hand.

Speaking he said, "The Advairan captains, three Galaxian captains, the hunters. Then he looked at me, cleared his throat, Shila, Basco, Dred, Fina Dris, all come aboard the transport." Standing in front of the others the messenger said to them, "relax we will return soon." Taking us to the chambers of the general it was a big room, very elegant Several minutes later the man appeared.

He was not exactly what I expected. He was very tall to be a human. Bigger than Basco. I think as Shila, if I was older I would mate him for sure. Basco was a handsome man with muscles oh yeah. My mind went to the time he saw me naked. Shila was the worst for that. I do believe she would go naked all the time if she could. It never seemed to bother her for someone to see her that way. Now that I think about it, it doesn't bother me either.

The general made his way to the center of the chambers. I could tell he was a made, man. The way he walks you could tell he was very confident in himself. In his voice, when he spoke you could tell he spoke with authority. I listen as he talked.

"I am the general." He said. I focused on Shila. I didn't know the bitch could do that. I'll kick her ass for not telling me, she smiled as my thoughts reached her. She told me with her thought it had come to her several days ago. I thought Claxton's could do that. It was my belief Shila's mind was getting stronger, strong to be a human. I knew nothing about her or her past ancestors. The general spoke clearly as it brought me back.

"I am the ruler here on Eden. No ship comes to port without my approval, none leave without it. If one tries to leave you would be destroyed. The ship the Claxton and your king are on. I know the captain very well. Captain Lux has come here for many years." He looked at the Advairan, and then to the Galaxian. "I feel there is tension between you. Yet you fight for the same reason." I also was told the Advairan once had trade with Galaxo, before the overthrow of King Icol.

The general said, "I could go on for hours, maybe for days." Looking a Basco, would it not be talking. The hunters stand, Basco stand. The general said as he looked at Shila. "Who stands for you little one?"

Dris, Dred, and Fina stood, we stand for our self's. Dred stood beside me looking down. The general called to him by name. Dred's head came up,

"Ah yes, you wondered how I know you. Let me tell you, sir, I know all of you by name. Yet I've never met you. I thought, wonder how he knows that. Shila turned to look at me. The bounty has been lifted on Icol and Tenna the general said. Looking at the hunters, go with them to help them. Return here, I'll see you compensated." In a half bow, the hunters replied, as you wish."

"To the Advairan captain, "you have earned the right to lead. I know you are proud people. I have been in contact with your government. We have spoken of replacing Icol to the throne. This man Drex is a moron. I'm surprised someone has not already killed him. Someone needs to kill him." "I jumped up, "That's my job sir." The general smiled that smile.

"Shila I believe you; I really do."

"Now there is another matter. Bliss traveling with Bunn from Gara that gives you seven ships. You will also be accompanied by six of my ships, fully armed battleships like you have never seen." Well now I've been quiet, I thought it was my turn.

I ask the general, "Why is this you will send ships?"

"Fina it is as this, Icol and Tenna are not with Lux. You see three days ago a ship left here going to the Star of Joni. Joni is a very ruthless planet. They don't like humans. Icol and Tenna left going to the Moon of Corning."

He looked at Shila, "It is where Shila saw Icol at the stream.

I do believe it is a place where his ancestors were from. I have been informed the captain has been captured. Someone on the moon has befriended Icol and Tenna. He has them hidden away. I was told it was the Palatonians that did this."

I stood, "General I do thank you for your help, really we need to go."

He replied, "Yes I know Shila. Much distance between you and the moon."

The general said, "One more thing. You will have thirteen ships in all. That should scare away anyone."

One captain said, "There will be more sir. When we leave your orbit, a message will be sent to our world, other ships will come."

"Then go," the general said, "the Moon of Corning is as it is on Eden. It is always beautiful." Shila said she couldn't wait to meet Icol and Tenna. As we went aboard the transport to the big ship.

Three hours later the call came to leave the pads. All ships went into the darkness of space. On the ship, Basco approached the captain. We had our council. Shila's father was with us now.

Basco said to Shila, "When we reach Corning your father must stay on the ship until we see what we face. Shila agreed.

Fina asks Basco, "How long before we arrive?"

Basco replied, Fina I'm told three weeks. Other ships will join us before we arrive."

I ask, "How many more?"

Basco said, "I'm not sure Fina."

Dris ask a question, I suppose we should have all ask. Yet we were warriors. What do we know, of these Palatonians?"

Basco simply said, "Nothing."

In our room Shila said, I'm so tired. let's get out of these clothes I want to meditate. Doing as she suggested our robes fell to the floor. Shila said now that better. I had to agree at least we locked the door. Three weeks was not as forty-eight days. I thought we will be there in no time. I'm not sure what we will face, I told Shila we need to go there, she agreed. Going beyond the galaxies, to another universe, with our minds as one. Shila and I flew through the darkness of space.

Shila said to me "Look that where I saw him." Shila was pointing to a stream. Shila's thought came to me like rushing water in a stream. Looking through the sky I saw several ships in space.

Dris spoke to us. I said to him, "You finally did it." From nowhere Basco appeared in front of me so did Dred. There Shila pointed he is underground.

Basco said to me, "Fina we wait." Well anyone could see this made Shila mad.

Shila said, "I did not come all this way for nothing." Basco told her, it won't be for anything. A strange sound brought us back I looked at Shila, we are being attracted. Placing our clothes on we ran into the corridor. Basco, Dred, Dris was in the corridor, as we turn the corner, we ran into them. Running to the bridge Basco called.

The captain said, "The hunters fired on us, then left."

Shila asks the captain, "How is that possible, were in hyperspace. Dred, you can't fire weapons in hyperspace. Dred agreed. Shila's thoughts went wild, she was pissed off again. Trust me, I read every tiny cell in her small ass brain. I told her this later.

Basco asks, "Did we take damage."

The captain said, "No." Dred had left for his room. I told Shila I was going to Dred, talk to my brother. Inside his room, he had started his meditation.

looking up at me, "Sister you cannot come with me. Yet wait for me here, I will be awhile I'm sure." We were only two weeks away from the moon's orbit. I noticed as I looked through the portal it was a strange universe. There was a red light in space.

I walk to the bridge, I ask the captain, "What are the red lights." Showing me on the star chart he called them gas stars. Leaving him I went to the galley Basco and Dris was having tea.

I made a cup talking to them. Just a short time had passed since the hunters had fired on us.

Basco said, "You look puzzled little one."

I said, "Basco in our training in the Claxton city, we were told you cannot fire in hyperspace. That's what it all about. Hyperspace was to run from a fight if you were being attracted. Your enemy can follow only if they get caught up in your stream. What I'm asking is how can you teach one thing and another thing happens."

Basco said, "Shila I can't answer your question. I do not know. I think the only good thing to come from this is, now we know where our king is." I told Basco yes at least we know that.

I told them I was going to bed. Fina came to the room with me as we talked about the events. I told her I wanted to go back again. As hard as I tried, I could not clear my mind. Somehow, I fell asleep. The next morning Fina and I were in the galley when the men came in. Dris and Basco started to talk to me about the things we saw.

"Shila," Basco said, "I saw the ships, I saw the men. Icol and Tenna are in trouble. In that cave, is the safest place they could be." I told him I wish I was there now.

Dris said, "What about me?"

I answered, "Yes Dris, you too." Basco took my hand such a strong hand, I love this man.

Basco asks, "Where did Fina go?" I told him she went back to check on Dred.

"Dred, what about Dred," Basco asks? He told Fina he was going to meditate; said she could not go with him. Dred told her she must wait here. Basco rubbed his face with his hand.

"I wonder," Basco said. I told Basco I think he went to the city of the ancient, city of the Claxton's. Hours had passed I went to Fina. Fina was sitting beside Dred.

I ask Fina, "Do you know where he is?"

Fina replied, "He is lost Shila."

Later in the day as it was in space, Dred opened his eyes.

Fina held on to him.

Dred was weak, "Where did you go," Fina ask? To a land, no one has been before, a land of more than just wise. A place that was long ago but is no more."

I looked at Fina, "He has gone draft."

Dred said, "I found them, I've only heard the ancients talk of them. Yet I thought it was only a legend." Fina and I help Dred to the bed.

I ask Dred, "Why are you so weak?"

"Little one, too much in the mind. It takes a lot of mine will, to go, where I went, I must rest. Tell Basco to meet me in the galley for tea when I awaken."

Dred went fast asleep. Fina and I found Dris went back to the galley. Several of the Advairan guards were sitting in the galley. We tried not to mix with them. Trouble was something we did not want. Yet there is always someone that manages to piss me off. Two of the guards started with Dris. Dris started to move Fina grabbed his hand.

The guard said, "Let the girl come to me. I have something for her. Well, you know me, being a girl, I did not know which one he was talking about. I do know something was wrong with me. I was moody, I get mad quickly, my stomach ached all the time. Well, today was no different than any other day. I started to move when Basco came through the door.

"Is there a problem here," Basco asks? I told him nothing I can't handle. Never taking my eyes off them.

Basco said to them, "If you want to fight, wait until we're on the ground." Basco knew as well as I did, someday it would come to a head.

Basco said to them, "You're an Advairan guard, fight with us." The guard looked at me, then back to Basco. The guard stood for what seemed several seconds.

The guard said, "I don't think females should carry weapons." Basco told him, these two women are better warriors than you will ever be.

He said to Basco, "Someday we'll see."

Jumping to a fighting stance, "Let's do it now," I said. I took my sword from my belt handed it to Fina.

Give your weapons to the guard. "Unless you're afraid of a female." From behind me, the captain stood. The fight was over before it started. The guard was on the floor with a broken nose. Our captain said to the others.

"Take him to lock up."

I said to the captain, so did Basco, "We'll need him."

It didn't take long for the fight to spread through the ship. When the guards saw us, they would stand aside. Fina and I walk back to the galley. Six guards were having tea. Fina and I wondered if we should go in.

One guard said, "We'll leave if you want to come in."

The guards said, "We want no trouble with you Shila."

"I don't want trouble with you either. If you fight me here on this ship, will you continue to fight me on the ground? Will we be by our self's when we reach the surface. We can't do this without you. I understand you are not used to seeing a woman doing what I'm doing. You must understand what we face in our world without our king. We're supposed to be friends. You're helping me, my friends, by giving us a ride."

"I'm sorry about your friend, he should not have said what he did about me." The guards looked at me with that skeptical look.

"Oh, I said, "You only heard one side of the story. It wasn't nice what he said. However, I'll let it go just to place my king back on the throne. My friends and I try hard to do this quest."

One guard said, "Shila, we heard you picked the fight."

"I have never picked but one fight, it was with a Galaxian guard."

One of them asks, "What happen in the fight?"

"I killed him," I said. "I do not wish to kill you, as your friend, I just wanted him to see I mean what I say."

Everyone looked at each other. I turned to see Basco. I told him what Dred said.

Basco asks, "What happen to him?" I told him Dred will tell you, Basco nodded. I left with Fina for our room, I started to cry. Fina took my hand and held me.

"Shila what is wrong with you," she asks? I told her my stomach was hurting so bad, I was shaking, sweaty. I told her I was hot all the time.

"Fina I ask, "What is wrong with me?"

Fina asks, "Shila are you bleeding from your bottom?"

I said, "Yes sometimes, Fina I'm scared. I have these mood changes."

Fina said, "Shila your cycle has started, you are becoming a woman. This happens to Claxton's also. Once a Claxton female has her cycle it only happens every couple of years. Remember when Dris saw us naked. My cycle had happened. I wanted to mate with something. Sometimes it drives me up the wall. I've only had two cycles. I started very early."

I said, to Fina, "I'm not sure a Claxton can have a human baby, or a human can have a Claxton."

"I think it is the same," Fina said. Our bodies are the same. If a female has a child, she must have a cycle. Come Shila, let me show you what to do." I told her I remember in the Claxton city I begin once then it went away. Fina showed me how to fold the material so I didn't soil my clothes.

I ask her, "How long does this last?"

Fina answered, "It can and will vary. Sometimes five to seven days sometime longer."

I said, "Well now that I knew what it is, I can take care of the problem."

Fina said, "Shila you will need to take care not to be with a man, you could become pregnant."

I said, "That will not happen until my king is back on the throne."

Fina said, "Shila if you wish I'll take care of Dris for you."

"Smiling, I replied to her pea ass comment, "Fina you're a

"Bitch." She laughed out loud.

Traveling through space with no more trouble. I walked to the cell where the guard was lying on the bed.

I ask him, "Please, let me talk to you?"

"Shila, he said, "I never mint you harm."

Replying, I said, "You came at me."

He said, "It was because the others were there." The guard was looking at me, as men would do. I stood in front of him my body was full. Fuller than it was when I left. My hair was long and dark, hanging to my waist. I told him I was sorry.

"Shila, he said, "You are a beautiful woman." Well, I thought I was now. Yesterday I was a girl, I said nothing of this to him. I told him I was spoken for as I left him.

I said, "Thank you, I will talk to the captain for your release." Walking down the corridor I meet Dris and Fina. I told them I was going to bed.

Fina agreed, she was tired too."

The night as it was, I tried to meditate. Taking my clothes off was the last thing I remember; I went fast to sleep. What seemed hours later I woke up with someone calling my name. Where was I? I Was dreaming, I had to be. A very old man, I do mean old, calling me to a high mountaintop.

"Who are you," I ask?

He said, "My name is not important Shila. What is important is you? Shila you are part of our Earth family." Standing in front of this man, he changed his body to a strange being. Looking at this strange being in front of me was scary.

I said, "Wow, I'm pretty sure I'm not."

"Your king, he is the blood of royalty." He was from a planet that once stood."

"Shila," he said. "As he changed his body to a man. You have been chosen to go forth to defend him." Well, I thought, tell me something I don't know.

"Shila," he said, "we have watched for hundreds of years the Moon of Spores, and the Moon of Corning. So far, the

Palatonian have not mistreated them too badly. Once we fought the Palatonians, we won the war of the planets. You must do the same. When the time is right, we will come."

"Go Shila, tell your captain to stop his fleet. Tell him to wait for the other ships. Tell him this, as the dream started to fade."

"Wait, wait." I ask, "Who are you? What is your name?" I woke up Fina shaking me.

"Shila, who are you talking to. "Where were you, I couldn't find you, I jumped to the floor.

Fina embraced me, "What is wrong with you Shila?"

I ask her, "How long have I been asleep?"

Fina said, "All night Shila." I just went to sleep Fina.

Fina continued asking me what was wrong. She kept saying its morning. I was about to wake you. I told Fina I must see the captain. Running for the door Fina shouted. Shila put some clothes on. I was so excited, I forgot to dress. Placing my robe on I thought, I wish we had other clothes to wear. Maybe someday we will. I told Fina I was going to see the captain.

She asks, "You want some company?" I told her always by my side, my sister.

Fina ask me, "What is going on?" I told her about the experience. I might need you to back me.

Fina replied, "Always Shila, if it's the truth." Fina and I dashed for the bridge.

I ask the captain, "May I enter the bridge?" He made a jester with his hand to enter. I told him of the dream.

Shaking his head, "Shila, you want me to stop this fleet until the other ships come from home, because you had this dream."

"Yes, captain," I said, "you must do as the dream said," Basco said nothing. Dred the one that Nevers says much looked at me like he was reading my thoughts.

"Captain," Dred said, "I would do as Shila has instructed you to do. It is hard for outsiders that do not believe in our ways, yet it is always the same. As a ship comes to the plains, we can see this, we know this will take place." The captain said as he stood from his chair.

"Pilot is their ships on the scope." No was the reply.

"There is nothing sir, nothing at all."

"Captain, I would not ask you, if it wasn't important. Two hours sir that's all."

Looking skeptical at me our captain said, "Pilot, bring the fleet to a stop."

I did not believe he would do it. Calls started to come from the other ships. The Galaxian ships were confused. Even through the ages of time they did not know what was to come, neither did I. I told Basco this, he just shook his head.

Basco said, "Shila, you have stopped the fleet when we need to be in flight."

"Basco, I don't know what is to happen. I only know we are to find Icol."

Basco looked at me, "Is there more."

"Yes." I kind of looked at each one listening to me. We are to fight these Palatonians. Trust me Basco we will win; the others will come. We had been stopped about thirty minutes when the pilot announced.

"Ships on the scope sir. Maybe an hour out."

The captain turned to me, "Well little one, seems you were right, or a coincidence."

Dred spoke, "No captain, she was right. I know it's hard to listen to a fourteen-year-old female. Shila is protected by the ancients, listen to her she gets her guidance from them. She has been to the planet that disappeared." I looked at Dred fast. "Listen to her, I promise you will see the power you will never see again. I hate to see her leave; she will be great with her people."

Fina jumped up, "She is going nowhere." Dred, our father said for us to protect her."

Dont worry my sister, you will be asked to go too." Something was wrong here. Where did he go? What did he see? Dred has said nothing since he woke up.

Dred said, "Basco, on The Moon of Corning your king hides in a cave, we were there. In the orbit of the moon, there were many ships. Shila knew this would come. Therefore, she asks the captain to stop the fleet."

Basco said, "I know this Dred, she is strong with power, I'm not sure how."

"Basco, Shila is not only protected by the Claxtons but she is also protected by the ancient of your ancestors."

Fina asks Dred, "What did you mean, I'll be asked to go too?"

Dred said, "There will be a great fight between the Advairan, Galaxian, and the Palatonians. Basco, we must fight them. Basco, in deep meditation I went to the most remote parts of all universe. I found your people of long ago. The planet that was and is no more, yet it is still." Sipping his tea for several moments.

Basco said," You make no sense Dred," Basco look around the room at the rest of us.

Dred replied, "Wait until you see what is to come, then you say that. Dris, Basco all of you, started on this planet from a man with a past from there. Shila not so much, you from Corning ancestors and a place called Earth. You are like your mother, her mother, her mother, all the way to a woman named Lola. A native of Earth, Lola was the blood of Mya."

I sit with my mouth open in shock at what I heard. Dred kept talking it was the way they repopulated their world, thousands of years ago. From Maoke, Bota to Kohl."

I looked at Dred. "Dred this Maoke, did you talk to him on this quest of yours."

Dred said, "Yes, Shila, I was with him. He was very old, he told me they were to believe Leah was the last until Leah's sister was found. He said to me, we would meet again. He also said he would come to you." I told Dred as I looked at Basco. He did Dred I'm my dream. One hour had passed when the captain called to us.

"The ships have arrived." He said. I told Basco there not going to listen to a fourteen-year-old girl. Basco the men will not take orders from a woman. I told Basco to tell the captain to take us within range of the moon then give us a shuttle to the floor. We will go to the place where I saw Icol. Then you pick me, five good guards. When we leave the ship, tell the captain to continue.

Tell the Platonians why we are here. Don't trust them, watch them very closely. If they start to fight, blow them out of orbit. Basco, tell the captain we will do our fighting from the ground. We will take Tenna and Icol home.

Basco asks, "Dred you agree with what she has said?"

"Everything Shila has said has been told to us." I looked out the portal there were a lot of ships thirty in all.

The captain said, "Now what Shila?"

"Captain, Basco will tell you what must be done. I'm sure no one wants to take orders from a girl."

"Shila," the captain said. "You have been right so far.

"Basco would be a better choice," I said. Basco started to tell him what we wanted. When a blast hit us.

The pilot announced, "Captain it's the hunters." They fired two more rounds. It was the last two they will ever fire. The Galaxian ship blew them apart.

CHAPTER
28

On the surface of the moon, Icol and Tenna were hiding like animals, they were hunted like one. The Palatonians searched the stream up and down. Icol was still recovering from his experience at the pool. Icol told Tenna, I want to look again.

Tosh said, "Icol maybe you should wait to Look, too much staring into the pool could scramble your brain some. I have seen all of this. Your people are coming. The Palatonians will fight they are warriors. I've read about them in the archives. They fought in the war of the planets. The planet that disappeared almost destroyed the planet of Plano.

Plano rebuilt, conquered the Moons and Xon. It was said that the King of Xon and several others locked themselves in a chamber one night. The next day, when the door was opened, no one was in the room. There was no way out."

Tenna asks, "How do you think that could happen?"

Tosh said, "I have no idea. I'm not that smart. I have always heard; they will come if ever needed."

A rumbling sound came from above. A guard dropped a rock down the hole to see what would come out. Several minutes later, a guard started down.

Tosh said, "We cannot let this happen." Tosh climbed to a flat place placed a stick so whoever it was would step on it. The guard fell yelling for help. Three feet he fell. I give out a sound like an animal. I could see two others pull him out. That will teach you to go in a hole.

The guard said, "there's a wild animal in there, I heard it growl. Let's go there no one here."

The night was coming as the sun went down over the mountains. My thought went to the people of the city.

Tenna said, "Maybe we should not build a fire" Icol agreed. Days turned to over a week since we had come inside the cave. In my thoughts, I wondered what was going on outside. When it was full dark Tenna did climb to the top coming back he told us what he had seen.

He said, "There were five men camped at the water's edge."

Later Tenna crawled to the top of the hole I followed him. We found our target. Tenna went one way I went the other. Tenna walked to the target first, then me. A guard went for a weapon I took him. Tenna walked in slashing one guard was running, the other's dead.

I ask Tenna, "Are we safer in the cave or should we move to some other place."

Tenna said, "I believe we are much safer in the cave than outside." Looking around their camp, I told Tenna they left their supplies. Tenna and I carried all we could, we took them back to Tosh.

Going back to the hole carefully not to disturb anything, down the hole we went Tosh helping with the supplies. Tosh wanted to know what happened. Tenna told him one guard got away the other's dead. Tosh said, "Well that will bring them all to the stream." I took a flat rock to the top placed it to the outside. It looks as if the hole was a crack in the rock.

The moon's sun had descended, darkness had come again. Tosh had been talking for hours.

Tenna said," I'm going to rest." Tosh had laid back, pulled the blanket over him as it was cool in the cave; with the dampness from the water.

My thoughts took me to a faraway place. Places I've never been before. I didn't remember going to sleep. This I thought, must be a dream. I was looking for something. I did not remember losing anything, except for the last twenty years of my life.

Where was Tenna, and Tosh? There was no one here. I turned to see her arms stretched. She fell into my arms as she knew where she belonged. Shara, oh Shara how I have longed for this moment. A faint whisper in my ear. How much longer, Icol please come soon. I sit up looking around, I was sweating my heart pounding. Was it a dream or did I go there?

I laid back on the blanket. Tenna was looking out through the falls.

Tosh said, "They're a lot of guards out there." Tenna had gone to the top of the hole, it was full daylight outside.

Coming back down Tenna said, "Sire there is no one on the top. If they come, we will need to climb in a hurry." I told Tenna not to worry about me I'll keep up.

Sitting behind the rock wall, rock had been thrown through the falls, hitting the wall we were behind. I told Tenna there anxious to know if something is in here.

Tenna said, "Ah sire, I do believe someone will die today."

Tosh said, "I've never seen this before."

Tenna said, "I heard them say there's nothing in there, yet they continue the search."

One guard said, "This is where it happened. They got to be here. I'll go into the water myself. I'll see if there is anything under the falls."

The guard said, "Their millions of gallons of water coming over the falls. Rocks, logs that can hit you in the head."

Wading in the water one said, "Cover your head with your arms." Walking on appearing from the falls showing himself Tenna smacked him over the head with a log.

Tenna said with a smile, "You see sire I told you." Placing him on the log Tenna pushed him back through the falls so all the guards could see.

One guard said, "Crazy fool, I told him. Didn't I tell him, I told him." Once again, we were safe, at least for a while. My thought was for how long.

I told Tenna of the dream as he made tea. A warm drink was nice to hold. It was still cool in the cave. Tosh told us they would search for a while then go back to the city. They will wait for a while. I assure you, they will come back.

Tosh said as we had our tea, "He read in the archives when he was a boy. The Palatonians searched four years for a man on a planet called Earth. I don't think they wanted to find him. I think they loved this Earth so much they didn't want to go home. From the writing of Kohl, he said he never liked the

Palatonians. Only one of them could you trust.

I do believe his name was Cam. Cam and Bota went flying across space. It is a good story. I told him maybe someday maybe I will read it.

Tosh said, "you should Icol, your part of his legacy. Kohl left here with the ship to build what is called Galaxo."

Tosh asks," Icol have you never read your archives?" I told Tosh not all of it. There's another story I liked about Kohl. How his wife before they mated stole his ship. His first mate Comp feared her, not only did she still it once she did it again. She would wear him out having sex, while he would sleep, she would steal the ship. Icol started laughing.

Tenna asks, "Sire did you find it humorous?"

Icol said, "You know Tenna, it's just like a woman to do that. Remember the time we were to take the scruple going to the north. Shara took my sword. Remember I told you she said I could have it back when I took her to bed."

Tenna replied, "Ah yes, sire, I see it runs in the family."

Tenna and Tosh sit all day telling of our existence. Over three hundered years ago I must admit we have not advanced that much. We were not even the size of Corning. Tosh said later the city was not always this big. Then he started telling another story of a prince named Ject, that ran with Bota.

Through the years they were together many flights they did take. Ject left on a mission with Bota twenty-five years later, they returned. Bota stayed in the city for a while then left one day back to the ancient city. Their quest to Earth was always promising. They would come here to trade with Quad. He would have all kinds of things. Payment would always be with stones that were found everywhere in their world.

It is written in our archives these stones were in the streets in the water in homes. There was no value to the people. They never wanted anything. It is said everything they wished for was there. It is written there were so many stones in this fall, they called it rainbow falls because the sun shined on the stones making the stones glow.

Icol said, "I to read of stone in the archives. In the two days I've been in the archives I did read quite a bit. We do find a few stones in our world. The stones are different in color they have no value to us. Tenna broke the conversation with a word.

"Sire tonight when it is full dark, I will make a small search around the falls. I won't be gone long." My thought went back to Gara.

"Oh, you mean like the time on Gara, when you left me in the rock didn't return until daybreak."

Tenna said, "Sire your memories have returned."

I ask Tosh, "How much of the archives have you read?"

Replying, "I was almost finished up to the time, where I was born." Tenna told me of the Palatonians taking your parents away.

"They did Icol," Tosh said. "That's why I want to leave with you. I would be loyal to you Icol." I told him I knew he would. I think that would be a good start. Sipping my tea, sitting around the fire my thought ran wild. What was going to happen I could not say.

I said to Tenna, "Let yourself go. This girl you call Shila, find her." Tenna looked at Tosh, Tosh told Tenna, go to the pool let it take you there. The pool was not real water, it was more of an illusion. How it works I can't say.

Tenna faced the pool moments later he was fast asleep or was he. Tenna woke up what seemed hours. He was shaking as if he was cold.

Tenna said through trembles lips, "I wish never to do that again."

Tosh asks, "Can you talk yet?"

Tenna nodded his head, "I think so."

I ask Tenna, "Tell me what you have seen?"

"Sire they are coming, thirty ships maybe. Perhaps tomorrow, she is a warrior. I'm afraid sire destruction follows. This Shila has been chosen to return you to power by the ancient of Claxton city. There also is another power that goes with her. I could not see it, yet it was there. There is more sire, she wishes to free the people of Corning for their help."

"I tell you sire, the group that follows her, I see this will happen. All that comes sire will stand by you as I have. I need rest sire before they come. I will not go out tonight as planned."

Tenna went to his blanket laid down. Before closing his eyes, He said, "Sire she is strong this one."

Inside their room, Shila and Fina felt the ship come from hyperspace to impulse.

Fina opened her eyes, "This is it," I said. "You ready."

"Shila as long as I'm by your side, I'll always be ready," I told Fina we may not be so lucky this time.

Fina said, "It is what it is." Dris and Basco waited outside the door.

"Basco said, "Shila the captain said the shuttle is ready." I did not pick others Shila. I feel the least in numbers we are the better we will be. Now little one, we must go." I told him we need to talk.

He asks, "Shila isn't this what you wanted?"

"Basco I'm not a leader you are, I will follow you."

Basco said to me, "Ah Shila, you're doing a great job, Dred said as much. Shila I have no problem following you. You are a warrior, a Claxton warrior." I told him before we went out to the shuttle.

"Fina and I have gone into great meditation. There is a great war going to happen."

Basco said, "I know Shila, let's go to the moon."

Luck was with us as we dropped from orbit. I counted several Palatonians ships. We heard them call the other ships. The commander called to our ships told them this was Palatonian airspace. Our captain told them our king was on the ground, we want to retrieve him. He was told if your king is on the ground, he is a prisoner of the Palatonian guard.

Running fast and low as we entered the atmosphere our

pilot told us what was happening.

"Should I answer them Shila," I told him no?"

Dred broke in," If you answer, they will find us." Through the scope, I showed the pilot where to land.

Looking for a suitable place, "There," I said. "We will walk from here."

The Palatonians were not looking for us, so we had that working for us. They didn't even know we were here. Sitting the craft down walking off the ship to the forest we were asked to help cover the craft. I fell to one knee.

Basco asks, "Shila are you ready?" Tears filled my eyes as I turned to him. My throat had a big lump in it. I was shaking.

Fina grabbed me, "What is wrong with you?"

I said, "My King is out there. There're men I must kill, everything is coming together. Just as the old ones said in the city of the ancient.

The pilot asks, "Should I stay or return to the big ship." I told him to stay where he was.

It was very early morning. I told him if we are not back by this time tomorrow go back to the ship do not vary from the course. I told him to stay in the shuttle you may need to leave fast.

Dred, Dris, Fina looked at me, "Let's go Shila." I told Basco beyond the stream the small ridge there's a bigger stream. This is where we will find Icol. Crawling to the top of the ridge there, Basco look.

Fina said, "I'll take care of the first fire." Upstream a lone man waits, daylight had caught him out. He was working his way to the small outcrop of rocks.

Looking at Basco I ask, "Who is that?".

Basco looked down, "By the Gods, it's Icol. I'm as sure as I am sitting here beside you Shila. Shila, look behind him, several guards were trying to catch him. I could see Icol was trying to hide. I told Basco I'll go this way maybe we can cut them off.

Basco said, "I hope he can hide from them."

Icol had gone out instead of Tenna. Tenna was resting from his ordeal with the pool. Time had slipped away daylight had caught Icol out. We could see Fina as she walks to the fire. The two guards stood; they stand no more. She told me later they wanted to have their way with her.

Fina said, "You know Shila, that pissed me off." I ask them as they went for their weapons, where were you when I was ready. Both men picked up their weapons; they will never do that again.

I took care of the men at the fire. I was running for the rocks when a big limb was thrown to my head. Falling to my back. I looked up into the eyes of a being I had only heard of.

"Tenna it's me." Dropping my robe to show the seal of the Claxton's on my shoulder.

Tenna reached out his hand, "Come little princess." Everyone, we must hurry several guards are coming, they're closing in on Icol. Just a small way up the stream there was a fight going on. Tenna looked at me, I pointed this way we can come in from behind. I was running full out, Tenna was behind me.

I've never seen Tenna in action before just stories. Trust me they were all true. My thought was wow. Moving as he did as well as the others there were twenty guards on the ground. Twenty guards were dead. There was not a scratch on any of us. Icol turned to Shila. I saw her fall to one knee.

Shila said, "My King," I choked up again.

Icol said, "Rise, all of you, give me your sword." Touching me and the other, "You are now a Galaxian guard, you are free."

"I said, "My king until I finish what I started, then and only then will any of us be free."

I could not get enough of talking to the man. It was as the weight had been lifted from my shoulder. Icol embraced Basco.

"It is good to see you, my friend," Basco said the same.

Tenna said to Basco, "Often my friend have I thought of

you."

Basco said as he looked at Icol. "Sire I had no idea you were in a prison, you or Tenna. If so, I would have come for you. Drex is a madman I know he is your blood, yet he is evil."

Icol said, "He is everything you say. I have seen him in my dreams. He will pay for what he has done."

Fina said, "The old ones of the mountain say Shila will be the one to do just that." Icol looked at Shila.

I read his thoughts; he didn't want me to kill him. This I would do, no matter what. If my king gets in my way, well we will see. I told Icol these are our people. It's only a different time, yet we come from here.

We never ask for a fight with these Palatonians. We must fight them and free our people. I said to Icol, this is the very land our ancestors came from. I know on Galaxo our queen is held in a cell; we must free our people before we go home.

We sat talking for several minutes when we heard a great explosion. Tenna said it comes from the city. Tenna yelled, "we must retrieve Tosh." Tosh had come to the top of the cave by the time we had reached the hole. Coming through the hole Tenna gave him a hand.

Tenna said, "Tosh these are my people from Galaxo. Tosh looked at ShIla, you are exactly what I had expected you to be, all of you are. I feel there is much trouble in the city, looking at Tenna, "can you help us. Captain lux is being held on his ship; it is in port now."

Tenna asks, "How do you know this." Tenna told Tosh to go back to the cave, take his craft to the city we will leave know. Try not to get caught trying to see what we are going into."

We made our way to the bottom of the falls waited for Tosh to come through the fall with the craft. Going down, following the stream to the large lake there must have been two hundered people waiting. Icol walked to them.

Tenna said, "This is what I was talking about." A man approached Icol.

I am Prior, "The smoke you see is from the Palatonians. We left last evening when they arrived. There were over a hundered of them, Redda said there's more in orbit. He has been taken to the port. Redda has been beaten placed in his quarters with the Advairan captain. If we are to die, then we wish to die in a place we love."

Icol said to him, "I can't tell you no one will not die if you want your freedom you could stand with us. I am Icol direct descendant of Kohl."

Shila came to Icols side. "My family come from here over three hundred years ago. Stand with my king, if you wish to be free, fight with us."

One said, "We are not fighters, we're a peaceful race. "

I said, "As your family of Boldlygo were." Several heads come up. How do you know about this? Kohl was born on Boldlygo, so were several others."

"We have no weapons," Prior said. A bag was thrown in front of them.

Tenna said, "These are the weapons of the guards. Take them each time you take one down take his weapon."

One said, "If we do this we will be destroyed by the ships in orbit." Shila told them we have thirty ships in orbit fully armed. I would not worry too much about that. A noised come up over the ridge Tosh had returned.

Tosh stopped his craft just short of Icol. "There must be at least one hundered of them on the ground. Icol there's only seven of us."

Prior said, "There is many more, we need more weapons."

Tosh said, "Well let me help, Tosh picked up two big bags from the craft. "Maybe this will help, there were over a hundered weapons."

Icol said, "Now will you fight."

Basco told us to break up into small groups. Each one of us, with some of them.

Basco asks Tosh, "Did you see where these people are?"

Tosh took a stick drew a picture in the dirt. Placed rocks in the dirt where everyone was. Everyone stood over the drawing, then broke up into small parties with a given time to strick.

Each of us went to a different part of the city. I took my small crew to the port. A small craft had landed. My thought went to a hot bath. I thought how tired I was just to fight more. I did not pay that much attention to the ship that landed. The hatch open Bliss and Tankko walked off. The fighting on the ground was almost over.

Tankko said, "Little one, we have watched from orbit. That's where we did our fighting. You did well on the ground." I told him for over four hours. Tankko said, "Shila, all the ship except one was destroyed."

"Where is the one," I ask?

Tankko replied, "Shila there is always one that gets away. There was a celebration a feast was planned.

Redda and Prior ask Icol, "Maybe we can form an alliance with you, after all, we are family."

I said, "my king," as I bowed to him, "this is not over if I may." I looked at my father walked to Basco took his hand," Stand with me."

Basco said, "Shila you know I will." I turned to Icol, my king you are to take a ship go to Galaxo, on the Plains you will find a farmhouse by the Trions. You will find a guard his name is Nordic. He will show you a cave, wait for us there."

Icol said, "Shila. I made you a Galaxian guard, not a ruler."

I bowed to Icol saying, "I'm only looking out for your wellbeing my king. I have Basco with me. I was pissed off again, Fina since this. The others stood, "we are with you to Shila."

Basco said to Tenna, "Take him with Tankko and Bliss, wait for us. We will be there soon take one Advairan ship, one Galaxo ship."

Tenna said to Icol, "I wish to stay with them. Sire you need to leave."

Icol said to Tenna, "You just want to fight." Tenna bowed

to the words.

Icol said as he walked to Shila. "I do think you for what you do Shila. You as well as anyone knows my place is with you. I will lead you if you wish." Shila told him it was not a good idea. Sire, there is no one to take your place if you die.

Icol smiled, "My wife, she should be the ruler now." Well, I had to agree with that, yet I said nothing.

Icol said, "My place is with you. I must go, see what you do. After all, I am a Claxton warrior too Shila." I had heard the stories of Tenna and Icol. I guess I had forgotten about them. Icol for the first time showed the seal on his forearm. Lux came to Icol.

Lux said, "Icol we have come too far to stop now. I have been with you for several years, for your help on the ship for the rescue now. I'm forever in your debt. My crew will also come with you."

Several ships had come to port. The Advairan captain that brought us here came to Basco.

He asks, "What is the plan?"

Redda said as he came forward, "Go to their planet destroy them. Plano is several hours away. If you don't, they will return. It will be much worst when they come."

Icol said, "I have a better idea. We will follow them. I will go to their king, or government, or whatever. I'll talk to them under the escort of course. Making our plans to leave.

Fina and I said, "We liked Redda plan better." I said as much to Basco. I will let Icol make his pledge to them. I will make mine.

I still had only one thing in my mind. The same thing that was there when Basco took me from his cabin. That was to kill Drex. I wanted to kill Drex. Basco told me once to let it build inside of me. I swear that's what keeps me going. The long hours of training, the fights, the lives I've taken.

I have said I would kill anyone that stood in my way. I will stand beside Icol when he makes his pledge. If I don't like what is said, I'll kill their king, with my friends by my side, I fear nothing. Just a few of us were an army. We will fight to our death to protect our king our ancestors pulse ourselves.

We prepared to leave, Fina and I went to our quarters. I wanted out of my clothes if only for a while. I also needed a bath as the spray fell on my body I thought of the pools in the city of the Claxton's. I will always remember the pools when I take a bath.

Coming from my bath Fina and I talk about things I suppose women talk about. What I am saying, I never had a female to talk with. Somehow, I do remember three females once. I do believe two of them were my mother's sisters. However, this I cannot be sure of. Fina told me as I toweled my body.

"Shila your body has reached its full potential." Since my cycle had started; I have noticed it myself, so did Dris.

Fina said, "If I become pregnant my breast would become fuller."

I ask, "How she would know this?"

Fina replied, "I'm more intelligent than you Shila." When she said that, I turned to say without moving my lips.

I smiled at her. "Fina, you're a bitch." Then we both laughed out loud. My friend was right, I left Galaxo over a year ago I was showing breasts not like what I have known. I've noticed men looking when I pass them, always whispering little thing as they do when Fina pass. Being the only two females on a ship trust me we get a lot of looks.

A knock on the door made me aware of my presence. I turned to see Basco and Dris.

Basco said, "Shila, I've told you and Fina, to keep the door locked." I told him I thought it was locked. Tying my robe Basco told me and Fina to come to the galley. Walking past the deck shuttles were coming from the other ships. Icol had sent for all the captains. In the galley, plans were being made to talk to the Plano government.

Icol wanted to see this planet. I wanted to kill Drex. Whatever happens, that would always be. Drex hurting my friend, my family, my people. You can do whatever you want to me, hurt my family I will find you and kill you plain and simple.

Icol told me himself he wanted to kill Drex. I told him he had other things to do. I told him that is my destiny.

The whole fleet had come to a stop, just outside the sensors of Plano. Icol talked to all the captains, one hour later all captains went back to their ships a short trip in hyperspace would bring us to the orbit of Plano.

CHAPTER 29

Three hundered years had passed. The war of the planets was just fading memories. Even to this day, no one could explain what happened. Plano had taken control of both moons, even Xon. Plano was at one time allies of Boldlygo. Both Moons alone with Xon now lived under Palatonians law. Our captain made the call. Eight ships came fast.

Icol the captain said, "They fly the crown of the planet that disappeared, it's the same as your ship."

Icol said, "That's impossible, our ships are here."

The pilot called. "Captain we're being held."

The lead ship answered, "We know your intention, may we join you." I thought that's thirty-eight ships.

The captain said, "We are from the Moon of Spores."

The captain asks, "Who are you loyal to?"

The captain replied. "I have lived under Plano laws. I'm loyal to the Boldlygo high command, they're no longer here, yet I am." I looked at Icol, how many ships did they have, Word was given for them to move into the fleet.

Our fleet came from hyperspace just inside the orbit of Plano. The captain sent his message.

"We wish to have a council with you king or your government." Orders were given to take a shuttle to come to the floor of the planet. Several went inside the shuttle. On, the pad we waited for the captain to talk to the command, the message was taken to the king. On a parchment, a sentry handed it to his king.

Reading the parchment, the king said, "That's impossible, it can't be. Why was I not told of this when you returned from the moon? You did not tell me it was with people from Boldlygo." Walking to the Huge glass window the king's mind went back to the war of the planets.

"Sentry, I was a small boy when they come and destroyed our world. Bring them before me."

The Sentry left, "As you wish my King."

Several sentries were sent to the pad to escort us. Telling us to give up our weapons.

"Well, the first one they said that to was me."

I whispered to one, "I'll give it up when I run you through." Now are we going to your king, or do you die here? To me, it makes no difference."

The king knew the power they had. He also knew of their intelligence. The war of the planet proved to be brutal, thousands of people died. Only a few of them were killed, only from Xon One afternoon late they came without warning, destroying everything. We rebuilt sent our ships for them, the planet was gone.

Now I wonder, where have they been for all these years. I will find them and destroy this place. The King stood looking out the window at all that was beautiful.

A sentry called to him. Turning to see, the king did not see the natives of Boldlygo. He was staring in the eyes of Icol, and the Claxton. Me and the others beside him.

Walking to his throne each one was introduced by name.

Icol said to him, "We have come to ask your counsel. We ask for the impendence for the Moons." The king just looked at them saying nothing. I started to speak, as he stepped forward.

"Females are not allowed to speak in council." He answered. The king knew the power the females had. Their power in the council. The ones he read of in their archives. The ones they called the Three. There were others just as powerful. April, Marie, Tressa still there were others. The king just sat looking.

"Why have you returned," he asked?

Icol said, "Excuse me, sir."

"Over three hundered years ago your planet disappeared. I demand you tell me."

I stood there feeling helpless. I spoke to Fina in our mind thought. Then I started to speak. The chief started to speak as he reached for me, I took him down. Three more sentries' come running in. We were at a standoff with the king in the middle.

Yelling at the top of his voice, "Enough. Sentry's leave now, we are more civilized than this." Weapons were drawn.

King Won said, "I know who you are. I know the power of your people. We fought a fight to the end. The Centaurian were destroyed, the Valorians almost destroyed, was that not enough. Tell me where you have been."

No one said a word. We all just looked at each other, as to say what is he talking about.

Icol said, "King Won, "We are not from the plant of Boldlygo. Yet we are descendants of the ones that were. We are here to stop a fight, not start one." I looked at Fina, she was smiling. "Shila be quiet."

I said, "None since, let's fight."

King Won said, "You must be silence female."

I replied, "Is this the way you do all your women?" I turned to leave.

"Icol," I said. "Finish this or I will."

King Won said, "I'm afraid you will become prisoners. You will soon tell me where you're from." I froze in my tracks. I was five feet away staring into his eyes.

I said, "Don't piss me off."

Icol questioned the king saying. "I thought you said, we were more civilized than this."

Basco said, "We have an army in orbit thirty-eight ships in all. We have destroyed most of your ships."

You fool do you think you can come here, without me knowing about your past. "Sentrys." He called. There were at least fifty men rushing in. I drew my sword faster than I have ever. I backlashed him across the face. Won give out a scream, the fight was on. Tenna was all over the floor. Basco was fighting three. I went for the king. Blood was flowing from his face. He stumbled backward fell onto the floor.

I placed my sword to his throat, "Get up slowly King Won," I said. You're as Drex. Your no man, in fact, you nothing. Tell them to stop or 'I'll end you here and now." I looked at Dris he had got nicked on the arm blood had stained his shirt.

I ask the king, "Sir how does it feel to be captured by a female. Your fleet is surrounded."

Won said, "Doesn't matter, I have you." I told him you have nothing. I'm going to destroy your planet again."

He boasted, "You would not dare." Blood was oozing from Won, from the slice across his face.

I said to him, "Give the word, or I swear you a swift death, I promise." I drew my blade back to thrust when Fina screamed. I could not tell what was wrong. I could see she was not wounded. A strong wind blew as a craft hit the wall. King Won fell to the ground.

"No, no it's happening again," he said." Stop Won shouted stop." The sentry's laid their weapons on the floor.

"Go," Won said. "Just go."

Icol asks, "What about the Moons?"

Won answered, "You may leave, the moons are mine. Dred and Fina walked toward the king.

Dred said, "Let them go. If you don't, we will destroy you."

King Won replied, "Go I will give you an answer tomorrow. You must return to your ship." I told him that will not happen we like it here. I turned to sit in his chair.

"Fina, don't I look good on a throne."

"You do look like a princess Shila," Fina said. I think we will overrun you take this place it is a beautiful castle; don't you think Fina." We were taunting him.

I said, "I have already captured you. I don't think I will let you go."

"Basco, I think he comes with us to the ship. I have a place for him to sleep. I looked at the chief justice, I suppose you're in charge chief."

Icol looked at me kind of strange. Walking down a long hallway that took ages to build. I told him I sure would hate to see all of this destroyed. I took hold of him pushed him into the window that seemed to go forever.

I got close to his face, "Look at your world, you called us

fools for coming here. I'm sure three hundred years ago the King said the same."

"He was my father," Won said. I told him it would seem if people don't beacon to your every call you try to conquer them. You will never conquer us; we have just overrun you. You will go with us. Passing by the pad King Won said to the sentry. "Tell the fleet to stand down."

"King," I said. "Tell them to come to port all of them. Won if I see one ship leave the surface, I'll take it as an act of war." Walking onto the ship I noticed how everyone was looking at me. I noticed it before, even Icol. What was happening, what was I doing, was I doing something wrong. On the ship, I took King Won placed him with two Advairan guards. I told King Won a female captured you. How is that going to look to your people?

Won said nothing he just kept walking. Icol called for a council in the galley. Icol was giving his speech I found boring. I left my home my father escaped with his life. I've trained hard placed myself in harm's way. Killed people with no remorse to place Icol back on the throne. He just kept on talking then it was over.

Fina shook me, "What is it, Fina," I asked?

Icol said to me, "Shila, will you stand." I never heard his speech I had no idea what he said.

"Today Shila, you and your friends fought like an army. You fought as the guards you are. We would like to hear from you. Shila, I have heard you say you're no leader. Well, today you led. Please, Shila speak."

I looked at my teacher, the man I most respected. The flow of his strength is what keeps me going. Basco was a beautiful man, if not for him where would I be. In the castle with Drex, the one I wanted to kill.

"Go ahead Basco said," Remember on the mountain when the Claxton's came. I told you to stand your ground, it's the same here. Stand your ground." Dris looked upon this as it was his sister.

Then I heard him say, not my sister, I love her with my heart. I must talk to Fina of this."

I walked to Icol, speaking to a guard. Moments later the guard came into the room with King Won. He started to speak as I stood in front of him.

"King Won," I said. "You will get your chance to speak. In my council, you speak when spoken to. We destroyed your fleet on Curning. In the beautiful hallway, I ask you how you would like to see your planet destroyed. Three hundered years ago you have wondered where the people from Boldlygo had gone."

"They left to keep from destroying you. They were tired of fighting you and the Centaurian. They were more powerful than you could imagine. When they come, they won't stop this time?" The king's head snapped.

"What, what did you say?"

"Oh King, I forgot to tell you when we need them; they will come. I think you need to go to your room think of this."

I looked at Icol, "We need to be forceful," I bowed to him.

Icol said, "What do you think we should do?"

I said, "The guards can do nothing on this ship. We need to deploy to the ground."

Icol replied, "We are outnumbered Shila." I told him I know we are outnumbered in men, not in power.

Icol said, "Shila, what does that mean?" I told Icol when we need them they will come.

Stepping from Icol I told him I was going to take a bath. Fina and Dris were talking about something. Everything stood as I left the council. Basco and Dred touched my shoulder as I passed. All I wanted to do was shed my clothes. That is just what I did. Toweling my body as Fina entered our room.

Fina saying, "I'm next." Fina sat on the bed after her shower.

"Shila," she said. "What are we to do?"

I smiled at her, "Fight I hope."

Fina replied, "Shila you're reckless." I told her I'm not reckless I'm a Claxton warrior.

I ask Fina, "Do you not think it would be the best thing. Take the fight to them, before they bring it to us."

Fina dropped her head, "Yes Shila, that's exactly what I would do."

I said," That's what we were taught in the city, even Basco said that."

Fina said, "Shila there is another problem."

"Ok, I said. "What is the problem?" I told Shila Dris saw you when Basco held you. He said it was the first time he had ever seen you as a sister. He said it's not what he wanted for you. I told Fina I love Dris with my heart. I hope he knows that. I always saw him when we were small. He would come to our store in the village. Maybe I should tell him I love him.

Fina said, "That would help." There was a knock on the door. Placing my robe on I walk to the door Dris stood looking at me. I reached for him kissed him long and hard. I even gave him a little taste of the tongue, Dris backed up.

Dris said, "Wow, I have forgotten what I come here for," he said. I told him as he stood in front of me, how much I loved him. He backed up closed the door I looked at Fina, she was smiling there was another knock.

Opening the door, Dris said, "Icol would like to see you when you rise, in the galley." Well, I had to do it again. I pulled Dris in the doorway. I kissed him again, I told him again, I love you Dris now go to bed. I closed the door dropped my robe, sat on the bed I needed to relieve some stress; meditation was the best way.

I was taught in my training to meditate. Fina said it was the best way to find your enter self, I agreed. First, you must be able to clear your mind, all things must be left behind. It only took several minutes to do what I needed to do. Somehow, I found myself in the city of Corning. Someone took my arm, looking to my right I saw Fina.

Our thought was the same. We saw smoke buildings destroyed, people dying, it was destroyed after we left. Fina and my mine thoughts separated as we came back to our room. I jumped up as Fina grab me.

"I'll kill him," I told Fina I must see Basco and Icol. Fina and I ran to the galley.

Icol said, "Thought you would be asleep by now." Basco could tell something was wrong.

Basco stood from the table, "Shila what is wrong?" Basco could see the tears in my eyes.

"Corning has been destroyed," I said.

Fina said, "Shila, wants to kill the King."

Icol said to the guards, "Bring the king to me." King Won was brought to Icol.

Icol asks, "Did you destroy Corning?"

Won said, "Yes, I did send ships to do just that." I drew my sword kill Won there in front of Icol. Several guards were watching this.

One guard said, "Did you see that." I placed the sword back in its sheath.

"No more talk." I took the king placed him in a shuttle, everyone watched. I said, "Well I can't fly this thing I need a pilot."

Basco said, "You also need clothes." I looked down I had on only my robe. I wondered if they saw my naked body. I was pissed off, I didn't care. Icol tried to stop me.

Tenna said, "I will fly it for you, little one."

"Give me five minutes," I said. "It is time for us to fight." I looked around everyone ran for their weapons. Fina and I were the first to return each guard that came in.

"We will fight with you Shila," they said. "We have sent word to all of the ships." Tenna, Basco the rest got on board the shuttle we went to the surface.

CHAPTER 30

A small ship landed on Galaxo. Drex had no idea who had landed. There was no one there to greet the ship. All his ships as he said had left, ran as a coward would. Drex had sent two guards to the landing pad. The ramp went down the captain thought it was strange there were no ships or anyone around to greet them. As the captain walked toward the castle two-guard appeared.

One said, "We have never seen a ship like yours before, where are you from."

The captain said, "Eden, I'm here to deliver a message to your king. I'll give it to you; I will be on my way." Taking the message, the guard watched the ship as it went into the darkness of space. Roaring until it was out of sight. The guard walked to the chambers of Drex.

The guard said. "Sire the ship was from Eden."

Drex replied, "I know nothing of Eden."

"The captain left this message for you." The guard said. Handing the message to Drex the guard bowed walked out. Drex opened the message his heart almost stops. He knew the writing after twenty years; he knew the writing. The message simply read.

"I'm coming for you," it was signed, Icol.

Drex called the guard back, "Bring that ship back."

The guard said, "How do I do that, we have no ships they've all left."

Drex was mad, walking to the fire he burned the letter. His world was breaking up, Drex felt helpless. His men had turned against him, his ships left. He also knew his plan for a son grew less. His thought turned to Shara; she would give me a son. She would be the only woman to do this.

When he thought of her his loins hurt. He needed her, from her beautiful lips to her beautiful breast. Over twenty years since she has been with a man. Could she not have just one feeling for me.

"Guards, Drex called, bring me the queen. If she refuses to

come, break down the door." Several guards were still loyal to Icol, even after all this time. They would help bring things to the cell to help Shara fortified the room. Shara and Lama had braced and made locks on the door. It would take an army of rams to break it down. The guards stood outside the cell, looking through the window,

"Shara, Drex ask for you to come. He said for us to break down the door if we had to."

Shara never said a word neither did Lama. Walking around the room then to the door.

Shara asks, "Does he have my husband?"

The guard replied, "No."

I ask, "Does he have his head?"

The guard said, "No."

I ask, "Was Icol on the ship that left,"

Again, he said, "No."

I said, "Well then I suppose you need to break it down."

I said to Lama," Stand back." Looking through the window the guard saw the weapons on the floor.

"Where did you get those weapons," he asked?

I said, "They just flew through the window one day. I will show you what I will do with them if you break down the door.

The guard said, "We're coming in." Two guards caring a ram started beating on the door pounding as hard as they could. It wasn't going anywhere.

I said to them, "The first one to enter the room dies."

Lama said, "I will take the next one." The guards kept ramming the door.

I ask, "Ah what's the matter? Big boys as yourself can't knock down a little door." Drex came down the corridor.

"What is the meaning of this?" "Shara," Drex screamed, "open this door, I'm going to kill you here and now."

With the baby voice that Drex hated. "Ah what the matter king. Boys the big bad King can't get in."

"You bitch, when I do, I swear I will kill you Shara, and the bitch with you." Drex made another mistake he placed his arm through the window. Lama took a sword ran it through Drexs biceps. The blade on one side the handle on the other. Drex tried to pull his arm out. Lama took the arm of a chair started beating Drex's arm with it.

When she stopped, Drex was screaming his arm was a mess, it was bloody, bruised, blood dripping to the floor.

I laughed, "How is your arm Drex?" The guard stood in disbelief.

Lama walked to the window, "How is your arm father?" My king is coming soon. Drex stood by the door, with his arm still through the window. Lama walked to the door took the handle in her hand pulled it slowly out of Drex's arm. Drex fell backward.

"How is your arm father," she asked?

"You bitch," Drex said, "I'll kill you for that." The two guards picked him from the floor.

Drex screamed, "Shara, I will kill you for this. Shara you will die I promise you." I told Lama he is desperate the next time he might win.

Lama said, "Well if we are to die, my lady, we will die together. We will die here waiting for our men. I fear my lady Nordic is long dead." I told her to never give up.

Lama said, "He has been gone a long time." I told her I feel he is waiting for Icol to return.

"Lama, I said, "There is so many waiting, I'm waiting for him myself."

I took a peace; of parchment, I wrote my thought on it. [*This is Queen Shara, Queen to Icol we have had another encounter with Drex. We have fought him off again. I don't know how much longer we can last. Lama is still with me. She has recovered from the beating Drex bestowed on her. All the girls that come here, Drex has killed them. My heart goes to each family. Please tell Lama's mother she is well. Always remember my love and thought are with you as I hope yours are with me. I to suffer, he does mean to kill both of us. He will kill me first; without me, he surely will kill Lama.*]

I took the note dropped it from the window. I looked at Lama she had cut the last piece of bread. Now we were out of food.

My lady, please come, share this with me. It's not going to be enough for both of us. Yet something will happen. You are the one who said don't give up.

We spent the evening talking. For the past four months, she had been with me. We had become very close. I brought her back from near death; this was for sure. In my heart, Lama will be the daughter I will never have. There were times I have asked myself why Icol and I never had children, I promise you it wasn't because we didn't try. Then Drex, that horrible man, took everything away.

Talking to Lama, was something I found easy to do. I stood walked to the window, nighttime had come again to Galaxo. The sun was going down as it showed its last light over the Trions. Lights were coming on throughout the village. Lama helps me with the chair. She was holding it as I climbed up to the window. Our candles were in short supplies too.

What bothered me was the material we needed to make our cycle pads. We both were close we were completely out, Drex made sure of that. Same with our food then it occurred to me, we have no water. We needed a bath, it had been a while since we had a bath; my hair was oily, my body needed a bath. I took Lama in my arms. I told her tonight we may not have a bath, yet we still have each other.

Sleeping as I could, my thought went to Icol. I could see him standing in front of me. Seeing him walking toward me, taking his hands kissing him on the lips. My love, I feel Drex will overtake me. Knowing you're alive keeps me from giving up. I want to run to you. I find in my dreams I do just that. Each time I do I can feel the power of your love. The kind of love that should be shared between two people.

I had no idea how long I had been asleep. Turning on to my side a voice called to me. I looked at the door it was locked. I pinched myself, I was awake. There was someone in our room. I looked around there was no one. I turned to my side when the voice called Shara, daughter of Biel come to me. I knew I was awake, turning to look at Lama.

"She will be fine Shara, now close your eyes, let your mind go to a happy place."

I ask, "Please who are you?"

The voice said., "Shara let yourself go in deep meditation." Flying through the aero of space, opening my eyes I found myself standing on top of a mountain. Looking out over a beautiful valley where animals walked. I thought how beautiful.

Someone took my hand, I looked at her, she was so beautiful. Looking into her blue eyes, I thought the bluest I've ever seen.

Dressed in a yellow rode she said to me, "Come with me, Shara."

I ask again, "Who, are you? Am I dreaming?"

She asked, "Does it feel like a dream Shara?"

I said, "It is impossible to do this. I have read in our history before I was a prisoner. I know this was not the first time this had happened. She wanted me to go with her, the only thing about this was, there was no place to go but down.

"Shara, come with me," she said.

I ask her, "Come where?"

She said, "Believe me, Shara."

I said, "I do believe in you, yet I know you not."

"You are a descendant of Biel. Biel was a descendant of Corning. Kohl was a native of Boldlygo. Just as your husband was a descendant of Kohl. It sounds complicated it's not. Shara, you will see him again, I promise. Now come we haven't much time."

When she told me, I would see Icol again, I let myself go. Flying she showed me all that was. She showed me what would be. I saw my husband with many ships. Icol was with many men. I saw a small girl running, a girl I've never seen before. She was fighting, slashing, stabbing doing all she could to reach Drex.

I turned to her as she said, "Shara we must go." I found myself back in my room.

"We will meet again Shara."

"Please my lady, who are you?"

"I am Kayla, first Queen of all Boldlygo." I was wide awake now, where have I heard that name before.

Three hundered years since the planet disappeared. Why had she come to me, better yet how did she come to me? There was a knock on the door turning over I noticed my feet were wet. Looking down I saw dried leaves and sand on the floor. How could this be? I looked at Lama, she was still sleeping. The knock came again, the sun had not come up the stars fill the night sky, yet a knock.

"My lady," a voice called, in a low whisper. I did not know the voice I was hearing.

Lama raised, "My lady," she said. I told her someone was at the door. Who would that be at this hour? I told Lama I had no idea, the voice called again, my lady please wake up. I walked to the door open the small window, a man was waiting, he was not a guard.

"Who are you," I ask?

He replied, "My lady I have found my way through the castle dressed as a guard, no one noticed me. Besides everyone is sleeping."

The man outside the window I had no idea who he was or what he wanted. Maybe Drex sent him to kill me. All my thought went wild.

"My lady," he said, "I have fruit, bread, the women have given you things you will need." I took the thing he pushed through the window and passed them to Lama.

The old man said, "I was walking on the plains two days ago. There was a man who was a guard here in the castle. He told me what the people already knew. Now everyone will know. My lady a message to the little one, you also. He told me to tell you Icol was alive. He is now fighting for his life. He is with others from here."

"He is with Basco, Dred a Claxton. The little one with you. Nordic said he would come for her. If he made his move now, he would be killed. My lady the Claxton's will stand with Icol. He is coming I must leave now before the guards awake. I will try to come again."

I looked at Lama, your man is coming for you, as is mine, she had started to cry.

"Lama, I ask? "Why are you crying?"

Lama embraced me, "My lady," Lama said through tears, "I knew he was not dead. I knew he was out there somewhere. Now at least I have hope." I told her to never give up." I cut the bread, Lama, and I had it with the fruit. There were several different kinds of fruit. The bread was the best I've ever had. If I live to leave this place, I will find the maker and reward them. Lama laid down, soon was asleep again so was I. The sun had come to the morning sky. I lay on the floor on the mat.

Lama asks, "You awake my queen."

I answered her, "I am Lama. I have something to tell you. I think I had a dream." I told her of the dream she looked at me in disbelief.

"Do you think it was a dream, my lady?" What I said to her next, Lama looked draft at me.

"Are you well, "My lady?"

"Lama you have been here for almost five months. You know as well as I, not one person has been in this cell, you know this."

"I do my lady," she answered. I told her to look at the floor. Lama kneeled touched the sand, it was damp.

She asked, "How could this get here?" Lama asks me to show her my feet. Lama asks, "You went outside without me?" My feet were dirty, Lama sat down on the chair.

"Lama, I don't know how this happened, I thought it was a dream." My feet were dirty all over. I said to her we both need a bath.

Lama said, "My lady, my father has deprived me of the luxury of what I need."

I said, "Lama taking her hand. I can't explain what has happened. The only thing I know, that I wish for, is for Icol to come soon." I stood to walk to the table, "I wish for a bath."

Lama said in a low voice, "Me too my Queen. "Other than a drink of water it was scarce. Drex had the water flow stopped. I knew what the bastard thought. He thought I would beg him to turn it on.

I sit in this prison waiting for Icols return. I know before I could let him have me, I would have a bath. Believe me, I dearly wanted him to take me to bed. A bath I must have first.

Lama asks, "My lady, on my wedding day, would you be my maid of honor. I will ask Icol to give me away." I told her I'm sure he will do just that.

We were eating a piece of bread when the voice of Drex sounded. He appeared with a ram and three guards.

"Break it down," he said.

The guards said, "Sire why."

Drex said, "Break the damn door down now. These two bitches, they die today."

"Sire I will not help you kill them. I have been with you from the beginning. I will not kill them. You can kill me is one thing. I will not kill the queen or your daughter."

Drex took a sword the fastest I've ever seen. Made a swing at the guard. Moving with a countered the move took a piece of Drexs shoulder. Blood was oozing from the cut.

Drex said, "I'll kill you for that." Drex made his move the other guards stood to watch. I shouted guards your next if you open this door. The guards stood helpless against the wall. Looking at me then to Drex not knowing what to do. I must say the guard was holding his own. Drex thrust with his sword missed. The guard cut Drex across the leg. The cut went deep blood was rushing to the floor.

I shouted to the guard, "Kill him, he would have done this

to you."

Drex screamed. "Shut up Shara, you're in enough trouble." Yelling through the small door I said to the guards.

"Give me the sword, I will kill him myself." Drex was not sure now what to do.

I said, "Drex you are king, yet your fighting for your life. You're no King Drex you're not even a man."

"Break down that damn door," Drex screamed. Blood was staining the floor.

"I will not kill you, sire." Drex smiled that evil smile.

"That's too bad for you. I will kill you here and now." Drex shouted to the other guards to kill him.

"I shouted, "Let Drex do his dirty work." I said again, "when Icol comes I'll have you placed in prison for life," the guards stopped. I suppose they thought prison would be better than death. One guard said as he threw down his sword.

"I will not kill another person for you. Today I leave this place." The others followed. "Sire, I will not kill you, if you persist in this, I will cut you up.

I laughed out loud, "Drex your world is falling apart. King Drex, how do you do what you do. You're no King. Look at you are bleeding on the floor."

"Shara, when I kill whatever this is, I promise you I will kill you and the bitch with you." Lama touched my shoulder I stood aside.

"Father, the bitch you speak of is your daughter, believe me, father."

Drex screamed, "Ran for the door." Screaming through his teeth, "don't ever call me that. Shara, open this door, now." Blood was oozing from his cuts.

Lama called again, "Father you need to see the doctor. Father your bleeding so."

Drex standing outside the door still screaming. The guards stood waiting to see what would happen. I told Drex the loss of blood is making you delirious. Drex stood looking through the window. His shirt was soaked with blood. His pants were soaked to the knee on the right side.

I said, "Drex your dying." Drex staggered to the wall.

"Shara, he said. "I will return, I will kill you and that bitch with you," I called the guard to the door. I told him to watch behind him he may return.

"Guard listen to me. Go through the garden, there's a Huge tree. Behind the tree is a hole in the wall, that will take you outside, go to the plains Somewhere there's a house. There's a guard there, his name is Nordic."

The guard said, "I know him."

I said, "Go tell him what has happened. You cannot stay here Drex will have you killed. Now go tell Nordic, wait there for Icol.

CHAPTER 31

I did as the Queen requested. I eased my way through the castle down the steps to the ground level. I passed two guards, I told them what had happened.

"He is going to kill us all," I'm the one that fought him. I cut him twice I'm leaving, do not try to stop me." Drexs first in command, a man that would kill his father if Drex told him to.

"If I see you again, I will kill you."

Bowing to him I said, "Until then." I left for the hole in the wall. How could she know of this? Shara had been locked up for twenty years.

I found a natural place where a big tree had fallen it was a hideaway. Behind the castle, I waited for the guards to come from the plains for the day. I made my way around the walls of the castle to the road. I was headed to the plains. Looking behind me there was nothing. In front of me were the Trions showing their peaks.

There were several people on the road to the castle. Coming up to a house I had been several times, the house of Basco. Basco was a warrior of the old school. I remember several years ago Basco would come to the training area, train the guards in the art of self-defense. I never knew why we had no one to fight. I ask just that once.

Basco would tell of the city of the Claxton's. How he was trained, he would tell all that ask the question of why we train. Basco replied to each, better to train than to be caught off guard. It took me several years to understand that. When Drex took power from his brother, then I knew what Basco meant. I did not agree with what Drex did when I found out the queen was alive, I started seeing the difference. Drex sleeping with his daughters was even worst.

I stopped at the house of Basco. The plains were not safe at night that has been told to us our lifelong. There are animals here, yet I've never heard of anyone being attracked. I walked out back to gather dried sticks to start a fire. I took a small package from my pack, made a crude dinner. I started to look around. Basco had a cellar under his house it would appear no one has found it.

Opening the door, I thought to myself. Wow, Basco was a knowing man. Basco had put supplies up for days to come. I took a small number of dried fruits, a container of fruit. I placed the door back, so It didn't look disturbed.

The night was coming to Galaxo. I built my fire as the warmth of the fire raced through the open air of the big room. It wasn't long before the room was warm somewhere in the night, I fell asleep. It was the first time in a while I slept like this, in quite some time. Lying in bed I could see the morning was coming. Through the window the light sky told me the sun would soon be up, I needed to move. Something moved outside there was no mistaking it was human.

Listening carefully, I moved to the shadow of the room. In front of the room, the door opened from the stoop. A voice said, someone here if so speak now. Stepping from the shadows it was Iams, one of Drex guards. He was in the hall with Drex as we fought. Iams saw me come from the shadows.

"Nonik," he said. I told him I could not kill her.

Iams asks, "Where is Rea?" I told Iams Drex killed him.

I said to Iams, "I see Drex has sent you to bring me back."

"Konik," Drex said If I brought you back alive, he would let me live." Iams did not see my sword. I brought it up to his throat before he knew. Stepping back to the wall, "You can try," I said. "Iams I will kill you." He pushed my sword from his throat.

"Nonik, I have no intentions of taking you back. I'm going with you by the way where are you going." I offered tea to Iams.

Taking the tea, he asks, "Where are you going." I told him away that's all. Maybe to the mountains of the Trions. Maybe to see the Claxton's.

Iams said, "Maybe you will be killed. I suppose if you look for them. What if we just go to the plains to the bottom of the mountain wait. I promise you they will show up." Iams and I packed a bag, I told him to find a shirt.

I ask him, "What did Drex say if you brought me back dead."

Iams smiled, "He said he would kill me."

I said, "He doesn't play very well does he." I said as Iams looked around Basco's house for clothes I told him, we may haft to fight our friends. They will come I assure you, Drex will send them. If you're not back by the end of the week.

I told Iams I look for a friend, all I know he is on the plains. He must dodge the patrols Drex has not sent for him because he thinks he is dead. Drex sent him into the mountains. The queen told me where to find him. We need to move.

Iams found some old clothes changed we left for the plains. It was late afternoon when we stopped running. Most of the day Iams and I ran. As we were in good shape. A huge tree where we stopped with tall grass all around was a perfect place for a crude camp. Iams started to stand when a scruple passed by within fifty yards. I grabbed him pulling him down.

"You see Iams," I said. "Drex has sent them to look for you." The guards were our friends, you will see they will keep coming."

I ask Iams, "Should we call to them?"

"Iams said sure if they want to fight, we can kill them take their scruple," I told him I like the way you think. Iams yelled at them. Iams was waist-high in the grass as the scruple come back. The two guards saw him wave. Stopping beyond the tall grass, they could not see me lying flat on the ground.

Iams asks them, "Did Drex had sent you?"

They replied by saying, "Yes Drex thought you would need some help." lying in the grass I could tell the talk was going to be short.

One of the guards said to Iams, "If you find Nonik you will kill him." I stood to speak to them the fight was on I told them I'm not going back. I wait for Icol.

"Then you die now," the guard said. I killed the one that

spoke turning to see Iams, he was fighting for his life. I was not worried, I was slashing and cutting the guard, he went down. The guard that Iams was fighting made a mistake he made a slash he missed, Iams didn't. It was over, now we had a scruple. Now It will be easier, at least we don't have to run.

All the years I have been here, well, all my life. I told Nonik I've never been this far before. I thought about how anyone could live in a remote place like the plains. The land was fertile, the water pure. Yet I had no desire to live here. We stopped at a rock formation, made a camp just short of sunset.

I ask Iams, "You've heard the stories of the plains not being safe at night."

Iams said, "I have been told all my life. Yet I've never heard anything happening on the plains."

I slept soundly. I suppose Iams did also. Awaking me as the stars left the morning sky. Iams poured me a cup.

Iams asks me again, "Where are we going?" I told him to see a friend.

"Do I know this friend," Nonik?

"Yes, you do Iams, we look for Nordic."

Iams said, "You look for a dead man. Nordic is a long time dead from Galaxo my friend."

I sipped my tea looking at him, "You believe that."

"Yes, Nonik I do," Iams said.

I said to Iams, "The queen told me to come here, I'm going on, you can tell Drex you killed me. Take the hand of the other guard. Tell Drex it is my hand. I'm going to find Nordic, tell him what is going on. I'll try to stay hidden, wait for Icol.

"Icol," Iams said in disbelief. "Brother Icol is dead so is the queen."

"Iams, two days ago in the east towers, I had a council with Queen Shara." Iams had a shocked look on his face.

Iams said, "So it is true, she is alive." Where do you think Icol is? I find it hard to believe he is alive." I told Iams I couldn't be sure, the Queen said he is alive. She said Icol and the Claxton are together.

Iams ask, "Why do you think the Claxton has not overrun Drex and freed the Queen."

I answered, "Iams, I only know she is alive. Maybe the Claxton are waiting for the same thing. Maybe they're waiting for Icol. You know they may be looking for him."

Iams said to me, "I truly would love to meet a Claxton, Just one. I was two years old when the overthrow took place. I hear of them, yet no one I know has ever seen one, maybe this Basco has." I told Iams Basco was trained by the Claxton's. He is one of the few that has ever been to the city. That's why Drex wanted him so bad. Basco would die before he would tell Drex where the city lies.

Iams said, "Well I still would like to meet one." A voice from the tree and tall grass came alive with a response. Iams and I came off the ground so fast, sword in hand.

"Who's there," I ask? "Show yourself."

The voice asks, "What would you do if you met a Claxton. Would you fight him or befriend him?"

Iams said, "I would offer him a cup of tea, then my hand. If he declined, then my blade."

"Then you would die, my friend." Stepping from behind the tree was Nordic. Standing in front of the two, they both had a huge smile on their face. Iams passed me a cup of tea.

Nordic said, "You're the first humans I've seen in a month. Other than the guards, I hide from them."

Nonik said, "Well you are alive?" Sipping our tea, Nordic's hand moved to his sword.

I ask, "are you here to take me back?"

Nonik said, "No my friend we're here to join you. We were informed by the queen where to find you. She said wait here for Icol."

Nordic asks, "Nonik, you have spoken to the queen."

Nonik said, "I have two days ago. A word from the little one, she said she waits for you. Nordic sipped his tea, "I wait to be with her. The guards do patrol here I said, the cabin also. We need to move." The sun had reached midday as we started to move.

Nonik asks, "How much further?"

Nordic said, "Well if you had stayed on the course you were on; you would be there. Only a few miles more."

Loading our things into the scruple, it was as Nordic said it was a short way. Hidden in a valley was a small house.

Nonik, "Well my friend you have done well." I told the boys it belongs to a friend; a man and his daughter. The guard killed her mother for hiding the girl from Drex. I found their writing on the table. The girl was hiding for hours in a hole, listening to the guard's torcher her mother. The guards killed her in front of the girl looking up from the cellar.

Somewhere there was a fight with the guards at the Trions. The guard killed her and her father. There was another man from the village. The Claxton's brought them here. I buried them outback.

Walking into the house, I ask, "What is happening in the castle." Nonik told of the fight with Drex. How Shara and Lama had built up the wall.

Nordic said, "I carried a lot of material to them. I give them swords too."

Iams asks, "So that's where they got them." Sitting in silence for what seemed several minutes we talked about several things.

Nonik asks, "When do you think Icol will come?"

"I don't know brother, soon I hope," I answered.

Iams said, "I don't know how we can survive." I told them we have food here. I plan to live here with Lama when this is over."

Iams asks, "What is your next action?" I told them I had planned to go to the Trions. I had already started my journey when I spotted you. I waited for you to rest. You know when we were kids, the plains were not safe at night, there's nothing to that. I slept in the same place you did. I walked several miles after dark. The moon was so beautiful; the night was clear I tell you living in the village, we never saw this at night. I told them in two days there will be a full moon, we will leave then.

Nonik asks, "leave to where?"

"Why Nonik," I said. "We are going to find these Claxton's; you want to meet."

Nonik said, "Then my friend you lead us to our death." I told them we will carry our weapons; we need to go to the cave of the Trions. We will wait there, the Claxton's, they will come, I assure you.

We talked for a while, I ask for a place to sleep.

Nordic said, "Anywhere."

I ask Nordic, "What about the patrols sent to the mountains."

Nordic said, "Drex sends them every day. We will be protected I assure you."

Nonik said, "You assure me."

I said, "Watch, you will see little brother."

Iams ask. "Nordic who do you fight for, the one with the queen or yourself."

I replied, "I fight for our freedom, I fight to rid the castle of a madman. I fight for Icol our King. I tell you now if I had known he was alive, I would have gone to him long ago. I would have found him as Basco has."

Nonik asks, "How do you know Basco has found him."

"Brother, you did not see what I saw when they left Galaxo. That's another story. Nonik told us he was going to sleep,"

Iams and Nonik stayed with me for two days. Looking for the patrols every day we talked about and planned for the journey to the Trions. The main topic we talked about every day, where was Icol. We had no idea why he has not come. We didn't know if he was alive or dead. Hearsay was all we had.

Iams said, "the journey you talk of Nordic, well I was on patrols there very often. I never saw a cave. I do remember hearing about the fight. I know you were there, I sure you know what you're talking about. I ask Nordic about the scar on the arm."

I smiled then said, "Trophy from a sixteen-year-old Claxton female. She cut me, so I could show the guard, so they would run out of the cave. She killed two of them. The storekeeper's daughter Shila, killed three. Basco the Claxton Dred Basco son killed the others. I tell you boys; I don't want to fight a Claxton. If Drex and his guard knew what I no, they would run now."

The morning before we left, I was in the field. Nonik walked to the small cabin I used as a barn. I didn't hear the scruple. Sixteen men pulled in front of the house. Drex had sent them for us. Iams was alone in the house. Walking outside to the stoop stopping at the edge.

"Iams," one guard said. "What are you doing here?"

"I suppose the same as you, looking for something," Iams answered.

The guard said, "Looks as if you found something, this place is nice. Who lives here?"

Iams said, "A man Drex, killed his wife and daughter. They refused to give their daughter to Drex for his pleasure. How about your daughter she is of age, yet?"

"Now look Iams, "I don't like it either, he is our king?" Iams shouted he was stalling. He was trying to buy time for me and Nonik to come from behind the house. Three against sixteen, we were going to die, this I had no doubt.

I said, "Drex is no king. He is a man in power to use the power as he, please. If he doesn't like the way these are going, if they don't go as he wants, he kills, he'll kill you. Rea, he killed him. He is still trying to kill the queen. The girl in the tower his daughter. You've heard the stories, you know it to be true, I wait for Icol."

The guard stepped from the scruple. Drawing his sword took the point drawled a line in the dirt. Walked from one side to the other. That's your line cross it, you die. Taking my sword, I stepped from the stoop. He died there; one guard tried to come from the scruple he never made it. I took my knife threw it at another; took him in the chest. I thought three-down thirteen to go. The other scruple took off. There were five left."

I said, "Well fellows, what will it be?" All five come with swords in hand. I drew up as Nonik, and Nordic come around the house.

I said to them, "If you cross the line in the dirt, they will kill you." Nordic laughed out loud.

The guard said, "Well, either way, you will die. This is treason against the king." Nordic stared at the guard.

The guard said, "You are supposed to be dead."

"Yet here I am," Nordic said. "Drex is no king, he will fall if you stand with him, you will die or be placed in a prison."

Five guards listen to me talk. I told them of the queen. I told them of the girls Drex had killed. Like always, there are a few stupid people. The five of them came at once. I suppose they got tired of talking. I do say it was a good fight. Nonik took a cut across the hand that was it. Several minutes it was over, they were dead. We placed them in a grave. In the middle of the afternoon, we packed up headed for the cave in the Trions.

CHAPTER 32

Our ships landed on the surface, looking down the ramp the chief justice waited. Fina and I walk to him with the King. Each of us had him under the arm. Throwing him to the ground.

I said to the chief, "He is dead. I killed him as I'll kill you."

The chief replied, "you're a stupid girl, a female speaking to me." Before he finished saying the phrase Fina cut him across the face. Over five hundred troops come from everywhere. The Advairan and Galaxian guards ran from the ships. Still, we were outnumbered.

We were fighting with everything we had, it seemed all was lost. I ran for the chief, lasers flashed, there was an explosion in space. Large balls of fire. I ran for the ship to call the other. I was going to tell the captains to blow up the city. I called my ship to break orbit to join the destruction of the city. There were hundreds of people dead.

Some of the old ones remembered the war of the planet. Some remembered the destruction. The fight went on. On the third day of the fight, the chief justice came with a peace offering.

I was waiting on the bridge with the captain. A sentry walked to the captain, whispered something. Replying he said, "I'll tell her. Shila it appears the chief would like a counsel with you." I looked at Basco and Fina

Basco said," I suppose we should see what's on the chief mind." I walked from the ship. the smell of smoke lingered. Fighting still prevailed in the city. I walked to the chief. I ask, "what is on your mind? Hundreds of people have died. For what chief?

Chief justice said, "Female take your people leave, my world. If you leave now, I'll let you live. If you stay here, you will die. There will be others coming from Xon you can't win." I walk to the chief, with Fina beside me. He reached out took hold of me, placing a knife to my throat. Fina killed him, the fight was on again. I ran to the ship that was in port.

I called to the captain, "Have you seen other ships," I ask?

The captain replied, "twenty-five ships in all Shila. What should we do?" I told him to take them out. There was silence for a moment.

"Shila may I suggest something." The captain asks. I told him anything that will help.

The captain said, "Let me break orbit, take all the ships out of range, I'll leave one here to watch. I'll come in from behind." I looked at Basco, he agreed it would work. I think I know what he has in mind.

Tenna said, "We should send scouts to the city. We need to see what is happening. I'll take the princess with me, we'll be fine." I looked at Fina.

She said, "I'll be fine Shila, I promise." As Tenna and Fina move to the streets she moved her lips to say I was a bitch. We both laughed. Basco looked at Dris.

"Don't ask me, father," Dris said.

Tenna and Fina walked the streets as if they were part of the city. There were people everywhere digging through the rubbish of the destruction Tenna told me later the old one was remembering the war of the planets.

Some of the people ask, "Why has this happen again?" Tenna and Fina came to us and give their report. I told them we need to take it to Icol. I bowed to Icol as we entered the galley. Tenna told Icol the Palatonians were going to attract us again. Sire, the old ones have spoken to me of the old war.

"Shila what do you think," Icol asks?

"My King, I only know they're keeping me from my destiny," Icol said to Basco in a whisper.

Icol turned to me, "Shila come to me, please. You fifteen years old. You have proven to be a very powerful warrior. I have waited for many years to place my brother in prison."

My king, "that will not happen" I said. "It was told by the old one in the mountains of Trion. It was said, I would be the one to kill Drex. He is your brother; I will kill him Icol." Fina and Dris and Dred came to my side. Icol looked at us.

Fina said, "My king, we will protect her on her journey."

Dris said as he kneeled to Icol. You are our true king, please don't try to stop us. You might stop us, who will stop Dred."

Icol said, "I won't try to stop you, you have my word." I told them this fight we must win somehow. Dred spoke for the first time in days. Dred was a warrior of the highest. Dred could fight better than ten of us. Tenna, Dris, Basco, Dred, and me, I swear one hundered guards could not take us. I was thankful Dred was on our side.

Looking around Icol asks again. "So, what is the next move Shila?" Thousands of ideas went through my mind.

"My king, we know the Palatonians have sent word to Xon. We know their coming. We also know they will be here in the next few hours. What we don't know is if their ground troop. We much watch for this. Bliss is monitoring there move of the ships. Tenna also thinks of their troopships. We know two of the ships have stopped. We don't know why.

Dred asks, "Shila what of your vision?"

I looked at Dred, "That's all it was Dred, a vision."

Dred said, "What was it they said, when you need us, we will come?"

"Well Dred, we need them," I said.

Dred said, "Shila, don't lose your faith. I went there, Shila there real."

Icol asks, "Dred what is real." I told Icol of the dream or vision I had of the old's one of Boldlygo. Icol had heard the stories, knew their powers. He read of them in the archives.

I told Dred we can't wait for them to come. Standing in front of Icol I told him I wanted to go home. Icol let's end this, Tankko came to us, standing in the galley door.

I ask, "Tankko you have something to say?"

"Tankko said, "Bliss said the ships from Xon have arrived. They're just sitting there. We have called to then; we flew a shuttle close to them there was no response."

Basco said, "Well that is strange. It's as if something has

taken hold of them."

Dred said, "This could be it." I told him to believe as you wish.

Icol said to me, "Shila you and Fina go get some rest, you will need it. If something happens, I'll come for you." I thought as I stood there. I looked at Dred then at Basco, they both nodded to me.

I said, "Very well, Fina come with me it would appear we need rest." In our room, I don't remember much. Lying on the bed is all I remember. Someone called to me. I could hear them call my name. Shila came to me, I awaken, looking all around, there was total darkness.

I called, "Fina where are you." Trying to see into the darkness a small light appeared. It seemed to come closer, getting bigger.

A voice said, "Don't be afraid."

"I'm not afraid of a light," I said.

The voice said, "You remind me of my mother when she was a young woman." It was a man's voice, yet I could not see him.

"Take my hand, come with me," the voice said.

"Where to this time, shall we go to the top of another mountain?"

The voice said again," Take my hand." I reached out, a hand reached from the light took mine, away we went.

I couldn't believe how fast we were moving. From what I knew of space we were moving so fast passing planets, going through galaxies. I've never moved so fast. This had to be a dream. A vast field of stars, then a clearing, and a beautiful valley of lights.

I said out loud, "Ah, another mountaintop." Looking down I said out loud, "I've been here before." I was looking at this beautiful valley. I swear I saw a herd of Unicorns. I've only heard of them, no one has ever seen one.

"Where are we," I ask?

A man appeared," the Marder-to-goes. It means mountains

of beauty."

I said, "I know, I read of this in the archives of our world." There was silence for a moment.

I said, "That was long ago when our world was free and peaceful. Who are you and why have you brought me here? I need to be with my people there's a war going on."

The man said, "come with me Shila, they're some people you must meet."

I looked at him, "I'll come with you when you tell me who you are, why you have brought me here?"

"Take my hand." He said. In seconds we were in a beautiful courtyard. The suns on this planet had come up, I thought what a beautiful place. Walking through a very large room I took to be the chamber of the council. There were several people there. Everyone stood as I entered.

"Welcome Shila," A woman's voice said. I had seen her somewhere before. Maybe in a vision. The man that brought me here went to the end of the table; he was embraced by another beautiful woman.

"Well my love, she said what have you brought us? Shila, she said welcome to Boldlygo."

My heart was pounding so hard. I swear it was coming through my chest. A small tinkle of sweat rolled down my face. A shiver ran through me like a chill.

"This is not real, I said out loud, it's got to be a dream."

The man said, "I am Zin, King of our world." Pushing out his hand this is my wife Tressa. I looked around the table. Everyone appeared to be human. some appeared to be from other planets.

The King said, "The others will give you their names."

"Fax, Zin called, you first."

I am called Fax, "Once King of Xon."

I said, "Your ships are attracting us. We are at war with them and the Palatonians."

Fax said, "Shila there not my ships. I have been here, over

three hundered years." Then the others stated their names.

"I am Kikki, my husband the great Bota."

I ask Bota, "How long have you been here?"

Bota replied to me, "I have lost time Shila. I have been here since the beginning, with Maoke. I was Maoke head scientist."

"Who," I ask?

Bota replied, "Maoke."

I said, "He came to me in a dream once."

A female asks, "Was it a dream Shila? We have been to your queen, one of your warriors, that is with you. The other members stood and gave their names. I knew them all, one female said, "I am Leah."

I said, "You're Zin's mother?" Turning to look at the man beside her, "you must be Dorn, her husband? I told them I've read about all of you. In our archives of long ago, history before our king was overrun by his brother. We are at war, even as we speak."

"Shila that is why you're here. First, have some breakfast." Zin said.

"Eat," I said. "If this is real, it does appear to be, I'm too excited to eat. There's some much I want to ask. There's not enough time."

Bota ask. "Shila, why has the Palatonian destroyed Corning."

Bota looked at Zin. "Speak Bota, Quad has been destroyed," I told them Quad was not in power, he has passed on. Redda severed as governor. Redda is a descendant of Quad. The Palatonians came after the war of the planets. Conquered everything.

Standing I said to them, "I fear for my world, there's only several thousand of us. It's the Claxton's, I fear for them."

Bota said, "I have met these being once. Ject and I on one of our crusades. They're good people, furious warriors."

"Yes, they are," I said. "I too am a Claxton warrior. I dropped my shoulder showed them the seal, tell me why you brought me here." Another voice said it was another female.

"I'm April, my husband Tyler. Shila, we have watched you for a while."

Zin said, "Shila we brought you here to stay."

I was already standing, I said, my destiny is not of your world. I must fulfill it or die trying.

Zin said, "There are others there, we want here also. Your husband to be and Fina." Tears were flowing down my face I was all choked up.

I said, "This is a beautiful place, you once fought for your world, just as I am fighting for mine. I suppose anyone would want to live here, please I can't stay. Even as we speak, I may be needed." I looked at Dorn, he was like Basco a beautiful person.

He said, "Shila, relax, all the women said to me without moving their mouth, how is it possible. Another female stood.

"I am Shasta"

"I'm Adair, sister to Leah. Things aren't always as they seem Shila."

"Shasta said, "father."

Dorn replied, "Well daughter I have not done that in quite some time." I looked at Dorn before my eyes, he changed his body to something. Bota and Kikki changed also. Then they changed back.

"See Shila your world, our world, the world of the Palatonians. Thing sometimes isn't what they seem." I didn't know what to say. I stood there staring.

Zin stood as two others came into the room. They were introduced, Mea, Henery. One big happy family, I thought.

Zin stood, "Shila I did bring you here to stay. I do understand what you say. Most everyone here has only seen war once on this planet. My father on his journeys to Earth has seen many. He rescued Mea from a war country. That's how he met my mother. After all the years there still very much in love."

I ask, "Will take you back?"

"Shila, we told you and the warrior, when you need us, we

will come. There is still much to talk about, some other time. This Shila I promise. Shila with all that you see, and what you hear, we will do as *we* say. You must do as we say. I fell to one knee.

"I'm truly sorry Zin, I can't stay. I need to be with my people, be with my man, stand beside him. In my heart, I know you are all-powerful. Zin please help me fight them, help me to destroy them. I know in the archives it is written you are a peaceful race."

"Yes, we are," Zin said.

I said, "When something brought death and destruction to your world, you intervened, help me. I just want to full fill my destiny."

Zin said, "Yes, Shila I'm sure you do, killing Drex is what you were born to do. You just did not know it at the time. You had to find out from the Claxton's.

I ask, "How could you, possible no that?"

Zin said, "Things are not what they seem little one." Tressa took me by the hand.

Tressa said, "Someone you must meet." Tressa told me something I would never guess.

"Shila you are the first person that has been on Boldlygo for over three hundered years," I told Tressa it is so beautiful here.

Tressa said, "It was almost destroyed when I was eighteen. Trust me Shila my people are very powerful; my husband has more power than all of us together. There are some here that have powers. They were born on Earth-like Leah. She at one time scared me." Tressa said with a smile, "she still does. It wasn't just me, my Opa said Leah scared him sometimes. You know Shila you are a look-alike of Leah and Adair. I told her I noticed that.

I ask, "How could that be, coming from a different world?"

Tressa said, "All in time Shila."

Walking by an opening with a view that was breathtaking, off in a meadow I saw what appeared to be several Unicorns.

I ask Tressa, "Are they real?"

"Yes, silly," she replied. Tressa knocked on a door, a man and woman stood. She had long white hair. He was tall with a muscular body. I went to my knees pushed out my hand.

"My lady," I said.

Tressa asks, "what's wrong Shila?"

"Rise child," the woman said, "Shila we have watched you for several years. Just in the past few years, you have grown up. From your mother's people through countless generations to you."

I looked at the man, "You are Omega, and you are Kira?"

"I said, "You are so beautiful. I never thought you would look as you do."

Tressa asks "Shila how did you know who they were?"

"Kira said, "My daughter, she has just begun her journey."

"Mother she will not stay, we have already asked.

Kira said, "let's go join the others."

Kira, you and Omega said you have watched me. How, who am I.?" We were asked long ago by Ira, to watch after you after all you are a descendant of Lola." I got choked up again, I do that a lot it seems.

Kira said, "Lola was a descendant of Destiny. Destiny lived on Corning. She left for Earth thousands of years ago. She started our family in a country called Russia."

I ask, "Then how did I come into existence? Through DNA, from Lola when she was brought here. We took her DNA stored it. Lola was married to Comp. They chose to live on Earth. As you have chosen to go back to your world."

"I must go back Kira," I said.

Kira said, "Relax Shila, we are taking care of it as we speak. Enjoy yourself talk to us." Then in my state of mind, I realized why the ship had stopped Kira, Omega, Tressa took their place. I was the only one standing.

I said, "My name is Shila, I'm from a world called Galaxo. I had no idea this could happen or would. I still think I'm dreaming as I've said before. I've only read about you in the archives. Kira and Omega have told me I am a descendant of Lola, how I'm still not sure."

"Tressa has asked of my mother," I told her I never knew her, she died when I was one year old. My father raised me."

Zin said, "That is sad, that your mother died. My father saw this on Earth." "Zin, it does happen, I said, "You saw it in your war of the planets, it does happen I've seen it. I've done it, I'm not proud of it."

Tressa said, "Shila if you followed back Lola descendent. Eleven generations you will carry on the bloodline, you will marry Dris. You will have a daughter to carry the blood. I tell you now with each generation the blood becomes stronger."

I ask, "What does that mean, I'm not strong?"

Leah said," You will become more powerful than you think. You already are strong. You and Fina together are very strong. Your daughter will be very powerful." Zin held up his hand. "Something else I need to know, I ask.

Zin said, "You must do as I say, it's time to go. Tell your king to go aboard the ship. I jumped up, "No," I said.

"Shila please listen to me, leave Plano. When you need us, we will come?"

I set up in bed, "My words Fina. How long have I been asleep? You should not have let me sleep so long."

Fina replied, "Shila you have been here in this room for five minutes." I told Fina I need to see Icol. I started to the door, looked to see if I was dressed, I was. I had a habit of rushing off naked. Gathered around a table in the galley Basco was talking to Icol.

I ran into the galley, "Icol, pull all of our forces, we must leave the surface now they're coming."

Dred said to me. "Shila were you there?"

"Their coming Dred." From everywhere came an explosion. Running to the portal I could see the ships were descending to the surface, our troops were running for the ship.

Basco Fina and I ran as hard as we could to the ramp. There was chaos in the yard men were dying my group was outside fighting.

I shouted, "Let's go, everyone gets on board now, come on hurry." Tankko was right they were troopships. I looked as we all went aboard captain give the word to leave for space. "All our ships lifted to the darkness of space without losing a single ship.

The captain said, "The Palatonians, they're flowing us."

I said, "They will follow, they will return to the surface." Everyone looked at me strangely as the ships turned.

I could not comprehend what was going to happen next. I sat quietly with my eyes closed. I felt Fina when she touched my hand.

She whispered a low voice in my ear, "I'm here let it go bitch." We were out of range of the Palatonians. They had returned to the planet's surface. I suppose they were sitting around rejoicing their victory. No doubt bragging of the way we ran. They had no way of knowing what was about to happen to them.

Icol said to me, "Little one, I've never seen you so quiet."

Fina said to the captain, "Stop the fleet." The planet of Plano was well in sight. We were about hundreds of miles in space. We were close enough to witness the format of what was to come.

I stood up in a hazy state, "Icol, I said, "Tell the Advairan thanks for their help. If they like, they may return home. The ships from the Moon of Spores too." For several minutes I watched through the scope.

I said to all that heard my voice. "I will see this planet destroyed."

Icol replied, "How Shila we have not enough people. I winked at him, took his hand kneeled before my king.

I stood, "My king, watch the power of our people. The people of long ago, my blood, the blood of Mya, the blood of

Lola. Royal blood that stills flows through my veins."

Icol looked at Basco, "Basco, is she saying."

Basco said, "I'm not sure what she is saying."

I said, "Icol remember your reading of Destiny of Corning. She passed it to Lola our Earth mother. I someday will go to this Earth. I will go to find our people that still live, that remember Destiny."

Icol looked puzzled, "What does she have to do with this Shila?"

"Icol you are my king, how is it you do not know? Destiny lived on Corning. She went to Earth to start our earth family. When our ancestors came back to Earth several hundered years later they found Lola. Lola came to Boldygo while she was there, her DNA was taken. It was passed to someone in Corning. My mother's four-generation until it came to me. I am Royal Blood. As Fina, I too am a princess Icol."

Dris said, "Shila you make no sense." A strange sound in our ears. A gray light appeared on the wall of the ship A hole appeared, Mea, Zin, Tressa, Leah, stepped through. Everyone fell to their knees.

Zin took my hand, "Shila, come, see the power of your people." The planet of Plano started to spin. A vortex opens in space. We watched as the planet of Plano disappeared. Zin turned to Icol.

King Icol, "I know you would love to be home, go to Corning, help them before you go home. All that witness this will have something to talk about for hundreds of years to come. Basco, Dred, Tenna, Dris, stood with their mouth open, as Zin and the others stepped back through the portal.

Zin turned to look at me before going through the portal, "Shila we will meet you again," The portal closed. Icol stood looking at me, "What just happen Shila?" There is no need for me to explain. Just as the old one said.

Icol asks again, "What just happen?"

Fina said, "My king you are in the presence of a true princess.

A very powerful one, it would seem." From that day, the crew looked at me differently. They would stand aside when we met in the corridor. I was glad it was over.

I said to the others. "When I return home, I will write of this in the archives. Each of you should do the same. I will write about all our journeys together."

CHAPTER 33

We did as Zin and Tressa said. We went to Corning. We found it to be as Fina and I had for seen. The captains of the Advairan fleet and the ships from the Moon accompanied us to Corning. For them, it was a war they had never seen before. As for the descendants of Spores, it was a remembering of a war long past. The war of the planets was a bloody one for some. Redda met us at the landing. Redda had a broken arm. Tenna and Icol ask of Tosh. Redda dropped his head.

"I'm truly sorry, he asks of you with his last breath." Icol walked to a platform.

"Please," he said. "Give me your attention. I can never repay you for the bravery you have shown or the loyalty. We have lost some friends and love ones over the past few weeks. Some will say casualties of war; others will say a bad thing. To the Advairan. Thank you, please go home to your family's. Write as Shila has said in your archives. Let's hope nothing ever happens like this again. I truly think you." Icol got grand thanks from all.

The Advairan captains said, "We will leave if you need us, come to us. King Icol my government will call." I stood with my sister watching this take place, I was thankful to be a part of it. I was thankful we were still alive. My friends and I left our world what seemed like a lifetime ago, to what we are now. We found our king we will help rebuild what was destroyed.

The Advairan left, so did the people from Spores. Each left us with an invitation to come as we wish.

They said as the last ship closed. "Shila you will always be welcome." We worked long and hard this day. A sentry was sent to us with a message to come to the ship. Icol and Tenna were sitting having tea. Entering the galley Icol stood welcomed us.

"Shila," Icol said. "It has been four days. We have waited for you to come to us."

"My king, "What is it you wait for?"

Icol said, "I wish for you to tell what happened to the planet of Plano."

I said, "Icol, you have witnessed with your own eyes the power of our people. Sire back to Kohl, He was from Boldlygo. Our people on Earth. They thought it all ended with Leah and Adair. The DNA on Corning I'm part of that. These people are the most powerful in the cosmos."

"I believe that Shila," Icol said. I put my hand up.

"Sire, please I can't explain what has happened. Power to the people for whatever it was, it worked. Just be thankful it happens."

Icol said, "Have more tea." I looked at him, I just wanted to go do what was needed then go home. Fina said to me with her mind thoughts.

"Shila, Icol is afraid of you." He is worried about your power. I have no power Fina, except my own.

I ask, "Icol are you afraid of me?" A gentle hand touched my shoulder. There was no need to look. It was Basco, I have felt his touch many times.

Basco said, "Sire, I think as the little one does. I think you are afraid of her."

Icol said, "Basco, I'm afraid of what she can do. Shila is very strong, she is stronger than anyone I've ever met. What I fear is the same as my brother. I fear she will rise against me."

I said, "That will never happen." Going to one knee, I told Icol, sire, if you wish when we return you home, I will leave. I was asked to come to Boldlygo to live my life. There I can live forever with Dris looking at him when we are married. No one said a thing. Tenna looking around, Dred never saying a word.

Dris said, "You know, I'm still considered a kid. Yet the Claxton's say I'm a warrior. You Icol everyone else would have been destroyed long ago if not for Shila. You should be grateful. Grateful she is on your side. She has freed you to go home. Shila has saved your ass."

Basco looked at his son. "Dris this is your king you speak to."

"Yes, father I know who he is. After all, once again we did save his ass. He speaks to us the way he does. I feel as Shila we will leave Galaxo."

I stood," I have nothing else to say except when we get to Galaxo, I'll fulfill my destiny, I will leave Galaxo. My king, I will kill Drex, this I promise you. I do mean as I've said before if anyone stands in my way, I will kill them. Sire as far as me trying to overrun you that will never happen. Now if you will excuse me."

Fina and I went to Redda, he said, "It would be ok to go to the archives." Fina and I spent the rest of the day reading. The day passed into the night. I was tired I spoke to Fina. She never answered, looking around Fina lay on a table, she was fast asleep with books under her head for a pillow.

Crossing my arms lying my head on them, I closed my eyes, went back in time. It was as always, it was real. How does this happen? I opened my eyes I was in a strange place. Where was I? A woman's voice said to me.

"Shila," she said. "Yes, I'm Shila." She stepped from the shadows. I knew her not.

I said to her, "I'm dreaming again?"

"Are you dreaming Shila," she asks? The bloodline of Lola will not end with you. As a native of Boldlygo we to have waited for you. Amazing how you can't hurry time, and how time never waits. Everything must be in place for time to take its place, just as Plano."

"Remember Shila, there is always a beginning, always an end. A start to a finish. Everything has its place, just as you, here on Corning. The reasons, you came back here, to the place you are now."

I said, "Yes, that, where am I now?"

"Shila you will find that out someday," she said. Come with me take my hand." I never said a word, I knew she would not hurt me. If I was dreaming, well I would wake up. Across the spaces of time too long ago, to the age of time to my world.

I said to her, "Where are we?"

"Shila tell me what you see, do you know the woman," she asks?

"I can't say I have ever seen her, or the boys or man with her. Who are they," I ask?

"Come Shila, they cannot see you. What you see is only in your thought. I let you see what was. The woman is Lola and her husband Comp."

I looked at her. "Yes, Shila, the very blood that flows through your veins, many years have gone by since this day. The people on Boldlygo always gave a coin so they would know their people. You will go to Earth with your husband by your side. Find our people bring them back. Bring them to your world."

I looked at her skeptically like. "I have not full filled my destiny yet."

"Oh Shila," she said. "It will be as you wish. Remember what I said. Everything in its place."

I ask her, "Have you been to my people before?"

She replied, "I have been to your queen."

Taking me by the hand she said, "It's time to go."

I ask, "Wait, who are the children?"

"The girl is Nancy; the boys are Ira and Mekon."

"No way," I said.

"Come Shila, we must go." Taking me to another place of my own time. I realized where I was.

Looking up, "Who are you," I ask?

She smiled, "I am Kayla, the first queen of all Boldlygo." Then she was gone. Fina was shaking me.

"Shila," she said. "Who were you talking to."

I said, "Fina, when this is over, I'm going to Earth; it will make me very happy if you come with me."

Fina said, "My lady I'm a princess like you. I will follow you as my brother will. How much did you read Shila?" I held up a book.

Fina said, "Oh my." I told her I have learned so much. I was with someone tonight. Someone over a thousand years old. I was with Ira's wife. The human he met on Earth. When Lola gave him life. Zin never told me, about that, Mekon too.

Fina asks, "Who was Ira's mother?" I told her Lola. Mary niece of Lola was Mekon's mother.

Fina smiled, "Shila it sounds so troublesome. She moved her lips to say you're a bitch." We both laughed out loud. I wanted to keep reading.

Fina said, "It's way past daylight, I'm hungry let's go. I wish I could read until it was all gone, I told her. Walking outside the sun was bright. It was also high in the sky. Redda called for us to join him.

Redda said, Shila, it will be time for you to leave soon. Your king needs to go home. Icol must do what needs to be done."

I said, "Redda, it a long journey to go, another fight to fight." The war with the Palatonians was over. There have been sensors placed in space. The Xonians will not bother you." I told Redda sometimes in the future I will go to Earth. I'll stop here and see you.

Redda asks, "Shila what happen to Plano?" Some say it was you that destroyed it.

I smiled, "Redda, I wish I had that kind of power. That comes from the old ones of Boldlygo." Redda looked shocked.

"You mean." he tried to find the words they would not come.

I said, "Zin, Dorn, Leah the others. Redda, you will never have to worry about the Palatonians again."

We lingered for a while with Redda. Fina had her meal. I had a cup of tea. I find tea here was a different kind of tea. It was nothing as we had on Galaxo.

Redda asks, "Shila, why do you want to go to Earth." I told him Zin asks me to go, then Kayla.

"Kayla," Redda asks? I told him Kayla was Ira's wife from Earth.

Redda said, "I've read of Ira, he was powerful."

I replied, "His grandson wow. Zin over the years has learned to create portals," Redda looked at me.

I said, "A portal, you can step from here to there across galaxies in a single step. That's power Redda."

Redda said, "Yes, I suppose it is Shila. Yet I will hate to see you leave."

"I will come back to see you again, maybe you will come to this Earth with me," I said.

Redda said, "I'm happy here Shila." Three days later we said our goodbyes to Redda, boarded our ship left Corning.

Dred made way to space than to hyperspace. We had several meetings on the ship. Everyone talked about what we were to do. In each counsel, I noticed Icol would stare at me. Fina also noticed this. Basco brought me back to reality.

Basco said, "I think, the best thing to do, would be to go to the plains first. The guard we met on the trail to the Trions we sent to the plains, we were to meet him." I noticed Dred standing in the do I walked to him. Dred nodded to me.

"Shila, we must see your king," he announced.

I said, "let's go." Fina walking to the galley. I asked her to come with us. Dred told Icol of the vision. Icol there is a cave at the foot of the Trions, someone waits there. The Claxton's are leaving the mountain. They will be there for the fight.

Tenna stood, "He speaks the truth, they are coming. There's a large group of them I have seen this."

My heartbeat fast. I wanted another fight. I wanted to see my father's store. I had told Basco of the tunnel long ago.

Icol asks, "Basco what should we do?"

Basco said, "We should go to the cave, pick up the men then land outside the castle, walk the rest of the way." I smiled as they talked. I lust for the feeling of my blade going in and out of Drex's stomach. I long to kill him, I wanted to kill him. The men I've killed before it was something needed to be done. Drex, I wanted to see the look on his face when my sword goes to the hilt. I wanted to withdraw it, thrust it again, and again.

I wanted to see what was in his eyes as the last breath leaves his body. Just before he dies, I want to whisper in his ear.

"Drex, how does it feel to know you will never have me as you desired." Then push him away as I claim victory. I'll have Fina, Dris, Dred, by my side. Then and only then will we be free.

CHAPTER 34

Drex was still in pain. The cut on his leg was bad, the worst he had ever received. When he stood and tried to walk the pain was so severe the pain ran up the spine. His shoulder was hurting, yet not as bad as the leg. Drex screamed as the doctor told him another inch it would have got the main artery.

What was happening to his world? He was losing control of his men. His men were leaving him. I'm a good king. I've always given my men the best. I've always given them the girls when I was finished with them. Now people laugh at me, mock me for my right as a king, to have any woman or all of them.

Drexs thoughts went to the Claxton's, why can't I find them. A Claxton woman, I've always wanted one. Maybe someday I will. I looked out the window, turned for my bed. My guards, death to all that turn their hands on the king. I needed rest, lying on the bed my eyes closed I was almost asleep when a guard called.

"Sire may I approach." He asks?

"Enter," I said. "Sire a patrol has returned they bring word." Drex asks, "Word of what?"

"Sire a guard has reports Nordic, Iams, Konik has been seen at the base of the Trions."

I laid in bed thinking. I raised on one arm.

"That's impossible, Nordic is dead," I said.

"Sire they have been seen in a cave at the path of the Trions." Drex thought for a moment.

Drex asks, "Was it not you that told me he was dead."

"I saw him fall, Sire," I did. "We did not wait we were undermanned. That day we flew back here." I lie back, so the man was alive, along with the ones I sent to find him." I told the guard to bring their family put them in chains."

"Sire," the guard said. "They have no family. It has been said your daughter in the towers Nordic wants to marry her, said you give her to him." Drex told the guard to leave.

Turning to leave the guard said, "Sire one other thing."

"Yes, what know?"

The patrol reported the move of many Claxton's. They're coming from the mountain."

Raising my head, "What did you say. Bring the guard to me now."

"As you wish sire."

Drex thought as the guard left, what was the Claxton's up to. Why were they coming from the mountain? How many were there? Were they coming here to the castle? Then I thought what do I with Shara, and Lama. The guard did say Nordic was to marry her. Well, I'll take care of that bitch this time. How do I get to them if ever I wanted a woman dead it was those two?

"Yes, Lama she meant nothing to me. I should find her mother and kill her for not having a son. I should kill them all. Lama was just another female. I never had problems until she came alone. For over twenty years I've tried to take Shara. I did give her everything. Then she treats me as she does. How could she, I was the king. She looked at me as if I was not there. I think I will never have her. If I can't have her no one will. I will kill her and the tramp with her.

How would I do that, the thought left me as the sentry entered the room. "Sire, at your request." I staggered to the left.

"Sire can I help you." Tell me, sentry, tell me what you have seen. The guard Nordic, Iams, Nonik. I have seen them in a cave at the base of the Trions. We left to report this to you. I saw a group of Claxton's on a path coming down the mountains to the plains.

I ask, "How many would you say?"

The sentry replied, "Maybe a hundered."

Drex asks, "Why did you not engage them?"

"Sire four men against a hundered Claxton's, I'm not stupid sire. The three guards, we had no orders as we thought they were dead."

Drex smiled, "Yes sentry, there is always an answer. How strong are our forces?"

"Sire I'm only a sentry, I do not know this. If you will excuse me, I'll send the head guard to you."

"Very well," Drex said. "Go tell all to wait in my ready room."

"As you wish sire."

"Wait," Drex said. "Are you loyal to me?"

"Yes, sire for seventeen years." Drex was up to something. He sat in silence for several minutes.

I have a task for you, "There are two females in the tower. I want them dead, do it for me I'll reward you ten folds, of anything you want."

The sentry asks, "Who, are they?" I told him it doesn't matter, just kill them. If you can't do it find someone that will. How hard can it be to kill two women? Turning from the window I almost fell. The pain was horrible.

Maybe now after all these years, now I can have some peace. I caught a chill, thinking of Shara dead. Such beauty what a waste. Lama was so beautiful, damn them for what they have done to me. The head guard came in.

"Sire," the sentry said. "You wish to see me."

I ask him," How strong are our guards and sentry's."

"We can stand a good fight. Sire if we had the ships we could do better."

Drex said, "guard when they return, kill all of them."

The guard asks, "Sire where do you think they are?"

Drex said, "They're probably in orbit over the planet waiting."

"Waiting sire, waiting for what?"

"Sire, I have a headcount, we had about three hundred men."

Drex said, "Go ready all for a battle with the Claxton's."

"Sire we're no match for the Claxton's."

Drex said, "Guard there's only a hundred of them."

"Sire, one hundered Claxton's is like one thousand of us."

Drex said, "I give the sentry a job, is he reliable." I told him he was, only been with us for a while. Sire, may I ask the job."

Drex said, "He is going to kill the queen and the bitch with her."

"Sire if he knows who it is, he won't do it."

Replying, "Then you better not let him find out," Drex said. "As you wish sire."

Things do have a way of working out. My dear brother, when he does return, he'll find Shara dead he will lose all his faith. I knew saying this it was only a few days before Icol comes. I've heard the talk. I know the signs, the Claxton's coming from the mountain. Nordic the others they'll come here for a reason. Maybe try to overrun the castle. The people will fight with Icol that I'm sure of.

Walking to the east tower, holding to the wall for support. I tapped lightly on the door, in a low whisper.

"Shara," I whispered her name long and low S- h- a- r- a." The small window opened, a voice softly called, "father."

"I screamed at the bitch, "I've told you never call me that. Screaming I ask, "Where is Shara?"

A voice said, "I'm here Drex. Has my husband returned? Do you have his head, should I make our wedding plans?"

"Damn you, Shara, for all that has happened to me. Damn the bitch with you." "Oh Drex, you mean your daughter."

"Shara," I said in a scream. "I have someone coming to kill you both, today. Shara, you know what I say is true." A silence came over me.

"Oh Drex," I replied. "You know I was wondering what makes a poor pitiful man like you. Way back when the wrong person died. Drex it should have been you that died instead of your mother and father. I mean, after all, you did kill both. A man that can't kill two people yet can kill his parents. Yet a man can't even break down a door." I was taunting him.

"You will die, Shara, this I promise you."

"Father please," Lama said.

Drex said, "I told you never to call me that."

Lama said, "You are my father, I love you. Even after all

you have done, I still love you." Drex was speechless. Lama was close to the door. Drex could not see her in her right hand, Lama had a rung from the chair. Between her and Shara sitting on the floor rubbing it to sharpen it to a point. Finally, the day had come, so she could use it.

Drex had his face close to the window, Lama waited, waited for the moment. Drex closed his eyes. His face close to the window.

"Shara you don't know how long I've waited for this day to come, someone, I could employee to kill you."

Drex came close to the window. He was cautious since the sword went through his arm. Yet Lama knew it was close enough. His eyes closed Lama pushed the rung through the window as hard as she could. Drex started to speak when the rung went into his mouth coming out his jowl. Blood was pouring from his mouth running down his throat staining his clothes. Going into spasms a choking sound like he was trying to speak.

Drex staggered down the corridor. Two guards came running, he was spitting blood.

Drex screamed, "Find that sentry. Tell him they die today."

After Drex left, the guards said, "You would think by now he would leave them alone." In the tower, I looked stunned.

I said, "Lama you tried again."

"I hate him, my lady. There was a time I wish I could kill him. All I think of now is I want to kill him."

I said, "Oh Lama, I do believe you." Lama sat with the rung in her hand. She had retrieved it.

Lama smiled at me, "Well my lady, it works just fine." As directed the sentry went to Drex. Talk between them, Drex explained.

"Sire, just what is it I'm to do," the sentry ask?

"There are two women in the tower, I want them dead. Whatever it takes I want it done."

"I understand," the sentry replied.

"Sire what do I do with the bodies? Do you wish to see

them?"

Drex thought for a moment. "I do not wish to see them. Take them out of the castle through the wall to the backgrounds, bury them both."

"As you wish sire." the sentry turned to leave. "Sire, you did say ten folds?"

Drex expressed, "Yes ten."

"My king that won't be necessary. I'm following your orders. I am a sentry."

Drex said, "Then go, kill them both." It was late morning when the sentry stood by the door of the tower.

"My lady," he called. Shara opened the window the sentry was the same one that brought the bread and fruit.

"My lady, Drex has ordered me to kill you and the girl." Passing a loaf of bread to us. He told me to take your bodies out of the castle. I have a plan I'm going to get you out of here, you must do as I say.

I handed them a bag, Lama asks, "What is in it.?" I told her blood from an animal. Shara took it from Lama.

She said, "I understand." Lama looked a little scared.

"When I tell you, open the door pour the blood over you, and the girl. There're a few guards that I know will come to take you out of the cell. Drex will probably want to see you. Pour the blood on your arm so it will drop off as we pass. Please lie still I'll let you know when we are safe."

The sentry sat outside the cell. A faint sound he heard behind him. He turned to see Drex standing in the corridor.

Drex asks, "Have you done it?" The sentry stood with a blood-soaked shirt, his arms were bloody.

"Yes, sire it is done." The cell was a bloody mess. Lama and Shara laid on top of a makeshift carrier, the cover was soaking up the blood. Drex told the guards to carry them outside the wall. Drex stood in front of the guards. Drex said, "Finally a real man." Then asked, "How did you, do it?"

"I have been here before sire, they knew me. I had no idea

who she was the queen. I suppose now, it doesn't matter." I told them I had bread and fruit they open the door; I cut both. I kept on slashing cutting stabbing until it was done. Sire, you didn't hear the screams, it is something I wish not to hear again. Sire I wish to do this myself." The guards that carried them out will be the only help I'll need.

"Go then," Drex said. "When it is finished come to me."

"As you wish sire."

Drex went back to his chambers. Thoughts running through his mind. Finally, I can get some rest, finally there dead. They cannot hurt me again. I thought, Shara was dead, so was Lama. I closed my eyes. The early morning sky seemed to hang low as if it knew what had happened. I had them killed. A tear fell from the corner of my eye, running down my face.

I turned to the right side; my left side was still bandaged from the wound Lama had inflicted on me. She stood waiting for me to get close when the time was right well, let me say, it hurt. They hurt me their last time, the bitch. Now I would sleep. Several hours had passed, darkness had come to Galaxo. The people had gone to their homes, lights were everywhere. The guard that killed Shara had returned. Walking to Drex door.

"Sire," he said.

Drex said to him, "Enter."

"Sire we dug the graves in the hills behind the castle. Dug them deep pushed rocks on top so they could not be seen. Sire did you know there's a trail that goes over the hill. Do you know where it goes?" I believe sire it goes over the mountains to the north." I sat listening, waiting for the sentry to speak.

I said to him, "It goes nowhere." I knew it went to the village to the north. It is said half breeds lived there. Humans and Claxton's mixed. Wonder why I never sent guards there.

The sentry said, "It is on that trail in the curve to the back of the castle is where we buried them." I told the sentry to leave me. Wait what is your name.

"Mick, Sire." I watched him go I stopped him again.

Galaxian

"How old are you sentry?"

"Twenty-two sire." I waved him on, walking away he held himself proud. Reminded me of someone from long ago. Thoughts ran through my mind. He knew what he had done. It did not seem to bother him. I looked at myself in the glass. I was scared for life, smiling I whispered, "It's over," she is dead.

CHAPTER 35

I left the chambers of Drex little did he know my Queen, and her guest was very much alive. The guards in I could trust, the ones that were still loyal to Icol, carried them from the castle. Blood was flowing down their arms. I was hopeful Drex would not lift the cover or they would not move, at least until we left the castle. Drex had no idea that I had betrayed him. He never would.

Going through the wall Shara and Lama were uncovered. I told them to follow me. We have a place of safety for you until dark comes. I told them one of my men went ahead to a dear friend.

My queen when the time is right, we will take you and Lama there. A bath will be prepared for you, fresh clothes will also be ready for you. You will get a hot meal, my lady. We have a place of safety for you. My men will keep you hidden until.

Lama looked at me, "Until what?"

I smiled, "Until Icol gets here. Maybe in two days, you will see your man to Lama."

Shara said, "Icol comes."

I said again, "In two days my lady. You will see what I say is true."

They both said at the same time, "You know this how."

I walked to them, gave them a cloth to wipe the blood from the arms. "I got you out of the castle, didn't I. You must trust me." We waited under a deadfall of a Huge tree that had fallen for some reason many years ago. The branches and leaves had made a natural shelter.

I could tell the queen and Lama were scared. I told them if someone did come by, they could not see us. We were completely hidden. My Queen with you gone, Drex will let down his guard. You will no longer be a thorn in his side.

Shara said, "I fought him for over twenty years, always trying to bed me. Only for his pleasure. I hate him always did. Even at a small boy in the streets of the village, always showing off. I was Something he thought he must have. Something he wanted to possess. He would bring my mother and father fruits all the time. I found out later he had taken them from the storekeepers without payment."

Lama sat quietly for several minutes, "Several months, I've been a prisoner in the tower. The only good thing about this was meeting you my lady, you and Nordic."

I ask, "Tell me, sentry, what is it you are called."

"I am Mick, not a common name."

"Your mother and father, who are they," I ask? "I mean there is something about you, how old are you."

"I said, "Old enough my lady, my mother was human, she raised me the best she could. She tried to hide me from Drex and his army."

Lama sat up, "Hid you, hid you for what reason?" I knew as I Lama talked, she was a smart girl.

Replying, "Let's just say, if Drex had found me, he surely would have killed me." Shara stood looking around.

I ask, "My lady can I help you with something." Reaching into my pack, I give her bread I had raped in cloth, it's all I have.

"Mick it will be enough, it's thoughtful of you," I said. There was a slight movement outside, a twig broke. Someone comes, I placed my hand up as to be quiet, there was silence for a moment.

I said in a whisper, "It's my men."

Lama asks, "Your men." I told her not to worry she is safe all the guards and sentry's Drex has, five of them is all I could trust There the oldest one. They were here served for your husband. My lady, they despise Drex for what he has done. When I told them you were alive, they went crazy. The first time I came to you, Drex had sent me to find what I could about Nordic."

"I was to find him and kill him. Looking at Lama I told her I fought him. In a field on the plains, we fought hard. I took his blade away. Beat him down to have the blood of a human in me, I almost killed him. I was sent to do just that. He called

Shara in the name of my Queen I'm sorry. Well, that stopped me."

I ask him, "What do you know of a queen?"

Nordic answered, "I know she is alive. I called her name because I can't help her, now kill me. That is what Drex sent you here for; is it not." Nordic had been careful not to leave a trail. Yet I found it was not so hard to follow. Shara stood again, so did Lama.

Lama said, "You keep saying the blood of a human. Why do you say that Mick? Why did your mother hide you from Drex? You speak of your mother not a word of your father. Why?"

I looked around to see where my men were. The guard that approached the deadfall said all was good in the castle, Drex was asleep. I told him to go to the village, make arrangements to receive the queen. I told him to have their bath ready with fresh clothes for them and us, tell no one."

"As you wish," he said. The guard left through the shadows. I told Shara and Lama to stay here, do not leave. You must not go out until I return. Please, do not go outside the deadfall. They both nodded their heads.

Shara asks, "Where are you going?" I told them I would be back shortly, something I must do.

I had seen three guards head up the trail, to the place I told Drex I had dug the graves. I wanted to see what they were up to. Leaving the women, I eased my way out of the deadfall walking up the sloping grade.

I stood in the shadows of the late evening, watching the men. I watched them move rocks around. I stepped from the trees.

One guard said to me as I walked up. "You the one that did this," I told them I was. You were never going to do it.

The guard replied, "You killed the queen and the daughter of Drex."

I said to them walking around, "What will you do if Icol

Galaxian

does come back. Will, you run or fight with Drex. Will you fight for the life you have, or for the one he will give you in prison on Advair." There was silence for several minutes.

One asks, "What do you know of a prison on Advair?"

I said, "Everyone knows Drex, sent Icol and Tenna there. They also know he has escaped."

"How do you know this," the guard said ask?" He pulled his sword?" You're the new sentry, you have been here only a few months. How can you know this?" I told them everyone knows. He looked at me as he pointed his sword.

"I bet you did not kill them. I bet they're not dead, you only made it appear that way. You pushed the rocks down on this place. If Drex wanted us to dig up the bodies, we can't now. I'm going to tell Drex this."

"I can't let you do that," I said.

"You're going to stop me," he asks? I told him no. I am going to stop all three of you. Stopping you would let the others run to Drex. No, I'm going to kill all three of you.

The mistake was made; they will make no more. They started laughing throwing their head back I took my blade pushed hard into one of their stomachs. Before the other two could stop laughing I thrust the middle one. One left he came at me. I tell you; I didn't know why Drex had them as a guard, they couldn't fight. I rolled their bodies in a ravine, darkness was coming to Galaxo one more.

I made my way back to the queen. She and Lama sat with their arms around each other. I could tell they were very afraid. They both looked at me they were shaking as they were cold.

I ask them, "What is wrong?"

Lama said, "We was afraid you would not return."

"Lama, if I had not returned, my men would have carried on." It was a beautiful night, I said as much.

Shara said, "My nights have been as days since Icol had been gone. Always living with the threat of Drex. So many times, he came to me. Each time I would push him away. I tried

345

so many times to have the guard try to get me out. They were as afraid of Drex, as anyone. I know, I saw him kill several. Mick, if I die before I see my husband, please tell him I did wait."

I looked at the two women, "My lady if you or Lama die it will be after I draw my last breath. I will fight to that point; this I promise you."

Lama looked at me strangely. She was still trying to determine who or what I was? I did appear to them to be human. The silence was broken by Lama.

"Mick, she said, "I do want to think you for what you have done for us. You keep saying the human blood in you. Your half-human tell us what you mean." I dropped my head. Then looked at Shara.

"My lady, my mother was one of your handmaidens. My father was Tenna. I'm half-human, half Claxton." I took the scarf from my head, so my ears would show. They were kind of pointed not as much as the Claxton's.

I said, "All my life my mother made me wear this scarf. She would never let me play very long with the others. My mother's dead. It was some time ago on the plains, I buried her. I lived with the family. I was gone into the Trions when Drex sent his guards for the daughter. The old man got away with the girl not before the girl saw the guards kill her mother."

"Urea, his daughter, and a girl named Pru. They went to the Trions with a man from the village named Pena. Drexs guards found them kill all except Pur. Pru escaped with the Advairan. I do not know where she is now. My lady, I am a warrior, loyal to Icol, the true king. I'm waiting for his return, him and my father Tenna."

"I went to the Trions, I never found the Claxton's. I did find their signs. They watched every move I made. Yet I still don't know why they did not come to me. The talk was going on between us when I singled them to silence.

In a low whisper, I said to them, "Someone comes."

"Mick," the guard called, "it is arranged. It is time to leave."

Easing from the deadfall one of the men stayed behind to watch our trail. Just in case someone follows. Working around the wall through a hole then to the house where plans had been made for the queen and Lama.

Down the steps, we walked through a cellar door. We waited for anything. Inside the room, two women waited. Lama and Shara took off their hoods the women caught their breath, both kneeled tears filled their eyes.

"My lady," they said.

"Shara said please don't kneel to me." On the left two tubs of water were waiting. Lama's mother was one of the women. She took her daughter in her arms as tears flowed down, her face.

I said, "My lady please you must take a bath, Lama, too. This must be done so we can leave before the sun."

The two women started to remove their clothes. The man handed me a bag of clothes. He said, "for you and the others." Thanking him I walked outside, where the other men were keeping watch. Changing our clothes, we waited for the queen. An hour had passed when the two appeared. The man told us we could pass the guards they were asleep. A little herb in the tea.

Going around the corner I could see the gate was down, the guard was asleep. Making our way from the village to the road to the plains was an easy walk. The sun was up by the time we reached the house of Basco. I looked at the girls, I could see they were ready for sleep. I was thankful for the house.

The morning sun had turned the sky into an orange glow. Walking through the door I saw a shadow across the room, a man jumps me. Knocking him down I drew my sword.

"Wait, wait," he said.

"Who are you," I ask?

He replied, "I am Iams." Lama said, turning to see her. Lama said, "He is one of Drex's guards."

He said, "I was one. I have been with Nordic and Nonik.

There at the cave at the Trions. He saw the Queen as she took off the hood. "My lady, I was ordered to find and kill Nordic, I left to join him. We left the plains to the Trions waiting for Icol. There's over a hundered Claxton's in the hills waiting.

"Icol is coming, within two days he will arrive, I have a scruple hid. We wait here until dark, I'll take you there. I told him; I know where it is. I am a half Claxton. He looked at me with that look. I pushed my hair back to show my ears. You would think the red hair would be enough. Only Claxton's has red hair.

"I will be damn, Iams said. I told him if you lie I will kill you.

Iams said, "I do not lie. I want Drex out of power as much as anyone. I want him dead." Everyone was in the house when the sound of a scruple come into the yard. I told Iams to go to the door. I smiled you still have your uniform on. Dirty as he was, he walked to the door.

The guards walk to the door as Iams walked outside. One of the guards knew him.

Iams, he said, "Iams you look rough."

Iams replied. "I've been gone for a month looking for Nordic and Nonik."

The guards said, "I thought they were dead."

Iams answered, "no, they're not dead." Showing the cut on the arm from a fight.

"You fought them," the guard ask?

Iams said, "I fought them. They ran to the scruple got away."

The guards ask, "what are you here at the house of Basco?" Iams told them he was going to get a bath before he went to Drex.

The guards said to Iams. "You do that Iams," he said, "Change your clothes too." The guards went aboard their scruple left.

I posted a guard outside the door to watch for anyone that may come. Tea had been made. I give Iams a cup sitting on the stoop.

I ask Iams, "Why are you here?"

Taking a drink of his tea Iams said, "I wanted to see what was going on. "My lady I speak the truth." Iams looked at Lama, "Your Nordic's woman?

"I will be," Lama said, "He has asked for me." Iams told her they wait at the cave, I promise." I came from the stoop, everything is good, the night is coming."

"My lady you and Lama go to the bedroom rest. Iams, and I will talk for a while." Sitting having our tea, Iams told me of the Claxton's coming from the mountain. They sent a runner ahead. Nordic and Nonik were having council when I told them I was coming here.

Iams said, "I must find out what is going on in the castle and the village." I told him it should be left alone. When darkness falls, we should take the scruple to go to the cave, wait there for Icol.

As we sat around the table Iams ask, "You know anything your people?"

I ask, "Which ones, the humans or the Claxton's."

Iams smiled, "The Claxton's of course." I told him I only know what my mother told me. There was a Claxton who came to me after I buried her. I told Iams my mother was human. She was the queen's handmaiden. She fell in love with a Claxton. I read somewhere the Claxton's could come and go as they pleased. Iams said, "you said a Claxton came to you, what did he want." I told him he trained me. The warrior stayed with me for several months, one morning he was gone.

Kohl and his wife settled on Galaxo hundreds of years ago. The Claxton's met them when they landed. Their story was told the chief of the Claxton's gave them exile here. He showed them the valley where the water is pure, the ground was fertile."

The chief____ told them they could build a castle. He told them no large building. The chief showed them where to build their hangers, for their ships. Time went on Kohl died, some said from his wife's passing. That's is in the writing. Kohl was over one thousand years old. Icol is a descendant of Kohl.

When I was about seven years old, I saw the Claxton's in the village. I remember they did come and go as they pleased. Then one day, they did not come again, it was when Drex took power. When Drex took over he killed all that was left, except Tenna, Icols right-hand man.

I said to Iams, "Tenna is my father. My mother had left the village before she gave birth to me. She told me I was a small boy when she came back. I always thought Tenna was dead. My mother's brother was Urea. He told me all I needed to know.

Drex sent Icol and Tenna to prison on Advair. My uncle told me that, how he knew this I can't say. It was said Icol and Tenna escaped over a year ago. I don't understand why it's taking him so long to come back." Iams sat on a log eating a slice of bread.

"A Claxton runner came to the cave the night I left," Iams said. He told us of the Claxton's coming from the mountains. They were coming to help Icol to take back the castle.

They want him dead. It was said he must not leave the village. What I don't understand is how they always know when a ship comes. I told Iams the Claxton's have a very powerful mind they can go anywhere with their thoughts.

Iams said, "Maybe they have a communications device we don't know of."

I looked at Iams, "I doubt that." I said.

Iams said, "You said, your mother died on the plains." I told him again she did. I dug the grave myself after I pulled my thought together, I went to the house of Urea. I worked with him for two years. That's when the Claxton came to me.

Drex started sending his patrols, taking what they wanted, that's when the guards saw the girl. The guards told Urea when she is of age, we will come for her. Now they're all dead, I want him dead I told Iams.

Iams said, "You need to get in line there are hundreds that want the same thing. If you take all the young girls in the village, they would be Drex, daughter. Can you imagine sleeping with your daughter? Well, you know Drex is not a normal man." I told him after two more days that will never happen again.

CHAPTER 36

Drex awakened with the sun on his face. Standing looking out the window, turning looking at his image he cursed Shara and Lama. I'm glad they're dead. Walking in the chambers two guards waited.

"Sire the three you sent to the back of the castle. Sire, they have not returned."

Drex said, "Send two guards, find them bring them to me."

"As you wish sire," then he was gone. Drex called to the sentry, who is left in the maiden chambers.

The sentry replied, "Two girls' sire, one is twenty-three the other thirteen."

I sat waiting for the sentries to return. I told the guard, when the sentry's return, let me know. I walked to the chambers where the two girls were. Walking into my sleeping chamber the two girls sat waiting. I told them to undress. The young one said to Drex.

"Do what you will with me sire, I'm here for you and you alone. I promise you I will not push you away." The older one said the same."

Drex was lying on the bed, the girls started to love him. The excitement was too much for Drex's face. He let out a scream both girls jumped back, "we're very sorry sire."

Drex said, "Only one of you, the young one." The pleasures, Drex had remembered come crashing through. The feeling of pleasure was full, the feeling he had not had in such a long while.

"More, more," he said. "Work it more." The girl gave out a scream, fell off Drex, with a jerking motion. The girl laid on the bed for several minutes. "Sire, may I speak freely?"

Drex said to her speak, "I will give you a son, you will see. Sire from this day I want no other man in me. You will be mine if you will have me."

Drex said as he lies on the bed with the other woman beside him. His hand was all over her. "A son you may have for me. From you, I only want my pleasures." What Drex said made the girl angry.

The older girl said, "Move, let me show him what a real woman can do."

The girl started to climb on Drex the girl said, "I'll show you a real woman." The girl took the blade Drex had by the bed, she made a violet swing, cutting the woman's head off.

Pointing the blade at Drex. "A son I will have. Remember, that could have been you." Drex looked at the beheaded woman lying on the floor. Blood was oozing from where the head once was.

For the first time, Drex felt fear. It was not from his brother coming home, not fear of the Claxton's coming from the mountain. Drex felt fear from a woman. All the years Drex had Shara in prison, his daughter he almost killed her, yet he was in control. This young woman sat with the sword in her hand looking at Drex he was excited, fully erected.

She said, "Now lie back." Drex did as the woman said, she was still holding the blade.

Placing one leg on each side of Drexs body. She raised just enough to take his penis in her hand. Stroking it to see the look on his face. She could tell this made him feel good.

She asks, "Do you like this, Drex"

Drex replied, "I do, put it in please I need you now." She guided his penis inside the lips of her sex canal rubbing it up and down. She let it play between the vaginal canal. She sat back on his penis until she sat on his stomach. Moving so vigorously, if nothing else Drex was a full man. She moaned just enough to let him know it won't belong.

Drex was all the way in, she tried to get all his penis in her as she could. She moved vigorously on top looking at Drex. She moves so fast, Drex screamed as he moved.

Drex, she said, "I love you, make it go deeper." This excited Drex never had he had a girl so full of excitement. For the second time, he was enjoying it.

She started screaming, "Don't lose it yet, please, please he was yelling, please.

"Oh, please stop."

Drex said, "Not so fast stop."

She yelled, "Now Drex, now let it go, oh Drex let it go." She was screaming so loud, moving vigorously she made a final scream. It was as if she was in pain. Then she fell off jerking as if she was freezing.

She was lying beside Drex, he looked at this young girl. Her breast was full to be her age. She had a full body not as full as Shara, yet it was nice.

Drex asks, "Will it always be like this."

She said, "Know my love, sometimes I promise you it will be better."

Drex asked the girl, "I need your name?"

Replying, she said, "My name is Venice. My mother said I was named from a planet somewhere." Drex raised in the bed.

Venice said, "Please stay with me please."

Drex said, "We need to get up, so the guards can clean up the mess you made." Looking at the floor she said, "Oh yes that. The bitch pissed me off. I did not want her to have you. I will give you a son, you will see." Drex called to the guards.

As the guards enter, they ask, "Sire what has happened? Sire the people from the village will ask of her. "That's why I called you to clean it up. I'll give you the right side of me."

"As you wish sire." He replied.

I turned to leave with my newfound woman. Somehow with her, I felt different. I had no idea what was going on. The only thing was it was a different feeling.

I called to the guards," Guard the sentry I sent, has he returned."

"No sire, he has not."

Drex said, "Find out, what is going on in the ranks now?"

Sending another sentry to check, walking through the wall in the back of the castle he saw nothing. Walking along the wall he saw the sentry all dirty.

"What has happened to you," he asked? The sentry told the guard he found the guards. Their bodies were rolled into a ravine. I moved rocks, dirt, wood there were no bodies where the graves were supposed to be.

Drex had promised the guard the right side for removing the body of the girl. He told the sentry this.

The guard asks, "Do you know who the two females were."

"Look," he said, I'm a sentry, it doesn't matter, he is my king."

I knew how he felt. I told him anyway the woman was the true queen of Galaxo. She was Queen Shara. The fourteen-year-old was Drex, daughter. Well, then it was true what people have said. I told him to do what you must, I'll stand beside you.

I simply said, "Icol is coming, do as you wish." I helped him off the ground, we went to Drex.

Entering the castle Drex asks, "What has happened to you?"

"Sire, the guards you sent will not be returning, they're dead. I found their bodies in a ravine, someone has killed them."

"Why are you so dirty," Drex asked?

Replying, "I alone sire, dug the dirt moved the rocks from the graves of the queen and your daughter. They are their sire, just as the sentry said. the one with the scarf.

Drex asks, "Where is that sentry, guards find him."

Venice said, "I was going to kill them myself. Now with Shara gone maybe, I can make you happy. Drex no more girls are to be brought to the castle."

Drex looked at her, "As you wish my dear. Guard, send a message to all in the village, there will be no more women brought to the castle.

Drex started to speak when a disturbance started outside. Facing the guards Drex told them to find out what was going on. Walking to the ground floor, then to the outside, the guard opened the door, Iams stood. The guard was staring at the man he thought was long dead," Iams," he said.

Instead of taking a bath, Iams came as he was. Thanks to

Shara for pointing it out. Shara told him if he appeared clean, Drex would have suspected something.

Everyone was asking me all kinds of questions. Everyone wanted to know if I had seen Icol or the Claxton.

I did manage to tell one of the storekeepers, Icol would be here in two days. I told him as I embraced him. I told him in a low whisper to spread the word to the ones he could trust; ones that are not loyal to Drex. While the sentry's spread the word the guards escorted me to Drex.

Drex said to his guards, "Go to the village, tell them I have found a queen."

There was a concern on all faces. Who was this girl Drex had found? Who was the mother, all looked on as word was passed? A woman came to the sentry, "what has happened to my daughter? She is a tall light-haired girl." I the guard did not tell her she was dead. He said to her, she is at the castle.

A woman with long black hair said, "he has chosen Venice, she is my daughter." The woman turned walked away.

Walking into the castle I was carried straight to Drex. The guards called to Drex.

"Sire Iams is here." Drex looked at me, I must have looked like a sad man. Standing in front of him, he shook his head.

Drex said to me, "Come here, Iams. What do you know of Nordic and Nonik?"

Iams said, "Sire I know they are alive."

Drex asks, "You know this for a fact?"

I said, "I do sire, I found them living in a farmhouse on a remote part of the plains. The other guards you sent I watch then kill everyone. Just two days ago I found Nordic and Konik. They were rushing in on me when a ship raced across the sky. They ran for their scruple. Sire for four-month I've looked for them. Only eating what I could find, sorry for the way I stand before you, I had no clothes for a bath, so I come here anyway to report."

Drex said to Iams, "You left me because you could not

kill the queen. You could not kill the one that said she was my daughter. Iams, I am surprised you fought Nordic when you could not even kill two women."

Jumping up I said, "Those two women were not trying to kill me. How dare you question my loyalty to you." Drex turned looked hard at Iams.

Drex said, "I have another task for you, Iams." Drex told the guard to take me to the place where the bodies were. Have him dig them up.

Iams looked in disbelief. "Surely sire, not even you would disturb the dead."

"Take him," Drex said with a stern voice.

Now I wasn't sure what was going on, or if he lied to Drex about the queen. Now Iams knew the queen was alive. This he told me later. We walked fast to get outside the wall.

Iams whispered to me, "we need to get away." Iams told the sentry to go retrieve two shovels for us to dig. They had no idea what was about to happen. When the sentry went for the shovel, we made a break in a hard run around the wall. We hid until the time was right. Approaching the gate just before sunset, when everyone was coming in.

The gate guard asks, "Where are you going?" I told them we were going looking for an old friend.

One of the guards said, "Iams take a bath." I told him when I'm free of the hole I will. We were well outside the gate, with the castle well behind us. Iams said, "Let run." That's what we did until we reached the house of Basco.

Mick was on watch when we walked up. Iams told him we need to leave now. We need to go to the Trions, they will be coming at first light when they find we have left. I walked to the back of the house stopped in my tracks. I could not believe my eyes. Lying on the bed was Lama and the queen.

I went to my knee; "My lady, I'm truly sorry for the way you have been treated. I am so glad you're not in that grave."

Shara replied, "Yes sentry, so am I."

Shara asks him, "What is Drex up to." I told her that Drex had taken two women to the castle. The girl called Venice killed one. Venice is to become queen. Drex will know by tomorrow you're not in the graves. He sent Iams and me to dig up the graves.

Shara asks him, "What is it your called?"

Replying, "I am Oyd, my lady."

Shara said, "Well Oyd, we need to move." It was almost dark outside. To me, it could not come fast enough. There was a noise as steel was hitting. Mick was in a fight with someone.

I and Iams dashed the outside. Mick could not see who had come up, it was Nordic. I yelled to Mick, as he jumped back.

Nordic said, "You fight well."

Mick replied, "Yes I do, I'm half Claxton. We have fought before." Nordic came closer to Mick.

"Yes, I see you now, something different."

Mick said, "I no longer wear the scarf."

"That's good son, whoever you are you are a warrior," Nordic said.

We stood talking for several minutes. Mick and I told Nordic of what has happened.

Nordic said, "Then you have the queen here."

"She is in the house Nordic, with your woman." Nordic ran to the house. Opening the door Shara stood with a sword in hand.

Nordic said, "My lady, I hope you won't need that." Shara dropped the sword she and Lama ran to me.

Shara gave me, an embrace. "Good to see you Nordic," she said.

Looking at Lama Nordic said, "My queen it's good to be seen."

Lama said to Nordic, "I knew you would come; our time is close, you must know what is happening." Iams told Nordic what is going on inside the castle.

Iams ask, "Why did you come here? You were supposed to

stay with Nonik."

Nordic said, "I come to see if I could find her, maybe try to help if I could." All that was going on, the time had gotten away for all.

The gray dawn of morning was upon us, I told everyone we need to go. Oyd came running in, scruple coming. Two guards, we had no lights on, it looked as if no one was here. Pulling up at the house of Basco one of the guards walked around the house, the other one walked to the porch.

Nordic whispered to Mick, "Your closest to the door. When he comes in, kill him."

Mick smiled, "Oh I have no problem doing that." Being very quiet yet ready for anything the door started to open.

The guard in the yard said, "Come on there's no one here. You could hear the guard say.

"Whatever happened to Basco, who lived here. He's been gone for a very long time. No one has seen him."

The guards said, "I could care less." The scruple left toward the castle.

CHAPTER 37

The sun had started to set over the Trions, two guards reported to Drex. All dirty from the digging, "Sire there is no grave. The three men were in the ravine as said. Someone has crossed you, sire."

Drex screamed pointed to Venice, "Go to the chambers." Venice left in a run; she could see Drex was mad, very disturbed.

Drex said, to the guards, talking between his teeth. "Find me that sentry, the one that wears the scarf. Find him bring him to me." Several hours had passed. Searching the village, the homes of everyone in the village, the sentry went back to Drex.

The gate guard said to sentry's, "Iams left this morning going to the hole in the wall." Drex said as he looked at all that stands before him.

"No one crosses me and lives. Go find them, Iams and the sentry with him find them, bring them to me."

Drex knew now that Queen Shara and Lama had escaped. Now he was scared. Drex walked to his quarters, Venice was looking out the window. Drex thought how beautiful she was even at thirteen, she was all woman.

"My love," Venice asks, "what can I do?"

Drex said with tears in his eyes. "For over twenty years I've had Shara in the towers, hidden away. She would be my shield if Icol ever returned."

Venice said, "Drex don't worry about her or of him. I truly do not believe he will ever return. Maybe if your brother has escaped, she will go to him. Maybe they will leave this world."

"Venice if Icol come back, and I truly believe he will, he will come here to kill me. I suppose Venice it's my faith."

Venice said, "what of your son." Drex told her you may have a son Venice; it will not be mine.

Drex said, "I can't believe she escape so easily. That damn sentry, I'll have his head for this." The guards waited outside of the castle, waiting on Drex to appear. Some of the people wanted to know what was going on.

Walking out on the pier Drex said," Bring me Iams and the

sentry. Bring the one that wears the scarf around his head. I'll give you anything you want." This is Venice if I die, she will carry on. Believe me, you had rather deal with me than her. Now go, you will be highly rewarded. People of Galaxo, believe me, she will carry on. Now go find the three men I speak of."

What Drex did not know was the guards would find the three. Yet they would never return. The house of Basco was the first stop. Outside the house, the head guard said to the men.

"Let's split up, one goes south one east, one west. Go to the edge of the planet if you must." Each searched for hours leading into the day, finding nothing. The guards decided to stop for the night, never being heard of again. The one to the south found the house of Urea. The same place where Nordic, Nonik, Iams was. They had left days before.

As the guards to the east searched for hours finding nothing, the sun had set.

One said, "We'll spend the night here." Lighting a light, starting the stove, each guard made a meal. Finding a cellar talking a few things, including a writing tablet.

Look one guard said, "Nordic was here, he wrote of his stay." The guards looked out the window after their meal. The night had come to the plains once more. The guards made their meal eating in silence for several minutes.

One said, "Tell me, why does no one go to the north. Every time a patrol is sent out, no one goes to the north. What is to the North? Some say it's just mountains. Some say other things. I remember once someone there is a village of half-breed Claxton's lived there. They would kill anyone that comes."

One said, "I don't believe that. If that was the case Drex would already have them killed. "it's just what I've heard," he said.

The gray morning sky showed the outline of the foothills of the Trions. Making a meal we gathered our thing loaded them into the Scruple. Walking around the house I could see why Nordic, stayed here so long.

I had been in the service of Drex for eighteen years. I wanted to see what was north. I told the other guards that were with me we would bypass the castle, go over the small hill to the north. Maybe we will find that city you told me about.

The guard smiled, "I tell you this, there is no one on this planet except us and the Claxton's. When the sun comes to the plains, we will leave to the north."

Now it is said the Claxton's were supreme warriors. The scruple that went west was going to find out what they have heard. One scruple six men.

One guard said, "Look, someone is there." Everyone searched the woods saw nothing. The scruple moved close to the base of the mountain. Close to the very trail to the path to the Claxton city. Yet the guards didn't know this.

The scruple stopped just a few hundered feet from the cave. Nonik thought as he looked around. Outside a scream then loud sound. In the dark of the cave with only the light from the outside, I looked up standing before me was a full-grown Claxton.

"I am Ra, do not be afraid." Thoughts in my mind, I'm dead. Standing up I told him, I'm not afraid of you. I know who you are. I don't know your name; I know you by your appearance.

He said to me, "Do not worry about the guards, there are others. One to the south that will be going to the north. One to the east, they will never return. There is over a hundred of Claxton's. We wait for Icol. "

I said to him, "I'm beginning to believe there is no such person."

Ra said, "Then you have been misled. A ship will come tomorrow, mid-day. Icol will be on that ship. The queen is on her way here."

I jump up, "Shara is coming here, how," I ask?

Ra said, "She and the girl that was with her, escaped with the help of a half-breed Claxton. Nordic and Iams, are bringing them here. They will arrive by sunrise." Ra told me to come with him. You can stay with us at our camp tonight.

I said, "I did not think the Claxton would let humans stay with them. With a voice, I'll never forget.

He said, "Sometimes there is the exception, we like the taste of the human when it is roasted." Then laughed out loud.

"Come, Konik, I was only as you say joking." Well, I did not know what to think after that. I wasn't sure I would be eaten, or what. In the camp, Claxton was coming and going, whispering to each other. Looking at me as to what piece they wanted.

A Claxton was coming to me. "Don't worry about the guards they're dead, lying on the floor of the plain." I thought good enough for them. Drex had sent them to their death. Yet it wasn't the first time that Drex had done this.

Ra sat back against a tree, he started to talk to me about Shila.

I said, "I know her only as a storekeeper's daughter. I was with the guards the morning she went to Basco, she never returned."

Ra kept talking he said, "Shila has become a strong warrior with my people. Shila will kill you if she or her family, as she says, is threatened. She was the first human female ever to be trained by the Claxton's. She has killed several men. Shila has been in combat on several planets."

I ask Ra, "How do you know this, have you seen this."

Ra said, "One only needs to look to see. I see with my mind, all Claxton's do. Don't forget Konik, a being's mind is more powerful than the sword."

I smiled at Ra, "I'll take the sword." I told him as I smiled at him. I'll admit humans are not as smart or intelligent as the Claxton's. We have not been trained to use our brains.

Ra said, "Shila can, Fina, Dred. Tenna." My head kind of came up.

"Tenna," I said, "Tenna was well respected in our village at one time."

Ra said, "He still is in mine." We sat talking about several things.

Ra said, "Shila has the blood of her ancient ancestors. She is not like other human women. She has the blood of Lola. Blood of Destiny, all come for the blood of Mya. My grandfather has seen this. Shila will defeat Drex in battle, she will kill Drex." I thought as I lie back. If she does, she will be the first to do what others have wanted to do for a very long time, even me.

There were Claxton's coming from the hills all around us. There were changing of the guards. I was not sure why we needed guards. Drex would not send guards at night.

Ra said to me, "Konik we will leave for the plains when it gets full dark. You're not afraid of the dark are you." I told him I was not. Yet I did say I thought we were on the plains.

Ra replied, "The ships will come further to the south. Will meet Nordic and Iams. The queen will be with him. By daybreak, all will come together."

I ask Ra, "When will the ship come?"

Ra said, "I'm not sure, I just know it will come."

I ask, "Then how does Nordic know we will be there?"

Ra said, "My friend, you ask a lot of questions." Ra told me to try to rest, you will need it. I sat down by a small tree. Looking around I fell asleep.

I did sleep very well, I must say. Then a soft hand touched my shoulder. "

"Konik," a voice said, "Time to go." I stood rubbed my eyes, looking around.

I said, "Wow did more of you come in while I was asleep."

Ra said, "The Claxton's want Drex gone. Yet each of them, know it will be Shila that kills Drex."

The morning had come once again to the world we lived in. I always have loved this planet, of course, I have never been anywhere else. Maybe someday I'll find myself on a ship going somewhere.

I ask Ra? "How many Claxton's are there?"

Replying, "Enough I suppose. Konik, we're all over the planet. Never seen unless we want to be seen. The scruple that went to the east will never be seen again. The one that is going north will never return."

I ask, "What of the others?"

Ra said, "You already know of them. When the ships land, we will join Icol and Tenna."

CHAPTER
38

I could not believe Icol. The help of Basco, the Claxton's, the Advairan, the people of Corning, and the Moon of Spores. Icol believes I am going to try to take his stupid throne. I don't want it. Since leaving home for almost two years. I've grown into a beautiful woman, a supreme warrior. I have made a wonderful friend with Fina. Sometimes I don't know where I would be without her.

Dris, the love of my life. Yet I could not let him in, not just yet. Basco well, what could I say of a man that took a young girl and treated her like a daughter. There's Dred; what can you say of a being that never said much, yet when he does, everyone listened.

Dred stood with me on Plano with his sister, side by side. Watching Dred fight was exciting. Dred would kill a person as fast as I would. Dred as his sister will always be with me.

The same as Dris, I feel Basco will go home after this. Me, I still had in my mind to go to Earth. I feel this will be later in the future.

We were two more days before home. I was in deep meditation when a soft hand touched my shoulder. It was a soft touch yet firm. A touch I've never felt before. My eyes open looking up, I could not believe what I saw. Tenna stood over me with his hands stretched out.

Tenna said, "Come with me Shila, we must talk."

I said, "Our King, should he not be here in this meeting."

"Shila Icol is the one that sent me; please, come." Tenna and I walked down the corridor. We entered a room with a table and two chairs.

I ask Tenna, "Where are we?"

"A place we can talk," Tenna said. "Much to talk about." You know I thought with all my training I was no fool. I could sense there was another presence in the room. In the room, I could see the outline of a man. I told Tenna, I will sit in this chair.

Tenna said, "Very well Shila, you're not a trusting person,

are you?"

I replied to him, "I'm trusting enough Tenna. It's the one in the shadows I'm not sure of."

Tenna said, "I'm not sure what you mean, Shila."

I ask Tenna, "What is this about?"

Tenna said, "Icol has asked me to talk to you about certain things."

I looked at him, "What things Tenna?" There was a silence for a minute. Tenna was looking down at the table.

I said again, "What things Tenna?"

Tenna said, "Icol is afraid, you will rise against him."

"Tenna I have said, all I want to do is place him back in power. Place him back on the throne. I want to remove his awful brother." I slapped the table stood up. "Tenna if I wanted the throne why would I fight so hard to place him back. Why would I help him, why would I do anything for him? Tenna I'm almost fifteen years old. If I wanted the throne why would I not just go kill Drex like I'm going to do and take it? You have been gone a long time Tenna. I believe you have grown soft." Well, I could see the rage in his eyes.

Tenna I said, "Believe me, I want nothing to do with his throne; except to try and protect it. When this is over, and it will be over soon. I will come to Icol ask him for a ship. If he won't give me one, I'll have one come to me."

Tenna looked skeptical at me. "What does that mean Shila?

I said to Tenna. "I'll call to the old one from the planet that disappeared. They will come when I need them."

"Oh, I see," Tenna said.

"Tenna I do not want my King's throne. That is for him and the queen. Tenna why do you think we left Galaxo. Look, I do not know the queen. I do know she will be there when we arrive. You're a Claxton Tenna, you have been gone too long. Have you forgotten how to meditate? Follow your heart, your mind. Tenna, can't you see who I am, can't you see what I stand for." We sat for several minutes just looking"

I stood up and said, "Is that all Tenna."

Tenna said, "No." Icol asks for you not to kill Drex." Well, now I was pissed off. I slammed the table as it moved from where it was. I drew my sword the fastest I've ever pulled it. It went to his throat before he could react. I applied just enough pressure. There was a horrid look in his eyes.

Tenna I said, "Do not get in my way. If you or anyone tries to stop me, from killing Drex, I will kill them, or I'll die trying. Tenna if I die someone else will take my place. You may stop me, Dris, Fina, even Basco. You will not stop Dred. Dred has sworn to his father to protect me. He will do just that. I looked at the shadow good enough for you Icol." I started for the door.

Icol came from the shadow. "You bother me Shila," I told him, Icol you should be honored I'm on your side. I have crossed several galaxies to find you, I have killed several. I have put my body in harm's way more than once for you, Just, to place you and the queen back on your throne. What is it you see in me you can't trust? Is it because I'm a woman? Maybe because I can call the old ones, your very ancestors. Ones you have said you read about. Icol I tell you now, it will be different when we return home.

When your brother is dead, and you're on the throne, then and only then will we be free. I turned to leave; please excuse me I have another thing to attend to.

"Shila," Icol said. "I'm not sure what it is about you that scares me. Yet the feeling is there. I feel a betrayal kind of feeling."

I said to him once more. "Icol I do not want your throne just a ship, a ship to go to Earth. It will take us several years to go there and return. I have my crew, there will be others here, Corning, the Moon of Spores. That is all I will say." I bowed to Icol, I said to him, "Goodnight my king.

Shila please do not kill Drex. I had not placed my sword back in the sheath. I turned so fast I pointed my sword.

I said with hate in my voice, "Tenna you need to talk to

him. Tenna you or my king need to stay out of my way. If you try to stop me Icol, that betrayal you speak of, I promise you, you will see it. While you were in prison you have a clue what Drex did. You have no idea what the people had to give up. He killed all the Claxton's that was left in the village.

Mothers and fathers give up their daughter, for his pleasure. Even his daughters, he took to bed. I made a promise to some, I would kill anyone that stands in my way."

Icol said, "I'll give you a ship Shila if you don't kill him. I know you have the right.

I looked at the two of them, "Stay out of my way or I'll kill you."

"Shila," Tenna said, that's treason against the king."

I said to them again, "Stay out of my way."

A voice spoke behind me, I never took my eyes from them I didn't need to it was Dred.

Dred said, "If she doesn't kill him I will."

Icol looked at Tenna, "See what I mean, she has too much power over them." I placed my sword back in the sheath.

"Icol tomorrow we will be in orbit above the planet of Galaxo. You have until then to give me the answer about the ship. My king do not betray me. Don't tell me one thing, do another." I left started back to my room.

I heard Dred say, "Tenna, I have seen in meditation the council has spoken. Drex dies or the humans will leave Galaxo. That is all I will say. I will follow Shila so will Fina, Basco, and Dris. We've all have pledge our loyalties to her. That was sworn in the city of the Claxton's."

"As she has said to the king. If something happens to her, I will carry on. I do not want to fight you. You must think about what this man has done."

Icol said, "He is still my brother."

Drex replied, "He has imprisoned you, your wife for over twenty years."

"I know what he has done Dred. As I've said, he is still my

brother. After tomorrow, he won't be any longer."

Leaving Icol and Tenna I went to my room to find Fina gone. Walking to the galley I told everyone what had happened. The crew said were with you Shila we want him dead.

"Shila we will follow you if you go to Earth. We wish, to be a part of it. Icol heard this as he walked behind me to the galley. Icol told Tenna again, see how powerful she is.

Tenna said, "Sire she is right. Drex must die. I've always wanted to kill him myself. Twenty years we were in prison, he took your chance to have a child. Who will carry on when you leave? Every day in prison I thought of ways to kill him."

"Tenna he is my brother; I can't do it."

Tenna said, "Don't worry, there are hundreds that will."

Icol jumped up, "I do not wish him dead. I am the King of Galaxo. The people must listen to me. Icol said Shila has won."

Tenna said, "Won what sire? She has fought hard to place you back in power. Look what she has done in the name of the king, Shila is right. Twenty years in prison. You must have an ill feeling of him. Think of all he has done. Prison on Advair is not good enough. No sire Shila will kill him." We sat in silence for a few minutes.

Icol said, "How do you expect to take over the castle when we arrive."

Tenna said, "There's going to be a fight. Drex my escape he may not. Even if he does sire, where would he go."

Icol looked at me. "Tenna you have stood beside me. You are a dear friend. Drex would go to the north. I've never told you Tenna, there's a small village there."

"Sire do you forget who I am. There's no place Drex can run. There's Claxton's all over the planet. It has been seen by the old ones that Shila will be the one to kill Drex. Stand in her way she will kill you.

Tenna asks, "Is that what you want after the fighting of the other planets. The coming to Corning, the fight on Plano. Sire is that what you want. Sire Dred told me of the meeting with the old ones. Shila has been tried several times, she has passed all trials that have been placed before her. Sire, I for one will not stand in her way. I will fight with her for all she has said I see; she tells the truth."

Icol looked at me, "You Tenna, you will stand against me." I will not stand against you, that I would never do. I will fight to place you back in power. You know as well as anyone, Drex needs to die. If he went to prison, he would escape, gather an army come again, you know this.

Tomorrow we will be on the plains. We'll meet with the guards and the Claxton's. We'll see what they say." Icol set quiet as I left him sitting at the table. I could see his thoughts went wild.

I sat long at the table after Shila left. Walking to the portal we were traveling so fast. Everything was a blur. Seeing the other ships was the only thing I could make out. The speed we were going I had no idea, yet to look at the ships it appeared we were sitting still, how I'm not sure.

My thought went back to Drex. I didn't want him dead. I wanted him in prison. I wanted him there, so I could go taught him. Let him see me with Shara. Maybe when I see her, I will ask her what she wants; then I will be content. Sipping a cup of tea, I thought of Shila. She has told me several times about what had happened. Yet why have I not asked Basco of this? I turned from the portal as someone entered the room.

A voice called, "Sire I'm captain of the ship. I have been for over fifty years. I took your father into space to several places."

"Captain, how can I help you," I ask?

"Sire, what Shila tells you is the truth. Your brother Drex, is as she says. I had no idea the queen was still alive. We were told by Drex she had been killed. He also told us you and the Claxton were also dead.

It was said later in the days to come a guard, had seen the queen. Word got back to Drex. He took his head in the square. He said this is what happens when someone defines me. Sire if a man ever needs killing its Drex.

I put my hands up, "Stop, I wish not to hear any more of this."

Sire before I left to join this crusade my daughter was taken to him. Drex had his way with her. I spoke to my wife, if it was a male child, I would kill the child myself. The child was born was a female. We named her from a planet we read of in the archives. We named her Venice. She is of age now she has I feel by now been taken to Drex. That's all I have to say, sire."

"You see sire there, are several that want him dead. Tomorrow sire, we will land on the plains. I hope you find the queen." The captain left me in the galley. Walking from the galley I told Tenna to find Basco and Dred. Have them come to my room?

Tenna asks, "Sire you want Shila there?" I told him I wanted to speak to just the two. Only moments had passed when Basco entered with Dred.

Basco asks, "Sire how may I help you?"

I ask, "Basco how did Shila become so powerful." I have in my thoughts wondered how she made them appear on the ship."

Dred said, "Shila did not do that. Shila is only a messenger of the old ones. The ones on the ship were from your world of long ago. Sire, I am a Claxton. I trained you when you were a small boy. Yet all this time you do not remember. Tenna was there, yet no one remembers me."

"I tell you now Shila is strong because of the blood that runs through her veins. Shila is not after your throne. She is after your brother for the thing he has done to the people of Galaxo, one other thing sire. Shila's power comes from what she feels. That is what makes her a supreme warrior. I truly think sire, that is what you fear.

Shila is a princess. If she wanted a throne she would go to the place of her mother and fathers' peoples. Shila would go back to Corning. She has also been asked to come to the planet that disappeared to live her life." I could not believe what I was hearing.

I said to them, "So I should give her a ship, let her go through the galaxies."

Dred said, "She can call to the ancients Icol if she so desires."

Basco said, "sire I've know you since you were born. I knew your mother and father. I was a young boy then." Reaching into my pocket I took a parchment unfolded it. "Sire I've waited until the time was right to give this to you. I suppose this will be as good as it will get."

I took the letter from Basco started to read it. I staggered, Tenna caught me. "Sire," Tenna said.

Icol said, "She is alive, Tenna this is from Shara. Basco is she alive."

"Sire she was when we left. You must understand, Shila came to me with this. That's what put the fire in her. We have been gone for almost two years."

I started to read the letter, it was no doubt that it was Shara's handwriting. My hands were shaking as I read the parchment.

I am queen Shara, wife of Icol. Drex has me held captive in the tower over the city. look at darkness a single light

"Sire, Shila was sweeping breadroot flour off the stoop where Drexs men tore open the bags. The note blew into the store. Sire as I have said that's what put the fire in her, she didn't know at the time of what was to be. I will say this. Shila will only get stronger as she grows. Sire from the Claxton's to the great one of Boldlygo, Shila has the blood of Lola, Destiny to the lifeblood of Mya."

I ask then, "So what do you think she will do."

Basco said, "Sire I say this, Shila will fulfill her Destiny. She will kill anyone that stands in her way. Sire on Plano you saw the warrior, not the woman. Shila is a strong-willed woman. Shila also has the respect of the people, just as you do. Sire you need to be more aggressive."

We at the castle or village lived in fear. Drex placed fear

in all the people. The cruel things he has done to all, even your queen. The people should not be afraid of their King and Queen. I will stand with Shila, my son. Fina, Dred even Tenna will stand."

"The captain of this ship wants to take her to Earth. She has the support of the crew." I turned looked out the portal, holding the parchment in my hand so be it then. I only wish for a small moment with him. I told my king, sire, I or the others can't promise you that.

I said as I left, "Shila is too powerful."

Walking to my sleeping room. I took my bath lie on the bed closed my eyes somewhere in the night I fell asleep. During the night as it is in space, she came to me. My love, you are so close to holding me once more. I am told tomorrow I to will hold you in my arms. Over twenty years we have been apart, tomorrow we will be together once more. Running to her touching her for what seemed hours. Just to be awakened by a rap on the door.

"Enter," I said. The door open, Fina stood in the doorway.

Fina asks, "Icol may I speak to you?"

I didn't know what to expect from her. Since I first met her in Corning she has not said much. She as her brother never says much. I have seen them several times, they just look and listen. Sometimes it is kind of scary the way they look at you. I told Fina to enter. "Fina, what is on your mind," I ask?

Replying Fina said, "The same thing that is on yours Icol."

"Fina I'm tired, I dont have time for games."

I said, "I wish not to play any games with you. You were dreaming of your wife. Wanting as you humans say sex." Well, she had my attention.

"Fina, how do you know what I was dreaming?" Fina walked around the room. I was still on the bed.

Fina said, "Tomorrow you will see your wife, she will be waiting on the plains." She had my attention now.

"Fina," I said, "Just how do you know this?"

Fina said, "The queen is with Nordic, Konik, Iams, and a

half breed Claxton."

I ask her again, "Fina how do you know this?"

"Icol, Icol," Fina said. "I like you, were taught to meditate. Even body separation, yet you choose not to practice it. Seriously I wondered how you let them capture you, or Tenna as Tenna is a supreme warrior."

I said, "Yes he is a warrior, there were too many of them."

"You know Icol, my father would tell me when I was a little girl. No retreat, no surrender."

"I'm sure Fina, your father has told you several things." My father told me to retreat to fight another day.

"Icol you are a king why are you afraid of a girl." There was silence from him. I told Fina I was not afraid of Shila. I'm afraid of her power. The things she can Do." I told him, Shila is strong.

Icol said, "Even you Fina have to admit she is powerful."

I said, "Shila is not powerful. She is chosen."

"Chosen by who Fina, surely not my people."

Fina said, "Shila is chosen by my people, the Claxton's. I was with her the night he called to her. In my life, I've heard of the old ones. I've never seen them until they called to her. She is chosen by the faith of your people of Corning. Chosen by the people of the planet long ago. Icol you need to embrace it."

Icol set quietly just looking at me as I continued to talk. Fina said something then, that caught my attention.

She said, "Icol with your own eyes, you've seen the power they have. It's the blood, there is no being on any planet, galaxy, or universe that can do what they can, or have done. Your people Icol, she can call to them. Icol Shila does not have to stay with you. She can go back to Corning. She has been asked to come to the planet of the ancient ones. If you stand in her way, she will destroy you. Then all she has done will be for nothing."

"Tomorrow we will be on the plains when you see your wife for the first time in over twenty years, let her tell you Drex must die." I started to leave then turned to face him. "Icol it doesn't matter to me either way. Drex will die, by the hands of Shila, this I promise you."

I left the room, I heard him say, "Not if she dies first." I looked around the door.

"They have to kill me first. There is always Dred, who will kill him."

Standing in my room alone I knew I was asking for too much. I knew Drex would die. I knew he would die at the hands of Shila. I knew he was bad; I knew he has done bad things. I suppose if I try to stop it the running to Shara was for nothing. If Shila kills him, if I band her, then an uprising from the people how do I win. My thought went to Shara. My love, I wish I could hold you.

CHAPTER 39

I was lying on the bed, when Fina, came into the room. I thought, where has she been.

I said, "Fina, I swear you can't sit still. What is with you."

Fina said, "Shila, I'm glad we're almost home. I want to see my father." Looking at her, a smile came to my face.

"Yes, Fina I would like to see him too. Fina, he would be proud of us, really proud." I thought, three weeks on a ship I want to feel the soil under my feet, drink fresh water and take a long bath. I wish I was in the pool of Claxton city.

Fina replied, "Wow, Shila it has been a long time. I've almost forgotten what it feels like. Oh, Shila that's where Dris saw us naked. Do you think he still remembers that?"

I replied, "You know how I feel of Dris. You're a bitch for saying that." Fina laughed out loud.

Fina said, "Well Shila, I got to keep you thinking." I told her I think all the time.

I ask her, "Where have you been?" She stood in silence then said.

"I was with Icol. He still has not recovered from the shock of going home."

I said to her, "He thinks I want the throne. All I want from him is a ship. Fina don't you think I deserve a ship to command. One with my captain." Fina just smiled.

Each passing moment, each mile through space, we, came closer to home. Closer to fulfilling my destiny. I swear each time I think of it I kind of tingle. Fina and I were in deep conversation when someone knocked on the door. I placed my finger to my lips.

"Fina, be quiet," I said in a low whisper. Moving from my bed to the floor I reached for my sword. I held up three fingers. Looking at Fina before I open the door, she stood ready with hers. Jerking the door open three guards stood completely in ah. I drew my sword started to thrust when one of them yelled.

"No, No, Shila we come to ask you something."

I ask, "Then why didn't you speak when you knocked."

The three said, "We were afraid Shila." Fina said as she looked at me. I knew that look, she wanted to play; I kind of nodded.

Fina said, "I think you lie; I think I'll just kill you anyway."

"Please we mean you no harm," he said. Fina grabbed one by his shirt pulled him close to her. In a low whisper, she said in a baby voice.

"I think I'll play with you first. You want to play with Fina. She said in a baby voice.

"Yes, he said, Fina, pushed him away. What did you say?"

He answered, "I mean no, no. Oh, I don't know what to say you have got me so confused. I forgot what I come here for." The guards took off running down the corridor. I looked at Shila she was on her bed laughing so hard.

"You're such a bitch, for doing that Fina. You scared the life from them."

Fina said, "Come on Shila, let's have some fun." We ran down the corridor after the guards. Running into the galley Basco, Tenna and Dris were having their evening tea. Tenna jumped as we entered. Fina said something in Claxton. Tenna pointed over his shoulder. Looking around, I saw them at a corner table in the back.

Basco asks, "What is going on Shila?"

Whispering I said, "We're having a little fun." I told Basco after this I needed to talk to him and Tenna before we dock of the thing that has happened.

"Basco," I said, "in twelve hours we will end our quest of two years. We will be back in our world. Then we can finish what we have started, my destiny. Basco, I want to go to Earth, will you come with me." Basco looked at Tenna, then at me.

Replying, "Shila how can I say no to you." Looking at the powerful man standing before me. Basco was so handsome, more than when we left. "Basco, have I told you I love you. I swear if not for Dris, I would take you and mate you here and now."

"Yes, Shila you have told me that. Now go play with Fina."

Basco asks, "What is Fina doing?" Looking around I said just watch. Fina was moving around in a circular motion. She was speaking in Claxton language. She smiled as I came close to her.

"My my Fina which one is it?" All three said at the same time.

"Which one is what," they ask?

"Well, Shila it's all three," Fina said.

One said, "We meant you no harm." Basco and Tenna were smiling.

One said, "What is happing here?" I told them they just got married to a Claxton.

"Oh no not me no way." One flew by Basco so fast his hair moved. The other two were in the corner.

Fina said, "Let's go to my room, I have plans for you."

"No way not me," he said.

Fina said in a baby voice, "You come here now."

The sentry said, "I just wanted to ask you if we could go to Earth with you, nothing else."

Fina said, "Then get out of here." Those two lefts so fast, one ran into the wall as he tried to make the corner.

Basco said, "that was cruel girls, what you did. They were the color of the clouds."

Fina and I sat with Tenna and Basco for over an hour. I wanted to take a nap, so did Fina. We excused ourselves. Fina and I went to our room got undressed sat on the floor lost our self in meditation. I have found out meditation and relaxation, well, it's a cleansing for the soul. It is also a way to relieve stress.

Fina's father told me once, I could go anywhere, see anything. That I find is the truth. Here and now we find ourselves on the floor of Galaxo. I Touched Fina's arm.

"Look, Fina, under the tree." Several people were standing in a small group waiting. From high in the Trions, to the North, over a hundred Claxton's were coming down the trail. Fina and

I were in the spirit in a meditated stage of mind, they could not see us.

Fina said to me, "Shila, he is a Claxton: He is what they call a half breed. They're several of them to the north in a village. My father told me that." I looked at the one Fina spoke of. The half breed as Fina said moved and drew his sword. That started the other. Nordic did the same. Nordic said in a low voice so only Mick could hear. "What's wrong Mick?

Mick said, "Someone is here; I swear it. I may be half-human, My Claxton since is working good."

Nordic asks, "Who do you think?"

Mick replied, "I'm not sure, whoever it is, they're strong with power."

Mick said to Nordic, "I'm going to the forest, I need to think." Mick walked away I saw the queen. She looked very tired; I went to her. The wind blew her hair, a chill come over her. She was a beautiful woman, yet she was tired. It won't be much longer my queen. Her eyes opened wide. In a low whisper, she asks, "Who is there?"

"It's Nordic, my lady, I'm here."

Shara said, "I swear Nordic, I feel the presence of something or someone."

Nordic said, "Mick feels it to my lady. Mick went to the forest."

Fina and I watched them for several minutes. Then walked to the forest where Mick was. Mick sat on the ground, closed his eyes. Mick went into deep thoughts. We sat watching him. Finally, he called out to us.

"Who are you, I know you're here?"

"I am Fina."

"He asks, "You are a Claxton?"

Fina said, "I am, this is Shila."

Mick said, "I have heard of that one. Why are you here in spirit?" I told him Tenna and Basco will be here tomorrow with Icol. We also will be here. Go to the queen tell her what I have said. Prepare to receive the king. In six hours, we will be here. Mick did as we ask. We stayed with him until he went to her. Mick told her what Fina and I said.

Shara said, "You talked to someone."

Mick said, "I did my lady. Fina and Shila."

Lama said, "My lady I believe him." Nordic said as much.

The night came as any on Galaxo. The moon came up, it was a beautiful night.

Konik said to Nordic, "Wish this was over."

Nordic asks, "For what reason?"

Konik replied, "To see if I survive."

Nordic said, "You will survive my friend."

Shara said, "After twenty years I will hold him once again." Shara took Lama's hand. "Soon Lama we will be free. Tell me, Mick, what is she like."

Mick asked, "Shila or Fina."

Shara said, "Both of them."

Mick said, "Shila is beautiful, she has long dark hair, blue eyes. Fina's hair is like the sunset. She too has blue eyes. She is a Claxton."

Mick said to Nordic, "we must prepare to welcome our king.

Nordic said, "Iams go to the camp of the Claxton's, tell them what has happened.

A voice from the trees said, "We are here, we saw what has happened, we're ready." Shila said there were eight ships. One ship will come to the floor until we secure the landing. Then Icol will come to meet his queen. Fina and I opened our eyes. We were back in our room on the ship.

Fina asks, "Shila what do we do now?"

I said, "Fina, I will go make one last plea to Icol."

"You want company Shila," Fina asks?

I said to my friend I have become to love. "Fina always by my side." In the corridor, several men stood. Tenna was one of them.

I ask him," Tenna come with us to see Icol." Entering the

galley Basco sat at a table with Dris. Icol was talking to the captain.

The captain said, "my king, ten hours we will be over the planet."

I ask, "Captain why ten hours, it's more like six? If you can't pilot the ship, maybe I need another captain."

Dred said, "I can pilot this very vessel."

I said, "You can be my captain." Icol in six hours you will reunite with your queen. She is expecting you on the floor of the planet. She is being protected by the guards and the Claxton's.

Icol looked at me, "You know this how." I told him Fina and I went there in meditations. Everyone looked at me.

The captain said, "You are a strange one Shila."

Dred said again," She does not lie, tell them what she wears." Fina told them everything we saw. There Is one other thing.

Icol said, "Yes Shila what is it?"

My king, "Basco took me two years ago to the Trions; alone with his son. I met Fina and Dred. My king, I worked hard to be what I am. We searched for you everywhere. On Corning, I found you just as I told Basco I would. We will land Queen Shara, will come aboard my King. I ask you to stay with her until then. My king, then you can come ashore and claim your throne. My king, if anyone tries to stop this, I will kill them. That throne is rightfully yours. At this moment, it belongs to the queen. I do not want your throne, my king."

"Open your heart, you will see what I say is true," I told him to open his arms I give him an embrace to show him the love I have for him. Bowing to one knee.

Icol said," Rise Shila." Talking my hand Icol said. "I admit Shila, I'm afraid of the power you possess. I know now what you want." I don't know what happened then.

A portal opened, everyone went to the floor except Fina. It would appear all were afraid. Zin stepped through the portal.

"King Icol, you have made a rightful decision," Zin said. Let Shila have her way. Someday we may share the same galaxy. In all galaxies, there is none as powerful as us. Shila has the blood of the ancients. Shila is our blood as you are Kohls. Remember King Icol, Kohl was from Boldlygo. Let her lead, then give her a ship of her choice. When the time is right, we will come to her. We will bring our people that want to return to Earth.

It has been over three hundered years, that we have been to Earth. My mother and father would dearly love to return, yet they no they never will. If not for them dying, I'm sure they would go. My queen and I would love to journey there. We have our world the world of humans that give us life thousands of years ago. Others played an important part in our history, yet not as the humans."

Zin, bowed to Shila, "My offer still holds good for you little princess, always will. Princess Fina, the offer is good for you and your people. Always remember we will come when you need us. King Icol to you and your victory." Zin stepped through the portal as it closed behind him.

Everyone looked at me. I was getting closer to my homeworld. the world I left what seemed a lifetime ago.

Tenna asks, "Shila what are your plans?" I told him, Tenna, you are the king's advisor. Basco Dred, Dris Fina, and I are warriors. You and Basco make the battle plans. Everyone knows my objective, I have only one. Sire, it hurts me to go against your wishes. However, when you see Queen Shara you will change your mind. Make your plans, I will follow you.

Dris, Fina, Dred spoke, "Shila we will be with you." I told them I would have it no other way. I told them we need to have a meal before we reach the planet. In the galley dining area, Icol made his speech to all. "Come sit with me please."

Icol said to me as I sat beside him. "Shila I'm scared, what if she doesn't want me."

"Sire she didn't wait twenty years to run away." We sat talking until I excused myself. Dris stopped me.

Dris said, "Shila we haven't had the chance to talk in several days." I told Dris I truly was sorry for that. Standing in front of him I got closer, kissed him softly.

"Dris, I said. "Our time is close. The longing to hold me, the wanting in your heart. You see why I keep pushing you away. I will leave you with this. I kissed him again, whispered in his ear. I love you Dris, always have, always will. Our time is close, after this, I will not push you away." Then I turned walked away to my room. Fina followed me to the room.

"Three hours Fina," I said. Lying on the floor of the cool ship we got undressed went into deep meditation. As the ship zoomed through space caring our bodies. Fina and I went to the village of Galaxo. It appeared to be a normal day. My father's shop was gone, well it was closed anyway. The castle looked different.

I said to Fina, "Something is wrong."

Fina replied, "Shila, I sense a feeling I cannot explain." Through the walls of the castle, to the room where the queen was imprisoned. We moved through the corridor of the castle. We went to the room of the man I was going to kill. Drex was in his chambers with a woman.

Venice, I knew her, we were friends once. She was being fitted for a wedding gown.

Fina touched my hand, "Surely not Shila. She is going to marry him after all he has done." I stood in disbelief. Thinking of the world with him still in charge, well that was going to change, soon. We left went to the courtyard behind the castle. By the gate, there were over two hundred men. The guards were training, they knew we were coming. One of the guards I knew. I had seen him before on the plains long ago.

"Fina," I said. They're getting ready."

Fina said, "We already are." Returning to reality, on the ship, I said to Fina, "we must tell Basco and Tenna."

Running through the corridor to the galley where Basco and Tenna were. Basco was drawing on parchment. Fina and I entered the room.

Basco asks, "Shila something you wish to say?" I told him

Fina and I had gone to the planet. We were in deep meditation, "they're waiting for us. they're training over two hundred men. Drex has guards placed all around the castle, except to the north."

Icol said, "That will be Drex's escape route."

"He won't escape," I said.

Basco replied, "I stood in front of him. "Shila something else."

I said, "He has taken a bride, her name is Venice. They're making wedding plans."

Icol said, "She is the captain's granddaughter. She is then Drexs daughter." Icol told the sentry to bring the captain to him. It was told to the captain about Venice.

The captain asks, "How do you know this?"

Icol pointed to me, "Shila, has seen this in her meditation."

"He had his way with my daughter, now with my granddaughter." She will give him a son.

The captain said, "my king, you cannot let this happen, I beg you." The captain walked away. I told him I would handle it; I promise we will stop the wedding. Fina and I returned to our room.

I said to Fina, "we will be home soon."

Fina said, "It has been a long time Shila. What do you think will happen to us?"

I looked at her, "I'm not sure what you mean Fina."

"Shila do you think we will stay friends, or will I go back to the mountain."

I said to her, "I thought you were going to Earth with me."

"If you wish Shila," Fina said.

"You are such a bitch Fina," I said. We both laughed at what was said. We embraced. I told Fina I will always need you with me, always Fina. Fina let me go as we felt the ship come from hyperspace.

We said at the same time, "We're home."

Fina and I started for the door. The men had already started down the corridor.

"Wait for us, you can't have all the fun," I said. Walking into the control room known as the bridge, the fleet came to a stop.

The captain asks, "Do we take a scruple or the ship down. We will not be detected by the castle unless Drexs guards are there."

I ask the captain, "Is it dark or daylight?"

Captain said, "It is mid-day."

I said, "Then take the ship. Captain tell the others to stay in orbit until called for." The captain sent the order to the other ships.

The ship broke away from the fleet. We sat waiting as it started its descent to the floor of the planet. The ship entered the atmosphere of our world, the pilot was given his landing instruction. The planet began to take on shape as the ship came closer. On the scope, I showed the pilot where Fina and I saw the others.

I said, "There, set down on the plains behind the wood line."

The large ship sat down so gracefully. Cutting the landing engine, the captain let the ramp down. It was a few steps to the edge of the forest. Waiting for several minutes, I told them this is where they will come. The Claxton's had seen us long before we come into sight. From the wood line, we stood with sword in hand.

Fina said, "Look!" There had to be over a hundered coming from the forest. The Claxton's were being led by the chief, Fina, and Dred's father. Fina ran swiftly to him. We waited as they embraced each other. Side by side as they walked to us. The chief acknowledged Basco. Then turned to Icol kneeling to one knee.

"You will not remember me; I was chief when Tenna brought you to the city I tell you now. We had no way of knowing you were in prison. Now, my friend, it's time we place you back where you belong."

Turning to say something the chief stared into the eyes of Tenna. Tenna walked to him, kneeling to one knee. I looked at Dred, Fina made a shoulder shrug.

Tenna stood up, "Father, it is good to see you."

The chief said, "My son it has been too long." As Tenna and the chief embraced each other, Mick saw this walk into the forest. I in my thoughts I could not explain what I just witness. Taking the hand of the chiefs.

He said, "I am very proud of you Shila, as I am of my daughter." Fina looked at her father.

"Why after all these years, you did not tell me Tenna was my brother. Dred did you know," Fina asks? Dred sad nothing.

Basco said, "I didn't know."

Fina said, "I've read all your journals. Tenna why did you not tell me when we met when you knew who I was. I have carried the image of you in my heart. I've always said I would always love the warrior called Tenna. Just as Shila loves Basco. Now I find you're my brother. I cannot believe it."

I ran to him, "Oh Tenna, this is so much more than I could ever expect." Everyone was talking when the chief said in a stern voice, so all could hear.

King Icol, "May I present your queen." The lines of people started to move apart. Shara was standing beside Lama, holding her hand. Shara was wearing a white and blue dress; her hair down midway of her back, curls laid over her shoulder. Shara started toward him. Icol broke into a run, laughing and crying as they both embraced each other.

Shara was crying so hard she said, "Finally. I have waited for this moment for so long, I love you." Tenna told Icol to take Shara to the ship.

"Sire," he said. "Wait until I come for you." Nordic, Konik, Iams came to Basco.

Nordic said to Shila, "Little one good to see you." I told them the others were on the ships in orbit. Tenna stood beside them as we talked of things to come.

I said, "Tenna there is someone here, you need to meet. He is a classic warrior; he is the one that took the queen from the castle. He took her and the girl. Tenna laughed hard when I told him what Mick did.

Tenna said, "We'll bring him here, we must think him."

"Fina, and I said. "Don't be surprised when you meet him."

"Surprise," Tenna said. "Shila, why would I be surprised. Tenna said where is this Mick."

"I'll find him Tenna," Fina replied, "stay with Shila." Tenna sat on a fallen tree looking around.

I said to Tenna, "You know if I live to be a hundered, I will never understand all the ways of the Claxton's."

Tenna said, "Shila I don't know all about the Claxton's."

"Tenna why did you not say you were the firstborn? Why did Dred not say?"

Tenna replied, "It was not my place to say."

I ask Tenna, "Since you have met her, been in a battle with her, what do you think of your little sister."

Replying, "She is a warrior Shila."

I said to Tenna, "That she is. She taught me very well, her and Dred. Basco taught me a lot. When I went to the city, the Claxton's taught me so much more."

Tenna asks, "Shila what do you wish to do of this. You said the elders of the city told you your destiny was to kill Drex. I tell you this: it is my belief you control your destiny. That was the trouble with my father, what he wanted for me, was not what I wanted. He let Icols father acquire me. Being with Icols father, and Icol, was my destiny, not my father's.

I told Tenna my Destiny was to kill Drex for the crimes he has imposed on my people. I told you when we met, let's not start again. Claxton was staring at Tenna. Some were pointing to him. Several Claxton's walked over.

They bowed, "Master Tenna."

Tenna put up a hand, "Do not call me master, I still believe a Claxton or human, should choose their destiny."

A warrior said, "You choose to live with humans, you see what it got you."

Tenna said, "My friend an experience I'll talk to my people, maybe someday my son.

Fina said, "how about today my brother?"

"How about what," Tenna asks?

Fina said, "Tell your son."

Tenna looked at Fina, "When I have one I will." Fina stepped aside, Tenna was looking into the eyes of Mick.

"Tenna your son, Mick," Fina said.

Tenna stood from his seat, "What kind of trickery is this."

Mick said, "It's no trick, I'm half Claxton." I could see Tenna's thoughts go to the time of long ago.

I remembered the maiden of the queen. The way I fell helplessly in love with a human. I remembered how Shara would let her come to me. The way she looked; she was so beautiful the human. I remembered the way she looked. Her face her hair, how she felt in my arm. It all came back to me at this moment.

Tenna said, "I knew we could mate." I was told we could not. "Where is she," Tenna asks?

Mick said, "Drex made it hard on us, mother kept me hid from him because I took your looks. Mick pulled the scarf from his sunset hair, to show Tenna the Claxton look.

Mick said, "I've waited for twenty-two years to stand before you. I always had hope you were still alive." Mick's eyes glassed over as tears streamed.

My mother said with her last breath, Mick he is still alive, somewhere. Wait for him, Tenna your father will return."

Tenna said, "I never knew of you."

Mick said, "I understand, Drex sent you away before she could tell you."

Mick asked, "Do you think it's too late to start."

Tenna replied, "I suppose not."

Mick asked, "May I be permitted to call you father?"

Tenna smiled, "It would be an honor." I poked Fina, "Dred is smiling."

"Oh, my" Fina said, "our family reunion is going well." Overhead a scruple flew, two guards headed straight to the castle.

Basco said, "Well Drex will know we're here."

The chief said, "Basco you and Tenna bring your council together. You must make your plans."

"Captain," the chief said, "You can bring the other ships to the ground."

The captain replied, "Why do you think their other ship?"

The chief said to him, "There's always another ship, captain."

There was so much I wanted to say to Tenna. So much I wanted to know. Fina stayed by him everywhere he went. I've never seen her do that. After all, Tenna was her brother. Dred never spoke of Tenna. I do remember once he said Tenna held the highest rank of a living warrior. Now Dred holds that rank. The Claxton chief met Mick. For some reason, I think he has known of him long before now.

Nordic told his part of the story, looking at the queen. The queen told us of the hole in the wall: no doubt Drex knows of this also. I feel he will be watching for us. The tunnel in Coe's store we can't go that way without being seen. The main gate is the only way. If it is closed, I'm not sure how we may enter.

Mick said, "There's only one way. Someone must go to the village. Once inside maybe you can overpower the guards on the gate."

Basco asks, "How will we know if the plan works?"

Mick said, "Candlelight. We at least need to try. Basco, we need at least fifteen men inside before darkness comes. Once inside we can overpower the guards. Then go to the hole. Maybe some can go through the tunnel Shila speaks of. I'm sure Drexs guards will think we'll wait until morning; we go tonight after the sun sets." Basco, Dred, Tenna were going over the plans.

The chief asks Tenna, "What he thought of this?"

Tenna said, "Whoever goes into the village must try not to bring attention to themselves." Fina and I sat listening as the men made their plans. Fina hardly took her eyes from Tenna. I also saw how she looked at Mick.

Now Basco and Dris were very handsome men. Mick was beautiful, there was something about him. Catching Fina's thoughts, I love him was the words I heard.

I looked at Fina, "What did you say?" She was smiling at me.

"What, I said nothing?"

"You're a bitch, you said, you loved him."

Fina said, "Shila, I swear you need help. You're always jumping to conclusions".

I put my arms around her, "I know what I heard, I also know you're a bitch."

"You're two of them Shila," Fina said.

Icol and Shara were walking toward me holding hands. Icol called to me, "come forward, please. Just the short time we have been here Shara has told me all the things Drex has done. Shila, do what you must."

I bowed to him, "Thank you, my king." There was a loud noise overhead. The other ships were here. Most of the men come to the wood line to see their king and queen. My father was with them. Going to him he took me in his arms.

"I could not be as proud of you as I am now Shila. I want to go home, go do what you must, I shall wait here."

I smiled at my father, "I have missed you so. I hope you can forgive me for the woman I've become."

"Shila," he said, "there's nothing to forgive, I've always known you were destined for bigger things. You were too smart as a child; you truly have the blood of the ancient ones."

Basco called me. I told my father goodbye; I will see him soon. Walking to Basco, Dred, Dris, Fina came to me. Basco started to speak when a voice called, it was Mick, "I'll be with them, he said.

Basco said, "Very well don't take chances. Try to get inside if you can: all we need is some of us to be inside when it starts. Someone to take the gate. Mick, you watch their back, it looks as if Fina will be with you. Fina gave that little smile as to say, I'm a princess bow before me. I'll bow to her, right after I kick her ass."

Basco told Iams to carry us on the scruple. Take them into the forest to the wall down the side no one will see you coming. When darkness falls watch for the guards to change then take the gate. We'll be waiting outside the gate. There's no need to tell the Claxton's, they know what needs to be done. After all the years they want a fight.

I said," Me too."

Fina said, "You scare me Shila."

I said to my friend, "I hope I do."

One hour later we mounted the scruples. Icol and Shara stood with Lama. "Lama, do you want to go home," Shara asks?

She replied, "My lady it's not over. I said to you long ago I would stay with you until it's over. My lady, I'll stay with you if you will let me." Shara took Lama's hand.

Basco said, "Iams will return for the others when the lights go up. Basco told Dris to take, take care of Shila, and the others.

Tenna said," It will be over soon."

My mind went blank for what seemed hours as the scruple took us through the forest. My thought took me back to the Trions. It was two years ago I left here. Look what I've become. A voice said to me, opening my eyes I was not in the scruple.

The voice said again, "Shila come."

"Who are you," I ask?

"Shila take this." It was a token the woman handed me. I've seen this before somewhere. The woman's face I could not see.

She said, "Things have changed since the last Earth journey. Kikki and the great Bota would have brought some of our people back. Three hundered years have passed. Take this coin, place a photo of it in a newspaper."

I ask, "What is a photo, and what is a newspaper?"

She said, "You will learn this as you go to Earth. Learn and read as you go to Earth Shila." The woman started to fade.

I ask, "Who are you?"

She simply said, "I am Kayla." I opened my eyes grabbed the side of the Scruple.

Fina laughed out loud, "You were asleep Shila." I open my hand there was the imprint of the coin. I thought to myself I must talk to Zin.

I never knew what hit the side of the scruple, it flew apart. Dris reached for me. Fina, Mick, Dred went rolling on the ground. I was completely dazed by the blast. It seemed the life was knocked from me. I could not breathe, in my mind, I was dying. Many thoughts went flashing before me. I thought I will never full fill my destiny. I turned my head to see Iams running to me.

Iams yelling, "Dris pick her up." That was the last thing I heard.

Dris was holding my hand when I came back to life. Opening my eyes, I could see darkness had come upon us. Dris was covered with blood, sitting holding my hand.

"You ok Shila," Dris asks?

"I ask, of the blood on him."

Dris said, "It's from a bloody nose. I thought you were dead Shila."

I ask him, "What happen?"

Dris answered, "They hit us with something, it was as if they knew we were coming. Iams could not return for the others. Iams and Nordic took the others to the castle. Fina wanted to stay here with you. Since my nose was bleeding bad, I stayed with you. The blast hit where you were sitting."

I said, "Help me up my love, we must go."

"Shila you're not ready, we should wait," Dris said. "You called me your love."

"Really Dris," I said. "Here, now, let's go." We made our way to the wall I admit my head throbbed badly. It felt as my chest was being pounded. I told Dris I got to stop.

Dris said, "I told you to wait."

"Dris, just give me a minute, let me gather my thoughts."

Dris said, "You won't last long in a fight if you ran up against Drex." I cleared my mind went to a place of joy. There I found solitude, peace in all parts of my body.

Returning to myself, I told Dris to place me in front of Drex get out of my way. Dris and I made our way to the wall.

Dris ask, "What did you do back there Shila?" I told Dris when you start and complete your meditation you will learn how to stop all that is.

Dris asks, "How are we to let the others know the scruple was destroyed?"

I said, "Basco knows if we don't show up, he will come, just trust that."

CHAPTER 40

Inside the castle, Drex guards went to him and reported the ships. They also reported the move of the Claxton's.

Drex asks, "Did you see him?"

The guard asked, "See who sire?"

"My brother," Drex asks?

"Sire, I do not know him. If I did know him, his image has left me." Drex looked at the other guard.

"Sire," he said. "I saw a man and a woman come from the trees. Sire, there were many on the ground pulse the ships."

Drex asks, "Did you see all the ships?"

He replied, "No sire, just the one." Drex thought, where are the others. Of course, they're still in orbit. Thoughts went through his mind he knew by now the other ships had come to the surface. Drex started to speak when another guard come to the chambers.

Sire we have destroyed a scruple, there were nobodies. The scruple was destroyed."

Drex said, "Go to the hole in the wall, take twenty men. Raise the gateman the walls. I'll show my brother." Venice ran to Drex, sword in her hand. Tears flowed from her eyes.

Venice said, "I will stand beside you. My love, I'm with child, a son you will have."

Drex took her hand, "Stand with me. Turning to the guards, if you do not have the guts to fight, leave now if you're not loyal to me, leave."

Drex said, "Go now protects you, king and queen." There was talk among the guards, some wanted to leave, Drex could feel it.

Drex said, "Venice is with child, she will give me a son. A son to carry on his rightful place. A son is what I have wanted for." Yet how can she have a child here? She would be cast from the village. Icol would never kill her. How could he, he didn't know of her.

"Venice, you must leave the castle. You must survive, when Icol comes he will kill me. Venice please, think of the child. I want you to leave," Drex said. Drex told her to go to the village to the north, I'll send guards with you.

Venice embraced Drex," I had rather be dead than to live without you. Drex by your side is where I belong if you die, I die, would you want your son to be without his father."

Drex stood in silence, his mind went to his father. The time Icol was away. The time his father would play with him in the garden. His mother would hold him, it was a time when life was much simpler. Then Icol returned, his perfect world ended, no one ever spoke of him. It was a time Drex remembered, then it was over.

Drex looked at Venice, "I would not want him to live without me." Drex took Venice by the hair and pulled her back. Taking the sword to push it hard into her stomach.

Venice said, "Do it, my love, do it."

Drex threw down the sword, "I can't." Falling to his knees. Venice placed her hand on top of his head.

Looking up at her, "I can't Venice Drex said.

Venice said, "Then get your ass, off this floor, let's end this. One way or the other."

There was a great disturbance outside. Drex and Venice ran to the window. People were running from their homes. Drex thought it's late for them to be out.

Drex shouted, "Go back to your homes or die."

"We have had enough of you Drex," shouted the crowd. "We're tired of your killing; we're tired of you." There was a noise from the hole. Drex took Venice's hand, "they're coming in my love."

Nordic, Nonik, and Iams, had made it to the gate. When the guards saw Nordic, the fight was on. Along the wall in back Konik, Mick, Fina had taken the guards.

I said, "Dris there, the light." Dris reached out to me kissed me long and hard. The kiss seemed to last for hours. I was not ready for it. It left me feeling weak at the bottom of my stomach. What was this new feeling I was having? He let me go, I tell you if it had been in another place, another time well it would be history.

I ask Dris, "What was that for?"

Dris said, "It was a just in case kiss."

I ask with a smile, "In case of what Dris?"

He replied, "In case I don't make it."

I said to him, "Well if you're ready, we need to run"

Dris said, "It was a moment in time my love." I agreed.

Nordic saw us come around the corner of the wall. He jumped behind us from the tower. Looking behind us, I could see the ships come into the hanger area. The Claxton's were all over the place. I shouted to the people as I ran by, go to your homes stay there. I ran to our store Nordic and Iams were behind me.

Down the stairs to the wall where Nordic torn the boards of. We raced through the tunnel; I grabbed the stool. Iams give me a boost through the hole. I saw Fina and Mick fighting for their life. I ran to them, looking at Fina fight she was fighting as ten men: she was that good. Mick was a full warrior he too was fighting. Dris ran fast to me.

"Duck," I said. A digger went past his head into the chest of a guard. The others were through the hole we were fighting, moving, turning flips. It was a trying time. Slashing, thrusting more were coming. I pushed Fina out of the way just in time my sword went to the hilt.

He said looking at me, his dying words came as drool coming from his mouth.

"You, you." I smiled at him, I told you the next time we meet, I would kill you. I withdrew my sword let him fall to the ground.

I shouted, "Fina, to the castle." The Claxton's had made their way to us we let them fight. Dris, Fina, Mick, and me, went into a hard run down the long corridor. The same one Drex would go to see the queen in the tower. I stopped at the door of the tower; it was unlocked. I peeped inside.

We turned to the other corridor hearing a door slam, sounds were coming from inside. Mick and Dris broke down the door. Several women were inside. I told them to stay inside.

Fina said, "Look Shila," as she walked around the room. I thought Drex had stopped bringing girls to the castle."

One said, "We are the queen's handmaidens."

"You are not," Fina said. "The queen is not in the castle." Fina pointed her sword at her.

"I'm sorry the queen to be."

I ask, "The queen to be, who is that?"

Fina said, "It's his daughter Shila."

One of the girls said, "She is with a child they plan to marry. She will give him a son." I told them to stay in the room if they come out, they could be killed.

Two of them said, "We just want to go home." I told her she would have her chance, for now, to stay here. Mick had watched the corridor.

"Shila," he said. "This way." Mick pointed the sword down the corridor. Several voices were coming from that room. I was thinking, where was Basco. I was sure he was doing his part.

Mick tried to open the door he said, "It is locked." I told them for what I could remember this would be Drexs chambers. This is what he calls the ready room, where he talks to his guards. I believe to the far side is his sleeping chambers. There is a room connected to his for guests. I can't remember him having a guest.

Dris placed his ear to the door then he jumped back quickly.

I whispered, "What is wrong Dris?"

Dris said, "The door clicked, it is unlocked." Mick tried the handle then backed up.

Mick said, "It is a trap."

I said, "Well of course it is."

"Let's not disappoint them," Fina said. Mick looked at Shila. "How do you want to do this?"

"Mick when you open the door, you and Fina place your

back against the wall go to the right. Dris and I will do the same, we will go to the left." The shadows from the light were in our favor the ones overhead I knocked out with my sword. I feel they won't expect four of us.

"Listen, I said, as we started to enter no retreat, kill everything in our way."

We move into the chambers as an animal in the forest. We could hear them talking inside. Mick opened the door enough, so we could hear. There was no mistaking. It was Drex's voice I would know that awful voice anywhere.

I heard him say, kill everyone that comes through that door' or be killed. The thought went through my mind. It's just as I always wanted it to be. Two years I've been gone, now I'm back, a full-grown woman. I looked at Fina as I thought, now it's my turn.

Mick pushed open the doorway, several diggers flew through the doorway down the corridor.

Fina smiled, "You are good."

I said, "Yes I had a good teacher." We ran through the door around the room thirty guards were waiting. That was no match for us, we went in swinging slashing thrusting, ten guards went to the floor. Mick, Fina, Dris were moving so gracefully it was almost a shame to miss. We were killing everyone. I had a cut on my arm, more like a scratch.

Dris had three on him, I threw a digger took one down. The fight lasted several minutes. I swear it felt like hours. There were several guards dead several wounded. The others threw down their swords.

Mick asked, "What are we to do with them Shila?" I told him, to take them to the tower and lock them in. I told the guards, pick up your wounded, go to the tower.

One of the guards asks, "What going to become of us." I told them I could kill you now. That I will have no problem with. I'm sure Icol will send you to prison on Advair. I know you don't want to die, nobody does. I assure you that you will not be set free.

One guard said, "Then let us help."

Fina jumped in between them, "That will not happen. You have fought a good fight; the victory is ours. I do not wish to fight you again. Now go to the towers as Shila has said."

I ask the guards, "Where is Drex."

He replied, "In his sleeping chambers with Venice."

Mick and Fina led the way to the tower locking them in. We went to Drexs chambers. I walked to the door knocked on the door, I could hear a woman's voice.

"Drex come out, "Your yellow coward. Your nothing, not even a man. Venice, I said how does it feel to be marrying your father. I mean Venice." Fina and Mick had returned from the tower. I was waiting at the door when it opened. A woman with a sword dashed at me. Fina pushed me out of the way as her sword went all the way through Venice. She let out a scream, Fina held her left arm.

Fina said, "You will never have your wedding day. You will never have a child." Venice tried to make words, looking at Fina then at me.

"Shila how could you do this to me," I told her I did nothing; it was all Fina. Fina withdrew her sword. Venice screamed again as she fell to the floor. On her knees, she died on the floor with her head bowed.

I called out, "she is dead Drex. Venice your daughter the one that was going to have your child. You are so low I can't even find the words to say what you are." For twenty years he had to listen to those words, echoing in his ears.

"Come on out Drex, it's just me and Fina she'll step aside." I kept calling him out, you are a miserable man. Drex there are no words for you, no way to describe you, with a deep breath I let it out you are nothing."

The fighting outside was going strong. Sometimes you could hear a guard scream. Even an explosion now and then. I kneel to the floor.

Fina said, "Shila he's here." Looking up. Drex was standing at the door.

I said, "Drex I must say, I'm surprised. You have put on a few pounds. You're bigger than I remember."

Drex said, "You know I should have lowered the age, so I could have taken care of you sooner."

"Oh Drex," I said. "As you did your daughter Lama. Poor Drex can't have a woman unless it's his daughter." Drex brought his sword up.

"Shila when I'm through carving you up, then your trashy Claxton friend, after all this time, I will have my way with you. The way it was meant to be."

"Drex," I said. "From the time I left here, two years have passed. I ran to the Claxton's where I knew I'd be safe. For two years I've been told killing you was my destiny. I never once thought it was going to be a pleasure."

Drex stood in the door smiling, well then come and get me. I started to make my move when Fina's sword went across my chest.

Fina said, "Shila, your too anxious, have you forgot what was taught to you. Never charge, wait, it will come to you, wait." From somewhere a knife was thrown. It passed Drexs head.

I said, "Someone is in the room with him." Drex made his move, so did the unseen guards there were three of them. Drex ran into the corridor.

"I yelled, run you, coward. Your no man you're a sick piece of nothing." Dris and Mick had started up the hallway.

Drex saw Mick, "You," he said. Mick ran for him. Drex was backing up when I swept his leg with my sword. Slashing out as he turned, he went to the floor.

"Do it," he shouted. "Kill me now."

I said, "Get up, you, worthless coward, fight me. If there is any sign of a man in, you fight me. You can't run I've made sure of that. Drex your guards are dead. It is just you and me Drex. I'm going to kill you, there is no one to help you." The fighting outside was almost over.

I said, "It is over Drex." Pulling himself up to a table for support Drex was bleeding from his legs. I had cut just above the knee to the side.

Drex made his move as the door opened. Icol and Shara stepped in.

Icol spoke to me, "Shila wait." Icol and Shara walked to him. I never took my eyes off him. Drex kind of staggered, brother help me, please.

Shara said, "Oh Drex, I will help you, give me a sword I'll kill you myself. When I'm through killing you, I'll let Lama, your kill you."

Drex tried to stand, "If I'm to die, then brother let me die by your hands." Icol started to speak, I knew what he was going to say. The words Drex said were the last words he'll ever say. In the chambers of my king, I killed his brother with no remorse, no regrets. I withdrew my sword, turned to Icol. Held up my sword, "Long live our king and queen." The chief of the Claxton's stood beside Icol.

"King Icol," the chief reached for my hand. "You have a warrior here, in the years to come I hope we never need them."

Icol said, "Yes I to hope this too."

"My king," I said. "I'll start by saying, I'll help with the cleanup. There is several in the towers do with them as you please." I took Dris by the hand Mick did Fina also. Her father saw this.

I said to the chief, "He's half-human, I see no problem with this. At least she's not his daughter."

Shara asks, "Where is Venice."

I said, "She is dead my lady, killed by Fina. She was trying to kill me." I bowed to Icol and Shara. I said, "the little girl left here two years ago to find her king, she grew up fast. My king," reaching out my hand, I led Shara and Icol to the throne. "I give you back what was always yours."